GHOST STORIES

GHOST STORIES

Henry James

Introduction and Notes by
MARTIN SCOFIELD
University of Kent at Canterbury

WORDSWORTH CLASSICS

This edition published 2001 by Wordsworth Editions Limited
8b East Street, Ware, Hertfordshire SG12 9HJ

ISBN 1 84022 422 3

Text © Wordsworth Editions Limited 2001
Introduction and Notes © Martin Scofield 2001

Wordsworth ® is a registered trademark of
Wordsworth Editions Limited

2 4 6 8 10 9 7 5 3 1

Typeset by Antony Gray
Printed and bound in Great Britain by
Mackays of Chatham, Chatham, Kent

CONTENTS

GENERAL INTRODUCTION

Wordsworth Classics are inexpensive editions designed to appeal to the general reader and students. We commissioned teachers and specialists to write wide ranging, jargon-free introductions and to provide notes that would assist the understanding of our readers rather than interpret the stories for them. In the same spirit, because the pleasures of reading are inseparable from the surprises, secrets and revelations that all narratives contain, it is suggested that you may find it more useful to read the Introduction after you have read the book.

General Adviser
KEITH CARABINE
Rutherford College
University of Kent at Canterbury

INTRODUCTION

I

Henry James (1843–1916) is mainly remembered and read today as a great realist novelist, the analyst and explorer of English and American morals and manners, perhaps the subtlest of all commentators on the late-nineteenth- and early-twentieth-century social scene. By 'realist' is meant, broadly, that he takes recognisable characters who inhabit the world of his time and puts them in situations which have the plausibility (if often also the oddity) of actual historical occurrence. James himself spoke of this quality (in a letter where he expressed a disinclination to 'cherish' the ghost story as a '*class* of fiction') as 'a close connotation, or close observation, of the real – or whatever one may call it – the familiar, the inevitable' (*Letters*, Vol. III, p.277).[1] His chosen form of the novel also allows

---

1 Letter of 27 April 1899 to Vernon Lee; cited in Lustig, p. 86. For full details of this and other references, see the Bibliography at the end of this Introduction.

that expansiveness and capaciousness, the exploration of character and event developing over time, that intricacy and complexity of relationships which we find in novels like *The Portrait of a Lady* (1881), *The Bostonians* (1886), *What Maisie Knew* (1897) and *The Ambassadors* (1903). But there was another side to his imagination that was drawn to the paranormal, the occult and the supernatural; to events and situations outside the ordinary expectations of experience; worlds of which the reality was called into question, and which perhaps exist only in the mind or in fiction. And to render this imaginative realm he also tends towards the more concentrated form of the short story or the 'novella'. This volume contains all the stories by James which can strictly be described as ghost stories, in that they all contain an apparition, or at least, in the case of 'The Private Life' and 'The Jolly Corner', a ghostly 'double'.

James was only partially interested, though he was aware of, that part of nineteenth-century scientific enquiry which explored the paranormal. His brother William James, the distinguished philosopher and psychologist and author of *The Varieties of Religious Experience* (1902), founded the American Society for Psychical Research which investigated ghostly and other paranormal phenomena. For two years he was president of the British Society of that name; and Henry James once read a paper by his brother to the British Society. Their father, Henry James Senior, was a writer on religious and social matters: in the 1840s he became a follower of the mystical writings of Swedenborg and underwent a kind of religious conversion. One of the factors contributing to this was a ghostly experience in which he was one evening beset by extreme terror at the sense of a 'damned shape' squatting invisibly in the corner of the room where he sat, 'beat upon meanwhile by an ever-growing tempest of doubt, anxiety and despair, with absolutely no relief from any truth I had ever encountered, save a most pale and distant glimmer of the Divine existence', a state of mind that it took him 'a good long hour' to get under control (James, ed. Edel, 1949, p. vi). Henry James himself records no such encounters of his own. But his famous dream of the Galerie d'Apollon in the Louvre Museum in Paris, in which he resisted a hostile force on the other side of a closed door and followed with a counter-attack leading to the routing of a figure who fled down the great expanse of the gallery, is recorded in his *Autobiography* as having the effect of 'a love-philtre or a fear-philtre which fixes for the senses their supreme symbol of the fair or the strange' (James, 1956, p. 196); and the dream's figure of a kind of double, the pursuer who becomes the pursued, the 'appalling', as

James puts it, who becomes the 'appalled', is surely related, by whatever mysterious psychological connections, to a similar doubling in 'The Jolly Corner'.

Above all, however, James's sense of the ghostly is a matter of literary imagination and artistry rather than any personal experience of or belief in the paranormal. Following his great predecessor Nathaniel Hawthorne, James often associated the supernatural with the genre of 'Romance'. In Romance the purely imaginary could co-exist alongside the everyday, and ghosts, spirits, demons and other creatures of a shadowy other world could suddenly rub shoulders, uncannily and shockingly, with creatures of flesh and blood. Hawthorne defined Romance as 'a neutral territory, somewhere between the real world and fairy-land, where the Actual and the Imaginary may meet, and each imbue itself with the nature of the other'.[2] This *meeting* of the actual and the imaginary is crucial in James's ghost stories. His stories are never pure fantasy: the supernatural always has a bearing on the world of human action, psychology and morality; and indeed it is the interpenetration of the two worlds that gives the stories their particular interest. 'It is as difficult . . . to trace the dividing-line between the real and the romantic,' James wrote, 'as to plant a milestone between north and south' (James, Vol. 2, 1984, p. 1067). And in another place: 'A good ghost-story . . . must be connected at a hundred points with the common objects of life' (James, Vol. I, 1984, p.742; cited in Lustig, 1994, p. 50). In his Preface to Volume XVII of the New York Edition of his works (1909), he spoke of that 'note' of 'the strange and sinister embroidered on the very type of the normal and easy' and, in relation to 'Sir Edmund Orme', of 'the indispensable history of somebody's *normal* relation to something' (James's emphasis; see below, pp. 20 and 16). It is notable that Sigmund Freud, in a famous essay, found the essence of the 'uncanny', that characteristic effect of many ghost stories, in the presence of the strange in the midst of the familiar or homely (*heimlich*) (Freud 1991, p. 220). Henry James's emphasis on 'somebody's *normal* relation to something' is expressing a similar idea, and James adds to it later in the same essay when he writes: 'The extraordinary is most extraordinary in that it happens to you and me, and it's of value (of value for others) but so far as visibly brought home to us' (see p. 17 below).

2 Nathaniel Hawthorne, *The Scarlet Letter and Selected Tales*, Penguin Books, Harmondsworth 1976, p. 66

This 'bringing home to us' lies of course at the heart of the matter, and also raises the question of form and style. The chosen form for James's ghost stories is the short story or (in the case of 'The Turn of the Screw') the *novella*, or 'beautiful and blest *nouvelle*' as James called it,[3] using the French term rather than the Italian for that story of somewhere around a hundred pages, longer than the 'short story' but not so long as a novel. The short story, one which may be read at a single sitting, has that advantage of unified impression and single effect which Poe famously saw as its great strength (May 1994, pp. 59–64). Or as James put it, speaking of one class of fairytale, it seeks an effect 'short and sharp and single, charged more or less with the compactness of anecdote' (see p. 4 below). For the ghost story, which aims to give a pleasurably disturbing shock, a *frisson* of the uncanny, to the reader, this quality would seem indispensable. The *nouvelle* prolongs this somewhat – though it is notable that 'The Turn of the Screw' was first published in twelve weekly instalments, each adding its 'short and sharp and single' effect.

Virginia Woolf, in her suggestive and elegant essay on James's ghost stories, points out how the element of disturbing shock, or *frisson* of the uncanny, is often mild and subtle (Woolf, 1966; Edel, 1963, pp. 47–54). In 'Sir Edmund Orme' the ghost does not terrify the narrator (though that is not to say it does not have its uncanny effect on the reader), and he comments: 'I am ready to answer for it to all and sundry that ghosts are much less alarming and much more amusing than was commonly supposed' (p. 80). More significantly, perhaps, the narrator feels a great sense of distinction and privilege in being vouchsafed a vision of the ghost of Sir Edmund. The ghost of Mrs Marden's wronged lover appears as a kind of moral guardian, both to punish Mrs Marden and to protect her daughter from committing a similar wrong, and perhaps too from being wronged herself. This last possibility is the cue for the narrator's involvement: he too, as the eventual wooer of Charlotte Marden, is being watched and warned. But the uncanny is still there in the quiet appearance of the ghost, a distinguished, soberly clad and human figure, at the church service. And it is there too, all the more effective for its impinging so surprisingly on the bustling scene of the sea-front in Brighton, in the sudden strange anxiety of Mrs Marden. It is ambiguous as to whether she sees Sir Edmund at this point, or whether her pang of guilt and anxiety arises simply from the

3 Preface to Vol. XV of the New York Edition of the novels and tales (James, Vol. 2, 1984, p. 1227)

conversation with the narrator: but if so, this is a large part of the point. Henry James's ghosts are liable to arise as much from within as from without: whatever their vivid perceptibility, they are often as much emanations from the psyche as visitants from 'another world'. Indeed, it is precisely the equivocation between the two that gives them their imaginative power.

II

In James's earliest ghost story, 'The Romance of Certain Old Clothes', the title suggests the Hawthornean influence. But the story suffers perhaps from the way the supernatural element is brought in only on the concluding page. The story of the rivalry between the two sisters is in the vein of a gentle comedy of manners, and the triumph of the younger and the jealousy of the elder are not given sufficient strength or virulence to give motive to the melodramatically violent ending. One feels the need of a more demonic hatred between the sisters to give some kind of psychological link with the supernatural revenge. As Woolf said (with less justification) of 'Owen Wingrave': 'The catastrophe has not the right relation to what has gone before.'

In 'The Ghostly Rental', on the other hand, although the atmosphere of the 'haunted' house is subtly done, the supernatural element is deliberately subverted by the revelation of the truth about the 'ghost': this could be seen as an anti-ghost story, a debunking of the genre. Nevertheless, despite its rationalistic explanation it does retain a haunting atmosphere, and the real guilt and transgression which lie behind the story, and the narrator's uneasy sense of trespassing upon a private tragedy, preserve a sense of 'haunting' which is metaphorical, but which raises the whole question of the status of metaphor in this realm: what does it mean to be 'haunted' by the past? The ghostly and the figurative are closely connected: ghosts are already 'figures' – whether in a supernatural, psychological or simply literary sense – and they can be seen as metaphors which suddenly become literal. Ghosts in James are constantly crossing these boundaries of definition. Even the living can become touched, through metaphor, with a ghostly unreality: so that in 'Sir Edmund Orme' the haunted Mrs Marden, appearing at a window, is momentarily taken for 'an apparition' by the narrator (p. 71), who later describes her as 'a flitting presence behind the pane' (p. 75).

The way in which being 'haunted by the past' – in the sense of past tradition – can suddenly become literal is illustrated by 'Owen

Wingrave', which is at the same time an example of the frequent concern in James's ghost stories with strongly felt social and moral dilemmas. This is a story about conceptions of courage and soldiership, a critique of a military ideal that looks back through the nineteenth and eighteenth centuries to the origins of ideas of heroism in the classical period of Greece and Rome. The story, as James relates in his Preface, was prompted by the glimpse of 'a tall quiet slim studious young man of admirable type' in Kensington Gardens (see p. 19 below). And the strengths of the story lie as much in its characterisations of the protagonist, his tutor, his fierce old grandfather and his formidable aunt, and in its evocation of the military traditions of the ancient house of Paramore, as in the supernatural element. Indeed the aunt, and (as Julia Briggs comments: Briggs, p. 150) even more the figure of the young Kate Julian who urges Owen on to his ghostly fate, are perhaps more disturbing figures than the unseen ghost itself. It was, after all, not so long after this story was written, that well-born ladies were giving white feathers to conscientious objectors and non-enlisting young men at the outset of the First World War, and the *Daily Mail*'s 'Little Mother' was exhorting the mothers of Britain to 'pass on the human ammunition of "only sons" to fill up the gaps'.[4] 'Owen Wingrave' is a remarkable study of British military family tradition, and its ghostly element can be seen simply as an uncanny dimension of the latter. It also perhaps indicates James's own relation to this tradition, his feeling for a 'studious' young man (not so unlike himself, perhaps) who aimed at a different kind of honour but who died sacrificed to the ghosts of the past. George Bernard Shaw's criticism of the story (in its later form as a play), made in a letter to James, is however very shrewd and telling: he argued forcefully that James had given in to the 'incubus' of the past in letting Owen be defeated.[5] James defended the story on the grounds of the artist's imaginative freedom (against Shaw's idea of art as 'encouragement'); and later responded with a note of exasperation: 'Really, really we would have howled at a surviving Owen Wingrave who would have embodied for us a failure – and an ineptitude' (James, *Letters* IV, p. 515). And so Owen is seen – surely effectively in terms of the atmosphere and sentiment of the story as a whole – as touching and heroic at the end. And in

4 Cited in Robert Graves, *Goodbye to All That*, Penguin Books, London 1986, p. 188
5 Bernard Shaw, *Collected Letters 1898–1910*, ed. Dan H. Laurence, Max Reinhardt, London 1972, pp. 827–8

James's revised version, which emphasises the 'victory' of Owen's courage, the phrasing is surely more in keeping with the rest than the first version: 'He was like a young soldier on the battlefield,' becomes, 'He was all the young soldier on the gained field' (p. 151).[6]

Responsibility to the dead, and to past tradition (the trammels of which have a tragic effect in 'Owen Wingrave'), is seen more positively in 'The Third Person' and (perhaps) in 'The Real Right Thing' – indeed in the former with a charming light comedy. In 'The Real Right Thing', George Withermore, the young friend and admirer of the writer Ashton Doyne, is asked by their mutual publisher, and at the insistence of Doyne's wife, to write a Life of the deceased. As he begins to work on the Life, among Doyne's papers and in Doyne's own study, he is immediately aware of how 'the place was full of their lost friend'. ' "It's here that we're *with* him," ' says Mrs Doyne; but Withermore feels rather that 'it was there he was with themselves' (p. 269). These still mainly figurative expressions of haunting presence gradually become more insistent and more literal. Withermore seems actually to encounter Doyne in his researches: 'Was it a matter of '67? – or but of the other side of the table?' (p. 272). He seems to be helped in finding papers, and as the narrative goes on the figurative casting of these events drops away and he 'heard documents on the table behind him gently shifted and stirred' (the use of passive past participles, rather than intransitive verbs, subtly helps to shift our perception). The ambiguity between metaphoric and literal haunting is increased by the way in which Mrs Doyne, whom he encounters unexpectedly on staircases and in corridors, seems herself to 'haunt' the protagonist. Gradually Withermore comes to be reassured and encouraged by the presence of Doyne, and when he begins to miss that feeling the way is open to the quiet climax of the story. Doyne's presence, which never for Withermore becomes quite visible, begins to intimate the former's hostility to the Life. The story is about the biographer's awareness of his responsibility to his subject, and perhaps suggests James's reservations about that form of writing.

In 'The Third Person', on the other hand, the responsibility to the past is carried out with a charming robustness. The two middle-aged spinsters who inherit a house and decide to live in it together become

6 The second version is printed in the present volume. The first version can be found in Vol. 9 of James, ed. Edel, 1962–4; and also in James, Vol. 2, ed. Bayley, 1999. For a different view of the relative merits of the two endings, see Bayley's Introduction, p. xii.

aware of a 'third person' who seems to be enjoining some task upon them. Marr, the story's location, is based on Rye in Sussex, James's home from 1907 to 1913. Rye had once been on the coast until the sea retreated, and was full of legends of smuggling: hence the nature of the ghost. This is James's one ghost story where the mood is gently comic: the character of the two ladies, one timid and retiring, the other more forthright and with more of a 'past', are done with great nicety; the ghost has a gruesomeness (its head has 'a dreadful twist') which prompts a smile more than a shudder, and its appeasing is the opportunity for a very minor but distinctive act of daring by one of the ladies. The supernatural presence here enjoins not guilt and sorrow, but a stimulus to adventurousness and almost to the recapture of youth. The influence of a past tradition is here not stifling but enabling and liberating.

Unlike many of the ghosts recorded in the annals of the Society for Psychical Research (of whom James complained that 'different things are done – though on the whole very little appears to be – by the persons appearing': see p. 7), ghosts in James's stories always appear with a purpose. They may warn, encourage or punish; they may corrupt; and sometimes they may provide one of the characters with an admonishing or enabling *alter ego*, or other self . 'The Private Life' is included here because, although no ghost appears, the story does contain a spectral double, the other self of Clare Vawdrey the great writer. The mood here is of sparkling social comedy – the setting is a fashionable gathering of distinguished friends in an Alpine hotel – but the story contains a serious parable of a writer's double life. The figure of Vawdrey was based on the poet Robert Browning, whose outward sociable presence in London society presented James with an enigma: how could, he asks in his 1909 Preface, 'this particular loud, sound, normal, hearty presence, all so assertive and so whole, all bristling with prompt responses and usual views', have written 'the immortal things'? (See p. 12). And so the imagining of the spectral double, encountered working in his room while his social self entertains his friends below, was born. The wonderfully comic counter case – that of Lord Mellifont – was drawn from the example of Frederick, Lord Leighton, the famous painter and Fellow of the Royal Academy, 'that most accomplished of artists and most dazzling of men of the world', who seemed to suggest a character 'so exclusive of any possible inner self that, so far from there being here a question of an *alter ego*, a double personality, there seemed scarce a question of a real and single one, scarce foothold or margin for any private and domestic *ego* at all' (p. 13). And so the private Lord Mellifont is not even a ghost, not an absent presence, but in a surprising encounter simply . . . but readers, if they have not already done so, must discover for themselves.

To reduce these stories to their bare scenarios invites the danger, of course, of ignoring how the thing is *done*, that element of 'representation' as James called it, that vivid treatment which brings forth a 'picture', some 'appreciable rendering of sought effects' through which the reader (and James implies also the writer himself) can begin 'to see and hear and feel' (p. 15). In 'The Jolly Corner', at any rate, this quality of representation is at its most intense. Here again we have an encounter with a double, and again one especially close to James, the man that James might have become had he stayed in America rather than travelling so extensively in Europe and finally settling in England. The story is set in New York, near where James lived for a time as a child. In 1904–5, James revisited the United States and spent much time rediscovering the scenes of his earlier life and of his American stories, and 'The Jolly Corner' seems to have been born out of that visit. Spencer Brydon's double, the figure that haunts the house on the jolly corner, and whom Brydon himself haunts when he goes to encounter him, is a 'ravaged' figure, who at first hides his face in his hands when finally encountered, and who then advances down on Brydon 'as for aggression'. He is in immaculate evening dress and has, Brydon, later surmises, 'a million a year'. He seems to be some kind of businessman (a figure with whom James was often preoccupied during these years; see Lustig, 1994, pp. 223ff.), familiar with 'downtown' and the world of money of which James was so conscious when he returned to the States in 1904, and which earlier in the story Brydon deprecates but also, as a new property owner, quite enjoys. The double is both powerful and abject, threatening and tragic. What gives the story its force is the powerful suspense with which James endows the exploration of the empty rooms; the sense of tracking and being tracked; the closed doors which Brydon had left open and the open doors which he had left closed; the build up to the encounter – so psychologically charged because it is an encounter with a potential self – with the figure set so eerily and yet so credibly in the ghostly silvery light cast by the actual side-lights and fan-tracery of the entrance to the hall.

'The Friends of the Friends' (in its first version entitled 'The Way It Came') also builds up its own kind of suspense, and it too has a kind of 'doubling'. It also involves a particular aspect of experience, relations between men and women, which preoccupies James in 'The Romance of Certain Old Clothes', in 'Sir Edmund Orme', in 'The

Third Person' (in a gently comic way) and above all in 'The Turn of the Screw'. The doubling is that of the male friend and the female friend of the woman narrator (none of the three is given a name in the story): both her friends have had a mysterious ghostly encounter with an absent parent at the moment of the latter's death. The narrator and other mutual friends have often tried to engineer a meeting between the 'visited' pair, who have this momentous experience and many other things in common, but without success. The continually deferred meeting comes, indeed, to have something both laughable and slightly uncanny about it. (The chances and accidents that prevent the meeting have that element of repetition which Freud saw as one of the marks of the uncanny.) The narrator is eventually engaged to be married to the man and is determined to arrange a successful meeting between her two friends before the wedding.

The precise complications that ensue need not be anticipated (or recapitulated) here. But the outcome of this appointment does not preclude another kind of encounter between the special pair. And the narrator is suddenly confronted with a peculiar jealousy: is she jealous of a ghost? The story raises questions about the nature of love, of its combination of the physical and spiritual. When Søren Kierkegaard, the Danish philosopher, lost his great love Regina to another man, he said (not entirely ironically) that while his rival had won her living self, he had won her eternal spirit. But in James's story the narrator is tormented by the idea that even after the woman's death her fiancé 'sees her'. And the encounters are felt, curiously, as far from purely spiritual. ' "She comes to you as she came that evening," I declared; "having tried it she found she liked it!" ' And she adds: 'those were the exact words – and far from "sketchy" they then appeared to me – that I uttered' (p. 173). The ghostly is here entangled strangely with the sexual; fantasy, phantasm and desire are inextricably linked.

III

The psychological and the ghostly – fantasy, phantasm and desire – are nowhere more ambiguously and subtly intertwined than in James's greatest ghost story, 'The Turn of the Screw'. None other of his stories has received such an extraordinary amount of critical attention. As well as its masterly narration, its telling use of frame and point of view, its unparalleled creation of atmosphere and suspense, the story has raised pressing questions – indeed has sometimes aroused pressing anxieties – about the nature of good and evil, childhood innocence and sexuality, heroism, psychological repression, the social class system, attitudes to women and the nature of literature itself. And the history of critical reaction to the story, in its changing methods and criteria, is almost, in little, the history of criticism in the twentieth century. Only a very cursory glimpse of that history can be given here, and the reader is referred to the Bibliography in this volume for further exploration.

It is fair to say that the question that has dominated critical discussion, and which in most cases underlies all other questions, is outwardly a simple one: are the ghosts 'real' or are they figments of the governess's disturbed imagination? From a certain point of view the question may be an artificial one: the story is fiction, so there is no way of going behind or outside it to some historical reality about which there might be further evidence. What constitutes the 'real' in fiction? Nor can one point to James's 'intentions': James's Preface (which I shall discuss in a moment) is simply a commentary on his own work, and has no final authoritative status (and it too has its ambiguities). But the story presents itself in broadly 'realistic' terms (except for the presence of the ghosts themselves) – it wonderfully demonstrates that quality of 'the strange and the sinister embroidered upon the very type of the normal and easy' that I have cited above – and so the reader may understandably be led to psychological interpretations.

James's own observations on the story in his Preface to Volume XII of the New York Edition (see below pp. 3–9), written some ten years after the story's first publication, were not of course the first 'critical reactions' but they are perhaps the logical place to begin. Even if we deny them authoritative status and recognise that they cannot remove the ambiguities of the story, they are uniquely interesting because they tell us something of how the writer thought about his work, and give us further pointers and material for interpretation. There are perhaps three main points to note: a certain equivocation in James's sense of the value of the story, which he begins by calling 'this perfectly independent and irresponsible little fiction'; a sense of his own power in controlling the response of the reader (he describes the tale as 'a piece of ingenuity pure and simple, of cold artistic calculation, an *amusette* to catch those not easily caught'); and a revelation of his aim to arouse the reader's imagination of the evil in the story by leaving it vague ('Make him *think* the evil, make him think it for himself, and you are released from weak specifications'). What the Preface does not do is give any clear suggestion of the 'psychological' reading of the story which has come to dominate so much later criticism. The protagonist is seen very much as a heroine fighting against an external evil: he has given her 'authority', he says, 'which is a good deal to have given her'. The only places where some critics have found a crevice, in this Preface, which might give some extra foothold for the psychological reading, are the remark about the '*amusette*' to catch the reader, and the passage where James speaks of 'our young woman's keeping crystalline her record of so many intense anomalies and obscurities – *by which I don't of course mean her explanation of them, a different matter*' (p. 6; my emphasis). But these remarks, too, have been interpreted in different ways.

The early reviewers of the story all read it straightforwardly as the tale of a heroic young governess struggling against supernatural forces of evil which threaten to corrupt two young children. They found it powerful but often disturbing. The *Independent* (5 January 1899) went so far as to describe it as 'the most hopelessly evil story that we have ever read in any literature' (Esch and Warren, 1999, p. 156) – a judgment which seems to be applied to the story itself, as much as to the ghosts. Clearly it aroused (as it still arouses) anxieties about the corruption of childhood innocence which were perhaps especially shocking to late-nineteenth-century readers, for the idea of the innocent child was something of a cult in popular Victorian fiction. F. L. Pattee in 1923 seems to have been the first to suggest publicly that the story was simply about the psychological disturbance of the governess, 'the record of a clinic' (Kimbrough, p.180), and Edna Kenton followed with an article in 1924 (Kimbrough, pp. 209–11). But it was not until Edmund Wilson's influential essay 'The Ambiguity of Henry James' in *Hound and Horn*, 1934, that the psychological (or in Wilson's case more particularly psychoanalytic) reading made its full impact.[7] Wilson, clearly influenced by the writings of Freud, argued that the governess was a case of neurotic 'sex repression', that she was in love with the children's guardian, and that Quint and Miss Jessel were the projection of her own sexual desires and fears. He took a number of details of the story (like the fact that the governess is day-dreaming of 'the master' just before her first vision of Quint or the more indubitable fact that only the governess is clearly stated to have seen the ghosts) and showed that they could be read in such a way as to support his argument. Wilson's theory had its opponents (most

---

7 Revised and reprinted in Wilson's *The Triple Thinkers*, London 1938, where Wilson admitted greater ambiguity in the story than he had earlier argued. He modified his views again in a republication of *The Triple Thinkers* in 1948, and added a further Postscript in 1959.

notably, perhaps, A. J. A. Waldock, who asked how, if the governess's
vision of Quint was a product of her imagination, she could describe
him in such accurate detail that Mrs Grose the housekeeper, who had
of course known Quint before his death, could recognise him
immediately);[8] but many other critics later provided variations and
additions to Wilson's basic view, which after all answers to a modern
tendency to prefer psychological to transcendental explanations.

Why did (and does) the story arouse such intense critical interest?
One answer of course is that the power and subtlety of James's
writing itself creates an atmosphere and tension that grip the reader
whatever his or her subsequent interpretation of the story. Then
there is the eminence of James himself, whom many have seen as the
greatest novelist of the turn of the century, and especially fine and
creative in his moral and reasonable discriminations of human
behaviour.[9] Here, in this story, we see this eminently sane observer of
the human world suggesting a dark, irrational and uncanny evil
which is not fully explained in natural terms. So is James entirely in
control of his material? Are there elements here (perhaps elements
arising from his own psyche) which his moral sense cannot fully
encompass and explain?[10] There are also broader cultural reasons for
the interest in this story: it can be read in Christian and parabolic
terms as a struggle between the forces of light (represented by the
governess) and the forces of darkness (represented by Quint and
Jessel), and has been related in this way to many of the great
presentations of this theme in past literature.[11] Or it can be read, as
we have seen, in modern, 'scientific' and psychological terms as the

8 A. J. A. Waldock, 'Mr Edmund Wilson and *The Turn of the Screw*', *Modern Language Notes*, Vol. LXII, April 1947; repr. in Willen, 1969
9 For a classic statement of this view, see F.R. Leavis, *The Great Tradition*, Penguin Books, London 1966, Chapter 3.
10 F. R. Leavis, in a passing mention of the story, found in it a 'curious suggestion of abnormality' in 'the preoccupation with indefinite evil', relating it to a 'morbidity' which he also found in James's story 'The Altar of the Dead' (Leavis, 1962, p. 230). He modified this view in a later discussion which contrasted the story, to its disadvantage, with *What Maisie Knew*, and relegated it to the status of 'a non-significant thriller, done, nevertheless, with the subtlety of a great master'. He also found a critical 'perversity' in the view that 'focuses the evil . . . in the governess' (Leavis, 1967, p. 77). And, in a similar vein, Peter Coveney found in the story 'a suggestiveness . . . which makes for the sense of its psychic dishonesty' (Coveney,1967, p. 212).
11 See Robert Heilman, '*The Turn of the Screw* as Poem', *University of Kansas City Review*, Vol. XIV, Summer 1948, pp.277–89; repr. in Kimbrough, 1966, pp. 214–28

study of the governess's neurosis. It thus challenges two great paradigms of explanation, the religious and the scientific, and raises just those doubts and anxieties about the validity of each that have been so much in the forefront of intellectual debate since the latter part of the nineteenth century. It also, more specifically, raises questions of attitudes to women and to children's sexuality which were already pressing in James's day (the figure of the governess was particularly problematic for Victorian readers), and have perhaps come into even more prominence in the last fifty years.

Shoshona Felman, in a complex and interesting essay,[12] has argued that those critics who try to decide unequivocally between the two main opposing positions on the story, and to impose their view by rational and quasi-legalistic demonstration, may be making the same mistake that the governess herself makes in seeking 'mastery' of interpretation. Her attempt at mastery may be heroic, but it is also destructive, since it results in the death of Miles (unless, that is, one takes the broadly Christian reading that holds that although Miles has died his soul has been saved from the evil of Quint). The ambiguities of the story may be such that *both* readings can be equally well supported from the text, and so difference of interpretation has to rest in the end on the particular 'world-view' of the critic, and the critical reading will have validity less because it corresponds to some objectively demonstrable evidence in the text, and more because it answers to the views and preoccupations of a particular time. This is a view which has in recent decades, of course, been held of literature and criticism in general.

At any rate, it seems unsatisfactory to accept either of the two main views exclusively. It is the psychological view which has received overwhelming endorsement and variation in the last sixty years or so. But as Peter Beidler suggests (Beidler, 1975, p. 140), despite its variety of interest and undeniable productiveness, there are signs recently of dissatisfaction with it. And even if one takes the psychological view, many questions still remain unanswered. Unless the governess has made up the story from beginning to end (a singularly unproductive, indeed rather pointless reading), we know from Mrs Grose that Quint and Miss Jessel existed, that they were almost certainly lovers, that they were both closely involved with the

12 Shoshona Felman, 'Writing and Madness (Literature/Philosophy/Psycho-analysis)', *Yale French Studies*, Vols 55–6, 1977, pp. 94–113, 185–207; repr. in Felman, 1985 ; and repr. in shorter versions in Esch and Warren, 1999, pp. 196–228, and Beidler, 1995, pp. 193–206

children and that they both died in mysterious circumstances. James said that the 'private source' of the story was an anecdote he heard from E. W. Benson, the Archbishop of Canterbury, about corrupt servants, the ghosts of whom tried to lure the children of their former household into destruction. The idea of the abuse of children, that is, seems to have been at the very root of the story. And the governess's hallucination of the 'ghosts' (if we read the story that way) does not preclude the possibility of the children's having been harmed psychologically and morally by Quint and Miss Jessel. The governess's fantasies would then be a 'reification', as it were, of the persisting influence of the sinister pair. The vaguely suggested reasons for Miles's expulsion from school also play their part here. In this light the story has a particular kind of moral and psychological interest, since it involves that notoriously difficult area – of which we have seen distressing real-life cases in recent years in relation to child-abuse – of the adult perception of childhood sexual awareness, the problems of thinking of it in terms of 'guilt' and 'innocence', and the dangers of making adult inferences about children's behaviour, and of projecting adult conceptions and awarenesses into the minds of children. An approach which sees the irresolvable ambiguity of the story, to some extent along Felman's lines, is one which would do justice to this complexity.

In its simplest form the psychological reading would seem to reduce the story to a clinical case history in which we can place the governess's experience at a safe distance from ourselves. But it is not in that spirit we enjoy reading it. If we focus exclusively on problems of interpretation we may forget to do justice to the artistry with which James creates his atmosphere and his rendering of the governess's state of mind. Virginia Woolf points to the chilling effect of the silence at Bly, in particular to the governess's recollection of the moment before she sees Quint for the first time: 'I can hear again, as I write, the intense hush in which the sounds of evening dropped. The rooks stopped cawing in the golden sky, and the friendly hour lost for the unspeakable minute its voice' (p. 191 below). Or one might recall the uncanny precision of those little misunderstandings or slippages of expression that give glimpses of dark secrets, like the early conversation with Mrs Grose about the master:

'He seems to like us young and pretty!'
'Oh he *did*,' Mrs Grose assented: 'it was the way he liked everyone!' She had no sooner spoken indeed than she caught herself up. 'I mean that's *his* way – the master's.'

I was struck. 'But of whom did you speak first?'
She looked blank, but she coloured. 'Why of *him.*'
'Of the master?'
'Of who else?'   [pp. 186–7]

At innumerable points in the story there are formulations that lend
themselves to ambiguous interpretation by the characters or by the
reader. What is it that the governess claims the children 'know'
(p. 205) when she returns from the episode with Flora and the figure
of Miss Jessel beside the lake? Whom is Miles addressing as 'you
devil!' in his impassioned response, at the climax of the drama, to the
governess's question, 'Whom do you mean by "he"?'– the figure of
Quint, or the governess herself? (p. 266). Our answers will depend
on our interpretation of the story as a whole.

    At the heart of the story lies the ambiguity of the perception of evil
(how do we distinguish between what is outside us and what is merely
in our minds?). Without its ambiguity, and its atmosphere of mystery
and terror, the story would hardly have aroused the interest it has. Its
telling (including the important effect of Douglas's narrative in the
'frame') also induces, surely, a considerable amount of sympathy for
the governess: not only do we see things from her point of view but
we also share her sympathies, her sense of her own task, her self-
doubts and terrors, her moments of robust common sense. (We
particularly warm to her, I think, when she dismisses with a brisk
' "Stuff and nonsense!" ' Miles's claim that the things he 'sometimes
said' at school were 'too bad' for the masters to write home [p. 265].)
She is also often just as critical of her own motives as her many
subsequent critics. The reading that sees the governess as the heroic
protectress of the children is still a satisfying one. But perhaps
questioning and uncertainty are fundamental to the reading experience here; and the demands and pleasures of fiction are not to be
overruled by any demands for a univocal interpretation. In the end
we read ghost stories because we desire fictional mystery – the raising
of unanswered questions – as well as an interpretation of the world
around us. Perhaps the imagination needs and benefits from the
arousal of dubiety and fictional fear, and feels what James himself
calls 'the need and the love of wondering' (p. 14); so that we value the
story both as a compelling interpretative conundrum and as one that
arouses (again in James's words) 'the dear old sacred terror' (p. 3).

                                            MARTIN SCOFIELD
                                University of Kent at Canterbury

SELECT BIBLIOGRAPHY

NOTE Dates in brackets, placed after the date of an edition, are the dates of the first publication.

Works by Henry James

The Novels and Tales of Henry James (24 vols), New York Edition, Charles Scribner's Sons, New York 1907–9

The Complete Tales of Henry James (12 vols), ed. Leon Edel, Rupert Hart-Davis, London 1962–4.

The Ghostly Tales of Henry James, ed. Leon Edel, Rutger's University Press, New Jersey 1949 (consists of eighteen of James's tales involved with the supernatural or uncanny in a broad sense, with a general introduction and short critical and textual introductions to each tale)

Collected Stories (2 vols), selected and introduced by John Bayley, Everyman, London 1999

Selected Letters, ed. Leon Edel, Harvard University Press, Cambridge (Massachusetts) and London 1987

Letters (4 vols), ed. Leon Edel, Macmillan, London 1974–84

Literary Criticism (Vol. 1): *Essays on Literature, American Writers, English Writers*, ed. Leon Edel and Mark Wilson, The Modern Library of America, New York 1984

Literary Criticism (Vol.2): *French Writers, Other European Writers, the Prefaces to the New York Edition*, ed. Leon Edel and Mark Wilson, The Library of America, New York 1984

Autobiography, ed. Frederick W. Dupee, W. H. Allen, London 1956

Biography

Leon Edel, *The Life of Henry James* (revised edn. 2 vols), Penguin Books, Harmondsworth 1977 (5 vols. 1953–72)

Kenneth Graham, *Henry James: A Literary Life*, St Martin's Press, New York, 1995

Critical editions of The Turn of the Screw and of other ghost stories by Henry James:

Peter Beidler (ed.), *The Turn of the Screw*, Macmillan, London 1975 (includes James's Preface and material from Letters and Notebooks, and critical essays from different recent critical perspectives: reader-response, psychoanalytic, feminist, Deconstructionist and Marxist)

Deborah Esch and Jonathan Warren (eds), *The Turn of the Screw*, Norton Critical Editions (2nd Edition), W. W. Norton and Co., New York and London 1999 (includes textual variants, material from James's Preface, Letters and Notebooks, and criticism from the first Norton edition, with some changes in the early material and a number of more recent critical essays up to 1994)

Robert Kimbrough (ed.), *The Turn of the Screw*, Norton Critical Editions (1st Edition), W. W. Norton and Co., New York and London 1966 (includes textual variants, material from James's Preface, Letters and Notebooks, a number of early reviews and criticism up to 1957)

T. J. Lustig (ed.), *'The Turn of the Screw' and Other Stories*, Oxford World's Classics, 1992 (includes 'Sir Edmund Orme', 'Owen Wingrave' and 'The Friends of the Friends'; excerpts from James's Prefaces and Notebooks, a Chronology and variant textual readings)

Gerard Willen (ed.), *A Casebook on Henry James's 'The Turn of the Screw'* (2nd edition), Thomas Crowell Company, New York 1969 (1st edition 1959; includes material from James's Preface, Notebooks and Letters and nineteen critical essays from 1924–1967)

Other criticism of James's ghost stories

Peter Beidler, *Ghosts, Demons and Henry James: 'The Turn of the Screw' at the Turn of the Century*, University of Missouri Press, Columbia 1989 (includes a useful account of the relation of the story to the reports and investigations of the Society for Psychical Research, founded in 1882)

Julia Briggs, *Night Visitors: The Rise and Fall of the English Ghost Story*, Faber, London 1977

Leon Edel (ed.), *Henry James: A Collection of Critical Essays*, Prentice-Hall Inc., Englewood Cliffs 1963

Shoshona Felman, *Writing and Madness (Literature/Philosophy/Psychoanalysis)*, Cornell University Press, Ithaca 1985 (chapter on *The Turn of the Screw)*; excerpts reprinted in Beidler and Esch & Warren

T. J. Lustig, *Henry James and the Ghostly*, Cambridge University Press, Cambridge 1994 (the fullest and most thorough study of the 'ghostly', literal and figurative, across the whole range of James's writing)

Virginia Woolf, 'Henry James's Ghost Stories', in *Collected Essays*, Vol. 1, Hogarth Press, London 1966 (repr. in Edel 1963)

Related criticism of James's novels and stories

Edmund Wilson, 'The Ambiguity of Henry James', in *The Triple Thinkers*, Penguin Books, Harmondsworth, 1962 (1938; repr. in Willen, 1969)

F. R. Leavis, *The Great Tradition*, Penguin Books, Harmondsworth 1966 (1948; chapter 3)

F. R. Leavis, *The Common Pursuit*, Penguin Books, Harmondsworth 1962 (1952)

F. R. Leavis, *'What Maisie Knew'*, in *Anna Karenina and Other Essays*, Chatto & Windus, London 1967

Peter Coveney, *The Image of Childhood*, Penguin Books, Harmondsworth, 1967 (1957; chapter 8)

Related work on the supernatural in fiction

Sigmund Freud, 'The Uncanny', in *The Standard Edition of the Complete Psychological Works of Sigmund Freud*, Vol. XVI , The Hogarth Press and the Institute of Psychoanalysis, London 1991 (1955); also in *The Pelican Freud Library, Vol. XIV: Art and Literature*, ed. Albert Dickson, Penguin Books, Harmondsworth, 1987 (1985)

This perfectly independent and irresponsible little fiction rejoices, beyond any rival on a like ground, in a conscious provision of prompt retort to the sharpest question that may be addressed to it. For it has the small strength – if I shouldn't say rather the unattackable ease – of a perfect homogeneity, of being, to the very last grain of its virtue, all of a kind; the very kind, as happens, least apt to be baited by earnest criticism, the only sort of criticism of which account need be taken. To have handled again this so full-blown flower of high fancy is to be led back by it to easy and happy recognitions. Let the first of these be that of the starting-point itself – the sense, all charming again, of the circle, one winter afternoon, round the hall-fire of a grave old country-house where (for all the world as if to resolve itself promptly and obligingly into convertible, into 'literary' stuff) the talk turned, on I forget what homely pretext, to apparitions and night-fears, to the marked and sad drop in the general supply, and still more in the general quality, of such commodities. The good, the really effective and heart-shaking ghost-stories (roughly so to term them) appeared all to have been told, and neither new crop nor new type in any quarter awaited us. The new type indeed, the mere modern 'psychical' case, washed clean of all queerness as by exposure to a flowing laboratory tap, and equipped with credentials vouching for this – the new type clearly promised little, for the more it was respectably certified the less it seemed of a nature to rouse the dear old sacred terror. Thus it was, I remember, that amid our lament for a beautiful lost form, our distinguished host expressed the wish that he might but have recovered for us one of the scantest of fragments of this form at its best. He had never forgotten the impression made on him as a young man by the withheld glimpse, as it were, of a dreadful matter that had been reported years before, and with as few particulars, to a lady with whom he had youthfully talked. The story would have been thrilling could she but have found herself in better possession of it, dealing as it did with a couple of small children in an out-of-the-way place, to whom the spirits of certain 'bad' servants, dead in

the employ of the house, were believed to have appeared with the
design of 'getting hold' of them. This was all, but there had been
more, which my friend's old converser had lost the thread of: she
could assure him only of the wonder of the allegations as she had
anciently heard them made. He himself could give us but this
shadow of a shadow – my own appreciation of which, I need scarcely
say, was exactly wrapped up in that thinness. On the surface there
wasn't much, but another grain, none the less, would have spoiled
the precious pinch addressed to its end as neatly as some modicum
extracted from an old silver snuffbox and held between finger and
thumb. I was to remember the haunted children and the prowling
servile spirits as a 'value', of the disquieting sort, in all conscience
sufficient; so that when, after an interval, I was asked for something
seasonable by the promoters of a periodical dealing in the time-
honoured Christmastide toy, I bethought myself at once of the
vividest little note for sinister romance that I had ever jotted down.

Such was the private source of 'The Turn of the Screw'; and I
wondered, I confess, why so fine a germ, gleaming there in the
wayside dust of life, had never been deftly picked up. The thing had
for me the immense merit of allowing the imagination absolute
freedom of hand, of inviting it to act on a perfectly clear field, with no
'outside' control involved, no pattern of the usual or the true or the
terrible 'pleasant' (save always of course the high pleasantry of one's
very form) to consort with. This makes in fact the charm of my
second reference, that I find here a perfect example of an exercise of
the imagination unassisted, unassociated – playing the game, making
the score, in the phrase of our sporting day, off its own bat. To what
degree the game was worth playing, I needn't attempt to say: the
exercise I have noted strikes me now, I confess, as the interesting
thing, the imaginative faculty acting with the *whole* of the case on its
hands. The exhibition involved is in other words a fairytale pure and
simple – save indeed as to its springing not from an artless and
measureless, but from a conscious and cultivated credulity. Yet the
fairytale belongs mainly to either of two classes, the short and sharp
and single, charged more or less with the compactness of anecdote
(as to which let the familiars of our childhood, Cinderella and
Bluebeard and Hop o' my Thumb and Little Red Riding Hood and
many of the gems of the Brothers Grimm[1] directly testify), or else
the long and loose, the copious, the various, the endless, where,
dramatically speaking, roundness is quite sacrificed – sacrificed to
fullness, sacrificed to exuberance, if one will: witness at hazard almost
any one of *The Arabian Nights*.[2] The charm of all these things for the

distracted modern mind is in the clear field of experience, as I call it, over which we are thus led to roam; an annexed but independent world in which nothing is right save as we rightly imagine it. We have to do *that*, and we do it happily for the short spurt and in the smaller piece, achieving so perhaps beauty and lucidity; we flounder, we lose breath, on the other hand – that is we fail, not of continuity, but of an agreeable unity, of the 'roundness' in which beauty and lucidity largely reside – when we go in, as they say, for great lengths and breadths. And this, oddly enough, not because 'keeping it up' isn't abundantly within the compass of the imagination appealed to in certain conditions, but because the finer interest depends just on *how* it is kept up.

Nothing is so easy as improvisation, the running on and on of invention; it is sadly compromised, however, from the moment its stream breaks bounds and gets into flood. Then the waters may spread indeed, gathering houses and herds and crops and cities into their arms and wrenching off, for our amusement, the whole face of the land – only violating by the same stroke our sense of the course and the channel, which is our sense of the uses of a stream and the virtue of a story. Improvisation, as in *The Arabian Nights*, may keep on terms with encountered objects by sweeping them in and floating them on its breast; but the great effect it so loses – that of keeping on terms with itself. This is ever, I intimate, the hard thing for the fairytale; but by just so much as it struck me as hard did it in 'The Turn of the Screw' affect me as irresistibly prescribed. To improvise with extreme freedom and yet at the same time without the possibility of ravage, without the hint of a flood; to keep the stream, in a word, on something like ideal terms with itself: that was here my definite business. The thing was to aim at absolute singleness, clearness and roundness, and yet to depend on an imagination working freely, working (call it) with extravagance; by which law it wouldn't be thinkable except as free and wouldn't be amusing except as controlled. The merit of the tale, as it stands, is accordingly, I judge, that it has struggled successfully with its dangers. It is an excursion into chaos while remaining, like Bluebeard and Cinderella, but an anecdote – though an anecdote amplified and highly emphasised and returning upon itself; as, for that matter, Cinderella and Bluebeard return. I need scarcely add after this that it is a piece of ingenuity pure and simple, of cold artistic calculation, an *amusette*[3] to catch those not easily caught (the 'fun' of the capture of the merely witless being ever but small), the jaded, the disillusioned, the fastidious. Otherwise expressed, the study is of a conceived 'tone', the tone of suspected and felt trouble, of an inordinate and incalculable sort – the tone of tragic, yet of exquisite, mystification. To knead the subject of my young friend's, the supposititious narrator's, mystification thick, and yet strain the expression of it so clear and fine that beauty would result: no side of the matter so revives for me as that endeavour. Indeed, if the artistic value of such an experiment be measured by the intellectual echoes it may again, long after, set in motion, the case would make in favour of this little firm fantasy – which I seem to see draw behind it today a train of associations. I ought doubtless to blush for thus confessing them so numerous that I can but pick among them for reference. I recall for instance a reproach made me by a reader capable evidently, for the time, of some attention, but not quite capable of enough, who complained that I hadn't sufficiently 'characterised' my young woman engaged in her labyrinth; hadn't endowed her with signs and marks, features and humours, hadn't in a word invited her to deal with her own mystery as well as with that of Peter Quint, Miss Jessel and the hapless children. I remember well, whatever the absurdity of its now coming back to me, my reply to that criticism – under which one's artistic, one's ironic heart shook for the instant almost to breaking. 'You indulge in that stricture at your ease, and I don't mind confiding to you that – strange as it may appear! – one has to choose ever so delicately among one's difficulties, attaching one's self to the greatest, bearing hard on those and intelligently neglecting the others. If one attempts to tackle them all one is certain to deal completely with none; whereas the effectual dealing with a few casts a blest golden haze under cover of which, like wanton mocking goddesses in clouds, the others find prudent to retire. It was "déjà très-joli",[4] in "The Turn of the Screw", please believe, the general proposition of our young woman's keeping crystalline her record of so many intense anomalies and obscurities – by which I don't of course mean her explanation of them, a different matter; and I saw no way, I feebly grant (fighting, at the best too, periodically, for every grudged inch of my space) to exhibit her in relations other than those; one of which, precisely, would have been her relation to her own nature. We have surely as much of her own nature as we can swallow in watching it reflect her anxieties and inductions. It constitutes no little of a character indeed, in such conditions, for a young person, as she says, "privately bred", that she is able to make her particular credible statement of such strange matters. She has "authority", which is a good deal to have given her, and I couldn't have arrived at so much had I clumsily tried for more.'

For which truth I claim part of the charm latent on occasion in the extracted reasons of beautiful things – putting for the beautiful always, in a work of art, the close, the curious, the deep. Let me place above all, however, under the protection of that presence the side by which this fiction appeals most to consideration: its choice of its way of meeting its gravest difficulty. There were difficulties not so grave: I had for instance simply to renounce all attempt to keep the kind and degree of impression I wished to produce on terms with the today so copious psychical record of cases of apparitions. Different signs and circumstances, in the reports, mark these cases; different things are done – though on the whole very little appears to be – by the persons appearing; the point is, however, that some things are never done at all: this negative quantity is large – certain reserves and proprieties and immobilities consistently impose themselves. Recorded and attested 'ghosts' are in other words as little expressive, as little dramatic, above all as little continuous and conscious and responsive, as is consistent with their taking the trouble – and an immense trouble they find it, we gather – to appear at all. Wonderful and interesting therefore at a given moment, they are inconceivable figures in an *action* – and 'The Turn of the Screw' was an action, desperately, or it was nothing. I had to decide in fine between having my apparitions correct and having my story 'good' – that is producing my impression of the dreadful, my designed horror. Good ghosts, speaking by book, make poor subjects, and it was clear that from the first my hovering prowling blighting presences, my pair of abnormal agents, would have to depart altogether from the rules. They would be agents in fact; there would be laid on them the dire duty of causing the situation to reek with the air of Evil. Their desire and their ability to do so, visibly measuring meanwhile their effect, together with their observed and described success – this was exactly my central idea; so that, briefly, I cast my lot with pure romance, the appearances conforming to the true type being so little romantic.

This is to say, I recognise again, that Peter Quint and Miss Jessel are not 'ghosts' at all, as we now know the ghost, but goblins, elves, imps, demons as loosely constructed as those of the old trials for witchcraft; if not, more pleasingly, fairies of the legendary order, wooing their victims forth to see them dance under the moon. Not indeed that I suggest their reducibility to any form of the pleasing pure and simple; they please at the best but through having helped me to express my subject all directly and intensely. Here it was – in the use made of them – that I felt a high degree of art really required; and here it is that, on reading the tale over, I find my precautions justified. The essence of the matter was the villainy of motive in the evoked predatory creatures; so that the result would be ignoble – by which I mean would be trivial – were this element of evil but feebly or inanely suggested. Thus arose on behalf of my idea the lively interest of a possible suggestion and process of *adumbration*; the question of how best to convey that sense of the depths of the sinister without which my fable would so woefully limp. Portentous evil – how was I to save that, as an intention on the part of my demon-spirits, from the drop, the comparative vulgarity, inevitably attending, throughout the whole range of possible brief illustration, the offered example, the imputed vice, the cited act, the limited deplorable presentable instance? To bring the bad dead back to life for a second round of badness is to warrant them as indeed prodigious, and to become hence as shy of specifications as of a waiting anticlimax. One had seen, in fiction, some grand form of wrongdoing, or better still of wrong-being, imputed, seen it promised and announced as by the hot breath of the Pit[5] – and then, all lamentably, shrink to the compass of some particular brutality, some particular immorality, some particular infamy portrayed: with the result, alas, of the demonstration's falling sadly short. If *my* bad things, for 'The Turn of the Screw', I felt, should succumb to this danger, if they shouldn't seem sufficiently bad, there would be nothing for me but to hang my artistic head lower than I had ever known occasion to do.

The view of that discomfort and the fear of that dishonour, it accordingly must have been, that struck the proper light for my right, though by no means easy, short cut. What, in the last analysis, had I to give the sense of? Of their being, the haunting pair, capable, as the phrase is, of everything – that is of exerting, in respect to the children, the very worst action small victims so conditioned might be conceived as subject to. What would *be* then, on reflection, this utmost conceivability? – a question to which the answer all admirably came. There is for such a case no eligible *absolute* of the wrong; it remains relative to fifty other elements, a matter of appreciation, speculation, imagination – these things moreover quite exactly in the light of the spectator's, the critic's, the reader's experience. Only make the reader's general vision of evil intense enough, I said to myself – and that already is a charming job – and his own experience, his own imagination, his own sympathy (with the children) and horror (of their false friends) will supply him quite sufficiently with all the particulars. Make him *think* the evil, make him think it for himself, and you are released from weak specifications. This ingenuity I took pains – as indeed great pains were required – to apply; and with a success apparently beyond my liveliest hope. Droll enough at the same time, I must add, some of the evidence – even when most convincing – of this success. How can I feel my calculation to have failed, my wrought suggestion not to have worked, that is, on my being assailed, as has befallen me, with the charge of a monstrous emphasis, the charge of all indecently expatiating? There is not only from beginning to end of the matter not an inch of expatiation, but my values are positively all blanks save so far as an excited horror, a promoted pity, a created expertness – on which punctual effects of strong causes no writer can ever fail to plume himself – proceed to read into them more or less fantastic figures. Of high interest to the author meanwhile – and by the same stroke a theme for the moralist – the artless resentful reaction of the entertained person who has abounded in the sense of the situation. He visits his abundance, morally, on the artist – who has but clung to an ideal of faultlessness. Such indeed, for this latter, are some of the observations by which the prolonged strain of that clinging may be enlivened!

'The Private Life', 'Owen Wingrave',
'The Friends of the Friends', 'Sir Edmund Orme',
'The Real Right Thing' and 'The Jolly Corner'

I proceed almost eagerly, in any case, to 'The Private Life' – and at the cost of reaching for a moment over 'The Jolly Corner': I find myself so fondly return to ground on which the history even of small experiments may be more or less written. This mild documentation fairly thickens for me, I confess, the air of the first-mentioned of these tales; the scraps of records flit through that medium, to memory, as with the incalculable brush of wings of the imprisoned bat at eventide. This piece of ingenuity rests for me on such a handful of acute impressions as I may not here tell over at once; so that, to be brief, I select two of the sharpest. Neither of these was, in old London days, I make out, to be resisted even under its single pressure; so that the hour struck with a vengeance for 'Dramatise it, dramatise it!' (dramatise, that is, the combination) from the first glimpse of a good way to work together two cases that happened to have been given me. They were those – as distinct as possible save for belonging alike to the 'world', the London world of a time when discrimination still a little lifted its head – of a highly distinguished man, constantly to be encountered, whose fortune and whose peculiarity it was to bear out personally as little as possible (at least to *my* wondering sense) the high denotements, the rich implications and rare associations, of the genius to which he owed his position and his renown. One may go, naturally, in such a connection, but by one's own applied measure; and I have never ceased to ask myself, in this particular loud, sound, normal, hearty presence, all so assertive and so whole, all bristling with prompt responses and expected opinions and usual views, radiating all a broad daylight equality of emphasis and impartiality of address (for most relations) – I never ceased, I say, to ask myself what lodgement, on such premises, the rich proud genius one adored could ever have contrived, what domestic commerce the subtlety that was its prime ornament and the world's wonder have enjoyed, under what shelter the obscurity that was its luckless drawback and the world's despair have flourished. The whole aspect and *allure* of the fresh sane man, illustrious and undistinguished – no 'sensitive poor gentleman' he! – was mystifying; they made the question of who then had written the immortal things such a puzzle.

So at least one could but take the case – though one's need for relief depended, no doubt, on what one (so to speak) suffered. The writer of these lines, at any rate, suffered so much – I mean of course but by the unanswered question – that light *had* at last to break under pressure of the whimsical theory of two distinct and alternate presences, the assertion of either of which on any occasion directly involved the entire extinction of the other. This explained to the imagination the mystery: our delightful inconceivable celebrity was *double*, constructed in two quite distinct and 'watertight' compartments – one of these figured by the gentle man who sat at a table all alone, silent and unseen, and wrote admirably deep and brave and intricate things; while the gentleman who regularly came forth to sit at a quite different table and substantially and promiscuously and multitudinously dine stood for its companion. They had nothing to do, the so dissimilar twins, with each other; the diner could exist but by the cessation of the writer, whose emergence, on his side, depended on his – and our! – ignoring the diner. Thus it was amusing to think of the real great man as a presence known, in the late London days, all and only to himself – unseen of other human eye and converted into his perfectly positive, but quite secondary, *alter ego* by any approach to a social contact. To the same tune was the social personage known all and only to society, was he conceivable but as 'cut dead', on the return home and the threshold of the closed study, by the waiting spirit who would flash at that signal into form and possession. Once I had so seen the case I couldn't see it otherwise; and so to see it moreover was inevitably to feel in it a situation and a motive. The ever-importunate murmur, 'Dramatise it, dramatise it!' haunted, as I say, one's perception; yet without giving the idea much support till, by the happiest turn, the whole possibility was made to glow.

For didn't there immensely flourish in those very days and exactly in that society the apparition the most qualified to balance with the odd character I have referred to and to supply to 'drama', if 'drama' there was to be, the precious element of contrast and antithesis? – that most accomplished of artists and most dazzling of men of the world[1] whose effect on the mind repeatedly invited to appraise him was to beget in it an image of representation and figuration so exclusive of any possible inner self that, so far from there being here a question of an *alter ego*, a double personality, there seemed scarce a question of a real and single one, scarce foothold or margin for any private and domestic *ego* at all. Immense in this case too, for any analytic witness, the solicitation of wonder – which struggled all the while, not less amusingly than in the other example, towards the explanatory secret; a clear view of the perpetual, essential performer, consummate, infallible, impeccable, and with his high shining elegance, his intensity of presence, on these lines, involving to the imagination an absolutely blank reverse or starved residuum, no *other* power of presence whatever. One said it under one's breath, one really yearned to know: was he, such an embodiment of skill and taste and tone and composition, of every public gloss and grace, thinkable even as occasionally single? – since to be truly single is to be able, under stress, to be separate, to be *solus*,[2] to know at need the interlunar swoon of *some* independent consciousness. Yes, *had* our dazzling friend any such alternative, could he so unattestedly exist, and was the withdrawn, the sequestered, the unobserved and unhonoured condition so much as imputable to him? Wasn't his potentiality of existence public, in fine, to the last squeeze of the golden orange, and when he passed from our admiring sight into the chamber of mystery what, the next minute, was on the other side of the door? It was irresistible to believe at last that there was at such junctures inveterately nothing; and the more so, once I had begun to dramatise, as this supplied the most natural opposition in the world to my fond companion-view – the other side of the door *only* cognisant of the true Robert Browning. One's harmless formula for the poetic employment of this pair of conceits couldn't go much further than 'Play them against each other' – the ingenuity of which small game 'The Private Life' reflects as it can.

I fear I can defend such doings but under the plea of my amusement in them – an amusement I of course hoped others might succeed in sharing. But so comes in exactly the principle under the wide strong wing of which several such matters are here harvested; things of a type that might move me, had I space, to a pleading eloquence. Such compositions as 'The Jolly Corner', printed here not for the first time, but printed elsewhere only as I write and after my quite ceasing to expect it; 'The Friends of the Friends', to which I here change the colourless title of 'The Way It Came' (1896), 'Owen Wingrave' (1893), 'Sir Edmund Orme' (1891), 'The Real Right Thing' (1900), would obviously never have existed but for that love of 'a story as a story' which had from far back beset and beguiled their author. To this passion, the vital flame at the heart of any

sincere attempt to lay a scene and launch a drama, he flatters himself
he has never been false; and he will indeed have done his duty but
little by it if he has failed to let it, whether robustly or quite
insidiously, fire his fancy and rule his scheme. He has consistently
felt it (the appeal to wonder and terror and curiosity and pity and to
the delight of fine recognitions, as well as to the joy, perhaps sharper
still, of the mystified state) the very source of wise counsel and the
very law of charming effect. He has revelled in the creation of alarm
and suspense and surprise and relief, in all the arts that practise, with
a scruple for nothing but any lapse of application, on the credulous
soul of the candid or, immeasurably better, on the seasoned spirit of
the cunning, reader. He has built, rejoicingly, on that blest faculty of
wonder just named, in the latent eagerness of which the novelist so
finds, throughout, his best warrant that he can but pin his faith and
attach his car to it, rest in fine his monstrous weight and his queer
case on it, as on a strange passion planted in the heart of man for his
benefit, a mysterious provision made for him in the scheme of nature.
He has seen this particular sensibility, the need and the love of
wondering and the quick response to any pretext for it, as the
beginning and the end of his affair – thanks to the innumerable ways
in which that chord may vibrate. His prime care has been to master
those most congruous with his own faculty, to make it vibrate as
finely as possible – or in other words to the production of the interest
appealing most (by its kind) to himself. This last is of course the
particular clear light by which the genius of representation ever best
proceeds – with its beauty of adjustment to any strain of attention
whatever. Essentially, meanwhile, excited wonder must have a
subject, must face in a direction, must be, increasingly, *about*
something. Here comes in then the artist's bias and his range –
determined, these things, by his own fond inclination. About what,
good man, does he himself most wonder? – for upon that, whatever it
may be, he will naturally most abound. Under that star will he gather
in what he shall most seek to represent; so that if you follow thus his
range of representation you will know how, you will see where, again,
good man, he for himself most aptly vibrates.

All of which makes a desired point for the little group of
compositions here placed together; the point that, since the question
has ever been for me but of wondering and, with all achievable
adroitness, of causing to wonder, so the whole fairytale side of life has
used, for its tug at my sensibility, a cord all its own. When we want to
wonder there's no such good ground for it as the wonderful –
premising indeed always, by an induction as prompt, that this

element can but be at best, to fit its different cases, a thing of appreciation. What is wonderful in one set of conditions may quite fail of its spell in another set; and, for that matter, the peril of the unmeasured strange, in fiction, being the silly, just as its strength, when it saves itself, is the charming, the wind of interest blows where it lists, the surrender of attention persists where it can. The ideal, obviously, on these lines, is the straight fairytale, the case that has purged in the crucible all its *bêtises*[3] while keeping all its grace. It may seem odd, in a search for the amusing, to try to steer wide of the silly by hugging close the 'supernatural'; but one man's amusement is at the best (we have surely long had to recognise) another's desolation; and I am prepared with the confession that the 'ghost-story', as we for convenience call it, has ever been for me the most possible form of the fairytale. It enjoys, to my eyes, this honour by being so much the neatest – neat with that neatness without which *representation*, and therewith beauty, drops. One's working of the spell is of course – decently and effectively – but by the represented thing, and the grace of the more or less closely represented state is the measure of any success; a truth by the general smug neglect of which it's difficult not to be struck. To begin to wonder, over a case, I must begin to believe – to begin to give out (that is to attend) I must begin to take in, and to enjoy *that* profit I must begin to see and hear and feel. This wouldn't seem, I allow, the general requirement – as appears from the fact that so many persons profess delight in the picture of marvels and prodigies which by any, even the easiest, critical measure *is* no picture; in the recital of wonderful horrific or beatific things that are neither represented nor, so far as one makes out, seen as representable: a weakness not invalidating, round about us, the most resounding appeals to curiosity. The main condition of interest – that of some appreciable rendering of sought effects – is absent from them ; so that when, as often happens, one is asked how one 'likes' such and such a 'story' one can but point responsively to the lack of material for a judgement.

The apprehension at work, we thus see, would be of certain projected conditions, and its first need therefore is that these appearances be constituted in some other and more colourable fashion than by the author's answering for them on his more or less gentlemanly honour. This isn't enough; *give* me your elements, *treat* me your subject, one has to say – I must wait till then to tell you how I like them. I might 'rave' about them all were they given and treated; but there is no basis of opinion in such matters without a basis of vision, and no ground for that, in turn, without some communicated closeness of truth. There are portentous situations, there are prodigies and marvels and miracles as to which this communication, whether by necessity or by chance, works comparatively straight – works, by our measure, to some convincing consequence; there are others as to which the report, the picture, the plea, answers no tithe of the questions we would put. Those questions *may* perhaps then, by the very nature of the case, be unanswerable – though often again, no doubt, the felt vice is but in the quality of the provision made for them: on any showing, my own instinct, even in the service of great adventures, is all for the best *terms* of things; all for ground on which touches and tricks may be multiplied, the greatest number of questions answered, the greatest appearance of truth conveyed. With the preference I have noted for the 'neat' evocation – the image, of any sort, with fewest attendant vaguenesses and cheapnesses, fewest loose ends dangling and fewest features missing, the image kept in fine the most susceptible of intensity – with this predilection, I say, the safest arena for the play of moving accidents and mighty mutations and strange encounters, or whatever odd matters, is the field, as I may call it, rather of their second than of their first exhibition. By which, to avoid obscurity, I mean nothing more cryptic than I feel myself show them best by showing almost exclusively the way they are felt, by recognising as their main interest some impression strongly made by them and intensely received. We but too probably break down, I have ever reasoned, when we attempt the prodigy, the appeal to mystification, in itself; with its 'objective' side too emphasised, the report (it is ten to one) will practically run thin. We want it clear, goodness knows, but we also want it thick, and we get the thickness in the human consciousness that entertains and records, that amplifies and interprets it. That indeed, when the question is (to repeat) of the 'supernatural', constitutes the only thickness we do get; here prodigies, when they come straight, come with an effect imperilled; they keep all their character, on the other hand, by looming through some other history – the indispensable history of somebody's *normal* relation to something. It's in such connections as these that they most interest, for what we are then mainly concerned with is their imputed and borrowed dignity. Intrinsic values they have none – as we feel for instance in such a matter as the would-be portentous climax of Edgar Poe's 'Arthur Gordon Pym', where the indispensable history is absent, where the phenomena evoked, the moving accidents, coming straight, as I say, are immediate and flat, and the attempt is all at the horrific in itself. The result is that, to my sense, the climax fails – fails because it stops short, and stops short for want of connections. There *are* no connections; not only, I mean, in the sense of further statement, but of our own further relation to the elements, which hang in the void: whereby we see the effect lost, the imaginative effort wasted.

I dare say, to conclude, that whenever, in quest, as I have noted, of the amusing, I have invoked the horrific, I have invoked it, in such air as that of 'The Turn of the Screw', that of 'The Jolly Corner', that of 'The Friends of the Friends', that of 'Sir Edmund Orme', that of 'The Real Right Thing', in earnest aversion to waste and from the sense that in art economy is always beauty. The apparitions of Peter Quint and Miss Jessel, in the first of the tales just named, the elusive presence nightly 'stalked' through the New York house by the poor gentleman in the second, are matters as to which in themselves, really, the critical challenge (essentially nothing ever but the spirit of fine attention) may take a hundred forms – and a hundred felt or possibly proved infirmities is too great a number. Our friends' respective minds about them, on the other hand, are a different matter – challengeable, and repeatedly, if you like, but never challengeable without some consequent further stiffening of the whole texture. Which proposition involves, I think, a moral. The moving accident, the rare conjunction, whatever it be, doesn't make the story – in the sense that the story is our excitement, our amusement, our thrill and our suspense; the human emotion and the human attestation, the clustering human conditions we expect presented, only make it. The extraordinary is most extraordinary in that it happens to you and me, and it's of value (of value for others) but so far as visibly brought home to us. At any rate, odd though it may sound to pretend that one feels on safer ground in tracing such an adventure as that of the hero of 'The Jolly Corner' than in pursuing a bright career among pirates or detectives, I allow that composition to pass as the measure or limit, on my own part, of any achievable comfort in the 'adventure-story'; and this not because I may 'render' – well, what my poor gentleman attempted and suffered in the New York house – better than I may render detectives or pirates or other splendid desperadoes, though even here too there would be something to say; but because the spirit engaged with the forces of violence interests me most when I can think of it as engaged most deeply, most finely and most 'subtly' (precious term!). For then it is that, as with the longest and firmest prongs of consciousness, I grasp and hold the throbbing subject; *there* it is above all that I find the steady light of the picture.

After which attempted demonstration I drop with scant grace

perhaps to the admission here of a general vagueness on the article of
my different little origins. I have spoken of these in three or four
connections, but ask myself to no purpose, I fear, what put such a
matter as 'Owen Wingrave' or as 'The Friends of the Friends', such
a fantasy as 'Sir Edmund Orme', into my head. The habitual teller of
tales finds these things in old notebooks – which however but shifts
the burden a step; since how, and under what inspiration, did they
first wake up in these rude cradles? One's notes, as all writers
remember, sometimes explicitly mention, sometimes indirectly
reveal, and sometimes wholly dissimulate, such clues and such
obligations. The search for these last indeed, through faded or
pencilled pages, is perhaps one of the sweetest of our more pensive
pleasures. Then we chance on some idea we *have* afterwards treated;
then, greeting it with tenderness, we wonder at the first form of a
motive that was to lead us so far and to show, no doubt, to eyes not
our own, for so other; then we heave the deep sigh of relief over all
that is never, thank goodness, to be done again. Would we have
embarked on *that* stream had we known? – and what mightn't we
have made of this one *hadn't* we known! How, in a proportion of
cases, could we have dreamed 'there might be something'? – and
why, in another proportion, didn't we *try* what there might be, since
there are sorts of trials (ah indeed more than one sort!) for which the
day will soon have passed? Most of all, of a certainty, is brought back,
before these promiscuities, the old burden of the much life and the
little art, and of the portentous dose of the one it takes to make any
show of the other. It isn't however that one 'minds' not recovering
lost hints; the special pride of any tinted flower of fable, however
small, is to be able to opine with the celebrated Topsy that it can only
have 'growed'. Doesn't the fabulist himself indeed recall even as one
of his best joys the particular pang (both quickening and, in a
manner, profaning possession) of parting with some conceit of which
he can give no account but that his sense – of beauty or truth or
whatever – has been for ever so long saturated with it? Not, I hasten
to add, that measurements of time mayn't here be agreeably
fallacious, and that the 'ever so long' of saturation shan't often have
consisted but of ten minutes of perception. It comes back to me of
'Owen Wingrave', for example, simply that one summer afternoon
many years ago, on a penny chair and under a great tree in
Kensington Gardens, I must at the end of a few such visionary
moments have been able to equip him even with details not involved
or not mentioned in the story. Would that adequate intensity *all* have
sprung from the fact that while I sat there in the immense mild

summer rustle and the ever so softened London hum a young man should have taken his place on another chair within my limit of contemplation, a tall quiet slim studious young man, of admirable type, and have settled to a book with immediate gravity? Did the young man then, on the spot, just *become* Owen Wingrave, establishing by the mere magic of type the situation, creating at a stroke all the implications and filling out all the picture? That he would have been capable of it is all I can say – unless it be, otherwise put, that I should have been capable of letting him; though there hovers the happy alternative that Owen Wingrave, nebulous and fluid, may only, at the touch, have found *himself* in this gentleman; found, that is, a figure and a habit, a form, a face, a fate, the interesting aspect presented and the dreadful doom recorded; together with the required and multi-plied connections, not least that presence of some self-conscious dangerous girl of lockets and amulets offered by the full-blown idea to my very first glance. These questions are as answerless as they are, luckily, the reverse of pressing – since my poor point is only that at the beginning of my session in the penny chair the seedless fable hadn't a claim to make or an excuse to give, and that, the very next thing, the pennyworth still partly unconsumed, it was fairly bristling with pretexts. 'Dramatise it, dramatise it!' would seem to have rung with sudden intensity in my ears. But dramatise what? The young man in the chair? Him perhaps indeed – however disproportionately to his mere inoffensive stillness; though no imaginative response *can* be disproportionate, after all, I think, to any right, any really penetrating, appeal. Only, where and whence and why and how sneaked in, during so few seconds, so much penetration, so very much rightness? However, these mysteries are really irrecoverable; besides being doubtless of interest, in general, at the best, but to the infatuated author.

Moved to say that of 'Sir Edmund Orme' I remember absolutely nothing, I yet pull myself up ruefully to retrace the presumption that this morsel must first have appeared, with a large picture, in a weekly newspaper and, as then struck me, in the very smallest of all possible print – at sight of which I felt sure that, in spite of the picture (a thing, in its way, to be thankful for) no one would ever read it. I was never to hear in fact that anyone had done so – and I therefore surround it here with every advantage and give it without compunction a new chance. For as I meditate I do a little live it over, do a little remember in connection with it the felt challenge of some experiment or two in one of the finer shades, the finest (*that* was the point) of the gruesome. The gruesome gross and obvious might be charmless enough; but why shouldn't one, with ingenuity, almost infinitely refine upon it? – as one was prone at any time to refine almost on anything? The study of certain of the situations that keep, as we say, the heart in the mouth might renew itself under this star; and in the recital in question, as in 'The Friends of the Friends', 'The Jolly Corner' and 'The Real Right Thing', the pursuit of such verily leads us into rarefied air. Two sources of effect must have seemed to me happy for 'Sir Edmund Orme'; one of these the bright thought of a state of *unconscious* obsession or, in romantic parlance, hauntedness, on the part of a given person; the consciousness of it on the part of some other, in anguish lest a wrong turn or forced betrayal shall determine a break in the blest ignorance, becoming thus the subject of portrayal, with plenty of suspense for the occurrence or non-occurrence of the feared mischance. Not to be liable herself to a dark visitation, but to see such a danger play about her child as incessantly as forked lightning may play unheeded about the blind, this is the penalty suffered by the mother, in 'Sir Edmund Orme', for some hardness or baseness of her own youth. There I must doubtless have found my escape from the obvious; there I avoided a low directness and achieved one of those redoubled twists or sportive – by which I don't at all mean wanton – gambols dear to the fastidious, the creative fancy and that make for the higher interest. The higher interest – and this is the second of the two flowers of evidence that I pluck from the faded cluster – must further have dwelt, to my appraisement, in my placing my scene at Brighton, the old, the mid-Victorian, the Thackerayan Brighton;[4] where the twinkling sea and the breezy air, the great friendly, fluttered, animated, many-coloured 'front', would emphasise the note I wanted; that of the strange and sinister embroidered on the very type of the normal and easy.

This was to be again, after years, the idea entertained for 'The Jolly Corner', about the composition of which there would be more to say than my space allows; almost more in fact than categorical clearness might see its way to. A very limited thing being on this occasion in question, I was moved to adopt as my motive an analysis of someone of the conceivably rarest and intensest grounds for an 'unnatural' anxiety, a *malaise* so incongruous and discordant, in the given prosaic prosperous conditions, as almost to be compromising. Spencer Brydon's adventure however is one of those finished fantasies that, achieving success or not, speak best even to the critical sense for themselves – which I leave it to do, while I apply the remark as well to 'The Friends of the Friends' (and all the more that this last piece allows probably for no other comment).

The Romance of Certain Old Clothes

TOWARDS THE MIDDLE of the eighteenth century, there lived in the Province of Massachusetts a widowed gentlewoman, the mother of three children. Her name is of little account: I shall take the liberty of calling her Mrs Willoughby – a name, like her own, of a highly respectable sound. She had been left a widow after some six years of marriage, and had devoted herself to the care of her progeny. These young persons grew up in a manner to reward her zeal and to gratify her fondest hopes. The first-born was a son, whom she had called Bernard, after his father. The others were daughters – born at an interval of three years apart. Good looks were traditional in the family, and this youthful trio were not likely to allow the tradition to perish. The boy was of that fair and ruddy complexion and of that athletic mould which in those days (as in these) were the sign of genuine English blood – a frank, affectionate young fellow, a deferential son, a patronising brother, and a steadfast friend. Clever, however, he was not; the wit of the family had been apportioned chiefly to his sisters. Mr Willoughby had been a great reader of Shakespeare, at a time when this pursuit implied more liberality of taste than at the present day, and in a community where it required much courage to patronise the drama even in the closet; and he had wished to record his admiration of the great poet by calling his daughters out of his favourite plays. Upon the elder he had bestowed the romantic name of Viola; and upon the younger, the more serious one of Perdita,[1] in memory of a little girl born between them, who had lived but a few weeks.

When Bernard Willoughby came to his sixteenth year, his mother put a brave face upon it, and prepared to execute her husband's last request. This had been an earnest entreaty that, at the proper age, his son should be sent out to England, to complete his education at the University of Oxford, which had been the seat of his own studies. Mrs Willoughby fancied that the lad's equal was not to be found in the two hemispheres, but she had the antique wifely submissiveness. She swallowed her sobs, and made up her boy's trunk and his simple provincial outfit, and sent him on his way across the seas. Bernard was entered at his father's college, and spent five years in England, without great honour, indeed, but with a vast deal of pleasure and no discredit. On leaving the University, he made the journey to France. In his twenty-third year, he took ship for home, prepared to find poor little New England (New England was very small in those days) an utterly intolerable place of abode. But there had been changes at home, as well as in Mr Bernard's opinions. He found his mother's house quite habitable, and his sisters grown into two very charming young ladies, with all the accomplishments and graces of the young women of Britain, and a certain native-grown gentle *brusquerie*[2] and wildness, which, if it was not an accomplishment, was certainly a grace the more. Bernard privately assured his mother that his sisters were fully a match for the most genteel young women in England; whereupon poor Mrs Willoughby you may be sure, bade them hold up their heads. Such was Bernard's opinion, and such, in a tenfold higher degree, was the opinion of Mr Arthur Lloyd. This gentleman, I hasten to add, was a college-mate of Mr Bernard, a young man of reputable family, of a good person and a handsome inheritance, which latter appurtenance he proposed to invest in trade in this country. He and Bernard were warm friends; they had crossed the ocean together, and the young American had lost no time in presenting him at his mother's house, where he had made quite as good an impression as that which he had received, and of which I have just given a hint.

The two sisters were at this time in all the freshness of their youthful bloom; each wearing, of course, this natural brilliancy in the manner that became her best. They were equally dissimilar in appearance and character. Viola, the elder – now in her twenty-second year – was tall and fair, with calm grey eyes and auburn tresses; a very faint likeness to the Viola of Shakespeare's comedy, whom I imagine as a brunette (if you will), but a slender, airy creature, full of the softest and finest emotions. Miss Willoughby, with her candid complexion, her fine arms, her majestic height, and her slow utterance, was not cut out for adventures. She would never have put on a man's jacket and hose; and, indeed, being a very plump beauty, it is perhaps as well that she would not. Perdita, too, might very well have exchanged the sweet melancholy of her name against something more in consonance with her aspect and disposition. She was a positive brunette, short of stature, light of foot, with a vivid dark brown eye. She had been from her childhood a creature of smiles and gaiety; and so far from making you wait for an answer to your speech, as her handsome sister was wont to do (while she gazed at you with her somewhat cold grey eyes), she had given you the choice of half a dozen, suggested by the successive clauses of your proposition, before you had got to the end of it.

The young girls were very glad to see their brother once more; but they found themselves quite able to maintain a reserve of goodwill for their brother's friend. Among the young men their friends and neighbours, the *belle jeunesse*[3] of the Colony, there were many excellent fellows, several devoted swains, and some two or three who enjoyed the reputation of universal charmers and conquerors. But the homebred arts and the somewhat boisterous gallantry of those honest young colonists were completely eclipsed by the good looks, the fine clothes, the punctilious courtesy, the perfect elegance, the immense information, of Mr Arthur Lloyd. He was in reality no paragon; he was an honest, resolute, intelligent young man rich in pounds sterling, in his health and comfortable hopes, and his little capital of uninvested affections. But he was a gentleman; he had a handsome face; he had studied and travelled; he spoke French, he played on the flute, and he read verses aloud with very great taste. There were a dozen reasons why Miss Willoughby and her sister should forthwith have been rendered fastidious in the choice of their male acquaintance. The imagination of woman is especially adapted to the various small conventions and mysteries of polite society. Mr Lloyd's talk told our little New England maidens a vast deal more of the ways and means of people of fashion in European capitals than he had any idea of doing. It was delightful to sit by and hear him and Bernard discourse upon the fine people and fine things they had seen. They would all gather round the fire after tea, in the little wainscoted parlour – quite innocent then of any intention of being picturesque or of being anything else, indeed, than economical, and saving an outlay in stamped papers and tapestries – and the two young men would remind each other, across the rug, of this, that, and the other adventure. Viola and Perdita would often have given their ears to know exactly what adventure it was, and where it happened, and who was there, and what the ladies had on; but in those days a well-bred young woman was not expected to break into the conversation of her own movement or to ask too many questions; and the poor girls used therefore to sit fluttering behind the more languid – or more discreet – curiosity of their mother.

That they were both very fine girls Arthur Lloyd was not slow to discover; but it took him some time to satisfy himself as to the apportionment of their charms. He had a strong presentiment – an emotion of a nature entirely too cheerful to be called a foreboding – that he was destined to marry one of them; yet he was unable to arrive at a preference, and for such a consummation a preference was certainly indispensable, inasmuch as Lloyd was quite too gallant a fellow to make a choice by lot and be cheated of the heavenly delight of falling in love. He resolved to take things easily, and to let his heart speak. Meanwhile, he was on a very pleasant footing. Mrs Willoughby showed a dignified indifference to his 'intentions', equally remote from a carelessness of her daughters' honour and from that odious alacrity to make him commit himself, which, in his quality of a young man of property, he had but too often encountered in the venerable dames of his native islands. As for Bernard, all that he asked was that his friend should take his sisters as his own; and as for the poor girls themselves, however each may have secretly longed for the monopoly of Mr Lloyd's attentions, they observed a very decent and modest and contented demeanour.

Towards each other, however, they were somewhat more on the offensive. They were good sisterly friends, betwixt whom it would take more than a day for the seeds of jealousy to sprout and bear fruit; but the young girls felt that the seeds had been sown on the day that Mr Lloyd came into the house. Each made up her mind that, if she should be slighted, she would bear her grief in silence, and that no one should be any the wiser; for if they had a great deal of love, they had also a great deal of pride. But each prayed in secret, nevertheless, that upon *her* the glory might fall. They had need of a vast deal of patience, of self-control, and of dissimulation. In those days, a young girl of decent breeding could make no advances whatever, and barely respond, indeed, to those that were made. She was expected to sit still in her chair with her eyes on the carpet, watching the spot where the mystic handkerchief should fall. Poor Arthur Lloyd was obliged to undertake his wooing in the little wainscoted parlour, before the eyes of Mrs Willoughby, her son, and his prospective sister-in-law. But youth and love are so cunning that a hundred signs and tokens might travel to and fro, and not one of these three pair of eyes detect them in their passage. The young girls had but one chamber and one bed between them, and for long hours together they were under each other's direct inspection. That each knew that she was being watched, however, made not a grain of difference in those little offices which they mutually rendered, or in the various household tasks which they performed in common. Neither flinched nor fluttered beneath the silent batteries of her sister's eyes. The only apparent change in their habits was that they had less to say to each other. It was impossible to talk about Mr Lloyd, and it was ridiculous to talk about anything else. By tacit agreement, they began to wear all their choice finery, and to devise such little implements of coquetry, in the way of ribbons and topknots and furbelows as were sanctioned by indubitable modesty. They executed in the same inarticulate fashion an agreement of sincerity on these delicate matters. 'Is it better so?' Viola would ask, tying a bunch of ribbons on her bosom, and turning about from her glass to her sister. Perdita would look up gravely from her work and examine the decoration. 'I think you had better give it another loop,' she would say, with great solemnity, looking hard at her sister with eyes that added, 'upon my honour!' So they were forever stitching and trimming their petticoats, and pressing out their muslins, and contriving washes and ointments and cosmetics, like the ladies in the household of the Vicar of Wakefield.[4] Some three or four months went by; it grew to be mid-winter, and as yet Viola knew that if Perdita had nothing more to boast of than she, there was not much to be feared from her rivalry. But Perdita by this time, the charming Perdita, felt that her secret had grown to be tenfold more precious than her sister's.

One afternoon, Miss Willoughby sat alone before her toilet-glass combing out her long hair. It was getting too dark to see; she lit the two candles in their sockets on the frame of her mirror, and then went to the window to draw her curtains. It was a grey December evening; the landscape was bare and bleak, and the sky heavy with snow-clouds. At the end of the long garden into which her window looked was a wall with a little postern door, opening into a lane. The door stood ajar, as she could vaguely see in the gathering darkness, and moved slowly to and fro, as if someone were swaying it from the lane without. It was doubtless a servant-maid. But as she was about to drop her curtain, Viola saw her sister step within the garden and hurry along the path towards the house. She dropped the curtain, all save a little crevice for her eyes. As Perdita came up the path, she seemed to be examining something in her hand, holding it close to her eyes. When she reached the house, she stopped a moment, looked intently at the object, and pressed it to her lips.

Poor Viola slowly came back to her chair, and sat down before her glass, where, if she had looked at it less abstractedly, she would have seen her handsome features sadly disfigured by jealousy. A moment afterwards the door opened behind her, and her sister came into the room, out of breath, and her cheeks aglow with the chilly air.

Perdita started. 'Ah,' said she, 'I thought you were with our mother.' The ladies were to go to a tea party, and on such occasions it was the habit of one of the young girls to help their mother to dress. Instead of coming in, Perdita lingered at the door.

'Come in, come in,' said Viola. 'We've more than an hour yet. I should like you very much to give a few strokes to my hair.' She knew her sister wished to retreat, and that she could see in the glass all her movements in the room. 'Nay, just help me with my hair,' she said, 'and I'll go to mamma.'

Perdita came reluctantly, and took the brush. She saw her sister's eyes, in the glass, fastened hard upon her hands. She had not made three passes, when Viola clapped her own right hand upon her sister's left, and started out of her chair. 'Whose ring is that?' she cried passionately, drawing her towards the light.

On the young girl's third finger glistened a little gold ring, adorned with a couple of small rubies. Perdita felt that she need no longer keep her secret, yet that she must put a bold face on her avowal. 'It's mine,' she said proudly.

'Who gave it to you?' cried the other.

Perdita hesitated a moment. 'Mr Lloyd.'

'Mr Lloyd is generous, all of a sudden.'

'Ah no,' cried Perdita, with spirit, 'not all of a sudden. He offered it to me a month ago.'

'And you needed a month's begging to take it?' said Viola, looking at the little trinket; which indeed was not especially elegant, although it was the best that the jeweller of the Province could furnish. 'I shouldn't have taken it in less than two.'

'It isn't the ring,' said Perdita, 'it's what it means!'

'It means that you're not a modest girl,' cried Viola. 'Pray does your mother know of your conduct? does Bernard?'

'My mother has approved my "conduct", as you call it. Mr Lloyd has asked my hand, and mamma has given it. Would you have had him apply to you, sister?'

Viola gave her sister a long look, full of passionate envy and sorrow. Then she dropped her lashes on her pale cheeks and turned away. Perdita felt that it had not been a pretty scene; but it was her sister's fault. But the elder girl rapidly called back her pride, and turned herself about again. 'You have my very best wishes,' she said, with a low curtsey. 'I wish you every happiness, and a very long life.'

Perdita gave a bitter laugh. 'Don't speak in that tone,' she cried. 'I'd rather you cursed me outright. Come, sister,' she added, 'he couldn't marry both of us.'

'I wish you very great joy,' Viola repeated mechanically, sitting down to her glass again, 'and a very long life, and plenty of children.'

There was something in the sound of these words not at all to Perdita's taste. 'Will you give me a year, at least?' she said. 'In a year

I can have one little boy – or one little girl at least. If you'll give me your brush again I'll do your hair.'

'Thank you,' said Viola. 'You had better go to mamma. It isn't becoming that a young lady with a promised husband should wait on a girl with none.'

'Nay,' said Perdita, good-humouredly, 'I have Arthur to wait upon me. You need my service more than I need yours.'

But her sister motioned her away, and she left the room. When she had gone, poor Viola fell on her knees before her dressing-table, buried her head in her arms, and poured out a flood of tears and sobs. She felt very much better for this effusion of sorrow. When her sister came back, she insisted upon helping her to dress, and upon her wearing her prettiest things. She forced upon her acceptance a bit of lace of her own, and declared that now that she was to be married she should do her best to appear worthy of her lover's choice. She discharged these offices in stern silence; but, such as they were, they had to do duty as an apology and an atonement; she never made any other.

Now that Lloyd was received by the family as an accepted suitor, nothing remained but to fix the wedding day. It was appointed for the following April, and in the interval preparations were diligently made for the marriage. Lloyd, on his side, was busy with his commercial arrangements, and with establishing a correspondence with the great mercantile house to which he had attached himself in England. He was therefore not so frequent a visitor at Mrs Willoughby's as during the months of his diffidence and irresolution, and poor Viola had less to suffer than she had feared from the sight of the mutual endearments of the young lovers. Touching his future sister-in-law, Lloyd had a perfectly clear conscience. There had not been a particle of sentiment uttered between them, and he had not the slightest suspicion that she coveted anything more than his fraternal regard. He was quite at his ease; life promised so well, both domestically and financially. The lurid clouds of revolution were as yet twenty years beneath the horizon, and that his connubial felicity should take a tragic turn it was absurd, it was blasphemous, to apprehend. Meanwhile at Mrs Willoughby's there was a greater rustling of silks, a more rapid clicking of scissors and flying of needles, than ever. Mrs Willoughby had determined that her daughter should carry from home the most elegant outfit that her money could buy, or that the country could furnish. All the sage women in the county were convened, and their united taste was brought to bear on Perdita's wardrobe. Viola's situation, at this moment, was assuredly not to be envied. The poor girl had an inordinate love of dress, and the very best taste in the world, as her sister perfectly well knew. Viola was tall, she was stately and sweeping, she was made to carry stiff brocade and masses of heavy lace, such as belong to the toilet of a rich man's wife. But Viola sat aloof, with her beautiful arms folded and her head averted, while her mother and sister and the venerable women aforesaid worried and wondered over their materials, oppressed by the multitude of their resources. One day, there came in a beautiful piece of white silk, brocaded with celestial blue and silver, sent by the bridegroom himself – it not being thought amiss in those days that the husband-elect should contribute to the bride's trousseau.[5] Perdita was quite at a loss to imagine a fashion which should do sufficient honour to the splendour of the material.

'Blue's your colour, sister, more than mine,' she said, with appealing eyes. 'It's a pity it's not for you. You'd know what to do with it.'

Viola got up from her place and looked at the great shining fabric as it lay spread over the back of a chair. Then she took it up in her hands and felt it – lovingly, as Perdita could see – and turned about towards the mirror with it. She let it roll down to her feet, and flung the other end over her shoulder, gathering it in about her waist with her white arm bare to the elbow. She threw back her head, and looked at her image, and a hanging tress of her auburn hair fell upon the gorgeous surface of the silk. It made a dazzling picture. The women standing about uttered a little 'Ah!' of admiration. 'Yes, indeed,' said Viola, quietly, 'blue is my colour.' But Perdita could see that her fancy had been stirred, and that she would now fall to work and solve all their silken riddles. And indeed she behaved very well, as Perdita, knowing her insatiable love of millinery, was quite ready to declare. Innumerable yards of lustrous silk and satin, of muslin, velvet, and lace, passed through her cunning hands, without a word of envy coming from her lips. Thanks to her industry, when the wedding day came, Perdita was prepared to espouse more of the vanities of life than any fluttering young bride who had yet challenged the sacramental blessing of a New England divine.

It had been arranged that the young couple should go out and spend the first days of their wedded life at the country house of an English gentleman – a man of rank and a very kind friend to Lloyd. He was an unmarried man; he professed himself delighted to withdraw and leave them for a week to their billing and cooing. After the ceremony at church – it had been performed by an English parson – young Mrs Lloyd hastened back to her mother's house to change her wedding gear for a riding-dress. Viola helped her to effect the change, in the little old room in which they had been fond sisters together. Perdita then hurried off to bid farewell to her mother, leaving Viola to follow. The parting was short; the horses were at the door and Arthur impatient to start. But Viola had not followed, and Perdita hastened back to her room, opening the door abruptly. Viola, as usual, was before the glass, but in a position which caused the other to stand still, amazed. She had dressed herself in Perdita's cast-off wedding veil and wreath, and on her neck she had hung the heavy string of pearls which the young girl had received from her husband as a wedding gift. These things had been hastily laid aside, to await their possessor's disposal on her return from the country. Bedizened in this unnatural garb, Viola stood at the mirror, plunging a long look into its depths, and reading Heaven knows what audacious visions. Perdita was horrified. It was a hideous image of their old rivalry come to life again. She made a step towards her sister, as if to pull off the veil and the flowers. But catching her eyes in the glass, she stopped.

'Farewell, Viola,' she said. 'You might at least have waited till I had got out of the house.' And she hurried away from the room.

Mr Lloyd had purchased in Boston a house which, in the taste of those days, was considered a marvel of elegance and comfort; and here he very soon established himself with his young wife. He was thus separated by a distance of twenty miles from the residence of his mother-in-law. Twenty miles, in that primitive era of roads and conveyances, were as serious a matter as a hundred at the present day, and Mrs Willoughby saw but little of her daughter during the first twelvemonth of her marriage. She suffered in no small degree from her absence; and her affliction was not diminished by the fact that Viola had fallen into terribly low spirits and was not to be roused or cheered but by change of air and circumstances. The real cause of the young girl's dejection the reader will not be slow to suspect. Mrs Willoughby and her gossips, however, deemed her complaint a purely physical one, and doubted not that she would obtain relief from the remedy just mentioned. Her mother accordingly proposed on her behalf a visit to certain relatives on the paternal side, established in New York, who had long complained that they were able to see so little of their New England cousins. Viola was despatched to these good people, under a suitable escort, and remained with them for several months. In the interval, her brother Bernard, who had begun the practice of the law, made up his mind to take a wife. Viola came home to the wedding, apparently cured of her heartache, with honest roses and lilies in her face, and a proud smile on her lips. Arthur Lloyd came over from Boston to see his brother-in-law married, but without his wife, who was expecting shortly to present him with an heir. It was nearly a year since Viola had seen him. She was glad – she hardly knew why – that Perdita had stayed at home. Arthur looked happy, but he was more grave and solemn than before his marriage. She thought he looked 'interesting', – for although the word in its modern sense was not then invented, we may be sure that the idea was. The truth is, he was simply preoccupied with his wife's condition. Nevertheless, he by no means failed to observe Viola's beauty and splendour, and how she quite effaced the poor little bride. The allowance that Perdita had enjoyed for her dress had now been transferred to her sister, who turned it to prodigious account. On the morning after the wedding, he had a lady's saddle put on the horse of the servant who had come with him from town, and went out with the young girl for a ride. It was a keen, clear morning in January; the ground was bare and hard, and the horses in good condition – to say nothing of Viola, who was charming in her hat and plume, and her dark blue riding-coat, trimmed with fur. They rode all the morning, they lost their way, and were obliged to stop for dinner at a farmhouse. The early winter dusk had fallen when they got home. Mrs Willoughby met them with a long face. A messenger had arrived at noon from Mrs Lloyd; she was beginning to be ill, and desired her husband's immediate return. The young man, at the thought that he had lost several hours, and that by hard riding he might already have been with his wife, uttered a passionate oath. He barely consented to stop for a mouthful of supper, but mounted the messenger's horse and started off at a gallop.

He reached home at midnight. His wife had been delivered of a little girl. 'Ah, why weren't you with me?' she said, as he came to her bedside.

'I was out of the house when the man came. I was with Viola,' said Lloyd, innocently.

Mrs Lloyd made a little moan, and turned about. But she continued to do very well, and for a week her improvement was uninterrupted. Finally, however, through some indiscretion in the way of diet or of exposure, it was checked, and the poor lady grew rapidly worse. Lloyd was in despair. It very soon became evident that she was breathing her last. Mrs Lloyd came to a sense of her approaching end, and declared that she was reconciled with death. On the third evening after the change took place, she told her husband that she felt she would not outlast the night. She dismissed her servants, and also requested her mother to withdraw – Mrs Willoughby having arrived on the preceding day. She had had her infant placed on the bed beside her, and she lay on her side, with the child against her breast, holding her husband's hands. The night-lamp was hidden behind the heavy curtains of the bed, but the room was illumined with a red glow from the immense fire of logs on the hearth.

'It seems strange to die by such a fire as that,' the young woman said, feebly trying to smile. 'If I had but a little of such fire in my veins! But I've given it all to this little spark of mortality.' And she dropped her eyes on her child. Then raising them she looked at her husband with a long penetrating gaze. The last feeling which lingered in her heart was one of mistrust. She had not recovered from the shock which Arthur had given her by telling her that in the hour of her agony he had been with Viola. She trusted her husband very nearly as well as she loved him; but now that she was called away forever, she felt a cold horror of her sister. She felt in her soul that Viola had never ceased to envy her good fortune; and a year of happy security had not effaced the young girl's image, dressed in her wedding garments, and smiling with coveted triumph. Now that Arthur was to be alone, what might not Viola do? She was beautiful, she was engaging; what arts might she not use, what impression might she not make upon the young man's melancholy heart? Mrs Lloyd looked at her husband in silence. It seemed hard, after all, to doubt of his constancy. His fine eyes were filled with tears; his face was convulsed with weeping; the clasp of his hands was warm and passionate. How noble he looked, how tender, how faithful and devoted! 'Nay,' thought Perdita, 'he's not for such as Viola. He'll never forget me. Nor does Viola truly care for him; she cares only for vanities and finery and jewels.' And she dropped her eyes on her white hands, which her husband's liberality had covered with rings, and on the lace ruffles which trimmed the edge of her nightdress. 'She covets my rings and my laces more than she covets my husband.'

At this moment, the thought of her sister's rapacity seemed to cast a dark shadow between her and the helpless figure of her little girl. 'Arthur,' she said, 'you must take off my rings. I shall not be buried in them. One of these days my daughter shall wear them – my rings and my laces and silks. I had them all brought out and shown me today. It's a great wardrobe – there's not such another in the Province; I can say it without vanity now that I've done with it. It will be a great inheritance for my daughter, when she grows into a young woman.

There are things there that a man never buys twice, and if they're lost you'll never again see the like. So you'll watch them well. Some dozen things I've left to Viola; I've named them to my mother. I've given her that blue and silver; it was meant for her; I wore it only once, I looked ill in it. But the rest are to be sacredly kept for this little innocent. It's such a providence that she should be my colour; she can wear my gowns; she has her mother's eyes. You know the same fashions come back every twenty years. She can wear my gowns as they are. They'll lie there quietly waiting till she grows into them – wrapped in camphor and rose-leaves, and keeping their colours in the sweet-scented darkness. She shall have black hair, she shall wear my carnation satin. Do you promise me, Arthur?'

'Promise you what, dearest?'

'Promise me to keep your poor little wife's old gowns.'

'Are you afraid I'll sell them?'

'No, but that they may get scattered. My mother will have them properly wrapped up, and you shall lay them away under a double-lock. Do you know the great chest in the attic, with the iron bands? There's no end to what it will hold. You can lay them all there. My mother and the housekeeper will do it, and give you the key. And you'll keep the key in your secretary, and never give it to anyone but your child. Do you promise me?'

'Ah, yes, I promise you,' said Lloyd, puzzled at the intensity with which his wife appeared to cling to this idea.

'Will you swear?' repeated Perdita.

'Yes, I swear.'

'Well – I trust you – I trust you,' said the poor lady, looking into his eyes with eyes in which, if he had suspected her vague apprehensions, he might have read an appeal quite as much as an assurance.

Lloyd bore his bereavement soberly and manfully. A month after his wife's death, in the course of commerce, circumstances arose which offered him an opportunity of going to England. He embraced it as a diversion from gloomy thoughts. He was absent nearly a year, during which his little girl was tenderly nursed and cherished by her grandmother. On his return he had his house again thrown open, and announced his intention of keeping the same state as during his wife's lifetime. It very soon came to be predicted that he would marry again, and there were at least a dozen young women of whom one may say that it was by no fault of theirs that, for six months after his return, the prediction did not come true. During this interval, he still left his little daughter in Mrs Willoughby's hands, the latter assuring him that a change of residence at so tender an age was perilous to her health. Finally, however, he declared that his heart longed for his daughter's presence, and that she must be brought up to town. He sent his coach and his housekeeper to fetch her home. Mrs Willoughby was in terror lest something should befall her on the road; and, in accordance with this feeling, Viola offered to ride along with her. She could return the next day. So she went up to town with her little niece, and Mr Lloyd met her on the threshold of his house, overcome with her kindness and with gratitude. Instead of returning the next day, Viola stayed out the week; and when at last she reappeared, she had come only for her clothes. Arthur would not hear of her coming home, nor would the baby. She cried and moaned if Viola left her; and at the sight of her grief, Arthur lost his wits, and swore that she was going to die. In fine, nothing would suit them but that Viola should remain until the poor child had grown used to strange faces.

It took two months to bring this consummation about; for it was not until this period had elapsed that Viola took leave of her brother-in-law. Mrs Willoughby had shaken her head over her daughter's absence; she declared it was not becoming, and that it was the talk of the town. She had reconciled herself to it only because, during the young girl's visit, the household enjoyed an unwonted term of peace. Bernard Willoughby had brought his wife home to live, between whom and her sister-in-law there existed a bitter hostility. Viola was perhaps no angel; but in the daily practice of life she was a sufficiently good-natured girl, and if she quarrelled with Mrs Bernard, it was not without provocation. Quarrel, however, she did, to the great annoyance not only of her antagonist, but of the two spectators of these constant altercations. Her stay in the household of her brother-in-law, therefore, would have been delightful, if only because it removed her from contact with the object of her antipathy at home. It was doubly – it was ten times – delightful, in that it kept her near the object of her old passion. Mrs Lloyd's poignant mistrust had fallen very far short of the truth. Viola's sentiment had been a passion at first, and a passion it remained – a passion of whose radiant heat, tempered to the delicate state of his feelings, Mr Lloyd very soon felt the influence. Lloyd, as I have hinted, was not a modern Petrarch;[6] it was not in his nature to practise an ideal constancy. He had not been many days in the house with his sister-in-law before he began to assure himself that she was, in the language of that day, a devilish fine woman. Whether Viola really practised those insidious arts that her sister had been tempted to impute to her, it is needless to inquire. It is enough to say that she found means to appear to the very best advantage. She used to seat herself every morning before the great fireplace in the dining-room, at work upon a piece of tapestry, with her little niece disporting herself on the carpet at her feet, or on the train of her dress, and playing with her woollens balls. Lloyd would have been a very stupid fellow if he had remained insensible to the rich suggestions of this charming picture. He was prodigiously fond of his little girl, and was never weary of taking her in his arms and tossing her up and down, and making her crow with delight. Very often, however, he would venture upon greater liberties than the young lady was yet prepared to allow, and she would suddenly vociferate her displeasure. Viola would then drop her tapestry, and put out her handsome hands with the serious smile of the young girl whose virgin fancy has revealed to her all a mother's healing arts. Lloyd would give up the child, their eyes would meet, their hands would touch, and Viola would extinguish the little girl's sobs upon the snowy folds of the kerchief that crossed her bosom. Her dignity was perfect, and nothing could be more discreet than the manner in which she accepted her brother-in-law's hospitality. It may be almost said, perhaps, that there was something harsh in her reserve. Lloyd had a provoking feeling that she was in the house, and yet that she was unapproachable. Half an hour after supper, at the very outset of the long winter evenings, she would light her candle, and make the young man a most respectful curtsey, and march off to bed. If these were arts, Viola was a great artist. But their effect was so gentle, so gradual, they were calculated to work upon the young widower's fancy with such a finely shaded *crescendo*, that, as the reader has seen, several weeks elapsed before Viola began to feel sure that her return would cover her outlay. When this became morally certain, she packed up her trunk, and returned to her mother's house. For three days she waited; on the fourth, Mr Lloyd made his appearance – a respectful but ardent suitor. Viola heard him out with great humility, and accepted him with infinite modesty. It is hard to imagine that Mrs Lloyd should have forgiven her husband; but if anything might have disarmed her resentment, it would have been the ceremonious continence of this interview. Viola imposed upon her lover but a short probation. They were married, as was becoming, with great privacy – almost with secrecy – in the hope perhaps, as was waggishly remarked at the time, that the late Mrs Lloyd wouldn't hear of it.

The marriage was to all appearance a happy one, and each party obtained what each had desired – Lloyd 'a devilish fine woman,' and Viola – but Viola's desires, as the reader will have observed, have remained a good deal of a mystery. There were, indeed, two blots upon their felicity; but time would, perhaps, efface them. During the first three years of her marriage, Mrs Lloyd failed to become a mother, and her husband on his side suffered heavy losses of money. This latter circumstance compelled a material retrenchment in his expenditure, and Viola was perforce less of a great lady than her sister had been. She contrived, however, to sustain with unbroken consistency the part of an elegant woman, although it must be confessed that it required the exercise of more ingenuity than belongs to your real aristocratic repose. She had long since ascertained that her sister's immense wardrobe had been sequestrated for the benefit of her daughter, and that it lay languishing in thankless gloom in the dusty attic. It was a revolting thought that these exquisite fabrics should await the commands of a little girl who sat in a high chair and ate bread-and-milk with a wooden spoon. Viola had the good taste, however, to say nothing about the matter until several months had expired. Then, at last, she timidly broached it to her husband. Was it not a pity that so much finery should be lost? – for lost it would be, what with colours fading, and moths eating it up, and the change of fashions. But Lloyd gave so abrupt and peremptory a negative to her inquiry, that she saw that for the present her attempt was vain. Six months went by, however, and brought with them new needs and new fancies. Viola's thoughts hovered lovingly about her sister's relics. She went up and looked at the chest in which they lay imprisoned. There was a sullen defiance in its three great padlocks and its iron bands, which only quickened her desires. There was something exasperating in its incorruptible immobility. It was like a grim and grizzled old household servant, who locks his jaws over a family secret. And then there was a look of capacity in its vast extent, and a sound as of dense fullness, when Viola knocked its side with the toe of her little slipper, which caused her to flush with baffled longing. 'It's absurd,' she cried; 'it's improper, it's wicked'; and she forthwith resolved upon another attack upon her husband. On the following day, after dinner, when he had had his wine, she bravely began it. But he cut her short with great sternness.

'Once and for all, Viola,' said he, 'it's out of the question. I shall be gravely displeased if you return to the matter.'

'Very good,' said Viola. 'I'm glad to learn the value at which I'm held. Great Heaven!' she cried, 'I'm a happy woman. It's an agreeable thing to feel one's self sacrificed to a caprice!' And her eyes filled with tears of anger and disappointment.

Lloyd had a good-natured man's horror of a woman's sobs, and he attempted – I may say he condescended – to explain. 'It's not a caprice, dear, it's a promise,' he said – 'an oath.'

'An oath? It's a pretty matter for oaths! and to whom, pray?'

'To Perdita,' said the young man, raising his eyes for an instant, but immediately dropping them.

'Perdita – ah, Perdita!' and Viola's tears broke forth. Her bosom heaved with stormy sobs – sobs which were the long-deferred counterpart of the violent fit of weeping in which she had indulged herself on the night when she discovered her sister's betrothal. She had hoped, in her better moments, that she had done with her jealousy; but her temper, on that occasion, had taken an ineffaceable fold. 'And pray, what right,' she cried, 'had Perdita to dispose of my future? What right had she to bind you to meanness and cruelty? Ah, I occupy a dignified place, and I make a very fine figure! I'm welcome to what Perdita has left! And what has she left? I never knew till now how little! Nothing, nothing, nothing.'

This was very poor logic, but it was very good passion. Lloyd put his arm around his wife's waist and tried to kiss her, but she shook him off with magnificent scorn. Poor fellow, he had coveted a 'devilish fine woman', and he had got one! Her scorn was intolerable. He walked away with his ears tingling – irresolute, distracted. Before him was his secretary, and in it the sacred key which with his own hand he had turned in the triple lock. He marched up and opened it, and took the key from a secret drawer, wrapped in a little packet which he had sealed with his own honest bit of blazonry. *Teneo*, said the motto – 'I hold'. But he was ashamed to put it back. He flung it upon the table beside his wife.

'Keep it!' she cried. 'I want it not. I hate it!'

'I wash my hands of it,' cried her husband. 'God forgive me!'

Mrs Lloyd gave an indignant shrug of her shoulders, and swept out of the room, while the young man retreated by another door. Ten minutes later, Mrs Lloyd returned, and found the room occupied by her little step-daughter and the nursery-maid. The key was not on the table. She glanced at the child. The child was perched on a chair with the packet in her hands. She had broken the seal with her own little fingers. Mrs Lloyd hastily took possession of the key.

At the habitual supper-hour, Arthur Lloyd came back from his counting-room. It was the month of June, and supper was served by daylight. The meal was placed on the table, but Mrs Lloyd failed to make her appearance. The servant whom his master sent to call her came back with the assurance that her room was empty, and that the women informed him that she had not been seen since dinner. They had in truth observed her to have been in tears, and, supposing her to be shut up in her chamber, had not disturbed her. Her husband called her name in various parts of the house, but without response. At last it occurred to him that he might find her by taking the way to the attic. The thought gave him a strange feeling of discomfort, and he bade his servants remain behind, wishing no witness in his quest. He reached the foot of the staircase leading to the topmost flat, and stood with his hand on the banisters, pronouncing his wife's name. His voice trembled. He called again, louder and more firmly. The only sound which disturbed the absolute silence was a faint echo of his own tones, repeating his question under the great eaves. He nevertheless felt irresistibly moved to ascend the staircase. It opened upon a wide hall, lined with wooden closets, and terminating in a window which looked westward, and admitted the last rays of the sun. Before the window stood the great chest. Before the chest, on her knees, the young man saw with amazement and horror the figure of his wife. In an instant he crossed the interval between them, bereft of utterance. The lid of the chest stood open, exposing, amid their perfumed napkins, its treasure of stuffs and jewels. Viola had fallen backwards from a kneeling posture, with one hand supporting her on the floor and the other pressed to her heart. On her limbs was the stiffness of death, and on her face, in the fading light of the sun, the terror of something more than death. Her lips were parted in entreaty, in dismay, in agony; and on her bloodless brow and cheeks there glowed the marks of ten hideous wounds from two vengeful ghostly hands.

The Ghostly Rental

I WAS IN my twenty-second year, and I had just left college. I was at liberty to choose my career, and I choose it with much promptness. I afterwards renounced it, in truth, with equal ardour, but I have never regretted those two youthful years of perplexed and excited, but also of agreeable and fruitful experiment. I had a taste for theology, and during my college term I had been an admiring reader of Dr Channing.[1] This was theology of a grateful and succulent savour; it seemed to offer one the rose of faith delightfully stripped of its thorns. And then (for I rather think this had something to do with it), I had taken a fancy to the old Divinity School.[2] I have always had an eye to the back scene in the human drama, and it seemed to me that I might play my part with a fair chance of applause (from myself at least), in that detached and tranquil home of mild casuistry, with its respectable avenue on one side, and its prospect of green fields and contact with acres of woodland on the other. Cambridge,[3] for the lovers of woods and fields, has changed for the worse since those days, and the precinct in question has forfeited much of its mingled pastoral and scholastic quietude. It was then a College-hall in the woods – a charming mixture. What it is now has nothing to do with my story; and I have no doubt that there are still doctrine-haunted young seniors who, as they stroll near it in the summer dusk, promise themselves, later, to taste of its fine leisurely quality. For myself, I was not disappointed. I established myself in a great square, low-browed room, with deep window-benches; I hung prints from Overbeck and Ary Scheffer[4] on the walls; I arranged my books, with great refinement of classification, in the alcoves beside the high chimney-shelf, and I began to read Plotinus and St Augustine.[5] Among my companions were two or three men of ability and of good fellowship, with whom I occasionally brewed a fireside bowl; and with adventurous reading, deep discourse, potations conscientiously shallow, and long country walks, my initiation into the clerical mystery progressed agreeably enough.

With one of my comrades I formed an especial friendship, and we passed a great deal of time together. Unfortunately, he had a chronic weakness of one of his knees, which compelled him to lead a very sedentary life, and as I was a methodical pedestrian, this made some difference in our habits. I used often to stretch away for my daily ramble, with no companion but the stick in my hand or the book in my pocket. But in the use of my legs and the sense of unstinted open air, I have always found company enough. I should, perhaps, add that in the enjoyment of a very sharp pair of eyes, I found something of a social pleasure. My eyes and I were on excellent terms; they were indefatigable observers of all wayside incidents, and so long as they were amused I was contented. It is, indeed, owing to their inquisitive habits that I came into possession of this remarkable story. Much of the country about the old College town is pretty now, but it was prettier thirty years ago. That multitudinous eruption of domiciliary pasteboard which now graces the landscape, in the direction of the low, blue Waltham Hills, had not yet taken place; there were no genteel cottages to put the shabby meadows and scrubby orchards to shame – a juxtaposition by which, in later years, neither element of the contrast has gained. Certain crooked crossroads then, as I remember them, were more deeply and naturally rural, and the solitary dwellings on the long grassy slopes beside them, under the tall, customary elm that curved its foliage in midair like the outward dropping ears of a girdled wheatsheaf, sat with their shingled hoods well pulled down on their ears, and no prescience whatever of the fashion of French roofs – weather-wrinkled old peasant women, as you might call them, quietly wearing the native coif, and never dreaming of mounting bonnets, and indecently exposing their venerable brows. That winter was what is called an 'open' one; there was much cold, but little snow; the roads were firm and free, and I was rarely compelled by the weather to forego my exercise. One grey December afternoon, I had sought it in the direction of the adjacent town of Medford, and I was retracing my steps at an even pace, and watching the pale, cold tints – the transparent amber and faded rose-colour – which curtained, in wintry fashion, the western sky, and reminded me of a sceptical smile on the lips of a beautiful woman. I came, as dusk was falling, to a narrow road which I had never traversed and which I imagined offered me a short cut homeward. I was about three miles away; I was late, and would have been thankful to make them two. I diverged, walked some ten minutes, and then perceived that the road had a very unfrequented air. The wheel-ruts looked old; the stillness seemed peculiarly sensible. And yet down the road stood a house, so that it must in some degree have been a thoroughfare. On one side was a high, natural embankment, on the top of which was perched an apple-orchard, whose tangled boughs made a stretch of coarse black lace-work, hung across the coldly rosy west. In a short time I came to the house, and I immediately found myself interested in it. I stopped in front of it gazing hard, I hardly knew why, but with a vague mixture of curiosity and timidity. It was a house like most of the houses thereabouts, except that it was decidedly a handsome specimen of its class. It stood on a grassy slope, it had its tall, impartially drooping elm beside it, and its old black well-cover at its shoulder. But it was of very large proportions, and it had a striking look of solidity and stoutness of timber. It had lived to a good old age, too, for the woodwork on its doorway and under its eaves, carefully and abundantly carved, referred it to the middle, at the latest, of the last century. All this had once been painted white, but the broad back of time, leaning against the doorposts for a hundred years, had laid bare the grain of the wood. Behind the house stretched an orchard of apple-trees, more gnarled and fantastic than usual, and wearing, in the deepening dusk, a blighted and exhausted aspect. All the windows of the house had rusty shutters, without slats, and these were closely drawn. There was no sign of life about it; it looked blank, bare and vacant, and yet, as I lingered near it, it seemed to have a familiar meaning – an audible eloquence. I have always thought of the impression made upon me at first sight, by that grey colonial dwelling, as a proof that induction may sometimes be near akin to divination; for after all, there was nothing on the face of the matter to warrant the very serious induction that I made. I fell back and crossed the road. The last red light of the sunset disengaged itself, as it was about to vanish, and rested faintly for a moment on the time-silvered front of the old house. It touched, with perfect regularity, the series of small panes in the fan-shaped window above the door, and twinkled there fantastically. Then it died away, and left the place more intensely sombre. At this moment, I said to myself with the accent of profound conviction – 'The house is simply haunted!'

Somehow, immediately, I believed it, and so long as I was not shut up inside, the idea gave me pleasure. It was implied in the aspect of the house, and it explained it. Half an hour before, if I had been asked, I would have said, as befitted a young man who was explicitly cultivating cheerful views of the supernatural, that there were no such things as haunted houses. But the dwelling before me gave a vivid meaning to the empty words; it had been spiritually blighted.

The longer I looked at it, the intenser seemed the secret that it held. I walked all round it, I tried to peep here and there, through a crevice in the shutters, and I took a puerile satisfaction in laying my hand on the doorknob and gently turning it. If the door had yielded, would I have gone in? – would I have penetrated the dusky stillness? My audacity, fortunately, was not put to the test. The portal was admirably solid, and I was unable even to shake it. At last I turned away, casting many looks behind me. I pursued my way, and, after a longer walk than I had bargained for, reached the highroad. At a certain distance below the point at which the long lane I have mentioned entered it, stood a comfortable, tidy dwelling, which might have offered itself as the model of the house which is in no sense haunted – which has no sinister secrets, and knows nothing but blooming prosperity. Its clean white paint stared placidly through the dusk, and its vine-covered porch had been dressed in straw for the winter. An old, one-horse chaise, freighted with two departing visitors, was leaving the door, and through the uncurtained windows, I saw the lamp-lit sitting-room, and the table spread with the early 'tea', which had been improvised for the comfort of the guests. The mistress of the house had come to the gate with her friends; she lingered there after the chaise had wheeled creakingly away, half to watch them down the road, and half to give me, as I passed in the twilight, a questioning look. She was a comely, quick young woman, with a sharp, dark eye, and I ventured to stop and speak to her.

'That house down that sideroad,' I said, 'about a mile from here – the only one – can you tell me whom it belongs to?'

She stared at me a moment, and, I thought, coloured a little. 'Our folks never go down that road,' she said, briefly.

'But it's a short way to Medford,' I answered.

She gave a little toss of her head. 'Perhaps it would turn out a long way. At any rate, we don't use it.'

This was interesting. A thrifty Yankee[6] household must have good reasons for this scorn of time-saving processes. 'But you know the house, at least?' I said.

'Well, I have seen it.'

'And to whom does it belong?'

She gave a little laugh and looked away, as if she were aware that, to a stranger, her words might seem to savour of agricultural superstition. 'I guess it belongs to them that are in it.'

'But is there anyone in it? It is completely closed.'

'That makes no difference. They never come out, and no one ever goes in.' And she turned away.

But I laid my hand on her arm, respectfully. 'You mean,' I said, 'that the house is haunted?'

She drew herself away, coloured, raised her finger to her lips, and hurried into the house, where, in a moment, the curtains were dropped over the windows.

For several days, I thought repeatedly of this little adventure, but I took some satisfaction in keeping it to myself. If the house was not haunted, it was useless to expose my imaginative whims, and if it was, it was agreeable to drain the cup of horror without assistance. I determined, of course, to pass that way again; and a week later – it was the last day of the year – I retraced my steps. I approached the house from the opposite direction, and found myself before it at about the same hour as before. The light was failing, the sky low and grey; the wind wailed along the hard, bare ground, and made slow eddies of the frost-blackened leaves. The melancholy mansion stood there, seeming to gather the winter twilight around it, and mask itself in it, inscrutably. I hardly knew on what errand I had come, but I had a vague feeling that if this time the doorknob were to turn and the door to open, I should take my heart in my hands, and let them close behind me. Who were the mysterious tenants to whom the good woman at the corner had alluded? What had been seen or heard – what was related? The door was as stubborn as before, and my impertinent fumblings with the latch caused no upper window to be thrown open, nor any strange, pale face to be thrust out. I ventured even to raise the rusty knocker and give it half-a-dozen raps, but they made a flat, dead sound, and aroused no echo. Familiarity breeds contempt; I don't know what I should have done next, if, in the distance, up the road (the same one I had followed), I had not seen a solitary figure advancing. I was unwilling to be observed hanging about this ill-famed dwelling, and I sought refuge among the dense shadows of a grove of pines near by, where I might peep forth, and yet remain invisible. Presently, the newcomer drew near, and I perceived that he was making straight for the house. He was a little, old man, the most striking feature of whose appearance was a voluminous cloak, of a sort of military cut. He carried a walking-stick, and advanced in a slow, painful, somewhat hobbling fashion, but with an air of extreme resolution. He turned off from the road, and followed the vague wheel-track, and within a few yards of the house he paused. He looked up at it, fixedly and searchingly, as if he were counting the windows, or noting certain familiar marks. Then he took off his hat, and bent over slowly and solemnly, as if he were performing an obeisance. As he stood uncovered, I had a good look at him. He was, as I have said, a diminutive old man, but it would have been hard to decide whether he belonged to this world or to the other. His head reminded me, vaguely, of the portraits of

Andrew Jackson.[7] He had a crop of grizzled hair, as stiff as a brush, a lean, pale, smooth-shaven face, and an eye of intense brilliancy, surmounted with thick brows, which had remained perfectly black. His face, as well as his cloak, seemed to belong to an old soldier; he looked like a retired military man of a modest rank; but he struck me as exceeding the classic privilege of even such a personage to be eccentric and grotesque. When he had finished his salute, he advanced to the door, fumbled in the folds of his cloak, which hung down much farther in front than behind, and produced a key. This he slowly and carefully inserted into the lock, and then, apparently, he turned it. But the door did not immediately open; first he bent his head, turned his ear, and stood listening, and then he looked up and down the road. Satisfied or reassured, he applied his aged shoulder to one of the deep-set panels, and pressed a moment. The door yielded – opening into perfect darkness. He stopped again on the threshold, and again removed his hat and made his bow. Then he went in, and carefully closed the door behind him.

Who in the world was he, and what was his errand? He might have been a figure out of one of Hoffmann's tales.[8] Was he vision or a reality – an inmate of the house, or a familiar, friendly visitor? What had been the meaning, in either case, of his mystic genuflections, and how did he propose to proceed, in that inner darkness? I emerged from my retirement, and observed narrowly, several of the windows. In each of them, at an interval, a ray of light became visible in the chink between the two leaves of the shutters. Evidently, he was lighting up; was he going to give a party – a ghostly revel? My curiosity grew intense, but I was quite at a loss how to satisfy it. For a moment, I thought of rapping peremptorily at the door; but I dismissed this idea as unmannerly, and calculated to break the spell, if spell there was. I walked round the house and tried, without violence, to open one of the lower windows. It resisted, but I had better fortune, in a moment, with another. There was a risk, certainly, in the trick I was playing – a risk of being seen from within, or (worse) seeing, myself, something that I should repent of seeing. But curiosity, as I say, had become an inspiration, and the risk was highly agreeable. Through the parting of the shutters, I looked into a lighted room – a room lighted by two candles in old brass flambeaux,[9] placed upon the mantelshelf. It was apparently a sort of back parlour, and it had retained all its furniture. This was of a homely, old-fashioned pattern, and consisted of hair-cloth chairs and sofas, spare mahogany tables, and framed samplers hung upon the walls. But although the room was furnished, it had a strangely uninhabited look; the tables and chairs were in rigid positions, and no small, familiar objects were visible. I could not see everything, and I could only guess at the existence, on my right, of a large folding door. It was apparently open, and the light of the neighbouring room passed through it. I waited for some time, but the room remained empty. At last, I became conscious that a large shadow was projected upon the wall opposite the folding door – the shadow, evidently, of a figure in the adjoining room. It was tall and grotesque, and seemed to represent a person sitting perfectly motionless, in profile. I thought I recognised the perpendicular bristles and far-arching nose of my little old man. There was a strange fixedness in his posture; he appeared to be seated, and looking intently at something. I watched the shadow a long time, but it never stirred. At last, however, just as my patience began to ebb, it moved slowly, rose to the ceiling, and became indistinct. I don't know what I should have seen next, but by an irresistible impulse, I closed the shutter. Was it delicacy? – was it pusillanimity? I can hardly say. I lingered, nevertheless, near the house, hoping that my friend would reappear. I was not disappointed; for he at last emerged, looking just as when he had gone in, and taking his leave in the same ceremonious fashion. (The lights, I had already observed, had disappeared from the crevice of each of the windows.) He faced about before the door, took off his hat, and made an obsequious bow. As he turned away, I had a hundred minds to speak to him, but I let him depart in peace. This, I may say, was pure delicacy – you will answer, perhaps, that it came too late. It seemed to me that he had a right to resent my observation; though my own right to exercise it (if ghosts were in the question) struck me as equally positive. I continued to watch him as he hobbled softly down the bank, and along the lonely road. Then I musingly retreated in the opposite direction. I was tempted to follow him, at a distance, to see what became of him; but this, too, seemed indelicate; and I confess, moreover, that I felt the inclination to coquet a little, as it were, with my discovery – to pull apart the petals of the flower one by one.

I continued to smell the flower, from time to time, for its oddity of perfume had fascinated me. I passed by the house on the crossroad again, but never encountered the old man in the cloak, or any other wayfarer. It seemed to keep observers at a distance, and I was careful not to gossip about it: one inquirer, I said to myself, may edge his way into the secret, but there is no room for two. At the same time, of course, I would have been thankful for any chance sidelight that might fall across the matter – though I could not well see whence it was to come. I hoped to meet the old man in the cloak elsewhere, but as the days passed by without his reappearing, I ceased to expect it. And yet I reflected that he probably lived in that neighbourhood, inasmuch as he had made his pilgrimage to the vacant house on foot. If he had come from a distance, he would have been sure to arrive in some old deep-hooded gig with yellow wheels – a vehicle as venerably grotesque as himself. One day, I took a stroll in Mount Auburn cemetery – an institution at that period in its infancy, and full of a sylvan charm which it has now completely forfeited. It contained more maple and birch than willow and cypress, and the sleepers had ample elbow room. It was not a city of the dead, but at the most a village, and a meditative pedestrian might stroll there without too importunate reminder of the grotesque side of our claims to posthumous consideration. I had come out to enjoy the first foretaste of spring – one of those mild days of late winter, when the torpid earth seems to draw the first long breath that marks the rupture of the spell of sleep. The sun was veiled in haze, and yet warm, and the frost was oozing from its deepest lurking-places. I had been treading for half an hour the winding ways of the cemetery, when suddenly I perceived a familiar figure seated on a bench against a southward-facing evergreen hedge. I call the figure familiar, because I had seen it often in memory and in fancy; in fact, I had beheld it but once. Its back was turned to me, but it wore a voluminous cloak, which there was no mistaking. Here, at last, was my fellow-visitor at the haunted house, and here was my chance, if I wished to approach him! I made a circuit, and came towards him from in front. He saw me, at the end of the alley, and sat motionless, with his hands on the head of his stick, watching me from under his black eyebrows as I drew near. At a distance, these black eyebrows looked formidable; they were the only thing I saw in his face. But on a closer view I was reassured, simply because I immediately felt that no man could really be as fantastically fierce as this poor old gentleman looked. His face was a kind of caricature of martial truculence. I stopped in front of him, and respectfully asked leave to sit and rest upon his bench. He granted it with a silent gesture, of much dignity, and I placed myself beside him. In this position, I was able, covertly, to observe him. He was quite as much an oddity in the morning sunshine, as he had been in the dubious twilight. The lines in his face were as rigid as if they had been hacked out of a block by a clumsy woodcarver. His eyes were flamboyant, his nose terrific, his mouth implacable. And yet, after a while, when he slowly turned and looked at me, fixedly, I perceived that in spite of this portentous mask, he was a very mild old man. I was sure he even would have been glad to smile, but, evidently, his facial muscles were too stiff – they had taken a different fold, once for all. I wondered whether he was demented, but I dismissed the idea; the fixed glitter in his eye was not that of insanity. What his face really expressed was deep and simple sadness; his heart perhaps was broken, but his brain was intact. His dress was shabby but neat, and his old blue cloak had known half a century's brushing.

I hastened to make some observation upon the exceptional softness of the day, and he answered me in a gentle, mellow voice, which it was almost startling to hear proceed from such bellicose lips.

'This is a very comfortable place,' he presently added.

'I am fond of walking in graveyards,' I rejoined deliberately; flattering myself that I had struck a vein that might lead to something.

I was encouraged; he turned and fixed me with his duskily glowing eyes. Then very gravely – 'Walking, yes. Take all your exercise now. Some day you will have to settle down in a graveyard in a fixed position.'

'Very true,' said I. 'But you know there are some people who are said to take exercise even after that day.'

He had been looking at me still; at this, he looked away.

'You don't understand?' I said, gently.

He continued to gaze straight before him.

'Some people, you know, walk about after death,' I went on.

At last he turned, and looked at me more portentously than ever. 'You don't believe that,' he said simply.

'How do you know I don't?'

'Because you are young and foolish.' This was said without acerbity – even kindly; but in the tone of an old man whose consciousness of his own heavy experience made everything else seem light.

'I am certainly young,' I answered; 'but I don't think that, on the whole, I am foolish. But say I don't believe in ghosts – most people would be on my side.'

'Most people are fools!' said the old man.

I let the question rest, and talked of other things. My companion seemed on his guard, he eyed me defiantly, and made brief answers to my remarks; but I nevertheless gathered an impression that our meeting was an agreeable thing to him, and even a social incident of some importance. He was evidently a lonely creature, and his opportunities for gossip were rare. He had had troubles, and they had detached him from the world, and driven him back upon himself; but the social chord in his antiquated soul was not entirely broken, and I was sure he was gratified to find that it could still feebly resound. At last, he began to ask questions himself; he inquired whether I was a student.

'I am a student of divinity,' I answered.

'Of divinity?'

'Of theology. I am studying for the ministry.'

At this he eyed me with peculiar intensity – after which his gaze wandered away again. 'There are certain things you ought to know, then,' he said at last.

'I have a great desire for knowledge,' I answered. 'What things do you mean?'

He looked at me again awhile, but without heeding my question.

'I like your appearance,' he said. 'You seem to me a sober lad.'

'Oh, I am perfectly sober!' I exclaimed – yet departing for a moment from my soberness.

'I think you are fair-minded,' he went on.

'I don't any longer strike you as foolish, then?' I asked.

'I stick to what I said about people who deny the power of departed spirits to return. They *are* fools!' And he rapped fiercely with his staff on the earth.

I hesitated a moment, and then, abruptly, 'You have seen a ghost!' I said.

He appeared not at all startled.

'You are right, sir!' he answered with great dignity. 'With me it's not a matter of cold theory – I have not had to pry into old books to learn what to believe. *I know!* With these eyes I have beheld the departed spirit standing before me as near as you are!' And his eyes, as he spoke, certainly looked as if they had rested upon strange things.

I was irresistibly impressed – I was touched with credulity.

'And was it very terrible?' I asked.

'I am an old soldier – I am not afraid!'

'When was it? – where was it?' I asked.

He looked at me mistrustfully, and I saw that I was going too fast.

'Excuse me from going into particulars,' he said. 'I am not at liberty to speak more fully. I have told you so much, because I cannot bear to hear this subject spoken of lightly. Remember in future, that you have seen a very honest old man who told you – on his honour – that he had seen a ghost!' And he got up, as if he thought he had said enough. Reserve, shyness, pride, the fear of being laughed at, the memory, possibly, of former strokes of sarcasm – all this, on one side, had its weight with him; but I suspected that on the other, his tongue was loosened by the garrulity of old age, the sense of solitude, and the

need of sympathy – and perhaps, also, by the friendliness which he
had been so good as to express toward myself. Evidently, it would be
unwise to press him, but I hoped to see him again.

'To give greater weight to my words,' he added, 'let me mention
my name – Captain Diamond, sir. I have seen service.'

'I hope I may have the pleasure of meeting you again,' I said.

'The same to you, sir!' And brandishing his stick portentously –
though with the friendliest intentions – he marched stiffly away.

I asked two or three persons – selected with discretion – whether
they knew anything about Captain Diamond, but they were quite
unable to enlighten me. At last, suddenly, I smote my forehead, and,
dubbing myself a dolt, remembered that I was neglecting a source of
information to which I had never applied in vain. The excellent
person at whose table I habitually dined, and who dispensed
hospitality to students at so much a week, had a sister as good as
herself, and of conversational powers more varied. This sister, who
was known as Miss Deborah, was an old maid in all the force of the
term. She was deformed; and she never went out of the house; she sat
all day at the window, between a birdcage and a flowerpot, stitching
small linen articles – mysterious bands and frills. She wielded, I was
assured, an exquisite needle, and her work was highly prized. In spite
of her deformity and her confinement, she had a little, fresh, round
face, and an imperturbable serenity of spirit. She had also a very
quick little wit of her own, she was extremely observant, and she had
a high relish for a friendly chat. Nothing pleased her so much as to
have you – especially, I think, if you were a young divinity student –
move your chair near her sunny window, and settle yourself for
twenty minutes' 'talk'. 'Well, sir,' she used always to say, 'what is the
latest monstrosity in Biblical criticism?' – for she used to pretend to
be horrified at the rationalistic tendency of the age. But she was an
inexorable little philosopher, and I am convinced that she was a
keener rationalist than any of us, and that, if she had chosen, she
could have propounded questions that would have made the boldest
of us wince. Her window commanded the whole town – or rather, the
whole country. Knowledge came to her as she sat singing, with her
little, cracked voice, in her low rocking-chair. She was the first to
learn everything, and the last to forget it. She had the town gossip at
her fingers' ends, and she knew everything about people she had
never seen. When I asked her how she had acquired her learning, she
said simply – 'Oh, I observe!' 'Observe closely enough,' she once
said, 'and it doesn't matter where you are. You may be in a pitch-dark
closet. All you want is something to start with; one thing leads to

another, and all things are mixed up: shut me up in a dark closet and I will observe, after a while, that some places in it are darker than others. After that (give me time), and I will tell you what the President of the United States is going to have for dinner.' Once I paid her a compliment. 'Your observation,' I said, 'is as fine as your needle, and your statements are as true as your stitches.'

Of course Miss Deborah had heard of Captain Diamond. He had been much talked about many years before, but he had survived the scandal that attached to his name.

'What was the scandal?' I asked.

'He killed his daughter.'

'Killed her?' I cried; 'how so?'

'Oh, not with a pistol, or a dagger, or a dose of arsenic! With his tongue. Talk of women's tongues! He cursed her – with some horrible oath – and she died!'

'What had she done?'

'She had received a visit from a young man who loved her, and whom he had forbidden the house.'

'The house,' I said – 'ah yes! The house is out in the country, two or three miles from here, on a lonely crossroad.'

Miss Deborah looked sharply at me, as she bit her thread.

'Ah, you know about the house?' she said.

'A little,' I answered; 'I have seen it. But I want you to tell me more.'

But here Miss Deborah betrayed an incommunicativeness which was most unusual.

'You wouldn't call me superstitious, would you?' she asked.

'You? – you are the quintessence of pure reason.'

'Well, every thread has its rotten place, and every needle its grain of rust. I would rather not talk about that house.'

'You have no idea how you excite my curiosity!' I said.

'I can feel for you. But it would make me very nervous.'

'What harm can come to you?' I asked.

'Some harm came to a friend of mine.' And Miss Deborah gave a very positive nod.

'What had your friend done?'

'She had told me Captain Diamond's secret, which he had told her with a mighty mystery. She had been an old flame of his, and he took her into his confidence. He bade her tell no one, and assured her that if she did, something dreadful would happen to her.'

'And what happened to her?'

'She died.'

'Oh, we are all mortal!' I said. 'Had she given him a promise?'

'She had not taken it seriously, she had not believed him. She repeated the story to me, and three days afterwards, she was taken with inflammation of the lungs. A month afterwards, here where I sit now, I was stitching her grave-clothes. Since then, I have never mentioned what she told me.'

'Was it very strange?'

'It was strange, but it was ridiculous too. It is a thing to make you shudder and to make you laugh, both. But you can't worry it out of me. I am sure that if I were to tell you, I should immediately break a needle in my finger, and die the next week of lockjaw.'

I retired, and urged Miss Deborah no further; but every two or three days, after dinner, I came and sat down by her rocking-chair. I made no further allusion to Captain Diamond; I sat silent, clipping tape with her scissors. At last, one day, she told me I was looking poorly. I was pale.

'I am dying of curiosity,' I said. 'I have lost my appetite. I have eaten no dinner.'

'Remember Bluebeard's wife!'[10] said Miss Deborah.

'One may as well perish by the sword as by famine!' I answered.

Still she said nothing, and at last I rose with a melodramatic sigh and departed. As I reached the door, she called me and pointed to the chair I had vacated. 'I never was hardhearted,' she said. 'Sit down, and if we are to perish, may we at least perish together.' And then, in very few words, she communicated what she knew of Captain Diamond's secret. 'He was a very high-tempered old man, and though he was very fond of his daughter, his will was law. He had picked out a husband for her, and given her due notice. Her mother was dead, and they lived alone together. The house had been Mrs Diamond's own marriage portion; the captain, I believe, hadn't a penny. After his marriage, they had come to live there, and he had begun to work the farm. The poor girl's lover was a young man with whiskers from Boston. The captain came in one evening and found them together; he collared the young man, and hurled a terrible curse at the poor girl. The young man cried that she was his wife, and he asked her if it was true. She said, "No!" Thereupon Captain Diamond, his fury growing fiercer, repeated his imprecation, ordered her out of the house, and disowned her forever. She swooned away, but her father went raging off and left her. Several hours later, he came back and found the house empty. On the table was a note from the young man telling him that he had killed his daughter, repeating the assurance that she was his own wife, and declaring that he himself claimed the sole right to commit her remains to earth. He had carried the body away in a gig! Captain Diamond wrote him a dreadful note in answer, saying that he didn't believe his daughter was dead, but that, whether or no, she was dead to him. A week later, in the middle of the night, he saw her ghost. Then, I suppose, he was convinced. The ghost reappeared several times, and finally began regularly to haunt the house. It made the old man very uncomfortable, for little by little his passion had passed away, and he was given up to grief. He determined at last to leave the place, and tried to sell it or rent it; but meanwhile the story had gone abroad, the ghost had been seen by other persons, the house had a bad name, and it was impossible to dispose of it. With the farm, it was the old man's only property, and his only means of subsistence; if he could neither live in it nor rent it he was beggared. But the ghost had no mercy, as he had had none. He struggled for six months, and at last he broke down. He put on his old blue cloak and took up his staff, and prepared to wander away and beg his bread. Then the ghost relented, and proposed a compromise. "Leave the house to me!" it said; "I have marked it for my own. Go off and live elsewhere. But to enable you to live, I will be your tenant, since you can find no other. I will hire the house of you and pay you a certain rent." And the ghost named a sum. The old man consented, and he goes every quarter to collect his rent!'

I laughed at this recital, but I confess I shuddered too, for my own observation had exactly confirmed it. Had I not been witness of one of the captain's quarterly visits, had I not all but seen him sit watching his spectral tenant count out the rent-money, and when he trudged away in the dark, had he not a little bag of strangely gotten coin hidden in the folds of his old blue cloak? I imparted none of these reflections to Miss Deborah, for I was determined that my observations should have a sequel, and I promised myself the pleasure of treating her to my story in its full maturity. 'Captain Diamond,' I asked, 'has no other known means of subsistence?'

'None whatever. He toils not, neither does he spin[11] – his ghost supports him. A haunted house is valuable property!'

'And in what coin does the ghost pay?'

'In good American gold and silver. It has only this peculiarity – that the pieces are all dated before the young girl's death. It's a strange mixture of matter and spirit!'

'And does the ghost do things handsomely; is the rent large?'

'The old man, I believe, lives decently, and has his pipe and his glass. He took a little house down by the river; the door is sidewise to the street, and there is a little garden before it. There he spends his days, and has an old coloured woman to do for him. Some years ago, he used to wander about a good deal, he was a familiar figure in the town, and most people knew his legend. But of late he has drawn back into his shell; he sits over his fire, and curiosity has forgotten him. I suppose he is falling into his dotage. But I am sure, I trust,' said Miss Deborah in conclusion, 'that he won't outlive his faculties or his powers of locomotion, for, if I remember rightly, it was part of the bargain that he should come in person to collect his rent.'

We neither of us seemed likely to suffer any especial penalty for Miss Deborah's indiscretion; I found her, day after day, singing over her work, neither more nor less active than usual. For myself, I boldly pursued my observations. I went again, more than once, to the great graveyard, but I was disappointed in my hope of finding Captain Diamond there. I had a prospect, however, which afforded me compensation. I shrewdly inferred that the old man's quarterly pilgrimages were made upon the last day of the old quarter. My first sight of him had been on the 31st of December, and it was probable that he would return to his haunted home on the last day of March. This was near at hand; at last it arrived. I betook myself late in the afternoon to the old house on the crossroad, supposing that the hour of twilight was the appointed season. I was not wrong. I had been hovering about for a short time, feeling very much like a restless ghost myself, when he appeared in the same manner as before, and wearing the same costume. I again concealed myself, and saw him enter the house with the ceremonial which he had used on the former occasion. A light appeared successively in the crevice of each pair of shutters, and I opened the window which had yielded to my importunity before. Again I saw the great shadow on the wall, motionless and solemn. But I saw nothing else. The old man reappeared at last, made his fantastic salaam[12] before the house, and crept away into the dusk.

One day, more than a month after this, I met him again at Mount Auburn. The air was full of the voice of spring; the birds had come back and were twittering over their winter's travels, and a mild west wind was making a thin murmur in the raw verdure. He was seated on a bench in the sun, still muffled in his enormous mantle, and he recognised me as soon as I approached him. He nodded at me as if he were an old bashaw giving the signal for my decapitation, but it was apparent that he was pleased to see me.

'I have looked for you here more than once,' I said. 'You don't come often.'

'What did you want of me?' he asked.

'I wanted to enjoy your conversation. I did so greatly when I met you here before.'

'You found me amusing?'

'Interesting!' I said.

'You didn't think me cracked?'

'Cracked? – My dear sir – !' I protested.

'I'm the sanest man in the country. I know that is what insane people always say; but generally they can't prove it. I can!'

'I believe it,' I said. 'But I am curious to know how such a thing can be proved.'

He was silent awhile.

'I will tell you. I once committed, unintentionally, a great crime. Now I pay the penalty. I give up my life to it. I don't shirk it; I face it squarely, knowing perfectly what it is. I haven't tried to bluff it off; I haven't begged off from it; I haven't run away from it. The penalty is terrible, but I have accepted it. I have been a philosopher!

'If I were a Catholic, I might have turned monk, and spent the rest of my life in fasting and praying. That is no penalty; that is an evasion. I might have blown my brains out – I might have gone mad. I wouldn't do either. I would simply face the music, take the consequences. As I say, they are awful! I take them on certain days, four times a year. So it has been these twenty years; so it will be as long as I last. It's my business; it's my avocation. That's the way I feel about it. I call that reasonable!'

'Admirably so!' I said. 'But you fill me with curiosity and with compassion.'

'Especially with curiosity,' he said, cunningly.

'Why,' I answered, 'if I know exactly what you suffer I can pity you more.'

'I'm much obliged. I don't want your pity; it won't help me. I'll tell you something, but it's not for myself; it's for your own sake.' He paused a long time and looked all round him, as if for chance eavesdroppers. I anxiously awaited his revelation, but he disappointed me. 'Are you still studying theology?' he asked.

'Oh, yes,' I answered, perhaps with a shade of irritation. 'It's a thing one can't learn in six months.'

'I should think not, so long as you have nothing but your books. Do you know the proverb, "A grain of experience is worth a pound of precept"? I'm a great theologian.'

'Ah, you have had experience,' I murmured sympathetically.

'You have read about the immortality of the soul; you have seen Jonathan Edwards and Dr Hopkins[13] chopping logic over it, and deciding, by chapter and verse, that it is true. But I have seen it with these eyes; I have touched it with these hands!' And the old man held up his rugged old fists and shook them portentously. 'That's better!' he went on; 'but I have bought it dearly. You had better take it from the books – evidently you always will. You are a very good young man; you will never have a crime on your conscience.'

I answered with some juvenile fatuity, that I certainly hoped I had my share of human passions, good young man and prospective Doctor of Divinity as I was.

'Ah, but you have a nice, quiet little temper,' he said. 'So have I – now! But once I was very brutal – very brutal. You ought to know that such things are. I killed my own child:'

'Your own child?'

'I struck her down to the earth and left her to die. They could not hang me, for it was not with my hand I struck her. It was with foul and damnable words. That makes a difference; it's a grand law we live under! Well, sir, I can answer for it that *her* soul is immortal. We have an appointment to meet four times a year, and then I catch it!'

'She has never forgiven you?'

'She has forgiven me as the angels forgive! That's what I can't stand – the soft, quiet way she looks at me. I'd rather she twisted a knife about in my heart – O Lord, Lord, Lord!' and Captain Diamond bowed his head over his stick, and leaned his forehead on his crossed hands.

I was impressed and moved, and his attitude seemed for the moment a check to further questions. Before I ventured to ask him anything more, he slowly rose and pulled his old cloak around him. He was unused to talking about his troubles, and his memories overwhelmed him. 'I must go my way,' he said; 'I must be creeping along.'

'I shall perhaps meet you here again,' I said.

'Oh, I'm a stiff-jointed old fellow,' he answered, 'and this is rather far for me to come. I have to reserve myself. I have sat sometimes a month at a time smoking my pipe in my chair. But I should like to see you again.' And he stopped and looked at me, terribly and kindly. 'Some day, perhaps, I shall be glad to be able to lay my hand on a young, unperverted soul. If a man can make a friend, it is always something gained. What is your name?'

I had in my pocket a small volume of Pascal's 'Thoughts',[14] on the flyleaf of which were written my name and address. I took it out and offered it to my old friend. 'Pray keep this little book,' I said. 'It is one I am very fond of, and it will tell you something about me.'

He took it and turned it over slowly, then looking up at me with a scowl of gratitude, 'I'm not much of a reader,' he said; 'but I won't refuse the first present I shall have received since – my troubles; and the last. Thank you, sir!' And with the little book in his hand he took his departure.

I was left to imagine him for some weeks after that sitting solitary in his armchair with his pipe. I had not another glimpse of him. But I was awaiting my chance, and on the last day of June, another quarter having elapsed, I deemed that it had come. The evening dusk in June falls late, and I was impatient for its coming. At last, toward the end of a lovely summer's day, I revisited Captain Diamond's property. Everything now was green around it save the blighted orchard in its rear, but its own immitigable greyness and sadness were as striking as when I had first beheld it beneath a December sky. As I drew near it, I saw that I was late for my purpose, for my purpose had simply been to step forward on Captain Diamond's arrival, and bravely ask him to let me go in with him. He had preceded me, and there were lights already in the windows. I was unwilling, of course, to disturb him during his ghostly interview, and I waited till he came forth. The lights disappeared in the course of time; then the door opened and Captain Diamond stole out. That evening he made no bow to the haunted house, for the first object he beheld was his fair-minded young friend planted, modestly but firmly, near the doorstep. He stopped short, looking at me, and this time his terrible scowl was in keeping with the situation.

'I knew you were here,' I said. 'I came on purpose.'

He seemed dismayed, and looked round at the house uneasily.

'I beg your pardon if I have ventured too far,' I added, 'but you know you have encouraged me.'

'How did you know I was here?'

'I reasoned it out. You told me half your story, and I guessed the other half. I am a great observer, and I had noticed this house in passing. It seemed to me to have a mystery. When you kindly confided to me that you saw spirits, I was sure that it could only be here that you saw them.'

'You are mighty clever,' cried the old man. 'And what brought you here this evening?'

I was obliged to evade this question.

'Oh, I often come; I like to look at the house – it fascinates me.'

He turned and looked up at it himself. 'It's nothing to look at outside.' He was evidently quite unaware of its peculiar outward appearance, and this odd fact, communicated to me thus in the twilight, and under the very brow of the sinister dwelling, seemed to make his vision of the strange things within more real.

'I have been hoping,' I said, 'for a chance to see the inside. I thought I might find you here, and that you would let me go in with you. I should like to see what you see.'

He seemed confounded by my boldness, but not altogether displeased. He laid his hand on my arm. 'Do you know what I see?' he asked.

'How can I know, except as you said the other day, by experience? I want to have the experience. Pray, open the door and take me in.'

Captain Diamond's brilliant eyes expanded beneath their dusky brows, and after holding his breath a moment, he indulged in the first and last apology for a laugh by which I was to see his solemn visage contorted. It was profoundly grotesque, but it was perfectly noiseless. 'Take you in?' he softly growled. 'I wouldn't go in again before my time's up for a thousand times that sum.' And he thrust out his hand from the folds of his cloak and exhibited a small agglomeration of coin, knotted into the corner of an old silk pocket-handkerchief. 'I stick to my bargain no less, but no more!'

'But you told me the first time I had the pleasure of talking with you that it was not so terrible.'

'I don't say it's terrible – now. But it's damned disagreeable!'

This adjective was uttered with a force that made me hesitate and reflect. While I did so, I thought I heard a slight movement of one of the window-shutters above us. I looked up, but everything seemed motionless. Captain Diamond, too, had been thinking; suddenly he turned towards the house. 'If you will go in alone,' he said, 'you are welcome.'

'Will you wait for me here?'

'Yes, you will not stop long.'

'But the house is pitch dark. When you go you have lights.'

He thrust his hand into the depths of his cloak and produced some matches. 'Take these,' he said. 'You will find two candlesticks with candles on the table in the hall. Light them, take one in each hand and go ahead.'

'Where shall I go?'

'Anywhere – everywhere. You can trust the ghost to find you.'

I will not pretend to deny that by this time my heart was beating. And yet I imagine I motioned the old man with a sufficiently dignified gesture to open the door. I had made up my mind that there was in fact a ghost. I had conceded the premise. Only I had assured myself that once the mind was prepared, and the thing was not a surprise, it was possible to keep cool. Captain Diamond turned the lock, flung open the door, and bowed low to me as I passed in. I stood in the darkness, and heard the door close behind me. For some moments, I stirred neither finger nor toe; I stared bravely into the impenetrable dusk. But I saw nothing and heard nothing, and at last I struck a match. On the table were two old brass candlesticks rusty from disuse. I lighted the candles and began my tour of exploration.

A wide staircase rose in front of me, guarded by an antique balustrade of that rigidly delicate carving which is found so often in old New England houses. I postponed ascending it, and turned into the room on my right. This was an old-fashioned parlour, meagrely furnished, and musty with the absence of human life. I raised my two lights aloft and saw nothing but its empty chairs, and its blank walls. Behind it was the room into which I had peeped from without, and which, in fact, communicated with it, as I had supposed, by folding doors. Here, too, I found myself confronted by no menacing spectre. I crossed the hall again, and visited the rooms on the other side; a dining-room in front, where I might have written my name with my finger in the deep dust of the great square table; a kitchen behind with its pots and pans eternally cold. All this was hard and grim, but it was not formidable. I came back into the hall, and walked to the foot of the staircase, holding up my candles; to ascend required a fresh effort, and I was scanning the gloom above. Suddenly, with an inexpressible sensation, I became aware that this gloom was animated; it seemed to move and gather itself together. Slowly – I say slowly, for to my tense expectancy the instants appeared ages – it took the shape of a large, definite figure, and this figure advanced and stood at the top of the stairs. I frankly confess that by this time I was conscious of a feeling to which I am in duty bound to apply the vulgar name of fear. I may poetise it and call it Dread, with a capital letter; it was at any rate the feeling that makes a man yield ground. I measured it as it grew, and it seemed perfectly irresistible; for it did not appear to come from within but from without, and to be embodied in the dark image at the head of the staircase. After a fashion I reasoned – I remember reasoning. I said to myself, 'I had always thought ghosts were white and transparent; this is a thing of thick shadows, densely opaque.' I reminded myself that the occasion was momentous, and that if fear were to overcome me, I should gather all possible impressions while my wits remained. I stepped back, foot behind foot, with my eyes still on the figure and placed my candles on the table. I was perfectly conscious that the proper thing was to ascend the stairs resolutely, face to face with the image, but the soles of my shoes seemed suddenly to have been transformed into leaden weights. I had got what I wanted; I was seeing the ghost. I tried to look at the figure distinctly so that I could remember it, and fairly claim, afterwards, not to have lost my self-possession. I even asked myself how long it was expected I should stand looking, and how soon I could honourably retire. All this, of course, passed through my mind with extreme rapidity, and it was checked by a further movement on the part of the figure. Two white hands appeared in the dark perpendicular mass, and were slowly raised to what seemed to be the level of the head. Here they were pressed together, over the region of the face, and then they were removed, and the face was disclosed. It was dim, white, strange, in every way ghostly. It looked down at me for an instant, after which one of the hands was raised again, slowly, and waved to and fro before it. There was something very singular in this gesture; it seemed to denote resentment and dismissal, and yet it had a sort of trivial, familiar motion. Familiarity on the part of the haunting Presence had not entered into my calculations, and did not strike me pleasantly. I agreed with Captain Diamond that it was 'damned disagreeable'. I was pervaded by an intense desire to make an orderly and, if possible, a graceful retreat. I wished to do it gallantly, and it seemed to me that it would be gallant to blow out my candles. I turned and did so, punctiliously, and then I made my way to the door, groped a moment and opened it. The outer light, almost extinct as it was, entered for a moment, played over the dusty depths of the house and showed me the solid shadow.

Standing on the grass, bent over his stick, under the early glimmering stars, I found Captain Diamond. He looked up at me fixedly for a moment, but asked no questions, and then he went and locked the door. This duty performed, he discharged the other – made his obeisance like the priest before the altar – and then without heeding me further, took his departure.

A few days later, I suspended my studies and went off for the summer's vacation. I was absent for several weeks, during which I had plenty of leisure to analyse my impressions of the supernatural. I took some satisfaction in the reflection that I had not been ignobly terrified; I had not bolted nor swooned – I had proceeded with dignity. Nevertheless, I was certainly more comfortable when I had put thirty miles between me and the scene of my exploit, and I continued for many days to prefer the daylight to the dark. My nerves had been powerfully excited; of this I was particularly conscious when, under the influence of the drowsy air of the seaside, my excitement began slowly to ebb. As it disappeared, I attempted to take a sternly rational view of my experience. Certainly I had seen *something* – that was not fancy; but what had I seen? I regretted extremely now that I had not been bolder, that I had not gone nearer and inspected the apparition more minutely. But it was very well to talk; I had done as much as any man in the circumstances would have dared; it was indeed a physical impossibility that I should have advanced. Was not this paralysation of my powers in itself a supernatural influence? Not necessarily, perhaps, for a sham ghost that one accepted might do as much execution as a real ghost. But why had I so easily accepted the sable phantom that waved its hand? Why had it so impressed itself? Unquestionably, true or false, it was a very clever phantom. I greatly preferred that it should have been true – in the first place because I did not care to have shivered and shaken for nothing, and in the second place because to have seen a well-authenticated goblin is, as things go, a feather in a quiet man's cap. I tried, therefore, to let my vision rest and to stop turning it over. But an impulse stronger than my will recurred at intervals and set a mocking question on my lips. Granted that the apparition was Captain Diamond's daughter; if it was she, it certainly was her spirit. But was it not her spirit and something more?

The middle of September saw me again established among the theologic shades, but I made no haste to revisit the haunted house.

The last of the month approached – the term of another quarter with poor Captain Diamond – and found me indisposed to disturb his pilgrimage on this occasion; though I confess that I thought with a good deal of compassion of the feeble old man trudging away, lonely, in the autumn dusk, on his extraordinary errand. On the thirtieth of September, at noonday, I was drowsing over a heavy octavo, when I heard a feeble rap at my door. I replied with an invitation to enter, but as this produced no effect, I repaired to the door and opened it. Before me stood an elderly negress with her head bound in a scarlet turban, and a white handkerchief folded across her bosom. She looked at me intently and in silence; she had that air of supreme gravity and decency which aged persons of her race so often wear. I stood interrogative, and at last, drawing her hand from her ample pocket, she held up a little book. It was the copy of Pascal's 'Thoughts' that I had given to Captain Diamond.

'Please, sir,' she said, very mildly, 'do you know this book?'

'Perfectly,' said I, 'my name is on the flyleaf.'

'It is your name – no other?'

'I will write my name if you like, and you can compare them,' I answered.

She was silent a moment and then, with dignity – 'It would be useless, sir,' she said, 'I can't read. If you will give me your word that is enough. I come,' she went on, 'from the gentleman to whom you gave the book. He told me to carry it as a token – a token – that is what he called it. He is right down sick, and he wants to see you.'

'Captain Diamond – sick?' I cried. 'Is his illness serious?'

'He is very bad – he is all gone.'

I expressed my regret and sympathy, and offered to go to him immediately, if his sable messenger would show me the way. She assented deferentially, and in a few moments I was following her along the sunny streets, feeling very much like a personage in *The Arabian Nights*,[15] led to a postern gate by an Ethiopian slave. My own conductress directed her steps towards the river and stopped at a decent little yellow house in one of the streets that descend to it. She quickly opened the door and led me in, and I very soon found myself in the presence of my old friend. He was in bed, in a darkened room, and evidently in a very feeble state. He lay back on his pillow staring before him, with his bristling hair more erect than ever, and his intensely dark and bright old eyes touched with the glitter of fever. His apartment was humble and scrupulously neat, and I could see that my dusky guide was a faithful servant. Captain Diamond, lying there rigid and pale on his white sheets, resembled some ruggedly carven figure on the lid of a Gothic[16] tomb. He looked at me silently, and my companion withdrew and left us alone.

'Yes, it's you,' he said, at last, 'it's you, that good young man. There is no mistake, is there?'

'I hope not; I believe I'm a good young man. But I am very sorry you are ill. What can I do for you?'

'I am very bad, very bad; my poor old bones ache so!' and, groaning portentously, he tried to turn towards me.

I questioned him about the nature of his malady and the length of time he had been in bed, but he barely heeded me; he seemed impatient to speak of something else. He grasped my sleeve, pulled me towards him, and whispered quickly: 'You know my time's up!'

'Oh, I trust not,' I said, mistaking his meaning. 'I shall certainly see you on your legs again.'

'God knows!' he cried. 'But I don't mean I'm dying; not yet a bit. What I mean is, I'm due at the house. This is rent-day.'

'Oh, exactly! But you can't go.'

'I can't go. It's awful. I shall lose my money. If I am dying, I want it all the same. I want to pay the doctor. I want to be buried like a respectable man.'

'It is this evening?' I asked.

'This evening at sunset, sharp.'

He lay staring at me, and, as I looked at him in return, I suddenly understood his motive in sending for me. Morally, as it came into my thought, I winced. But, I suppose I looked unperturbed, for he continued in the same tone. 'I can't lose my money. Someone else must go. I asked Belinda; but she won't hear of it.'

'You believe the money will be paid to another person?'

'We can try, at least. I have never failed before and I don't know. But, if you say I'm as sick as a dog, that my old bones ache, that I'm dying, perhaps she'll trust you. She don't want me to starve!'

'You would like me to go in your place, then?'

'You have been there once; you know what it is. Are you afraid?'

I hesitated.

'Give me three minutes to reflect,' I said, 'and I will tell you.' My glance wandered over the room and rested on the various objects that spoke of the threadbare, decent poverty of its occupant. There seemed to be a mute appeal to my pity and my resolution in their cracked and faded sparseness. Meanwhile Captain Diamond continued, feebly: 'I think she'd trust you, as I have trusted you; she'll like your face; she'll see there is no harm in you. It's a hundred and thirty-three dollars, exactly. Be sure you put them into a safe place.'

'Yes,' I said at last, 'I will go, and, so far as it depends upon me, you shall have the money by nine o'clock tonight.'

He seemed greatly relieved; he took my hand and faintly pressed it, and soon afterwards I withdrew. I tried for the rest of the day not to think of my evening's work, but, of course, I thought of nothing else. I will not deny that I was nervous; I was, in fact, greatly excited, and I spent my time in alternately hoping that the mystery should prove less deep than it appeared, and yet fearing that it might prove too shallow. The hours passed very slowly, but, as the afternoon began to wane, I started on my mission. On the way, I stopped at Captain Diamond's modest dwelling, to ask how he was doing, and to receive such last instructions as he might desire to lay upon me. The old negress, gravely and inscrutably placid, admitted me, and, in answer to my inquiries, said that the captain was very low; he had sunk since the morning.

'You must be right smart,' she said, 'if you want to get back before he drops off.'

A glance assured me that she knew of my projected expedition, though, in her own opaque black pupil, there was not a gleam of self-betrayal.

'But why should Captain Diamond drop off?' I asked. 'He certainly seems very weak; but I cannot make out that he has any definite disease.'

'His disease is old age,' she said, sententiously.

'But he is not so old as that; sixty-seven or sixty-eight, at most.'

She was silent a moment.

'He's worn out; he's used up; he can't stand it any longer.'

'Can I see him a moment?' I asked; upon which she led me again to his room.

He was lying in the same way as when I had left him, except that his eyes were closed. But he seemed very 'low', as she had said, and he had very little pulse. Nevertheless, I further learned the doctor had been there in the afternoon and professed himself satisfied. 'He don't know what's been going on,' said Belinda, curtly.

The old man stirred a little, opened his eyes, and after some time recognised me.

'I'm going, you know,' I said. 'I'm going for your money. Have you anything more to say?' He raised himself slowly, and with a painful effort, against his pillows; but he seemed hardly to understand me. 'The house, you know,' I said. 'Your daughter.'

He rubbed his forehead, slowly, awhile, and at last, his comprehension awoke. 'Ah, yes,' he murmured, 'I trust you. A hundred and thirty-three dollars. In old pieces – all in old pieces.' Then he added more vigorously, and with a brightening eye: 'Be very respectful – be very polite. If not – if not – ' and his voice failed again.

'Oh, I certainly shall be,' I said, with a rather forced smile. 'But, if not?'

'If not, I shall know it!' he said, very gravely. And with this, his eyes closed and he sunk down again.

I took my departure and pursued my journey with a sufficiently resolute step. When I reached the house, I made a propitiatory bow in front of it, in emulation of Captain Diamond. I had timed my walk so as to be able to enter without delay; night had already fallen. I turned the key, opened the door and shut it behind me. Then I struck a light, and found the two candlesticks I had used before, standing on the tables in the entry. I applied a match to both of them, took them up and went into the parlour. It was empty, and though I waited awhile, it remained empty. I passed then into the other rooms on the same floor, and no dark image rose before me to check my steps. At last, I came out into the hall again, and stood weighing the question of going upstairs. The staircase had been the scene of my discomfiture before, and I approached it with profound mistrust. At the foot, I paused, looking up, with my hand on the balustrade. I was acutely expectant, and my expectation was justified. Slowly, in the darkness above, the black figure that I had seen before took shape. It was not an illusion; it was a figure, and the same. I gave it time to define itself, and watched it stand and look down at me with its hidden face. Then, deliberately, I lifted up my voice and spoke.

'I have come in place of Captain Diamond, at his request,' I said. 'He is very ill; he is unable to leave his bed. He earnestly begs that you will pay the money to me; I will immediately carry it to him.' The figure stood motionless, giving no sign. 'Captain Diamond would have come if he were able to move,' I added, in a moment, appealingly; 'but, he is utterly unable.'

At this the figure slowly unveiled its face and showed me a dim, white mask; then it began slowly to descend the stairs. Instinctively I fell back before it, retreating to the door of the front sitting-room. With my eyes still fixed on it, I moved backwards across the threshold; then I stopped in the middle of the room and set down my lights. The figure advanced; it seemed to be that of a tall woman, dressed in vaporous black crape. As it drew near, I saw that it had a perfectly human face, though it looked extremely pale and sad. We stood gazing at each other; my agitation had completely vanished; I was only deeply interested.

'Is my father dangerously ill?' said the apparition.

At the sound of its voice – gentle, tremulous, and perfectly human – I started forward; I felt a rebound of excitement. I drew a long breath, I gave a sort of cry, for what I saw before me was not a disembodied spirit, but a beautiful woman, an audacious actress. Instinctively, irresistibly, by the force of reaction against my credulity, I stretched out my hand and seized the long veil that muffled her head. I gave it a violent jerk, dragged it nearly off, and stood staring at a large fair person, of about five-and-thirty. I comprehended her at a glance; her long black dress, her pale, sorrow-worn face, painted to look paler, her very fine eyes – the colour of her father's – and her sense of outrage at my movement.

'My father, I suppose,' she cried, 'did not send you here to insult me!' and she turned away rapidly, took up one of the candles and moved towards the door. Here she paused, looked at me again, hesitated, and then drew a purse from her pocket and flung it down on the floor. 'There is your money!' she said, majestically.

I stood there, wavering between amazement and shame, and saw her pass out into the hall. Then I picked up the purse. The next moment, I heard a loud shriek and a crash of something dropping, and she came staggering back into the room without her light.

'My father – my father!' she cried; and with parted lips and dilated eyes, she rushed towards me.

'Your father – where?' I demanded.

'In the hall, at the foot of the stairs.'

I stepped forward to go out, but she seized my arm.

'He is in white,' she cried, 'in his shirt. It's not he!'

'Why, your father is in his house, in his bed, extremely ill,' I answered.

She looked at me fixedly, with searching eyes.

'Dying?'

'I hope not,' I stuttered.

She gave a long moan and covered her face with her hands.

'Oh, heavens, I have seen his ghost!' she cried.

She still held my arm; she seemed too terrified to release it. 'His ghost!' I echoed, wondering.

'It's the punishment of my long folly!' she went on.

'Ah,' said I, 'it's the punishment of my indiscretion – of my violence!'

'Take me away, take me away!' she cried, still clinging to my arm. 'Not there' – as I was turning towards the hall and the front door – 'not there, for pity's sake! By this door – the back entrance.' And snatching the other candles from the table, she led me through the neighbouring room into the back part of the house. Here was a door opening from a sort of scullery into the orchard. I turned the rusty lock and we passed out and stood in the cool air, beneath the stars. Here my companion gathered her black drapery about her, and stood for a moment, hesitating. I had been infinitely flurried, but my curiosity touching her was uppermost. Agitated, pale, picturesque, she looked, in the early evening light, very beautiful.

'You have been playing all these years a most extraordinary game,' I said.

She looked at me sombrely, and seemed disinclined to reply. 'I came in perfect good faith,' I went on. 'The last time – three months ago – you remember? – you greatly frightened me.'

'Of course it was an extraordinary game,' she answered at last. 'But it was the only way.'

'Had he not forgiven you?'

'So long as he thought me dead, yes. There have been things in my life he could not forgive.'

I hesitated and then – 'And where is your husband?' I asked.

'I have no husband – I have never had a husband.'

She made a gesture which checked further questions, and moved rapidly away. I walked with her round the house to the road, and she kept murmuring – 'It was he – it was he!' When we reached the road she stopped, and asked me which way I was going. I pointed to the road by which I had come, and she said – 'I take the other. You are going to my father's?' she added.

'Directly,' I said.

'Will you let me know tomorrow what you have found?'

'With pleasure. But how shall I communicate with you?'

She seemed at a loss, and looked about her. 'Write a few words,' she said, 'and put them under that stone.' And she pointed to one of the lava slabs that bordered the old well. I gave her my promise to comply, and she turned away. 'I know my road,' she said. 'Everything is arranged. It's an old story.'

She left me with a rapid step, and as she receded into the darkness, resumed, with the dark flowing lines of her drapery, the phantasmal appearance with which she had at first appeared to me. I watched her till she became invisible, and then I took my own leave of the place. I returned to town at a swinging pace, and marched straight to the little yellow house near the river. I took the liberty of entering without a knock, and, encountering no interruption, made my way to Captain Diamond's room. Outside the door, on a low bench, with folded arms, sat the sable Belinda.

'How is he?' I asked.

'He's gone to glory.'

'Dead?' I cried.

She rose with a sort of tragic chuckle.

'He's as big a ghost as any of them now!'

I passed into the room and found the old man lying there irredeemably rigid and still. I wrote that evening a few lines which I proposed on the morrow to place beneath the stone, near the well; but my promise was not destined to be executed. I slept that night very ill – it was natural – and in my restlessness left my bed to walk about the room. As I did so I caught sight, in passing my window, of a red glow in the north-western sky. A house was on fire in the country, and evidently burning fast. It lay in the same direction as the scene of my evening's adventures, and as I stood watching the crimson horizon, I was startled by a sharp memory. I had blown out the candle which lighted me, with my companion, to the door through which we escaped, but I had not accounted for the other light, which she had carried into the hall and dropped – heaven knew where – in her consternation. The next day I walked out with my folded letter and turned into the familiar crossroad. The haunted house was a mass of charred beams and smouldering ashes; the well-cover had been pulled off, in quest of water, by the few neighbours who had had the audacity to contest what they must have regarded as a demon-kindled blaze; the loose stones were completely displaced, and the earth had been trampled into puddles.

Sir Edmund Orme

THE STATEMENT APPEARS to have been written, though the fragment is undated, long after the death of his wife, whom I take to have been one of the persons referred to. There is however nothing in the strange story to establish this point, now perhaps not of importance. When I took possession of his effects, I found these pages, in a locked drawer, among papers relating to the unfortunate lady's too brief career – she died in childbirth a year after her marriage: letters, memoranda, accounts, faded photographs, cards of invitation. That's the only connection I can point to, and you may easily, and will probably, think it too extravagant to have had a palpable basis. I can't, I allow, vouch for his having intended it as a report of real occurrence – I can only vouch for his general veracity. In any case, it was written for himself, not for others. I offer it to others – having full option – precisely because of its oddity. Let them, in respect to the form of the thing, bear in mind that it was written quite for himself. I've altered nothing but the names.

If there's a story in the matter, I recognise the exact moment at which it began. This was on a soft still Sunday noon in November, just after church, on the sunny Parade. Brighton[1] was full of people; it was the height of the season and the day was even more respectable than lovely – which helped to account for the multitude of walkers. The blue sea itself was decorous; it seemed to doze with a gentle snore – if that *be* decorum – while nature preached a sermon. After writing letters all the morning, I had come out to take a look at it before luncheon. I leaned over the rail dividing the King's Road from the beach, and I think I had smoked a cigarette, when I became conscious of an intended joke in the shape of a light walking-stick laid across my shoulders. The idea, I found, had been thrown off by Teddy Bostwick of the Rifles and was intended as a contribution to talk. Our talk came off as we strolled together – he always took your arm to show you he forgave your obtuseness about his humour – and looked at the people, and bowed to some of them, and wondered who others were, and differed in opinion as to the prettiness of girls. About Charlotte Marden we agreed, however, as we saw her come towards us with her mother; and there surely could have been no one who wouldn't have concurred. The Brighton air used of old to make plain girls pretty and pretty girls prettier still – I don't know whether it works the spell now. The place was at any rate rare for complexions, and Miss Marden's was one that made people turn round. It made *us* stop, heaven knows – at least it was one of the things, for we already knew the ladies.

We turned with them, we joined them, we went where they were going. They were going only to the end and back – they had just come out of church. It was another manifestation of Teddy's humour that he got immediate possession of Charlotte, leaving me to walk with her mother. However, I wasn't unhappy; the girl was before me and I had her to talk about. We prolonged our walk; Mrs Marden kept me and presently said she was tired and must rest. We found a place on a sheltered bench – we gossiped as the people passed. It had already struck me, in this pair, that the resemblance between mother and daughter was wonderful even among such resemblances, all the more that it took so little account of a difference of nature. One often hears mature mothers spoken of as warnings – signposts, more or less discouraging, of the way daughters may go. But there was nothing deterrent in the idea that Charlotte should at fifty-five be as beautiful, even though it were conditioned on her being as pale and preoccupied, as Mrs Marden. At twenty-two she had a rosy blankness and was admirably handsome. Her head had the charming shape of her mother's and her features the same fine order. Then there were looks and movements and tones – moments when you could scarce say if it were aspect or sound – which, between the two appearances, referred and reminded.

These ladies had a small fortune and a cheerful little house at Brighton, full of portraits and tokens and trophies – stuffed animals on the top of bookcases and sallow varnished fish under glass – to which Mrs Marden professed herself attached by pious memories. Her husband had been 'ordered' there in ill health, to spend the last years of his life, and she had already mentioned to me that it was a place in which she felt herself still under the protection of his goodness. His goodness appeared to have been great, and she sometimes seemed to defend it from vague innuendo. Some sense of protection, of an influence invoked and cherished, was evidently necessary to her; she had a dim wistfulness, a longing for security. She wanted friends and had a good many. She was kind to me on our first meeting, and I never suspected her of the vulgar purpose of 'making up' to me – a suspicion of course unduly frequent in conceited young men. It never struck me that she wanted me for her daughter, nor yet, like some unnatural mammas, for herself. It was as if they had had a common deep shy need and had been ready to say: 'Oh be friendly to us and be trustful! Don't be afraid – you won't be expected to marry us.' 'Of course there's something about mamma: that's really what makes her such a dear!' Charlotte said to me, confidentially, at an early stage of our acquaintance. She worshipped her mother's appearance. It was the only thing she was vain of; she accepted the raised eyebrows as a charming ultimate fact. 'She looks as if she were waiting for the doctor, dear mamma,' she said on another occasion. 'Perhaps *you're* the doctor; do you think you are?' It appeared in the event that I had some healing power. At any rate, when I learned, for she once dropped the remark, that Mrs Marden also held there was something 'awfully strange' about Charlotte, the relation of the two ladies couldn't but be interesting. It was happy enough, at bottom; each had the other so on her mind.

On the Parade the stream of strollers held its course, and Charlotte presently went by with Teddy Bostwick. She smiled and nodded and continued, but when she came back, she stopped and spoke to us. Captain Bostwick positively declined to go in – he pronounced the occasion too jolly: might they therefore take another turn? Her mother dropped a 'Do as you like,' and the girl gave me an impertinent smile over her shoulder as they quitted us. Teddy looked at me with his glass in one eye, but I didn't mind that: it was only of Miss Marden I was thinking as I laughed to my companion. 'She's a bit of a coquette, you know.'

'Don't say that – don't say that!' Mrs Marden murmured.

'The nicest girls always are – just a little,' I was magnanimous enough to plead.

'Then why are they always punished?'

The intensity of the question startled me – it had come out in a vivid flash. Therefore I had to think a moment before I put to her: 'What do you know of their punishment?'

'Well – I was a bad girl myself.'

'And were you punished?'

'I carry it through life,' she said as she looked away from me. 'Ah!' she suddenly panted in the next breath, rising to her feet and staring at her daughter, who had reappeared again with Captain Bostwick. She stood a few seconds, the queerest expression in her face; then she sank on the seat again and I saw she had blushed crimson. Charlotte, who had noticed it all, came straight up to her and, taking her hand with quick tenderness, seated herself at her other side. The girl had turned pale – she gave her mother a fixed scared look. Mrs Marden, who had had some shock that escaped our detection, recovered herself; that is she sat quiet and inexpressive, gazing at the indifferent crowd, the sunny air, the slumbering sea. My eye happened to fall nevertheless on the interlocked hands of the two ladies, and I quickly guessed the grasp of the elder to be violent. Bostwick stood before them, wondering what was the matter and asking me from his little vacant disk if *I* knew; which led Charlotte to say to him after a moment and with a certain irritation: 'Don't stand there that way, Captain Bostwick. Go away – *please* go away.'

I got up at this, hoping Mrs Marden wasn't ill; but she at once begged we wouldn't leave them, that we would particularly stay and that we would presently come home to luncheon. She drew me down beside her and for a moment I felt her hand press my arm in a way that might have been an involuntary betrayal of distress and might have been a private signal. What she should have wished to point out to me I couldn't divine: perhaps she had seen in the crowd somebody or something abnormal. She explained to us in a few minutes that she was all right, that she was only liable to palpitations: they came as quickly as they went. It was time to move – a truth on which we acted. The incident was felt to be closed. Bostwick and I lunched with our sociable friends, and when I walked away with him, he professed he had never seen creatures more completely to his taste.

Mrs Marden had made us promise to come back the next day to tea, and had exhorted us in general to come as often as we could. Yet the next day when, at five o'clock, I knocked at the door of the pretty house it was but to learn that the ladies had gone up to town. They had left a message for us with the butler: he was to say they had suddenly been called and much regretted it. They would be absent a few days. This was all I could extract from the dumb domestic. I went again three days later, but they were still away; and it was not till the end of a week that I got a note from Mrs Marden. 'We're back,' she wrote: 'do come and forgive us.' It was on this occasion, I remember – the occasion of my going just after getting the note – that she told me she had distinct intuitions. I don't know how many people there were in England at that time in that predicament, but there were very few who would have mentioned it; so that the announcement struck me as original, especially as her point was that some of these uncanny promptings were connected with myself. There were other people present – idle Brighton folk, old women with frightened eyes and irrelevant interjections – and I had too few minutes' talk with Charlotte; but the day after this, I met them both at dinner and had the satisfaction of sitting next to Miss Marden. I recall this passage as the hour of its first fully coming over me that she was a beautiful liberal creature. I had seen her personality in glimpses and gleams, like a song sung in snatches, but now it was before me in a large rosy glow, as if it had been a full volume of sound. I heard the whole of the air, and it was sweet fresh music, which I was often to hum over.

After dinner I had a few words with Mrs Marden; it was at the time, late in the evening, when tea was handed about. A servant passed near us with a tray; I asked her if she would have a cup and, on her assenting, took one and offered it to her. She put out her hand for it and I gave it her, safely as I supposed; but as her fingers were about to secure it, she started and faltered, so that both my frail vessel and its fine recipient dropped with a crash of porcelain and without, on the part of my companion, the usual woman's motion to save her dress. I stooped to pick up the fragments and when I raised myself Mrs Marden was looking across the room at her daughter, who returned it with lips of cheer but anxious eyes. 'Dear mamma, what on earth *is* the matter with you ?' the silent question seemed to say. Mrs Marden coloured just as she had done after her strange movement on the Parade the other week, and I was therefore surprised when she said to me with unexpected assurance: 'You should really have a steadier hand!' I had begun to stammer a defence of my hand when I noticed her eyes fixed on me with an intense appeal. It was ambiguous at first and only added to my confusion; then suddenly I understood as plainly as if she had murmured 'Make believe it was you – make believe it was you.' The servant came back to take the morsels of the cup and wipe up the spilt tea, and while I was in the midst of making believe, Mrs Marden abruptly brushed away from me and from her daughter's attention and went into an other room. She gave no heed to the state of her dress.

I saw nothing more of either that evening, but the next morning, in the King's Road, I met the younger lady with a roll of music in her muff. She told me she had been a little way alone, to practise duets with a friend, and I asked her if she would go a little way farther in company. She gave me leave to attend her to her door, and as we stood before it I enquired if I might go in. 'No, not today – I don't want you,' she said very straight, though not unamiably; while the words caused me to direct a wistful disconcerted gaze at one of the windows of the house. It fell on the white face of Mrs Marden, turned out at us from the drawing-room. She stood long enough to show it *was* she and not the apparition I had come near taking it for, and then she vanished before her daughter had observed her. The girl, during our walk, had said nothing about her. As I had been told they didn't want me, I left them alone a little, after which certain hazards kept us still longer apart. I finally went up to London, and while there received a pressing invitation to come immediately down to Tranton, a pretty old place in Sussex belonging to a couple whose acquaintance I had lately made.

I went to Tranton from town, and on arriving found the Mardens, with a dozen other people, in the house. The first thing Mrs Marden said was 'Will you forgive me?' and when I asked what I had to forgive she answered 'My throwing my tea over you.' I replied that it had gone over herself; whereupon she said 'At any rate I was very rude – but sometime I think you'll understand, and then you'll make allowances for me.' The first day I was there she dropped two or three of these references – she had already indulged in more than one – to the mystic initiation in store for me; so that I began, as the phrase is, to chaff her about it, to say I'd rather it were less wonderful and take it out at once. She answered that when it should come to me I'd have indeed to take it out – there would be little enough option. That it *would* come was privately clear to her, a deep presentiment, which was the only reason she had ever mentioned the matter. Didn't I remember she had spoken to me of intuitions? From the first of her seeing me, she had been sure there were things I shouldn't escape knowing. Meanwhile there was nothing to do but wait and keep cool, not to be precipitate. She particularly wished not to become extravagantly nervous. And I was above all not to be nervous myself – one got used to everything. I returned that though I couldn't make out what she was talking of I was terribly frightened; the absence of a clue gave such a range to one's imagination. I exaggerated on purpose; for if Mrs Marden was mystifying I can scarcely say she was alarming. I couldn't imagine what she meant, but I wondered more than I shuddered. I might have said to myself that she was a little wrong in the upper storey;[2] but that never occurred to me. She struck me as hopelessly right.

There were other girls in the house, but Charlotte the most charming; which was so generally allowed that she almost interfered with the slaughter of ground game. There were two or three men, and I was of the number, who actually preferred her to the society of the beaters.[3] In short, she was recognised as a form of sport superior and exquisite. She was kind to all of us – she made us go out late and come in early. I don't know whether she flirted, but several other members of the party thought *they* did. Indeed, as regards himself, Teddy Bostwick, who had come over from Brighton, was visibly sure.

The third of these days was a Sunday, which determined a pretty walk to morning service over the fields. It was grey windless weather, and the bell of the little old church that nestled in the hollow of the Sussex down sounded near and domestic. We were a straggling procession in the mild damp air – which, as always at that season, gave one the feeling that after the trees were bare there was more of it, a larger sky – and I managed to fall a good way behind with Miss Marden. I remember entertaining, as we moved together over the turf, a strong impulse to say something intensely personal, something violent and important, important for *me* – such as that I had never seen her so lovely or that that particular moment was the sweetest of my life. But always, in youth, such words have been on the lips many times before they're spoken to any effect; and I had the sense, not that I didn't know her well enough – I cared little for that – but that she didn't sufficiently know *me*. In the church, a museum of old Tranton tombs and brasses, the big Tranton pew was full. Several of us were scattered, and I found a seat for Miss Marden, and another for myself beside it, at a distance from her mother and from most of our friends. There were two or three decent rustics[4] on the bench, who moved in farther to make room for us, and I took my place first, to cut off my companion from our neighbours. After she was seated, there was still a space left, which remained empty till service was about half over.

This at least was the moment of my noting that another person had entered and had taken the seat. When I remarked him he had apparently been for some minutes in the pew – had settled himself and put down his hat beside him and, with his hands crossed on the knob of his cane, was gazing before him at the altar. He was a pale young man in black and with the air of a gentleman. His presence slightly startled me, for Miss Marden hadn't attracted my attention to it by moving to make room for him. After a few minutes, observing that he had no prayer-book, I reached across my neighbour and placed mine before him, on the ledge of the pew; a manoeuvre the motive of which was not unconnected with the possibility that, in my own destitution, Miss Marden would give me one side of *her* velvet volume to hold. The pretext however was destined to fail, for at the moment I offered him the book, the intruder – whose intrusion I had so condoned – rose from his place without thanking me, stepped noiselessly out of the pew, which had no door, and, so discreetly as to attract no attention, passed down the centre of the church. A few minutes had sufficed for his devotions. His behaviour was unbecoming, his early departure even more than his late arrival; but he managed so quietly that we were not incommoded, and I found, on turning a little to look after him, that nobody was disturbed by his withdrawal. I only noticed, and with surprise, that Mrs Marden had been so affected by it as to rise, all involuntarily, in her place. She stared at him as he passed, but he passed very quickly, and she as quickly dropped down again, though not too soon to catch my eye across the church. Five minutes later, I asked her daughter, in a low voice, if she would kindly pass me back my prayer book – I had waited to see if she would spontaneously perform the act. The girl restored this aid to devotion, but had been so far from troubling herself about it that she could say to me as she did so: 'Why on earth did you put it there?' I was on the point of answering her when she dropped on her knees, and at this I held my tongue. I had only been going to say: 'To be decently civil.'

After the benediction, as we were leaving our places, I was slightly surprised again to see that Mrs Marden, instead of going out with her companions, had come up the aisle to join us, having apparently something to say to her daughter. She said it, but in an instant I saw it had been a pretext – her real business was with me. She pushed Charlotte forward and suddenly breathed to me: 'Did you see him?'

'The gentleman who sat down here? How could I help seeing him?'

'Hush!' she said with the intensest excitement; 'don't *speak* to her – don't tell her!' She slipped her hand into my arm, to keep me near her, to keep me, it seemed, away from her daughter. The precaution was unnecessary, for Teddy Bostwick had already taken possession of Miss Marden, and as they passed out of church in front of me I saw one of the other men close up on her other hand. It appeared to be felt that I had had my turn. Mrs Marden released me as soon as we got out, but not before I saw she had needed my support. 'Don't speak to anyone – don't tell anyone!' she went on.

'I don't understand. Tell anyone what?'

'Why, that you saw him.'

'Surely they saw him for themselves.'

'Not one of them, not one of them.' She spoke with such passionate decision that I glanced at her – she was staring straight before her. But she felt the challenge of my eyes and stopped short, in the old brown timber porch of the church, with the others well in advance of us; where, looking at me now and in quite an extraordinary manner, 'You're the only person,' she said; 'the only person in the world.'

'But *you*, dear madam?'

'Oh me – of course. That's my curse!' And with this she moved rapidly off to join the rest of our group. I hovered at its outskirts on the way home – I had such food for rumination. Whom had I seen and why was the apparition – it rose before my mind's eye all clear again – invisible to the others? If an exception had been made for Mrs Marden, why did it constitute a curse, and why was I to share so questionable a boon? This appeal, carried on in my own locked breast, kept me doubtless quiet enough at luncheon. After that repast I went out on the old terrace to smoke a cigarette, but had taken only a turn or two when I caught Mrs Marden's moulded mask at the window of one of the rooms open to the crooked flags.[5] It reminded me of the same flitting presence behind the pane at Brighton the day I met Charlotte and walked home with her. But this time my ambiguous friend didn't vanish; she tapped on the pane and motioned me to come in. She was in a queer little apartment, one of the many reception rooms of which the ground floor at Tranton consisted; it was known as the Indian room and had a style denominated Eastern – bamboo lounges, lacquered screens, lanterns with long fringes and strange idols in cabinets, objects not held to conduce to sociability. The place was little used, and when I went round to her we had it to ourselves. As soon as I appeared she said to me: 'Please tell me this – are you in love with my daughter?'

I really had a little to take my time. 'Before I answer your question will you kindly tell me what gives you the idea? I don't consider I've been very forward.'

Mrs Marden, contradicting me with her beautiful anxious eyes, gave me no satisfaction on the point I mentioned; she only went on strenuously: 'Did you say nothing to her on the way to church?'

'What makes you think I said anything?'

'Why the fact that you saw him.'

'Saw whom, dear Mrs Marden?'

'Oh you know,' she answered gravely, even a little reproachfully, as if I were trying to humiliate her by making her name the unnameable.

'Do you mean the gentleman who formed the subject of your strange statement in church – the one who came into the pew?'

'You saw him, you saw him!' she panted with a strange mixture of dismay and relief.

'Of course I saw him, and so did you.'

'It didn't follow. Did you feel it to be inevitable?'

I was puzzled again. 'Inevitable?'

'That you *should* see him?'

'Certainly, since I'm not blind.'

'You might have been. Everyone else is.' I was wonderfully at sea and I frankly confessed it to my questioner, but the case wasn't improved by her presently exclaiming: 'I knew you would, from the moment you should be really in love with her! I knew it would be the test – what do I mean? – the proof.'

'Are there such strange bewilderments attached to that high state?' I smiled to ask.

'You can judge for yourself. You see him, you see him!' – she quite exulted in it. 'You'll see him again.'

'I've no objection, but I shall take more interest in him if you'll kindly tell me who he is.'

She avoided my eyes – then consciously met them. 'I'll tell you if you'll tell me first what you said to her on the way to church.'

'Has she told you I said anything?'

'Do I need that?' she asked with expression.

'Oh yes, I remember – your intuitions! But I'm sorry to see they're at fault this time; because I really said nothing to your daughter that was the least out of the way.'

'Are you very very sure?'

'On my honour, Mrs Marden.'

'Then you consider you're not in love with her?'

'That's another affair!' I laughed.

'You are – you *are!* You wouldn't have seen him if you hadn't been.'

'Then who the deuce *is* he, madam?' – I pressed it with some irritation.

Yet she would still only question me back. 'Didn't you at least *want* to say something to her – didn't you come very near it?'

Well, this was more to the point; it justified the famous intuitions. 'Ah "near" it as much as you like – call it the turn of a hair. I don't know what kept me quiet.'

'That was quite enough,' said Mrs Marden. 'It isn't what you say that makes the difference; it's what you feel. *That's* what he goes by.'

I was annoyed at last by her reiterated reference to an identity yet to be established, and I clasped my hands with an air of supplication which covered much real impatience, a sharper curiosity and even the first short throbs of a certain sacred dread. 'I entreat you to tell me whom you're talking about.'

She threw up her arms, looking away from me, as if to shake off both reserve and responsibility. 'Sir Edmund Orme.'

'And who may Sir Edmund Orme be?'

At the moment I spoke she gave a start. 'Hush – here they come.' Then as, following the direction of her eyes, I saw Charlotte, out on the terrace, by our own window, she added, with an intensity of warning: 'Don't notice him – *never!*'

The girl, who now had had her hands beside her eyes, peering into the room and smiling, signed to us through the glass to admit her; on which I went and opened the long window. Her mother turned away and she came in with a laughing challenge: 'What plot in the world are you two hatching here?' Some plan – I forget what – was in prospect for the afternoon, as to which Mrs Marden's participation or consent was solicited, my own adhesion being taken for granted; and she had been half over the place in her quest. I was flurried, seeing the elder woman was – when she turned round to meet her daughter she disguised it to extravagance, throwing herself on the girl's neck and embracing her – so that, to pass it off, I overdid my gallantry.

'I've been asking your mother for your hand.'

'Oh indeed, and has she given it?' Miss Marden gaily returned.

'She was just going to when you appeared there.'

'Well, it's only for a moment – I'll leave you free.'

'Do you like him, Charlotte?' Mrs Marden asked with a candour I scarcely expected.

'It's difficult to say *before* him, isn't it?' the charming creature went on, entering into the humour of the thing, but looking at me as if she scarce liked me at all.

She would have had to say it before another person as well, for at that moment there stepped into the room from the terrace – the window had been left open – a gentleman who had come into sight, at least into mine, only within the instant. Mrs Marden had said 'Here *they* come,' but he appeared to have followed her daughter at a certain distance. I recognised him at once as the personage who had sat beside us in church. This time I saw him better, saw his face and his carriage were strange. I speak of him as a personage, because one felt, indescribably, as if a reigning prince had come into the room. He held himself with something of the grand air and as if he were different from his company. Yet he looked fixedly and gravely at me, till I wondered what he expected. Did he consider that I should bend my knee or kiss his hand? He turned his eyes in the same way on Mrs Marden, but she knew what to do. After the first agitation produced by his approach, she took no notice of him whatever; it made me remember her passionate adjuration to me. I had to achieve a great effort to imitate her, for though I knew nothing about him but that he was Sir Edmund Orme, his presence acted as a strong appeal, almost as an oppression. He stood there without speaking – young pale handsome clean-shaven decorous, with extraordinary light blue eyes and something old-fashioned, like a portrait of years ago, in his head and in his manner of wearing his hair. He was in complete mourning – one immediately took him for very well dressed – and he carried his hat in his hand. He looked again strangely hard at me, harder than anyone in the world had ever looked before; and I remember feeling rather cold and wishing he would say something. No silence had ever seemed to me so soundless. All this was of course an impression intensely rapid; but that it had consumed some instants was proved to me suddenly by the expression of countenance of Charlotte Marden, who stared from one of us to the other – he never looked at her, and she had no appearance of looking at him – and then broke out with: 'What on earth is the matter with you? You've such odd faces!' I felt the colour come back to mine, and when she went on in the same tone, 'One would think you had seen a ghost!' I was conscious I had turned very red. Sir Edmund Orme never blushed, and I was sure no embarrassment touched him. One had met people of that sort, but never anyone with so high an indifference.

'Don't be impertinent, and go and tell them all that I'll join them,' said Mrs Marden with much dignity but with a tremor of voice that I caught.

'And will you come – *you*?' the girl asked, turning away. I made no answer, taking the question somehow as meant for her companion. But he was more silent than I, and when she reached the door – she was going out that way – she stopped, her hand on the knob, and looked at me, repeating it. I assented, springing forward to open the door for her, and as she passed out she exclaimed to me mockingly: 'You haven't got your wits about you – you shan't have my hand!'

I closed the door and turned round to find that Sir Edmund Orme had during the moment my back was presented to him retired by the window. Mrs Marden stood there and we looked at each other long. It had only then – as the girl flitted away – come home to me that her daughter was unconscious of what had happened. It was *that*, oddly enough, that gave me a sudden sharp shake – not my own perception of our visitor, which felt quite natural. It made the fact vivid to me that she had been equally unaware of him in church, and the two facts together – now that they were over – set my heart more sensibly beating. I wiped my forehead, and Mrs Marden broke out with a low distressful wail: 'Now you know my life – now you know my life!'

'In God's name who is he – *what* is he?'

'He's a man I wronged.'

'How did you wrong him?'

'Oh awfully – years ago.'

'Years ago? Why, he's very young.'

'Young – young?' cried Mrs Marden. 'He was born before *I* was!'

'Then why does he look so?'

She came nearer to me, she laid her hand on my arm, and there was something in her face that made me shrink a little. 'Don't you understand – don't you *feel?*' she intensely put to me.

'I feel very queer!' I laughed; and I was conscious that my note betrayed it.

'He's dead!' said Mrs Marden from her white face.

'Dead?' I panted. 'Then that gentleman was – ?'

I couldn't even say a word.

'Call him what you like – there are twenty vulgar names. He's a perfect presence.'

'He's a splendid presence!' I cried. 'The place is haunted, *haunted!*' I exulted in the word as if it stood for all I had ever dreamt of.

'It isn't the place – more's the pity!' she instantly returned. 'That has nothing to do with it!'

'Then it's you, dear lady?' I said as if this were still better.

'No, nor me either – I wish it were!'

'Perhaps it's me,' I suggested with a sickly smile.

'It's nobody but my child – my innocent, innocent child!' And with this Mrs Marden broke down – she dropped into a chair and burst into tears. I stammered some question – I pressed on her some bewildered appeal, but she waved me off, unexpectedly and passionately. I persisted – couldn't I help her, couldn't I intervene? 'You *have* intervened,' she sobbed; 'you're *in* it, you're *in* it.'

'I'm very glad to be in anything so extraordinary,' I boldly declared.

'Glad or not, you can't get out of it.'

'I don't want to get out of it – it's too interesting.'

'I'm glad you like it!' She had turned from me, making haste to dry her eyes. 'And now go away.'

'But I want to know more about it.'

'You'll see all you want. Go away!'

'But I want to understand what I see.'

'How can you – when I don't understand myself?' she helplessly cried.

'We'll do so together – we'll make it out.'

At this she got up, doing what more she could to obliterate her tears. 'Yes, it will be better together – that's why I've liked you.'

'Oh we'll see it through!' I returned.

'Then you must control yourself better.'

'I will, I will – with practice.'

'You'll get used to it,' said my friend in a tone I never forgot. 'But go and join them – I'll come in a moment.'

I passed out to the terrace and felt I had a part to play. So far from dreading another encounter with the 'perfect presence', as she had called it, I was affected altogether in the sense of pleasure. I desired a renewal of my luck: I opened myself wide to the impression; I went round the house as quickly as if I expected to overtake Sir Edmund Orme. I didn't overtake him just then, but the day wasn't to close without my recognising that, as Mrs Marden had said, I should see all I wanted of him.

We took, or most of us took, the collective sociable walk which, in the English country-house, is – or was at that time – the consecrated pastime of Sunday afternoons. We were restricted to such a regulated ramble as the ladies were good for; the afternoons moreover were short, and by five o'clock we were restored to the fireside in the hall with a sense, on my part at least, that we might have done a little more for our tea. Mrs Marden had said she would join us, but she hadn't appeared; her daughter, who had seen her again before we went out, only explained that she was tired. She remained invisible all the afternoon, but this was a detail to which I gave as little heed as I had given to the circumstance of my not having Charlotte to myself, even for five minutes, during all our walk. I was too much taken up with another interest to care; I felt beneath my feet the threshold of the strange door, in my life, which had suddenly been thrown open and out of which came an air of a keenness I had never breathed and of a taste stronger than wine. I had heard all my days of apparitions, but it was a different thing to have seen one and to know that I should in all likelihood see it familiarly, as I might say, again. I was on the lookout for it as a pilot[6] for the flash of a revolving light, and ready to generalise on the sinister subject, to answer for it to all and sundry that ghosts were much less alarming and much more amusing than was commonly supposed. There's no doubt that I was much uplifted. I couldn't get over the distinction conferred on me, the exception – in the way of mystic enlargement of vision – made in my favour. At the same time, I think I did justice to Mrs Marden's absence – a commentary, when I came to think, on what she had said to me: 'Now you know my life.' She had probably been exposed to our hoverer for years, and, not having my firm fibre, had broken down under it. Her nerve was gone, though she had also been able to attest that, in a degree, one got used to it. She had got used to breaking down.

Afternoon tea, when the dusk fell early, was a friendly hour at Tranton ; the firelight played into the wide white last-century hall; sympathies almost confessed themselves, lingering together, before dressing, on deep sofas, in muddy boots, for last words after walks; and even solitary absorption in the third volume of a novel[7] that was wanted by someone else seemed a form of geniality. I watched my moment and went over to Charlotte when I saw her about to withdraw. The ladies had left the place one by one, and after I had addressed myself to her particularly, the three men who had been near gradually dispersed. We had a little vague talk – she might have been a good deal preoccupied, and heaven knows *I* was – after which she said she must go: she should be late for dinner. I proved to her by book that she had plenty of time, and she objected that she must at any rate go up to see her mother, who, she feared, was unwell.

'On the contrary, she's better than she has been for a long time – I'll guarantee that,' I said. 'She has found out she can have confidence in me, and that has done her good.' Miss Marden had dropped into her chair again, I was standing before her, and she looked up at me without a smile, with a dim distress in her beautiful eyes: not exactly as if I were hurting her, but as if she were no longer disposed to treat as a joke what had passed – whatever it was, it would give at the same time no ground for the extreme of solemnity – between her mother and myself. But I could answer her enquiry in all kindness and candour, for I was really conscious that the poor lady had put off a part of her burden on me and was proportionately relieved and eased. 'I'm sure she has slept all the afternoon as she hasn't slept for years,' I went on. 'You've only to ask her.'

Charlotte got up again. 'You make yourself out very useful.'

'You've a good quarter of an hour,' I said. 'Haven't I a right to talk to you a little this way, alone, when your mother has given me your hand?'

'And is it *your* mother who has given me yours? I'm much obliged to her, but I don't want it. I think our hands are not our mothers' – they happen to be our own!' laughed the girl.

'Sit down, sit down and let me tell you!' I pleaded.

I still stood there urgently, to see if she wouldn't oblige me. She cast about, looking vaguely this way and that, as if under a compulsion that was slightly painful. The empty hall was quiet – we heard the loud ticking of the great clock. Then she slowly sank down and I drew a chair close to her. This made me face round to the fire again, and with the movement I saw disconcertedly that we weren't alone. The next instant, more strangely than I can say, my discomposure, instead of increasing, dropped, for the person before the fire was Sir Edmund Orme. He stood there as I had seen him in the Indian room, looking at me with the expressionless attention that borrowed gravity from his sombre distinction. I knew so much more about him now that I had to check a movement of recognition, an acknowledgement of his presence. When once I was aware of it, and that it lasted, the sense that we had company, Charlotte and I, quitted me: it was impressed on me on the contrary that we were but the more markedly thrown together. No influence from our companion reached her, and I made a tremendous and very nearly successful effort to hide from her that my own sensibility was other and my nerves as tense as harp-strings. I say 'very nearly', because she watched me an instant – while my words were arrested – in a way that made me fear she was going to say again, as she had said in the Indian room: 'What on earth is the matter with you?'

What the matter with me was I quickly told her, for the full knowledge of it rolled over me with the touching sight of her unconsciousness. It was touching that she became in the presence of this extraordinary portent. What was portended, danger or sorrow, bliss or bane, was a minor question; all I saw, as she sat there, was that, innocent and charming, she was close to a horror, as she might have thought it, that happened to be veiled from her but that might at any moment be disclosed. I didn't mind it now, as I found – at least more than I could bear; but nothing was more possible than she should, and if it wasn't curious and interesting it might easily be appalling. If I didn't mind it for myself, I afterwards made out, this was largely because I was so taken up with the idea of protecting her. My heart, all at once, beat high with this view; I determined to do everything I could to keep her sense sealed. What I could do might have been all obscure to me if I hadn't, as the minutes lapsed, become more aware than of anything else that I loved her. The way to save her was to love her, and the way to love her was to tell her, now and here, that I did so. Sir Edmund Orme didn't prevent me, especially as after a moment he turned his back to us and stood looking discreetly at the fire. At the end of another moment, he leaned his head on his arm, against the chimney piece, with an air of gradual dejection, like a spirit still more weary than discreet. Charlotte Marden rose with a start at what I said to her – she jumped up to escape it; but she took no offence: the feeling I expressed was too real. She only moved about the room with a deprecating murmur, and I was so busy following up any little advantage I might have obtained that I didn't notice in what manner Sir Edmund Orme disappeared. I only found his place presently vacant. This made no difference – he had been so small a hindrance; I only remember being suddenly struck with something inexorable in the sweet sad headshake Charlotte gave me.

'I don't ask for an answer now,' I said; 'I only want you to be sure – to know how much depends on it.'

'Oh I don't want to give it to you now or ever!' she replied. 'I hate the subject, please – I wish one could be let alone.' And then, since I might have found something harsh in this irrepressible artless cry of beauty beset, she added, quickly vaguely kindly, as she left the room: 'Thank you, thank you – thank you so very much!'

At dinner, I was generous enough to be glad for her that, on the same side of the table with me, she hadn't me in range. Her mother was nearly opposite me, and just after we had sat down Mrs Marden gave me a long deep look that expressed, and to the utmost, our strange communion. It meant of course 'She has told me,' but it meant other things beside. At any rate I know what my mute response to her conveyed: 'I've seen him again – I've seen him again!' This didn't prevent Mrs Marden from treating her neighbours with her usual scrupulous blandness. After dinner, when, in the drawing-room, the men joined the ladies and I went straight up to her to tell her how I wished we might have some quiet words, she said at once, in a low tone, looking down at her fan while she opened and shut it: 'He's here – he's here.'

'Here?' I looked round the room, but was disappointed.

'Look where *she* is,' said Mrs Marden just with the faintest asperity. Charlotte was in fact not in the main saloon, but in a smaller into which it opened and which was known as the morning-room. I took a few steps and saw her, through a doorway, upright in the middle of the room, talking with three gentlemen whose backs were practically turned to me. For a moment my quest seemed vain; then I knew one of the gentlemen – the middle one – could but be Sir Edmund Orme. This time it *was* surprising that the others didn't see him. Charlotte might have seemed absolutely to have her eyes on him and to be addressing him straight. She saw me after an instant, however, and immediately averted herself. I returned to her mother with a sharpened fear the girl might think I was watching *her*, which would be unjust. Mrs Marden had found a small sofa – a little apart – and I sat down beside her. There were some questions I had so wanted to go into that I wished we were once more in the Indian room. I presently gathered however that our privacy quite sufficed. We communicated so closely and completely now, and with such silent reciprocities, that it would in every circumstance be adequate.

'Oh yes, he's there,' I said; 'and at about a quarter-past seven he was in the hall.'

'I knew it at the time – and I was so glad!' she answered straight.

'So glad?'

'That it was your affair this time and not mine. It's a rest for me.'

'Did you sleep all the afternoon?' I then asked.

'As I haven't done for months. But how did you know that?'

'As *you* knew, I take it, that Sir Edmund was in the hall. We shall evidently each of us know things now – where the other's concerned.'

'Where *he's* concerned,' Mrs Marden amended. 'It's a blessing, the way you take it,' she added with a long mild sigh.

'I take it,' I at once returned, 'as a man who's in love with your daughter.'

'Of course – of course.' Intense as I now felt my desire for the girl to be, I couldn't help laughing a little at the tone of these words; and it led my companion immediately to say: 'Otherwise you wouldn't have seen him.'

Well, I esteemed my privilege, but I saw an objection to this. 'Does everyone see him who's in love with her? If so there would be dozens.'

'They're not in love with her as you are.'

I took this in and couldn't but accept it. 'I can of course only speak for myself – and I found a moment before dinner to do so.'

'She told me as soon as she saw me,' Mrs Marden replied.

'And have I any hope – any chance?'

'That you may have is what I long for, what I pray for.'

The sore sincerity of this touched me. 'Ah how can I thank you enough?' I murmured.

'I believe it will all pass – if she only loves you,' the poor woman pursued.

'It will all pass?' I was a little at a loss.

'I mean we shall then be rid of him – shall never see him again.'

'Oh if she loves me I don't care how often I see him!' I roundly returned.

'Ah you take it better than *I* could,' said my companion. 'You've the happiness not to know – not to understand.'

'I don't indeed. What on earth does he want?'

'He wants to make me suffer.' She turned her wan face upon me with it, and I saw now for the first time, and saw well, how perfectly, if this had been our visitant's design, he had done his work. 'For what I did to him,' she explained.

'And what did you do to him?'

She gave me an unforgettable look. 'I killed him.' As I had seen him fifty yards off only five minutes before, the words gave me a start. 'Yes, I make you jump; be careful. He's there still, but he killed himself. I broke his heart – he thought me awfully bad. We were to have been married, but I broke it off – just at the last. I saw someone I liked better; I had no reason but that. It wasn't for interest or money or position or any of that baseness. All the good things were his. It was simply that I fell in love with Major Marden. When I saw *him* I felt I couldn't marry anyone else. I wasn't in love with Edmund Orme; my mother and my elder, my married, sister had brought it about. But he did love me and I knew – that is almost knew! – how much! But I told him I didn't care – that I couldn't, that I wouldn't ever. I threw him over, and he took something, some abominable drug or draught that proved fatal. It was dreadful, it was horrible, he was found that way – he died in agony. I married Major Marden, but not for five years. I was happy, perfectly happy – time obliterates. But when my husband died I began to see him.'

I had listened intently, wondering. 'To see your husband?'

'Never, never – *that* way, thank God! To see *him* – and with Chartie, always with Chartie. The first time it nearly killed me – about seven years ago, when she first came out. Never when I'm by myself – only with her. Sometimes not for months, then every day for a week. I've tried everything to break the spell – doctors and *régimes*[8] and climates; I've prayed to God on my knees. That day at Brighton, on the Parade with you, when you thought I was ill, that was the first for an age. And then in the evening, when I knocked my tea over you, and the day you were at the door with her and I saw you from the window – each time he was there.'

'I see, I see.' I was more thrilled than I could say. 'It's an apparition like another.'

'Like another? Have you ever seen another?' she cried.

'No, I mean the sort of thing one has heard of. It's tremendously interesting to encounter a case.'

'Do you call me a "case"?' my friend cried with exquisite resentment.

'I was thinking of myself.'

'Oh you're the right one!' she went on. 'I was right when I trusted you.'

'I'm devoutly grateful you did; but what made you do it?' I asked.

'I had thought the whole thing out. I had had time to in those dreadful years while he was punishing me in my daughter.'

'Hardly that,' I objected, 'if Miss Marden never knew.'

'That has been my terror, that she *will*, from one occasion to another. I've an unspeakable dread of the effect on her.'

'She shan't, she shan't!' I engaged in such a tone that several people looked round. Mrs Marden made me rise, and our talk dropped for that evening. The next day I told her I must leave Tranton – it was neither comfortable nor considerate to remain as a rejected suitor. She was disconcerted, but accepted my reasons, only appealing to me with mournful eyes: 'You'll leave me alone then with my burden?' It was of course understood between us that for many weeks to come there would be no discretion in 'worrying poor Charlotte': such were the terms in which, with odd feminine and maternal inconsistency, she alluded to an attitude on my part that she favoured. I was prepared to be heroically considerate, but I held that even this delicacy permitted me to say a word to Miss Marden before I went. I begged her after breakfast to take a turn with me on the terrace, and as she hesitated, looking at me distantly, I let her know it was only to ask her a question and to say goodbye – I was going away for *her*.

She came out with me and we passed slowly round the house three or four times. Nothing is finer than this great airy platform, from which every glance is a sweep of the country with the sea on the farthest edge. It might have been that as we passed the windows we were conspicuous to our friends in the house, who would make out sarcastically why I was so significantly bolting. But I didn't care; I only wondered if they mightn't really this time receive the impression of Sir Edmund Orme, who joined us on one of our turns and strolled slowly on the other side of Charlotte. Of what odd essence he was made I know not; I've no theory about him – leaving that to others – any more than about such or such another of my fellow mortals (and *his* law of being) as I have elbowed in life. He was as positive, as individual and ultimate a fact as any of these. Above all he was, by every seeming, of as fine and as sensitive, of as thoroughly honourable, a mixture; so that I should no more have thought of taking a liberty, of practising an experiment, with him, of touching him, for instance, or of addressing him, since he set the example of silence, than I should have thought of committing any other social grossness. He had always, as I saw more fully later, the perfect propriety of his position – looked always arrayed and anointed, and carried himself ever, in each particular, exactly as the occasion demanded. He struck me as strange, incontestably, but somehow always struck me as right. I very soon came to attach an idea of beauty to his unrecognised presence, the beauty of an old story, of love and pain and death. What I ended by feeling was that he was on my side, watching over my interest, looking to it that no trick should be played me and that my heart at least shouldn't be broken. Oh he had taken them seriously, his own wound and his own loss – he had certainly proved this in his day. If poor Mrs Marden, responsible for these things, had, as she told me, thought the case out, I also treated it to the finest analysis I could bring to bear. It was a case of retributive justice, of the visiting on the children of the sins of the mothers,[9] since not of the fathers. This wretched mother was to pay, in suffering, for the suffering she had inflicted, and as the disposition to trifle with an honest man's just expectations might crop up again, to my detriment, in the child, the latter young person was to be studied and watched, so that *she* might be made to suffer should she do an equal wrong. She might emulate her parent by some play of characteristic perversity not less than she resembled her in charm; and if that impulse should be determined in her, if she should be caught, that is to say, in some breach of faith or some heartless act, her eyes would on the spot, by an insidious logic, be opened suddenly and unpitiedly to the 'perfect presence', which she would then have to work as she could into her conception of a young lady's universe. I had no great fear for her, because I hadn't felt her lead me on from vanity, and I knew that if I was disconcerted it was because I had myself gone too fast. We should have a good deal of ground to get over at least before I should be in a position to be sacrificed by her. She couldn't take back what she had given before she had given rather more. Whether I asked for more was indeed another matter, and the question I put to her on the terrace that morning was whether I might continue during the winter to come to Mrs Marden's house. I promised not to come too often and not to speak to her for three months of the issue I had raised the day before. She replied that I might do as I liked, and on this we parted.

I carried out the vow I had made her; I held my tongue for my three months. Unexpectedly to myself there were moments of this time when she did strike me as capable of missing my homage even though she might be indifferent to my happiness. I wanted so to make her like me that I became subtle and ingenious, wonderfully alert, patiently diplomatic. Sometimes I thought I had earned my reward, brought her to the point of saying: 'Well, well, you're the best of them all – you may speak to me now.' Then there was a greater blankness than ever in her beauty and on certain days a mocking light in her eyes, a light of which the meaning seemed to be: 'If you don't take care I *will* accept you, to have done with you the more effectually.' Mrs Marden was a great help to me simply by believing in me, and I valued her faith all the more that it continued even through a sudden intermission of the miracle that had been wrought for me. After our visit to Tranton, Sir Edmund Orme gave us a holiday, and I confess it was at first a disappointment to me. I felt myself by so much less designated, less involved and connected – all with Charlotte I mean to say. 'Oh don't cry till you're out of the wood,' was her mother's comment; 'he has let me off sometimes for six months. He'll break out again when you least expect it – he understands his game.' For her these weeks were happy, and she was wise enough not to talk about me to the girl. She was so good as to assure me I was taking the right line, that I looked as if I felt secure and that in the long run women give way to this. She had known them do it even when the man was a fool for that appearance, for that confidence – a fool indeed on any terms. For herself she felt it a good time, almost her best, a Saint Martin's summer[10] of the soul. She was better than she had been for years, and had me to thank for it. The sense of visitation was light on her – she wasn't in anguish every time she looked round. Charlotte contradicted me repeatedly, but contradicted herself still more. That winter by the old Sussex sea was a wonder of mildness, and we often sat out in the sun. I walked up and down with my young woman, and Mrs Marden, sometimes on a bench, sometimes in a Bath-chair, waited for us and smiled at us as we passed. I always looked out for a sign in her face – 'He's with you, he's with you' (she would see him before I should) but nothing came; the season had brought us as well a sort of spiritual softness. Towards the end of April, the air was so like June that, meeting my two friends one night at some Brighton sociability – an evening party with amateur music – I drew the younger unresistingly out upon a balcony to which a window in one of the rooms stood open. The night was close and thick, the stars dim, and below us under the cliff we heard the deep rumble of the tide. We listened to it a little and there came to us, mixed with it from within the house, the sound of a violin accompanied by a piano – a performance that had been our pretext for escaping.

'Do you like me a little better?' I broke out after a minute. 'Could you listen to me again?'

I had no sooner spoken than she laid her hand quickly, with a certain force, on my arm. 'Hush! – isn't there someone there?' She was looking into the gloom of the far end of the balcony. This balcony ran the whole width of the house, a width very great in the best of the old houses at Brighton. We were to some extent lighted by the open window behind us, but the other windows, curtained within, left the darkness undiminished, so that I made out but dimly the figure of a gentleman standing there and looking at us. He was in evening dress, like a guest – I saw the vague sheen of his white shirt and the pale oval of his face – and he might perfectly have been a guest who had stepped out in advance of us to take the air. Charlotte took him for one at first – then evidently, even in a few seconds, saw that the intensity of his gaze was unconventional. What else she saw I couldn't determine; I was too occupied with my own impression to do more than feel the quick contact of her uneasiness. My own impression was in fact the strongest of sensations, a sensation of horror; for what could the thing mean but that the girl at last *saw*? I heard her give a sudden, gasping 'Ah!' and move quickly into the house. It was only afterwards I knew that I myself had had a totally new emotion – my horror passing into anger and my anger into a stride along the balcony with a gesture of reprobation. The case was simplified to the vision of an adorable girl menaced and terrified. I advanced to vindicate her security, but I found nothing there to meet me. It was either all a mistake or Sir Edmund Orme had vanished.

I followed her at once, but there were symptoms of confusion in the drawing-room when I passed in. A lady had fainted, the music had stopped; there was a shuffling of chairs and a pressing forward. The lady was not Charlotte, as I feared, but Mrs Marden, who had suddenly been taken ill. I remember the relief with which I learned this, for to see Charlotte stricken would have been anguish, and her mother's condition gave a channel to her agitation. It was of course all a matter for the people of the house and for the ladies, and I could have no share in attending to my friends or in conducting them to their carriage. Mrs Marden revived and insisted on going home, after which I uneasily withdrew.

I called the next morning for better news and I learnt she was more at ease, but on my asking if Charlotte would see me the message sent down was an excuse. There was nothing for me to do all day but roam with a beating heart. Towards evening, however, I received a line in pencil, brought by hand – 'Please come; mother wishes you.' Five minutes later, I was at the door again and ushered into the drawing-room. Mrs Marden lay on the sofa, and as soon as I looked at her I saw the shadow of death in her face. But the first thing she said was that she was better, ever so much better; her poor old fluttered heart had misbehaved again, but now was decently quiet. She gave me her hand

and I bent over her, my eyes on her eyes, and in this way was able to read what she didn't speak – 'I'm really very ill, but appear to take what I say exactly as I say it.' Charlotte stood there beside her, looking not frightened now, but intensely grave, and meeting no look of my own. 'She has told me – she has told me!' her mother went on.

'She has told you?' I stared from one of them to the other, wondering if my friend meant that the girl had named to her the unexplained appearance on the balcony.

'That you spoke to her again – that you're admirably faithful.'

I felt a thrill of joy at this; it showed me that memory uppermost, and also that her daughter had wished to say the thing that would most soothe her, not the thing that would alarm her. Yet I was myself now sure, as sure as if Mrs Marden had told me, that she knew and had known at the moment what her daughter had seen. 'I spoke – I spoke, but she gave me no answer,' I said.

'She will now, won't you, Chartie? I want it so, I want it!' our companion murmured with ineffable wistfulness.

'You're very good to me' – Charlotte addressed me, seriously and sweetly, but with her eyes fixed on the carpet. There was something different in her, different from all the past. She had recognised something, she felt a coercion. I could see her uncontrollably tremble.

'Ah if you would let me show you *how* good I can be!' I cried as I held out my hands to her. As I uttered the words, I was touched with the knowledge that something had happened. A form had constituted itself on the other side of the couch, and the form leaned over Mrs Marden. My whole being went forth into a mute prayer that Charlotte shouldn't see it and that I should be able to betray nothing. The impulse to glance towards her mother was even stronger than the involuntary movement of taking in Sir Edmund Orme; but I could resist even that, and Mrs Marden was perfectly still. Charlotte got up to give me her hand, and then – with the definite act – she dreadfully saw. She gave, with a shriek, one stare of dismay, and another sound, the wail of one of the lost, fell at the same instant on my ear. But I had already sprung towards the creature I loved, to cover her, to veil her face, and she had as passionately thrown herself into my arms. I held her there a moment – pressing her close, given up to her, feeling each of her throbs with my own and not knowing which was which; then all of a sudden, coldly, I was sure we were alone. She released herself. The figure beside the sofa had vanished, but Mrs Marden lay in her place with closed eyes, with something in her stillness that gave us both a fresh terror. Charlotte expressed it in the cry of 'Mother, mother!' with which she flung herself down. I fell on my knees beside her – Mrs Marden had passed away.

Was the sound I heard when Chartie shrieked – the other and still more tragic sound I mean – the despairing cry of the poor lady's death-shock or the articulate sob (it was like a waft from a great storm) of the exorcised and pacified spirit? Possibly the latter, for that was mercifully the last of Sir Edmund Orme.

The Private Life

I

WE TALKED OF LONDON face to face with a great bristling primeval glacier. The hour and the scene were one of those impressions that make up a little in Switzerland for the modern indignity of travel – the promiscuities and vulgarities, the station and the hotel, the gregarious patience, the struggle for a scrappy attention, the reduction to a numbered state. The high valley was pink with the mountain rose, the cool air as fresh as if the world were young. There was a faint flush of afternoon on undiminished snows, and the fraternising tinkle of the unseen cattle came to us with a cropped and sun-warmed odour. The balconied inn stood on the very neck of the sweetest pass in the Oberland, and for a week we had had company and weather. This was felt to be great luck, for one would have made up for the other had either been bad.

The weather certainly would have made up for the company; but it wasn't subjected to this tax, for we had by a happy chance the *fleur des pois*:[1] Lord and Lady Mellifont, Clare Vawdrey,[2] the greatest (in the opinion of many) of our literary glories, and Blanche Adney, the greatest (in the opinion of all) of our theatrical. I mention these first because they were just the people whom in London, at that time, people tried to 'get'. People endeavoured to 'book' them six weeks ahead, yet on this occasion we had come in for them, we had all come in for each other, without the least wire-pulling. A turn of the game had pitched us together the last of August, and we recognised our luck by remaining so, under protection of the barometer. When the golden days were over – that would come soon enough – we should wind down opposite sides of the pass and disappear over the crest of surrounding heights. We were of the same general communion, chalk-marked for recognition by signs from the same alphabet. We met, in London, with irregular frequency; we were more or less governed by the laws and the language, the traditions and the shibboleths[3] of the same dense social state. I think all of us, even the ladies, 'did' something, though we pretended we didn't when it was mentioned. Such things aren't mentioned indeed in London, but it was our innocent pleasure to be different here. There had to be some way to show the difference, inasmuch as we were under the impression that this was our annual holiday. We felt at any rate that the conditions were more human than in London, or at least that we ourselves were. We were frank about this, we talked about it: it was what we were talking about as we looked at the flushing glacier, just as someone called attention to the prolonged absence of Lord Mellifont and Mrs Adney. We were seated on the terrace of the inn, where there were benches and little tables, and those of us most bent on showing with what a rush we had returned to nature were, in the queer Germanic fashion, having coffee before meat.

The remark about the absence of our two companions was not taken up, not even by Lady Mellifont, not even by little Adney, the fond composer; for it had been dropped only in the briefest intermission of Clare Vawdrey's talk. (This celebrity was 'Clarence' only on the title-page.) It was just that revelation of our being after all human that was his theme. He asked the company whether, candidly, everyone hadn't been tempted to say to everyone else: 'I had no idea you were really so nice.' I had had, for my part, an idea that *he* was, and even a good deal nicer, but that was too complicated to go into then; besides it's exactly my story. There was a general understanding among us that when Vawdrey talked we should be silent, and not, oddly enough, because he at all expected it. He didn't, for of all copious talkers he was the most undesigning, the least greedy and professional. It was rather the religion of the host, of the hostess, that prevailed among us; it was their own idea, but they always looked for a listening circle when the great novelist dined with them. On the occasion I allude to, there was probably no one present with whom in London he hadn't dined, and we felt the force of this habit. He had dined even with me; and on the evening of that dinner, as on this Alpine afternoon, I had been at no pains to hold my tongue, absorbed as I inveterately was in a study of the question that always rose before me to such a height in his fair square strong stature.

This question was all the more tormenting that I'm sure he never suspected himself of imposing it, any more than he had ever observed that every day of his life everyone listened to him at dinner. He used to be called 'subjective and introspective' in the weekly papers, but if that meant he was avid of tribute no distinguished man could in society have been less so. He never talked about himself; and this was an article on which, though it would have been tremendously worthy of him, he apparently never even reflected. He had his hours and his habits, his tailor and his hatter, his hygiene and his particular wine, but all these things together never made up an attitude. Yet they constituted the only one he ever adopted, and it was easy for him to refer to our being 'nicer' abroad than at home. *He* was exempt from variations, and not a shade either less or more nice in one place than in another. He differed from other people, but never from himself – save in the extraordinary sense I shall throw my light upon – and he struck me as having neither moods nor sensibilities nor preferences. He might have been always in the same company, so far as he recognised any influence from age or condition or sex: he addressed himself to women exactly as he addressed himself to men, and gossiped with all men alike, talking no better to clever folk than to dull. I used to wail to myself over his way of liking one subject – so far as I could tell – precisely as much as another: there were some I hated so myself. I never found him anything but loud and liberal and cheerful, and I never heard him utter a paradox or express a shade or play with an idea. That fancy about our being 'human' was, in his conversation, quite an exceptional flight. His opinions were sound and second-rate, and of his perceptions it was too mystifying to think. I envied him his magnificent health.

Vawdrey had marched with his even pace and his perfectly good conscience into the flat country of anecdote, where stories are visible from afar like windmills and signposts; but I observed after a little that Lady Mellifont's attention wandered. I happened to be sitting next to her. I noticed that her eyes rambled a little anxiously over the lower slopes of the mountains. At last, after looking at her watch, she said to me: 'Do you know where they went?'

'Do you mean Mrs Adney and Lord Mellifont?'

'Lord Mellifont and Mrs Adney.' Her Ladyship's speech seemed – unconsciously indeed – to correct me, but it didn't occur to me that this might be an effect of jealousy. I imputed to her no such vulgar sentiment: in the first place because I liked her, and in the second because it would always occur to one rather quickly to put Lord Mellifont, whatever the connection, first. He *was* first – extraordinarily first. I don't say greatest or wisest or most renowned, but essentially at the top of the list and the head of the table. That's a position by itself, and his wife was naturally accustomed to see him in it. My phrase had sounded as if Mrs Adney had taken him; but it was not possible for him to be taken – he only took. No one, in the nature of things, could know this better than Lady Mellifont. I had originally been rather afraid of her, thinking her, with her stiff silences and the extreme blackness of almost everything that made up her person, somewhat hard, even a little saturnine. Her paleness seemed slightly grey and her glossy black hair metallic, even as the

brooches and bands and combs with which it was inveterately
adorned. She was in perpetual mourning and wore numberless
ornaments of jet and onyx, a thousand clicking chains and bugles[4]
and beads. I had heard Mrs Adney call her the Queen of Night,[5] and
the term was descriptive if you took the night for cloudy. She had a
secret, and if you didn't find it out as you knew her better, you at least
felt sure she was gentle unaffected and limited, as well as rather
submissively sad. She was like a woman with a painless malady. I told
her that I had merely seen her husband and his companion stroll
down the glen together about an hour before, and suggested that Mr
Adney would perhaps know something of their intentions.

Vincent Adney, who, though fifty years old, looked like a good little
boy on whom it had been impressed that children shouldn't talk in
company, acquitted himself with remarkable simplicity and taste of
the position of husband of a great exponent of comedy. When all was
said about her making it easy for him, one couldn't help admiring the
charmed affection with which he took everything for granted. It's
difficult for a husband not on the stage, or at least in the theatre, to be
graceful about a wife so conspicuous there; but Adney did more than
carry it off, the awkwardness – he taught it ever so oddly to make *him*
interesting. He set his beloved to music; and you remember how
genuine his music could be – the only English compositions I ever saw
a foreigner care for. His wife was in them somewhere always; they
were a free rich translation of the impression she produced. She
seemed, as one listened, to pass laughing, with loosened hair and the
gait of a wood nymph, across the scene. He had been only a little
fiddler at her theatre, always in his place during the acts; but she had
made him something rare and brave and misunderstood. Their
superiority had become a kind of partnership, and their happiness was
a part of the happiness of their friends. Adney's one discomfort was
that he couldn't write a play for his wife, and the only way he meddled
with her affairs was by asking impossible people if *they* couldn't.

Lady Mellifont, after looking across at him a moment, remarked to
me that she would rather not put any question to him. She added the
next minute: 'I had rather people shouldn't see I'm nervous.'

'*Are* you nervous?'

'I always become so if my husband's away from me for any time.'

'Do you imagine something has happened to him?'

'Yes, always. Of course, I'm used to it.'

'Do you mean his tumbling over precipices – that sort of thing?'

'I don't know exactly *what* I fear: it's the general sense that he'll
never come back.'

She said so much and withheld so much that the only way to treat her idiosyncrasy seemed the jocular. 'Surely he'll never forsake you!' I laughed.

She looked at the ground a moment. 'Oh at bottom I'm easy.'

'Nothing can ever happen to a man so accomplished, so infallible, so armed at all points,' I went on in the same spirit.

'Oh you don't know how he's armed!' she returned with such an odd quaver that I could account for it only by her being nervous. This idea was confirmed by her moving just afterwards, changing her seat rather pointlessly, not as if to cut our conversation short, but because she was worried. I could scarcely enter into her feeling, though I was presently relieved to see Mrs Adney come towards us. She had in her hand a big bunch of wild flowers, but was not closely attended by Lord Mellifont. I quickly saw, however, that she had no disaster to announce; yet as I knew there was a question Lady Mellifont would like to hear answered, without wishing to ask it, I expressed to her at once the hope that his lordship hadn't remained in a crevasse.

'Oh no; he left me but three minutes ago. He has gone into the house.' Blanche Adney rested her eyes on mine an instant – a mode of intercourse to which no man, for himself, could ever object. The interest on this occasion was quickened by the particular thing the eyes happened to say. What they usually said was only: 'Oh yes, I'm charming, I know, but don't make a fuss about it. I only want a new part – I do, I do, I do!' At present, they added dimly, surreptitiously and of course sweetly – since that was the way they did everything: 'It's all right, but something did happen. Perhaps I'll tell you later.' She turned to Lady Mellifont, and the transition to simple gaiety suggested her mastery of her profession. 'I've brought him safe. We had a charming walk.'

'I'm so very glad,' said Lady Mellifont with her faint smile; continuing vaguely, as she got up: 'He must have gone to dress for dinner. Isn't it rather near?' She moved away to the hotel in her leave-taking simplifying fashion, and the rest of us, at the mention of dinner, looked at each other's watches as if to shift the responsibility for such grossness. The head-waiter, essentially, like all head-waiters, a man of the world, allowed us hours and places of our own, so that in the evening, apart under the lamp, we formed a compact, an indulged little circle. But it was only the Mellifonts who 'dressed' and as to whom it was recognised that they naturally *would* dress: she exactly in the same manner as on any other evening of her ceremonious existence – she wasn't a woman whose habits could take account of anything so mutable as fitness – and he, on the other hand, with remarkable adjustment and suitability. He was almost as much a man of the world as the head-waiter, and spoke almost as many languages; but he abstained from courting a comparison of dress-coats and white waistcoats, analysing the occasion in a much finer way – into black velvet and blue velvet and brown velvet, for instance, into delicate harmonies of necktie and subtle laxities of shirt. He had a costume for every function and a moral for every costume; and his functions and costumes and morals were ever a part of the amuse-ment of life – a part at any rate of its beauty and romance – for an immense circle of spectators. For his particular friends indeed these things were more than an amusement; they were a topic, a social support and of course in addition a constant theme for speculative suspense. If his wife hadn't been present before dinner, they were what the rest of us probably would have been putting our heads together about.

Clare Vawdrey had a fund of anecdote on the whole question: he had known Lord Mellifont almost from the beginning. It was a peculiarity of this nobleman that there could be no conversation about him that didn't instantly take the form of anecdote, and a still further distinction that there could apparently be no anecdote that wasn't on the whole to his honour. At whatever moment he came into a room people might say frankly: 'Of course we were telling stories about you!' As consciences go, in London, the general conscience would have been good. Moreover it would have been impossible to imagine his taking such a tribute otherwise than amiably, for he was always as unperturbed as an actor with the right cue. He had never in his life needed the prompter – his very embarrassments had been rehearsed. For myself, when he was talked about, I had always had a sense of our speaking of the dead: it had the mark of that peculiar accumulation of relish. His reputation was a kind of gilded obelisk,[6] as if he had been buried beneath it; the body of legend and reminiscence of which he was to be the subject had crystallised in advance.

This ambiguity sprang, I suppose, from the fact that the mere sound of his name and air of his person, the general expectation he created, had somehow a pitch so romantic and abnormal. The experience of his urbanity always came later; the prefigurement, the legend paled then before the reality. I remember that on the evening I refer to the reality struck me as supreme. The handsomest man of his period could never have looked better, and he sat among us like a bland conductor controlling by a harmonious play of arm an orchestra still a little rough. He directed the conversation by gestures as irresistible as they were vague; one felt as if without him it wouldn't have had anything to call a tone. This was essentially what he contributed to any occasion – what he contributed above all to English public life. He pervaded it, he coloured it, he embellished it, and without him it would have lacked, comparatively speaking, a vocabulary. Certainly it wouldn't have had a style, for a style was what it had in having Lord Mellifont. He *was* a style. I was freshly struck with it as, in the *salle-à-manger*[7] of the little Swiss inn, we resigned ourselves to inevitable veal. Confronted with *his* high form – I must parenthesise that it wasn't confronted much – Clare Vawdrey's talk suggested the reporter contrasted with the bard. It was interesting to watch the shock of characters from which of an evening so much would be expected. There was however no concussion – it was all muffled and minimised in Lord Mellifont's tact. It was rudimentary with him to find the solution of such a problem in playing the host, assuming responsibilities that carried with them their sacrifice. He had indeed never been a guest in his life; he was the host, the patron, the moderator at every board. If there was a defect in his manner – and I suggest this under my breath – it was that he had a little more art than any conjunction, even the most complicated, could possibly require. At any rate, one made one's reflections in noticing how the accomplished peer handled the case and how the sturdy man of letters hadn't a suspicion that the case – and least of all he himself as part of it – was handled. Lord Mellifont expended treasures of tact, and Clare Vawdrey never dreamed he was doing it.

Vawdrey had no suspicion of any such precaution even when Blanche Adney asked him if he really didn't see by this time his third act – an enquiry into which she introduced a subtlety of her own. She had settled it for him that he was to write her a play and that the heroine, should he but do his duty, would be the part for which she had immemorially longed. She was forty years old – this could be no secret to those who had admired her from the first – and might now reach out her hand and touch her uttermost goal. It gave a shade of tragic passion – perfect actress of comedy as she was – to her desire not to miss the great thing. The years had passed, and still she had missed it; none of the things she had done was the thing she had dreamed of, so that at present she had no more time to lose. This was the canker in the rose, the ache beneath the smile. It made her touching – made her melancholy more arch than her mirth. She had done the old English and the new French,[8] and had charmed for a while her generation; but she was haunted by the vision of a bigger chance, of something truer to the conditions that lay near her. She was tired of Sheridan[9] and she hated Bowdler; she called for a canvas of a finer grain. The worst of it, to my sense, was that she would never extract her modern comedy from the great mature novelist, who was as incapable of producing it as he was of threading a needle. She coddled him, she talked to him, she made love to him, as she frankly proclaimed; but she dwelt in illusions – she would have to live and die with Bowdler.

It is difficult to be cursory over this charming woman, who was beautiful without beauty and complete with a dozen deficiencies. The perspective of the stage made her over, and in society she was like the model off the pedestal. She was the picture walking about, which to the artless social mind was a perpetual surprise – a miracle. People thought she told them the secrets of the pictorial nature, in return for which they gave her relaxation and tea. She told them nothing and she drank the tea; but they had all the same the best of the bargain. Vawdrey was really at work on a play; but if he had begun it because he liked her, I think he let it drag for the same reason. He secretly felt the atrocious difficulty and hung off, for illusion's sake, from the point of tests and tribulations. In spite of which nothing could be so agreeable as to have such a question open with Blanche Adney, and from time to time he doubtless put something very good into the play. If he deceived Mrs Adney, it was only because in her despair she was determined to be deceived. To her appeal about their third act he replied that before dinner he had written a splendid passage.

'Before dinner?' I said. 'Why, *cher grand maître*,[10] before dinner you were holding us all spellbound on the terrace.'

My words were a joke, because I thought his had been; but for the first time that I could remember, I noted in his face a shade of confusion. He looked at me hard, throwing back his head quickly, the least bit like a horse who has been pulled up short. 'Oh it was before that,' he returned naturally enough.

'Before that you were playing billiards with *me*,' Lord Mellifont threw off.

'Then it must have been yesterday,' said Vawdrey.

But he was in a tight place. 'You told me this morning you did nothing yesterday,' Blanche objected.

'I don't think I really know when I do things.' He looked vaguely, without helping himself, at a dish just offered him.

'It's enough if *we* know,' smiled Lord Mellifont.

'I don't believe you've written a line,' said Blanche Adney.

'I think I could repeat you the scene.' And Vawdrey took refuge in *haricots verts*[11].

'Oh do – oh do!' two or three of us cried.

'After dinner, in the salon, it will be a high *régal*,'[12] Lord Mellifont declared.

'I'm not sure, but I'll try,' Vawdrey went on.

'Oh you lovely sweet man!' exclaimed the actress, who was practising what she believed to be Americanisms and was resigned even to an American comedy.

'But there must be this condition,' said Vawdrey: 'you must make your husband play.'

'Play while you're reading? Never!'

'I've too much vanity,' said Adney.

The direction of Lord Mellifont's fine eyes distinguished him. 'You must give us the overture before the curtain rises. That's a peculiarly delightful moment.'

'I shan't read – I shall just speak,' said Vawdrey.

'Better still, let me go and get your manuscript,' Blanche suggested.

Vawdrey replied that the manuscript didn't matter; but an hour later, in the salon, we wished he might have had it. We sat expectant, still under the spell of Adney's violin. His wife, in the foreground, on an ottoman, was all impatience and profile, and Lord Mellifont, in the chair – it was always *the* chair, Lord Mellifont's – made our grateful little group feel like a social science congress or a distribution of prizes. Suddenly, instead of beginning, our tame lion began to roar out of tune – he had clean forgotten every word. He was very sorry, but the lines absolutely wouldn't come to him; he was utterly ashamed, but his memory was a blank. He didn't look in the least ashamed – Vawdrey had never looked ashamed in his life; he was only imperturbably and merrily natural. He protested that he had never expected to make such a fool of himself, but we felt that this wouldn't prevent the incident's taking its place among his jolliest reminiscences. It was only *we* who were humiliated, as if he had played us a premeditated trick. This was an occasion, if ever, for Lord Mellifont's tact, which descended on us all like balm: he told us, in his charming artistic way, his way of bridging over arid intervals (he had a *débit*[13] – there was nothing to approach it in England – like the actors of the Comédie Française),[14] of his own collapse on a momentous occasion, the delivery of an address to a mighty multitude, when, finding he had forgotten his memoranda, he fumbled, on the terrible platform, the cynosure of every eye, fumbled vainly in irreproachable pockets for indispensable notes. But the point of his story was finer than that of our other entertainer's easy fiasco; for he sketched with a few light gestures the brilliancy of a performance which had risen superior to embarrassment, had resolved itself, we were left to divine, into an effort recognised at the moment as not absolutely a blot on what the public was so good as to call his reputation.

'Play up – play up!' cried Blanche Adney, tapping her husband and remembering how on the stage a *contretemps*[15] is always drowned in music. Adney threw himself upon his fiddle, and I said to Clare Vawdrey that his mistake could easily be corrected by his sending for the manuscript. If he'd tell me where it was I'd immediately fetch it from his room. To this he replied: 'My dear fellow, I'm afraid there *is* no manuscript.'

'Then you've not written anything?'

'I'll write it tomorrow.'

'Ah you trifle with us!' I said in much mystification.

He seemed at this to think better of it. 'If there *is* anything you'll find it on my table.'

One of the others, at the moment, spoke to him, and Lady Mellifont remarked audibly, as to correct gently our want of consideration, that Mr Adney was playing something very beautiful. I had noticed before how fond she appeared of music; she always listened to it in a hushed transport. Vawdrey's attention was drawn away, but it didn't seem to me the words he had just dropped constituted a definite permission to go to his room. Moreover I wanted to speak to Blanche Adney; I had something to ask her. I had to await my chance, however, as we remained silent a while for her husband, after which the conversation became general. It was our habit to go early to bed, but a little of the evening was still left. Before it quite waned, I found an opportunity to tell Blanche that Vawdrey had given me leave to put my hand on his manuscript. She adjured me, by all I held sacred, to bring it at once, to give it to her; and her insistence was proof against my suggestion that it would now be too late for him to begin to read: besides which the charm was broken – the others wouldn't care. It wasn't, she assured me, too late for *her* to begin; therefore I was to possess myself without more delay of the precious pages. I told her she should be obeyed in a moment, but I wanted her first to satisfy my just curiosity. What had happened before dinner, while she was on the hills with Lord Mellifont?

'How do you know anything happened?'

'I saw it in your face when you came back.'

'And they call me an actress!' my friend cried.

'What do they call *me?*' I asked.

'You're a searcher of hearts – that frivolous thing, an observer.'

'I wish you'd let an observer write you a play!' I broke out.

'People don't care for what you write: you'd break any run of luck.'

'Well, I see plays all round me,' I declared; 'the air is full of them tonight.'

'The air? Thank you for nothing! I only wish my table-drawers were.'

'Did he make love to you on the glacier?' I went on.

She stared – then broke into the graduated ecstasy of her laugh. 'Lord Mellifont, poor dear? What a funny place! It would indeed be the place for *our* love!'

'Did he fall into a crevasse?' I continued.

Blanche Adney looked at me again as she had done – so unmistakeably though briefly – when she came up before dinner with her hands full of flowers. 'I don't know into what he fell. I'll tell you tomorrow.'

'He did come down then?'

'Perhaps he went up,' she laughed. 'It's really strange.'

'All the more reason you should tell me tonight.'

'I must think it over; I must puzzle it out.'

'Oh if you want conundrums, I'll throw in another,' I said. 'What's the matter with the Master?'

'The master of what?'

'Of every form of dissimulation. Vawdrey hasn't written a line.'

'Go and get his papers and we'll see.'

'I don't like to expose him,' I said.

'Why not, if I expose Lord Mellifont?'

'Oh I'd do anything for that,' I allowed. 'But why should Vawdrey have made a false statement? It's very curious.'

'It's very curious,' Blanche Adney repeated with a musing air and her eyes on Lord Mellifont. Then rousing herself she added: 'Go and look in his room.'

'In Lord Mellifont's?'

She turned to me quickly. '*That* would be a way!'

'A way to what?'

'To find out – to find out!' She spoke gaily and excitedly, but suddenly checked herself. 'We're talking awful nonsense.'

'We're mixing things up, but I'm struck with your idea. Get Lady Mellifont to let you.'

'Oh *she* has looked!' Blanche brought out with the oddest dramatic expression. Then after a movement of her beautiful uplifted hand, as if to brush away a fantastic vision, she added imperiously: 'Bring me the scene – bring me the scene!'

'I go for it,' I answered; 'but don't tell me I can't write a play.'

She left me, but my errand was arrested by the approach of a lady who had produced a birthday-book – we had been threatened with it for several evenings – and who did me the honour to solicit my autograph. She had been asking the others and couldn't decently leave me out. I could usually remember my name, but it always took me long to recall my date, and even when I had done so I was never very sure. I hesitated between two days, remarking to my petitioner that I would sign on both if it would give her any satisfaction. She opined that I had surely been born but once, and I replied of course that on the day I made her acquaintance I had been born again. I mention the feeble joke only to show that, with the obligatory inspection of the other autographs, we gave some minutes to this transaction. The lady departed with her book, and I then found the company had scattered. I was alone in the little salon that had been appropriated to our use. My first impression was one of disappointment: if Vawdrey had gone to bed, I didn't wish to disturb him. While I hesitated however I judged that my friend must still be afoot. A window was open and the sound of voices outside came in to me: Blanche was on the terrace with her dramatist and they were talking about the stars. I went to the window for a glimpse – the Alpine night was splendid. My friends had stepped out together; Mrs Adney had picked up a cloak; she looked as I had seen her look in the wing of the theatre. They were silent a while, and I heard the roar of a neighbouring torrent. I turned back into the room, and its quiet lamplight gave me an idea. Our companions had dispersed – it was late for a pastoral country – and we three should have the place to ourselves. Clare Vawdrey had written his scene, which couldn't but be splendid; and his reading it to us there at such an hour would be a thing always to remember. I'd bring down his manuscript and meet the two with it as they came in.

I quitted the salon for this purpose; I had been in his room and knew it was on the second floor, the last in a long corridor. A minute later my hand was on the knob of the door, which I naturally pushed open without knocking. It was equally natural that in the absence of its occupant the room should be dark; the more so as, the end of the corridor being at that hour unlighted, the obscurity was not immediately diminished by the opening of the door. I was only aware at first that I had made no mistake and that, the window-curtains not being drawn, I had before me a couple of vague star-lighted apertures. Their aid, however, was not sufficient to enable me to find what I had come for, and my hand, in my pocket, was already on the little box of matches that I always carried for cigarettes. Suddenly I withdrew it with a start, uttering an ejaculation, an apology. I had entered the wrong room; a glance prolonged for three seconds showed me a figure seated at a table near one of the windows – a figure I had at first taken for a travelling-rug thrown over a chair. I retreated with a sense of intrusion; but as I did so, I took in more rapidly than it takes me to express it, first that this was Vawdrey's room and second that, surprisingly, its occupant himself sat before me. Checking myself on the threshold I was briefly bewildered, but before I knew it I had called out: 'Hullo, is that you, Vawdrey?'

He neither turned nor answered me, but my question received an immediate and practical reply in the opening of a door on the other side of the passage. A servant with a candle had come out of the opposite room, and in this flitting illumination I definitely recognised the man whom an instant before I had to the best of my belief left below in conversation with Mrs Adney. His back was half-turned to me and he bent over the table in the attitude of writing, but I took in at every pore his identity. 'I beg your pardon – I thought you were downstairs,' I said; and as the person before me gave no sign of hearing I added: 'If you're busy I won't disturb you.' I backed out, closing the door – I had been in the place, I suppose, less than a minute. I had a sense of mystification which however deepened infinitely the next instant. I stood there with my hand still on the knob of the door, overtaken by the oddest impression of my life. Vawdrey was seated at his table, and it was a very natural place for him; but why was he writing in the dark and why hadn't he answered me? I waited a few seconds for the sound of some movement, to see if he wouldn't rouse himself from his abstraction – a fit conceivable in a great writer – and call out 'Oh my dear fellow, is it you?' But I heard only the stillness, I felt only the star-lighted dusk of the room, with the unexpected presence it enclosed. I turned away, slowly retracing my steps, and came confusedly downstairs. The lamp still burned in the salon, but the room was empty. I passed round to the door of the hotel and stepped out. Empty too was the terrace. Blanche Adney and the gentleman with her had apparently come in. I hung about five minutes – then I went to bed.

II

I slept badly, for I *was* agitated. On looking back at these queer occurrences (you'll see presently *how* queer!), I perhaps suppose myself more affected than in fact; for great anomalies are never so great at first as after we've reflected on them. It takes us time to use up explanations. I was vaguely nervous – I had been sharply startled; but there was nothing I couldn't clear up by asking Blanche Adney, the first thing in the morning, who had been with her on the terrace. Oddly enough, however, when the morning dawned – it dawned admirably – I felt less desire to satisfy myself on this point than to escape, to brush away the shadow of my stupefaction. I saw the day would be splendid, so that the fancy took me to spend it, as I had spent happy days of youth, in a lonely mountain ramble. I dressed early, partook of conventional coffee, put a big roll into one pocket and a small flask into the other, and, with a stout stick in my hand, went forth into the high places. My story isn't closely concerned with the charming hours I passed there – hours of the kind that make intense memories. If I roamed away half of them on the shoulders of the hills, I lay on the sloping grass for the other half and, with my cap pulled over my eyes – save a peep for immensities of view – listened, in the bright stillness, to the mountain bee and felt most things sink and dwindle. Clare Vawdrey grew small, Blanche Adney grew dim, Lord Mellifont grew old, and before the day was over I forgot I had ever been puzzled. When in the late afternoon I made my way down to the inn, there was nothing I wanted so much to learn as that dinner was at hand. Tonight I dressed, in a manner, and by the time I was presentable, they were all at table.

In their company again my little problem came back to me, so that I was curious to see if Vawdrey wouldn't look at me with a certain queerness. But he didn't look at me at all; which gave me a chance both to be patient and to wonder why I should hesitate to ask him my question across the table. I did hesitate, and with the consciousness of doing so came back a little of the agitation I had left behind me, or below me, during the day. I wasn't ashamed of my scruple, however: it was only a fine discretion. What I vaguely felt was that a public enquiry wouldn't have been fair. Lord Mellifont was there, of course, to mitigate with his perfect manner all consequences; but I think it was present to me that with these particular elements his lordship wouldn't be at home. The moment we got up therefore I approached

Mrs Adney, asking her whether, as the evening was lovely, she wouldn't take a turn with me outside.

'You've walked a hundred miles; hadn't you better be quiet?' she replied.

'I'd walk a hundred miles more to get you to tell me something.'

She looked at me an instant with a little of the odd consciousness I had sought, but hadn't found, in Clare Vawdrey's eyes. 'Do you mean what became of Lord Mellifont?'

'Of Lord Mellifont?' With my new speculation I had lost that thread.

'Where's your memory, foolish man? We talked of it last evening.'

'Ah yes!' I cried, recalling; 'we shall have lots to discuss.' I drew her out to the terrace and, before we had gone three steps, said to her: 'Who was with you here last night?'

'Last night?' – she was as wide of the mark as I had been.

'At ten o'clock – just after our company broke up. You came out here with a gentleman. You talked about the stars.'

She stared a moment, then gave her laugh. 'Are you jealous of dear Vawdrey?'

'Then it was he?'

'Certainly it was he.'

'And how long did he stay?'

She laughed again. 'You have it badly! He stayed about a quarter of an hour – perhaps rather more. We walked some distance. He talked about his play. There you have it all. That is the only witchcraft I have used.'

Well, it wasn't enough for me; so 'What did Vawdrey do afterwards?' I continued.

'I haven't the least idea. I left him and went to bed.'

'At what time did you go to bed?'

'At what time did *you?* I happen to remember that I parted from Mr Vawdrey at ten twenty-five,' said Mrs Adney. 'I came back into the salon to pick up a book, and I noticed the clock.'

'In other words, you and Vawdrey distinctly lingered here from about five minutes past ten till the hour you mention?'

'I don't know how distinct we were, but we were very jolly. Où voulez-vous en venir?'[16]

Blanche Adney asked.

'Simply to this, dear lady: that at the time your companion was occupied in the manner you describe, he was also engaged in literary composition in his own room.'

She stopped short for it, and her eyes had a sheen in the darkness.

She wanted to know if I challenged her veracity; and I replied that on the contrary I backed it up – it made the case so interesting. She returned that this would only be if she should back up mine; which however I had no difficulty in persuading her to do after I had related to her circumstantially the incident of my quest of the manuscript – the manuscript which at the time, for a reason I could now understand, appeared to have passed so completely out of her own head.

'His talk made me forget it – I forgot I sent you for it. He made up for his fiasco in the salon: he declaimed me the scene,' said Blanche. She had dropped on a bench to listen to me and, as we sat there, had briefly cross-examined me. Then she broke out into fresh laughter. 'Oh the eccentricities of genius!'

'Yes indeed! They seem greater even than I supposed.'

'Oh the mysteries of greatness!'

'You ought to know all about them, but they take me by surprise,' I declared.

'Are you absolutely certain it was Vawdrey?' my companion asked.

'If it wasn't he, who in the world was it? That a strange gentleman, looking exactly like him and of like literary pursuits, should be sitting in his room at that hour of the night and writing at his table *in the dark*,' I insisted, 'would be practically as wonderful as my own contention.'

'Yes, why in the dark?' my friend mused.

'Cats can see in the dark,' I said.

She smiled at me dimly. 'Did it look like a cat?'

'No, dear lady, but I'll tell you what it did look like – it looked like the author of Vawdrey's admirable works. It looked infinitely more like him than our friend does himself,' I pronounced.

'Do you mean it was somebody he gets to do them?'

'Yes, while he dines out and disappoints you.'

'Disappoints me?' she murmured artlessly.

'Disappoints *me* – disappoints everyone who looks in him for the genius that created the pages they adore. Where is it in his talk?'

'Ah last night he was splendid,' said the actress.

'He's always splendid, as your morning bath is splendid, or a sirloin of beef, or the railway service to Brighton. But he's never rare.'

'I see what you mean.'

I could have hugged her – and perhaps I did.

'That's what makes you such a comfort to talk to. I've often wondered – now I know. There are two of them.'

'What a delightful idea!'

'One goes out, the other stays at home. One's the genius, the other's the bourgeois, and it's only the bourgeois whom we personally know. He talks, he circulates, he's awfully popular, he flirts with you – '

'Whereas it's the genius *you* are privileged to flirt with!' Mrs Adney broke in. 'I'm much obliged to you for the distinction.'

I laid my hand on her arm. 'See him yourself. Try it, test it, go to his room.'

'Go to his room? It wouldn't be proper!' she cried in the manner of her best comedy.

'Anything's proper in such an enquiry. If you see him it settles it.'

'How charming – to settle it!' She thought a moment, then sprang up. 'Do you mean *now?*'

'Whenever you like.'

'But suppose I should find the wrong one?' she said with an exquisite effect.

'The wrong one? Which one do you call the right?'

'The wrong one for a lady to go and see. Suppose I shouldn't find – the genius?'

'Oh I'll look after the other,' I returned. Then as I had happened to glance about me I added: 'Take care – here comes Lord Mellifont.'

'I wish you'd look after *him*,' she said with a drop of her voice.

'What's the matter with him?'

'That's just what I was going to tell you.'

'Tell me now. He's not coming.'

Blanche looked a moment. Lord Mellifont, who appeared to have emerged from the hotel to smoke a meditative cigar, had paused at a distance from us and stood admiring the wonders of the prospect, discernible even in the dusk. We strolled slowly in another direction, and she presently resumed: 'My idea's almost as droll as yours.'

'I don't call mine droll: it's beautiful.'

'There's nothing so beautiful as the droll,' Mrs Adney returned.

'You take a professional view. But I'm all ears.' My curiosity was indeed alive again.

'Well then, my dear friend, if Clare Vawdrey's double – and I'm bound to say I think the more of him the better – his lordship there has the opposite complaint: he isn't even whole.'

We stopped once more, simultaneously. 'I don't understand.'

'No more do I. But I've a fancy that if there are two of Mr Vawdrey, there isn't so much as one, all told, of Lord Mellifont.'

I considered a moment, then I laughed out. 'I think I see what you mean!'

'That's what makes *you* a comfort.' She didn't, alas, hug me, but she promptly went on. 'Did you ever see him alone?'

I tried to remember. 'Oh yes – he has been to see me.'

'Ah then he wasn't alone.'

'And I've been to see *him* – in his study.'

'Did he know you were there?'

'Naturally – I was announced.'

She glared at me like a lovely conspirator. 'You mustn't *be* announced!' With this she walked on.

I rejoined her, breathless. 'Do you mean one must come upon him when he doesn't know it?'

'You must take him unawares. You must go to his room – that's what you must do.'

If I was elated by the way our mystery opened out I was also, pardonably, a little confused. 'When I know he's not there?'

'When you know he *is*.'

'And what shall I see?'

'You won't see anything!' she cried as we turned round.

We had reached the end of the terrace and our movement brought us face to face with Lord Mellifont, who, addressing himself again to his walk, had now, without indiscretion, overtaken us. The sight of him at that moment was illuminating, and it kindled a great backward train, connecting itself with one's general impression of the personage. As he stood there smiling at us and waving a practised hand into the transparent night – he introduced the view as if it had been a candidate and 'supported' the very Alps – as he rose before us in the delicate fragrance of his cigar and all his other delicacies and fragrances, with more perfections somehow heaped on his handsome head than one had ever seen accumulated before or elsewhere, he struck me as so essentially, so conspicuously and uniformly the public character that I read in a flash the answer to Blanche's riddle. He was all public and had no corresponding private life, just as Clare Vawdrey was all private and had no corresponding public. I had heard only half my companion's tale, yet as we joined Lord Mellifont – he had followed us, liking Mrs Adney, but it was always to be conceived of him that he accepted society rather than sought it – as we participated for half an hour in the distributed wealth of his discourse I felt with unabashed duplicity that we had, as it were, found him out. I was even more deeply diverted by that whisk of the curtain to which the actress had just treated me than I had been by my own discovery; and if I wasn't ashamed of my share of her secret any more than of having divided my own with her – though my own was, of the two mysteries, the more glorious for the personage involved – this was because there was no cruelty in my advantage, but on the contrary an extreme tenderness and a positive compassion. Oh he was safe with me, and I felt moreover rich and enlightened, as if I had suddenly got the universe into my pouch. I had learned what an affair of the spot and the moment a great appearance may be. It would doubtless be too much to say that I had always suspected the possibility, in the background of his lordship's being, of some such beautiful instance; but it's at least a fact that, patronising as such words may sound, I had been conscious of a certain reserve of indulgence for him. I had secretly pitied him for the perfection of his performance, had wondered what blank face such a mask had to cover, what was left to him for the immitigable hours in which a man sits down with himself, or, more serious still, with that intenser self his lawful wife. How was he at home and what did he do when he was alone? There was something in Lady Mellifont that gave a point to these researches – something that suggested how even to her he must have been still the public character and she beset with similar questionings. She had never cleared them up: that was her eternal trouble. We therefore knew more than she did, Blanche Adney and I; but we wouldn't tell her for the world, nor would she probably thank us for doing so. She preferred the relative grandeur of uncertainty. She wasn't at home with him, so she couldn't say; and with her he wasn't alone, so he couldn't show her. He represented to his wife and was a hero to his servants, and what one wanted to arrive at was what really became of him when no eye could see – and *a fortiori*[17] no soul admire. He relaxed and rested presumably; but how utter a blank mustn't it take to repair such a plenitude of presence! – how intense an *entr'acte*[18] to make possible more such performances! Lady Mellifont was too proud to pry, and as she had never looked through a keyhole, she remained dignified and unrelieved.

It may have been a fancy of mine that Mrs Adney drew out our companion, or it may be that the practical irony of our relation to him at such a moment made me see him more vividly: at any rate he never had struck me as so dissimilar from what he would have been if we hadn't offered him a reflection of his image. We were only a concourse of two, but he had never been more public. His perfect manner had never been more perfect, his remarkable tact never more remarkable, his one conceivable *raison d'être*,[19] the absolute single-ness of his identity, never more attested. I had a tacit sense that it would all be in the morning papers, with a leader, and also a secretly exhilarating one that I knew something that wouldn't be, that never could be, though any enterprising journal would give me a fortune for it. I must add, however, that in spite of my enjoyment – it was almost sensual, like that of a consummate dish or an unprecedented pleasure – I was eager to be alone again with Mrs Adney, who owed me an anecdote. This proved impossible that evening, for some of the others came out to see what he found so absorbing; and then Lord Mellifont bespoke a little music from the fiddler, who produced his violin and played to us divinely, on our platform of echoes, face to face with the ghosts of the mountains. Before the concert was over, I missed our actress and, glancing into the window of the salon, saw her established there with Vawdrey, who was reading out from a manuscript. The great scene had apparently been achieved and was doubtless the more interesting to Blanche from the new lights she had gathered about its author. I judged discreet not to disturb them, and went to bed without seeing her again. I looked out for her betimes the next morning and, as the promise of the day was fair, proposed to her that we should take to the hills, reminding her of the high obligation she had incurred. She recognised the obligation and gratified me with her company, but before we had strolled ten yards up the pass she broke out with intensity: 'My dear friend, you've no idea how it works in me! I can think of nothing else.'

'Than your theory about Lord Mellifont?'

'Oh bother Lord Mellifont! I allude to yours about Mr Vawdrey, who's much the more interesting person of the two. I'm fascinated by that vision of his – what-do-you-call-it?'

'His alternate identity?'

'His other self: that's easier to say.'

'You accept it then, you adopt it?'

'Adopt it? I rejoice in it! It became tremendously vivid to me last evening.'

'While he read to you there?'

'Yes, as I listened to him, watched him. It simplified everything, explained everything.'

I rose to my triumph. 'That's indeed the blessing of it. Is the scene very fine?'

'Magnificent, and he reads beautifully.'

'Almost as well as the other one writes!' I laughed.

This made her stop a moment, laying her hand on my arm. 'You utter my very impression! I felt he was reading me the work of another.'

'In a manner that was such a service to the other,' I concurred.

'Such a totally different person,' said Blanche. We talked of this difference as we went on, and of what a wealth it constituted, what a resource for life, such a duplication of character.

'It ought to make him live twice as long as other people,' I made out.

'Ought to make which of them?'

'Well, both; for after all they're members of a firm, and one of them would never be able to carry on the business without the other. Moreover, mere survival would be dreadful for either.'

She was silent a little; after which she exclaimed: 'I don't know – I wish he *would* survive!'

'May I on my side enquire which?'

'If you can't guess I won't tell you.'

'I know the heart of woman. You always prefer the other.'

She halted again, looking round her. 'Off here, away from my husband, I *can* tell you. I'm in love with him!'

'Unhappy woman, he has no passions,' I answered.

'That's exactly why I adore him. Doesn't a woman with my history know the passions of others for insupportable? An actress, poor thing, can't care for any love that's not all on *her* side; she can't afford to be repaid. My marriage proves that: a pretty one, a lucky one like ours, is ruinous. Do you know what was in my mind last night and all the while Mr Vawdrey read me those beautiful speeches? An insane desire to see the author.' And dramatically, as if to hide her shame, Blanche Adney passed on.

'We'll manage that,' I returned. 'I want another glimpse of him myself. But meanwhile please remember that I've been waiting more than forty-eight hours for the evidence that supports your sketch, intensely suggestive and plausible, of Lord Mellifont's private life.'

'Oh Lord Mellifont doesn't interest me.'

'He did yesterday,' I said.

'Yes, but that was before I fell in love. You blotted him out with *your* story.'

'You'll make me sorry I told it. Come,' I pleaded, 'if you don't let me know how your idea came into your head I shall imagine you simply made it up.'

'Let me recollect then, while we wander in this velvet gorge.'

We stood at the entrance of a charming crooked valley, a portion of the level floor of which formed the bed of a stream that was smooth with swiftness. We turned into it, and the soft walk beside the clear torrent drew us on and on; till suddenly, as we continued and I waited for my companion to remember, a bend of the ravine showed us Lady Mellifont coming towards us. She was alone, under the canopy of her parasol, drawing her sable train over the turf; and in this form, on the devious ways, she was a sufficiently rare apparition. She mostly took out a footman, who marched behind her on the highroads and whose livery was strange to the rude rustics. She blushed on seeing us, as if she ought somehow to justify her being there; she laughed vaguely and described herself as abroad but for a small early stroll. We stood together thus, exchanging platitudes, and then she told us how she had counted a little on finding her husband.

'Is he in this quarter?' I asked.

'I supposed he would be. He came out an hour ago to sketch.'

'Have you been looking for him?' Mrs Adney put to her.

'A little; not very much,' said Lady Mellifont.

Each of the women rested her eyes with some intensity, as it seemed to me, on the eyes of the other. 'We'll look for him *for* you, if you like,' said Blanche.

'Oh it doesn't matter. I thought I'd join him.'

'He won't make his sketch if you don't,' my companion hinted.

'Perhaps he will if *you* do,' said Lady Mellifont.

'Oh I dare say he'll turn up,' I interposed.

'He certainly will if he knows we're here!' Blanche retorted.

'Will you wait while we search?' I asked of Lady Mellifont.

She repeated that it was of no consequence; upon which Mrs Adney went on: 'We'll go into the matter for our own pleasure.'

'I wish you a pleasant excursion,' said her Ladyship, and was turning away when I sought to know if we should inform her husband she was near. 'That I've followed him?' She demurred a moment and then jerked out oddly: 'I think you had better not.' With this she took leave of us, floating a little stiffly down the gorge.

My companion and I watched her retreat; after which we exchanged a stare and a light ghost of a laugh rippled from the actress's lips. 'She might be walking in the shrubberies at Mellifont!'

I had my view. 'She suspects it, you know.'

'And she doesn't want him to guess it. There won't be any sketch.'

'Unless we overtake him,' I suggested. 'In that case we shall find him producing one, in the very most graceful and established attitude, and the queer thing is that it will be brilliant.'

'Let us leave him alone – he'll have to come home without it,' my friend contributed.

'He'd rather never come home. Oh he'll find a public!'

'Perhaps he'll do it for the cows,' Blanche risked; and as I was on the point of rebuking her profanity she went on: 'That's simply what I happened to discover.'

'What are you speaking of?'

'The incident of day before yesterday.'

I jumped at it. 'Ah let's have it at last!'

'That's all it was – that I was like Lady Mellifont: I couldn't find him.'

'Did you lose him?'

'He lost *me* – that appears to be the way of it. He supposed me gone. And then – !' But she paused, looking – that is smiling – volumes.

'You did find him, however,' I said as I wondered, 'since you came home with him.'

'It was he who found *me*. That again is what must happen. He's there from the moment he knows somebody else is.'

'I understand his intermissions,' I returned on short reflection, 'but I don't quite seize the law that governs them.'

Ah Blanche had quite mastered it! 'It's a fine shade, but I caught it at that moment. I had started to come home, I was tired and had insisted on his not coming back with me. We had found some rare flowers – those I brought home – and it was he who had discovered almost all of them. It amused him very much, and I knew he wanted to get more; but I was weary and I quitted him. He let me go – where else would have been his tact? – and I was too stupid then to have guessed that from the moment I wasn't there no flower would be – *could* be – gathered. I started homeward, but at the end of three minutes I found I had brought away his penknife – he had lent it to me to trim a branch – and I knew he'd need it. I turned back a few steps to call him, but before I spoke I looked about for him. You can't understand what happened then without having the scene before you.'

'You must take me there,' I said.

'We may see the wonder here. The place was simply one that offered no chance for concealment – a great gradual hillside without obstructions or cavities or bushes or trees. There were some rocks below me, behind which I myself had disappeared, but from which on coming back I immediately emerged again.'

'Then he must have seen you.'

'He was too absent, too utterly gone, as gone as a candle blown out; for some reason best known to himself. It was probably some moment of fatigue – he's getting on, you know, so that with the sense of returning solitude the reaction had been proportionately great, the extinction proportionately complete. At any rate, the stage was as bare as your hand.'

'Couldn't he have been somewhere else?'

'He couldn't have been, in the time, anywhere but just where I had left him. Yet the place was utterly empty – as empty as this stretch of valley in front of us. He had vanished – he had ceased to be. But as soon as my voice rang out – I uttered his name – he rose before me like the rising sun.'

'And where did the sun rise?'

'Just where it ought to – just where he would have been and where I should have seen him had he been like other people.'

I had listened with the deepest interest, but it was my duty to think of objections. 'How long a time elapsed between the moment you were sure of his absence and the moment you called?'

'Oh but a few seconds. I don't pretend it was long.'

'Long enough for you to be really certain?' I said.

'Certain he wasn't there?'

'Yes, and that you weren't mistaken, weren't the victim of some hocus-pocus of your eyesight.'

'I may have been mistaken – but I feel too strongly I wasn't. At any rate, that's just why I want you to look in his room.'

I thought a moment. 'How *can* I – when even his wife doesn't dare to?'

'She *wants* to; propose it to her. It wouldn't take much to make her. She does suspect.'

I thought another moment. 'Did he seem to know?'

'That I had missed him and might have immensely wondered? So it struck me – but with it too that he probably thought he had been quick enough. He has, you see, to think that – to take it mostly for granted.'

Ah – I lost myself – who could say? 'But did you speak at least of his disappearance?'

'Heaven forbid – *y pensez-vous*?[20] It seemed to me too strange.'

'Quite right. And how did he look?'

Trying to think it out again and reconstitute her miracle, Blanche Adney gazed abstractedly up the valley. Suddenly she brought out: 'Just as he looks now!' and I saw Lord Mellifont stand before us with his sketch-block. I took in as we met him that he appeared neither suspicious nor blank: he simply stood there, as he stood always everywhere, for the principal feature of the scene. Naturally he had no sketch to show us, but nothing could better have rounded off our actual conception of him than the way he fell into position as we approached. He had been selecting his point of view – he took possession of it with a flourish of the pencil. He leaned against a rock; his beautiful little box of watercolours reposed on a natural table beside him, a ledge of the bank which showed how inveterately nature ministered to his convenience. He painted while he talked and he talked while he painted; and if the painting was as miscellaneous as the talk, the talk would equally have graced an album. We stayed while the exhibition went on, and the conscious profiles of the peaks might to our apprehension have been interested in his success. They grew as black as silhouettes in paper, sharp against a livid sky from which, however, there would be nothing to fear till Lord Mellifont's sketch should be finished. All nature deferred to him and the very elements waited. Blanche Adney communed with me dumbly, and I could read the language of her eyes: 'Oh if *we* could only do it as well as that! He fills the stage in a way that beats us.' We could no more have left him than we could have quitted the theatre till the play was over; but in due time we turned round with him and strolled back to the inn, before the door of which his lordship, glancing again at his picture, tore the fresh leaf from the block and presented it with a few happy words to our friend. Then he went into the house; and a moment later, looking up from where we stood, we saw him, above, at the window of his sitting-room – he had the best apartments – watching the signs of the weather.

'He'll have to rest after this,' Blanche said, dropping her eyes on her watercolour.

'Indeed he will!' I raised mine to the window: Lord Mellifont had vanished. 'He's already reabsorbed.'

'Reabsorbed?' I could see the actress was now thinking of something else.

'Into the immensity of things. He has lapsed again. The *entr'acte* has begun.'

'It ought to be long.' She surveyed the terrace and as at that moment the head-waiter appeared in the doorway, she suddenly turned to address him. 'Have you seen Mr Vawdrey lately?'

The man immediately approached. 'He left the house five minutes ago – for a walk, I think. He went down the pass; he had a book.'

I was watching the ominous clouds. 'He had better have had an umbrella.'

The waiter smiled. 'I recommended him to take one.'

'Thank you,' Blanche said; and the Oberkellner[21] withdrew. Then she went on abruptly: 'Will you do me a favour?'

'Yes, if you'll do *me* one. Let me see if your picture's signed.'

She glanced at the sketch before giving it to me. 'For a wonder it isn't.'

'It ought to be, for full value. May I keep it a while?'

'Yes, if you'll do what I ask. Take an umbrella and go after Mr Vawdrey.'

'To bring him to Mrs Adney?'

'To keep him out – as long as you can.'

'I'll keep him as long as the rain holds off.'

'Oh never mind the rain!' my companion cried.

'Would you have us drenched?'

'Without remorse.' Then with a strange light in her eyes: 'I'm going to try.'

'To try?'

'To see the real one. Oh if I can get at him!' she broke out with passion.

'Try, try!' I returned. 'I'll keep our friend all day.'

'If I can get at the one who does it' – and she paused with shining eyes – 'if I can have it out with him, I shall get another act, I shall have my part!'

'I'll keep Vawdrey for ever!' I called after her as she passed quickly into the house.

Her audacity was communicable and I stood there in a glow of excitement. I looked at Lord Mellifont's watercolour and I looked at the gathering storm; I turned my eyes again to his lordship's windows and then I bent them on my watch. Vawdrey had so little the start of me that I should have time to overtake him, time even if I should take five minutes to go up to Lord Mellifont's sitting-room – where we had all been hospitably received – and say to him, as a messenger, that Mrs Adney begged he would bestow on his sketch the high consecration of his signature. As I again considered this work of art, I noted there was something it certainly did lack: what else then but so noble an autograph? It was my duty without loss of time to make the deficiency good, and in accordance with this view I instantly re-entered the hotel. I went up to Lord Mellifont's apartments; I reached the door of his salon. Here, however, I was met by a difficulty with which my extravagance hadn't counted. If I were to knock, I should spoil everything; yet was I prepared to dispense with this ceremony? I put myself the question and it embarrassed me; I turned my little picture round and round, but it gave me no answer I wanted. I wanted it to say, 'Open the door gently, gently, without a sound, yet very quickly: then you'll see what you'll see.' I had gone so far as to lay my hand on the knob when I became aware (having my wits so about me) that exactly in the manner I was thinking of – gently, gently, without a sound – another door had moved, and on the opposite side of the hall. At the same instant I found myself smiling rather constrainedly at Lady Mellifont, who, seeing me, had checked herself by the threshold of her room. For a moment, as she stood there, we exchanged two or three

ideas that were the more singular for being so unspoken. We had
caught each other hovering and to that extent understood each other;
but as I stepped over to her – so that we were separated from the
sitting-room by the width of the hall – her lips formed the almost
soundless entreaty: 'Don't!' I could see in her conscious eyes everything the word expressed – the confession of her own curiosity and the
dread of the consequences of mine. '*Don't!*' she repeated as I stood
before her. From the moment my experiment could strike her as an act
of violence I was ready to renounce it; yet I thought I caught from her
frightened face a still deeper betrayal – a possibility of disappointment
if I should give way. It was as if she had said: 'I'll let you do it if you'll
take the responsibility. Yes, with someone else I'd surprise him. But it
would never do for him to think it was I.'

'We soon found Lord Mellifont,' I observed in allusion to our
encounter with her an hour before, 'and he was so good as to give this
lovely sketch to Mrs Adney, who has asked me to come up and beg
him to put in the omitted signature.'

Lady Mellifont took the drawing from me, and I could guess the
struggle that went on in her while she looked at it. She waited to
speak; then I felt all her delicacies and dignities, all her old timidities
and pieties obstruct her great chance. She turned away from me and,
with the drawing, went back to her room. She was absent for a couple
of minutes, and when she reappeared I could see she had vanquished
her temptation, that even with a kind of resurgent horror she had
shrunk from it. She had deposited the sketch in the room. 'If you'll
kindly leave the picture with me, I'll see that Mrs Adney's request is
attended to,' she said with great courtesy and sweetness, but in a
manner that put an end to our colloquy.

I assented, with a somewhat artificial enthusiasm perhaps, and
then, to ease off our separation, remarked that we should have a
change of weather.

'In that case we shall go – we shall go immediately,' the poor lady
returned. I was amused at the eagerness with which she made this
declaration: it appeared to represent a coveted flight into safety, an
escape with her threatened secret. I was the more surprised therefore
when, as I was turning away, she put out her hand to take mine. She
had the pretext of bidding me farewell, but as I shook hands with her
on this supposition, I felt that what the movement really conveyed
was: 'I thank you for the help you'd have given me, but it's better as it
is. If I should know, who would help me then?' As I went to my room
to get my umbrella I said to myself: 'She's sure, but she won't put it to
the proof.'

A quarter of an hour later I had overtaken Clare Vawdrey in the pass, and shortly after this we found ourselves looking for refuge. The storm hadn't only completely gathered, but had broken at the last with extraordinary force. We scrambled up a hillside to an empty cabin, a rough structure that was hardly more than a shed for the protection of cattle. It was a tolerable shelter however, and it had fissures through which we could see the show, watch the grand rage of nature. Our entertainment lasted an hour – an hour that has remained with me as full of odd disparities. While the lightning played with the thunder and the rain gushed in on our umbrellas, I said to myself that Clare Vawdrey was disappointing. I don't know exactly what I should have predicated of a great author exposed to the fury of the elements, I can't say what particular Manfred[22] attitude I should have expected my companion to assume, but it struck me somehow that I shouldn't have looked to him to regale me in such a situation with stories – which I had already heard – about the celebrated Lady Ringrose. Her Ladyship formed the subject of Vawdrey's conversation during this prodigious scene, though before it was quite over he had launched out on Mr Chafer, the scarcely less notorious reviewer. It broke my heart to hear a man like Vawdrey talk of reviewers. The lightning projected a hard clearness upon the truth, familiar to me for years, to which the last day or two had added transcendent support – the irritating certitude that for personal relations this admirable genius thought his second-best good enough. It *was*, no doubt, as society was made, but there was a contempt in the distinction which couldn't fail to be galling to an admirer. The world was vulgar and stupid, and the real man would have been a fool to come out for it when he could gossip and dine by deputy. None the less my heart sank as I felt him practise this economy. I don't know exactly what I wanted; I suppose I wanted him to make an exception for *me* – for me all alone, and all handsomely and tenderly, in the vast horde of the dull. I almost believed he would have done so had he known how I worshipped his talent. But I had never been able to translate this to him, and his application of his principle was relentless. At any rate, I was more than ever sure that at such an hour his chair at home at least wasn't empty: *there* was the Manfred attitude, *there* were the responsive flashes. I could only envy Mrs Adney her presumable enjoyment of them.

The weather drew off at last and the rain abated sufficiently to allow us to emerge from our asylum and make our way back to the inn, where we found on our arrival that our prolonged absence had produced some agitation. It was judged apparently that the storm had placed us in a predicament. Several of our friends were at the door, who seemed just disconcerted to note we were only drenched. Clare Vawdrey, for some reason, had had the greater soaking, and he took a straight course to his room. Blanche Adney was among the persons collected to look out for us, but as the subject of our speculation came towards her she shrank from him without a greeting; with a movement that I measured as almost one of coldness, she turned her back on him and went quickly into the salon. Wet as I was I went in after her; on which she immediately flung round and faced me. The first thing I saw was that she had never been so beautiful. There was a light of inspiration in her, and she broke out to me in the quickest whisper, which was at the same time the loudest cry I have ever heard: 'I've got my *part!*'

'You went to his room – I was right?'

'Right?' Blanche Adney repeated. 'Ah my dear fellow!' she murmured.

'He was there – you saw him?'

'He saw *me*. It was the hour of my life!'

'It must have been the hour of his, if you were half as lovely as you are at this moment.'

'He's splendid,' she pursued as if she didn't hear me. 'He *is* the one who does it!' I listened, immensely impressed, and she added: 'We understood each other.'

'By flashes of lightning?'

'Oh I didn't see the lightning then!'

'How long were you there?' I asked with admiration.

'Long enough to tell him I adore him.'

'Ah that's what I've never been able to tell him!' I quite wailed.

'I shall have my part – I shall have my part!' she continued with triumphant indifference; and she flung round the room with the joy of a girl, only checking herself to say: 'Go and change your clothes.'

'You shall have Lord Mellifont's signature,' I said.

'Oh hang Lord Mellifont's signature! He's far nicer than Mr Vawdrey,' she went on irrelevantly.

'Lord Mellifont?' I pretended to enquire.

'Confound Lord Mellifont!' And Blanche Adney, in her elation, brushed by me, whisking again through the open door. Just outside of it she came upon her husband; whereupon with a charming cry of 'We're talking of *you*, my love!' she threw herself upon him and kissed him.

I went to my room and changed my clothes, but I remained there till the evening. The violence of the storm had passed over us, but the rain had settled down to a drizzle. On descending to dinner, I saw the change in the weather had already broken up our party. The Mellifonts had departed in a carriage and four, they had been followed by others, and several vehicles had been bespoken for the morning. Blanche Adney's was one of them, and on the pretext that she had preparations to make, she quitted us directly after dinner. Clare Vawdrey asked me what was the matter with her – she suddenly appeared to dislike him. I forget what answer I gave, but I did my best to comfort him by driving away with him the next day. Blanche had vanished when we came down; but they made up their quarrel in London, for he finished his play, which she produced. I must add that she is still nevertheless in want of the great part. I've a beautiful one in my head, but she doesn't come to see me to stir me up about it. Lady Mellifont always drops me a kind word when we meet, but that doesn't console me.

Owen Wingrave

I

'UPON MY HONOUR you must be off your head!' cried Spencer Coyle as the young man, with a white face, stood there panting a little and repeating, 'Really I've quite decided,' and, 'I assure you I've thought it all out.' They were both pale, but Owen Wingrave smiled in a manner exasperating to his supervisor, who however still discriminated sufficiently to feel his grimace – it was like an irrelevant leer – the result of extreme and conceivable nervousness.

'It was certainly a mistake to have gone so far; but that's exactly why it strikes me I mustn't go further,' poor Owen said, waiting mechanically, almost humbly – he wished not to swagger, and indeed had nothing to swagger about – and carrying through the window to the stupid opposite houses the dry glitter of his eyes.

'I'm unspeakably disgusted. You've made me dreadfully ill' – and Mr Coyle looked in truth thoroughly upset.

'I'm very sorry. It was the fear of the effect on you that kept me from speaking sooner.'

'You should have spoken three months ago. Don't you know your mind from one day to the other?' the elder of the pair demanded.

The young man for a moment held himself: then he quavered his plea. 'You're very angry with me and I expected it. I'm awfully obliged to you for all you've done for me. I'll do anything else for you in return, but I can't do that. Everyone else will let me have it of course. I'm prepared for that – I'm prepared for everything. It's what has taken the time: to be sure I was prepared. I think it's your displeasure I feel most and regret most. But little by little you'll get over it,' Owen wound up.

'*You'll* get over it rather faster, I suppose!' the other satirically exclaimed. He was quite as agitated as his young friend, and they were evidently in no condition to prolong an encounter in which each drew blood. Mr Coyle was a professional 'coach'; he prepared aspirants for the army, taking only three or four at a time, to whom he applied the irresistible stimulus the possession of which was both his secret and his fortune. He hadn't a great establishment; he would have said himself that it was not a wholesale business. Neither his system, his health nor his temper could have concorded with numbers; so he weighed and measured his pupils and turned away more applicants than he passed. He was an artist in his line, caring only for picked subjects and capable of sacrifices almost passionate for the individual. He liked ardent young men – there were types of facility and kinds of capacity to which he was indifferent – and he had taken a particular fancy to Owen Wingrave. This young man's particular shade of ability, to say nothing of his whole personality, almost cast a spell and at any rate worked a charm. Mr Coyle's candidates usually did wonders, and he might have sent up a multitude. He was a person exactly of the stature of the great Napoleon,[1] with a certain flicker of genius in his light blue eye: it had been said of him that he looked like a concert-giving pianist. The tone of his favourite pupil now expressed, without intention indeed, a superior wisdom that irritated him. He hadn't at all suffered before from Wingrave's high opinion of himself, which had seemed justified by remarkable parts; but today, of a sudden, it struck him as intolerable. He cut short the discussion, declining absolutely to regard their relations as terminated, and remarked to his pupil that he had better go off somewhere – down to Eastbourne,[2] say: the sea would bring him round – and take a few days to find his feet and come to his senses. He could afford the time, he was so well up:[3] when Spencer Coyle remembered how well up he was he could have boxed his ears. The tall athletic young man wasn't physically a subject for simplified reasoning; but a troubled gentleness in his handsome face, the index of compunction mixed with resolution, virtually signified that if it could have done any good he would have turned both cheeks. He evidently didn't pretend that his wisdom was superior; he only presented it as his own. It was his own career after all that was in question. He couldn't refuse to go through the form of trying Eastbourne or at least of holding his tongue, though there was that in his manner which implied that if he should do so it would be really to give Mr Coyle a chance to recuperate. He didn't feel a bit overworked, but there was nothing more natural than that, with their tremendous pressure, Mr Coyle should be. Mr Coyle's own intellect would derive an advantage from his pupil's holiday. Mr Coyle saw what he meant, but controlled himself; he only demanded, as his right, a truce of three days. Owen granted it, though as fostering sad illusions this went visibly against his conscience; but before they separated the famous crammer remarked: 'All the same, I feel I ought to see someone. I think you mentioned to me that your aunt had come to town?'

'Oh yes – she's in Baker Street.[4] Do go and see her,' the boy said for comfort.

His tutor sharply eyed him. 'Have you broached this folly to her?'

'Not yet – to no one. I thought it right to speak to you first.'

'Oh what you 'think right'!' cried Spencer Coyle, outraged by his young friend's standards. He added that he would probably call on Miss Wingrave; after which the recreant youth got out of the house.

The latter didn't, none the less, start at once for Eastbourne; he only directed his steps to Kensington Gardens,[5] from which Mr Coyle's desirable residence – he was terribly expensive and had a big house – was not far removed. The famous coach 'put up' his pupils, and Owen had mentioned to the butler that he would be back to dinner. The spring day was warm to his young blood, and he had a book in his pocket which, when he had passed into the Gardens and, after a short stroll, dropped into a chair, he took out with the slow soft sigh that finally ushers in a pleasure postponed. He stretched his long legs and began to read it; it was a volume of Goethe's poems. He had been for days in a state of the highest tension, and now that the cord had snapped the relief was proportionate; only it was characteristic of him that this deliverance should take the form of an intellectual pleasure. If he had thrown up the probability of a magnificent career it wasn't to dawdle along Bond Street nor parade his indifference in the window of a club. At any rate, he had in a few moments forgotten everything – the tremendous pressure, Mr Coyle's disappointment and even his formidable aunt in Baker Street. If these watchers had overtaken him there would surely have been some excuse for their exasperation. There was no doubt he was perverse, for his very choice of a pastime only showed how he had got up his German.

'What the devil's the matter with him, do *you* know?' Spencer Coyle asked that afternoon of young Lechmere, who had never before observed the head of the establishment to set a fellow such an example of bad language. Young Lechmere was not only Wingrave's fellow pupil, he was supposed to be his intimate, indeed quite his best friend, and had unconsciously performed for Mr Coyle the office of making the promise of his great gifts more vivid by contrast. He was short and sturdy and as a general thing uninspired, and Mr Coyle, who found no amusement in believing in him, had never thought him less exciting than as he stared now out of a face from which you could no more guess whether he had caught an idea than you could judge of your dinner by looking at a dish-cover. Young Lechmere concealed such achievements as if they had been youthful indiscretions. At any rate, he could evidently conceive no reason why it should be thought there was anything more than usual the matter with the companion of his studies; so Mr Coyle had to continue: 'He declines to go up. He chucks the whole shop!'

The first thing that struck young Lechmere in the case was the freshness, as of a forgotten vernacular, it had imparted to the governor's vocabulary. 'He doesn't want to go to Sandhurst?'

'He doesn't want to go anywhere. He gives up the army altogether. He objects,' said Mr Coyle in a tone that made young Lechmere almost hold his breath, 'to the military profession.'

'Why it has been the profession of all his family!'

'Their profession? It has been their religion! Do you know Miss Wingrave?'

'Oh yes. Isn't she awful?' young Lechmere candidly ejaculated.

His instructor demurred. 'She's formidable, if you mean that, and it's right she should be; because somehow in her very person, good maiden lady as she is, she represents the might, she represents the traditions and the exploits, of the British army. She represents the expansive property of the English name. I think his family can be trusted to come down on him, but every influence should be set in motion. I want to know what yours is. Can *you* do anything in the matter?'

'I can try a couple of rounds with him,' said young Lechmere reflectively. 'But he knows a fearful lot. He has the most extraordinary ideas.'

'Then he has told you some of them – he has taken you into his confidence?'

'I've heard him jaw by the yard,' smiled the honest youth. 'He has told me he despises it.'

'What *is* it he despises? I can't make out.'

The most consecutive of Mr Coyle's nurslings considered a moment, as if he were conscious of a responsibility. 'Why I think just soldiering, don't you know? He says we take the wrong view of it.'

'He oughtn't to talk to *you* that way. It's corrupting the youth of Athens.[6] It's sowing sedition.'

'Oh I'm all right!' said young Lechmere. 'And he never told me he meant to chuck it. I always thought he meant to see it through, simply because he had to. He'll argue on any side you like. He can talk your head off – I will say *that* for him. But it's a tremendous pity – I'm sure he'd have a big career.'

'Tell him so then; plead with him; struggle with him – for God's sake.'

'I'll do what I can – I'll tell him it's a regular shame.'

'Yes, strike *that* note – insist on the disgrace of it.'

The young man gave Mr Coyle a queer look. 'I'm sure he wouldn't do anything dishonourable.'

'Well – it won't look right. He must be made to feel *that* – work it up. Give him a comrade's point of view – that of a brother-in-arms.'

'That's what I thought we were going to be!' young Lechmere mused romantically, much uplifted by the nature of the mission imposed on him. 'He's an awfully good sort.'

'No one will think so if he backs out!' said Spencer Coyle.

'Well, they mustn't say it to *me*!' his pupil rejoined with a flush.

Mr Coyle debated, noting his tone and aware that in the perversity of things, though this young man was a born soldier, no excitement would ever attach to *his* alternatives save perhaps on the part of the nice girl to whom at an early day he was sure to be placidly united. 'Do you like him very much – do you believe in him?'

Young Lechmere's life in these days was spent in answering terrible questions, but he had never been put through so straight a lot as these. 'Believe in him? Rather!'

'Then *save* him!'

The poor boy was puzzled, as if it were forced upon him by this intensity that there was more in such an appeal than could appear on the surface; and he doubtless felt that he was but apprehending a complex situation when after another moment, with his hands in his pockets, he replied hopefully but not pompously: 'I dare say I can bring him round!'

II

Before seeing young Lechmere Mr Coyle had determined to telegraph an enquiry to Miss Wingrave. He had prepaid the answer, which, being promptly put into his hand, brought the interview we have just related to a close. He immediately drove off to Baker Street, where the lady had said she awaited him, and five minutes after he got there, as he sat with Owen Wingrave's remarkable aunt, he repeated several times over, in his angry sadness and with the infallibility of his experience: 'He's so intelligent – he's so intelligent!' He had declared it had been a luxury to put such a fellow through.

'Of course he's intelligent; what else could he be? We've never, that I know of, had but *one* idiot in the family!' said Jane Wingrave. This was an allusion that Mr Coyle could understand, and it brought home to him another of the reasons for the disappointment, the humiliation as it were, of the good people at Paramore, at the same time that it gave an example of the conscientious coarseness he had on former occasions observed in his hostess. Poor Philip Wingrave, her late brother's eldest son, was literally imbecile and banished from view; deformed, unsocial, irretrievable, he had been relegated to a private asylum and had become among the friends of the family only a little hushed lugubrious legend. All the hopes of the house, picturesque Paramore, now unintermittently old Sir Philip's rather melancholy home – his infirmities would keep him there to the last – were therefore gathered on the second boy's head, which nature, as if in compunction for her previous botch, had, in addition to making it strikingly handsome, filled with a marked and general readiness. These two had been the only children of the old man's only son, who, like so many of his ancestors, had given up a gallant young life to the service of his country. Owen Wingrave the elder had received his death-cut, in close quarters, from an Afghan sabre;[7] the blow had come crashing across his skull. His wife, at that time in India, was about to give birth to her third child; and when the event took place, in darkness and anguish, the baby came lifeless into the world and the mother sank under the multiplication of her woes. The second of the little boys in England, who was at Paramore with his grand-father, became the peculiar charge of his aunt, the only unmarried one, and during the interesting Sunday that, by urgent invitation, Spencer Coyle, busy as he was, had, after consenting to put Owen through, spent under that roof, the celebrated crammer received a vivid impression of the influence exerted at least in intention by Miss Wingrave. Indeed the picture of this short visit remained with the observant little man a curious one – the vision of an impoverished Jacobean[8] house, shabby and remarkably 'creepy', but full of character still and full of felicity as a setting for the distinguished figure of the peaceful old soldier. Sir Philip Wingrave, a relic rather than a celebrity, was a small brown erect octogenarian, with smouldering eyes and a studied courtesy. He liked to do the diminished honours of his house, but even when with a shaky hand he lighted a bedroom candle for a deprecating guest, it was impossible not to feel him, beneath the surface, a merciless old man of blood. The eye of the imagination could glance back into his crowded Eastern past – back at episodes in which his scrupulous forms would only have made him more terrible. He had his legend – and oh there were stories about him!

Mr Coyle remembered also two other figures – a faded inoffensive Mrs Julian, domesticated there by a system of frequent visits as the widow of an officer and a particular friend of Miss Wingrave, and a remarkably clever little girl of eighteen, who was this lady's daughter and who struck the speculative visitor as already formed for other relations. She was very impertinent to Owen, and in the course of a long walk that he had taken with the young man and the effect of which, in much talk, had been to clinch his high opinion of him, he had learned – for Owen chattered confidentially – that Mrs Julian was the sister of a very gallant gentleman, Captain Hume-Walker of the Artillery, who had fallen in the Indian Mutiny[9] and between whom and Miss Wingrave (it had been that lady's one known concession) a passage of some delicacy, taking a tragic turn, was believed to have been enacted. They had been engaged to be married, but she had given way to the jealousy of her nature – had broken with him and sent him off to his fate, which had been horrible. A passionate sense of having wronged him, a hard eternal remorse had thereupon taken possession of her, and when his poor sister, linked also to a soldier, had by a still heavier blow been left almost without resources, she had devoted herself grimly to a long expiation. She had sought comfort in taking Mrs Julian to live much of the time at Paramore, where she became an unremunerated though not uncriticised housekeeper, and Spencer Coyle rather fancied it a part of this comfort that she could at leisure trample on her. The impression of Jane Wingrave was not the faintest he had gathered on that intensifying Sunday – an occasion singularly tinged for him with the sense of bereavement and mourning and memory, of names never mentioned, of the faraway plaint of widows and the echoes of battles and bad news. It was all military indeed, and Mr Coyle was made to shudder a little at the profession of which he helped to open the door to otherwise harmless young men. Miss Wingrave might moreover have made such a bad conscience worse – so cold and clear a good one looked at him out of her hard fine eyes and trumpeted in her sonorous voice.

She was a high distinguished person, angular but not awkward, with a large forehead and abundant black hair arranged like that of a woman conceiving, perhaps excusably, of her head as 'noble', and today irregularly streaked with white. If however she represented for our troubled friend the genius of a military race, it was not that she had the step of a grenadier or the vocabulary of a camp-follower; it was only that such sympathies were vividly implied in the general fact to which her very presence and each of her actions and glances and tones were a constant and direct allusion – the paramount valour of her family. If she was military it was because she sprang from a military house and because she wouldn't for the world have been anything but what the Wingraves had been. She was almost vulgar about her ancestors, and if one had been tempted to quarrel with her one would have found a fair pretext in her defective sense of proportion. This temptation however said nothing to Spencer Coyle, for whom, as a strong character revealing itself in colour and sound, she was almost a 'treat' and who was glad to regard her as a force exerted on his own side. He wished her nephew had more of her narrowness instead of being almost cursed with the tendency to look at things in their relations. He wondered why when she came up to town she always resorted to Baker Street for lodgings. He had never known nor heard of Baker Street as a residence – he associated it only with bazaars and photographers. He divined in her a rigid indifference to everything that was not the passion of her life. Nothing really mattered to her but that, and she would have occupied apartments in Whitechapel if they had been an item in her tactics. She had received her visitor in a large cold faded room, furnished with slippery seats and decorated with alabaster vases and wax-flowers. The only little personal comfort for which she appeared to have looked out was a fat catalogue of the Army and Navy Stores, which reposed on a vast desolate table-cover of false blue. Her clear forehead – it was like a porcelain slate, a receptacle for addresses and sums – had flushed when her nephew's crammer told her the extraordinary news; but he saw she was fortunately more angry than frightened. She had essentially, she would always have, too little imagination for fear, and the healthy habit moreover of facing everything had taught her that the occasion usually found her a quantity to reckon with. He saw that her only present fear could have been that of the failure to prevent her nephew's showing publicly for an ass, or for worse, and that to such an apprehension as this she was in fact inaccessible. Practically, too, she was not troubled by surprise; she recognised none of the futile, none of the subtle sentiments. If Owen had for an hour made a fool of himself she was angry; disconcerted as she would have been on learning that he had confessed to debts or fallen in love with a low girl. But there remained in any annoyance the saving fact that no one could make a fool of *her*.

'I don't know when I've taken such an interest in a young man – I think I've never done it since I began to handle them,' Mr Coyle said. 'I like him, I believe in him. It's been a delight to see how he was going.'

'Oh I know how they go!' Miss Wingrave threw back her head with an air as acquainted as if a headlong array of the generations had flashed before her with a rattle of their scabbards and spurs. Spencer Coyle recognised the intimation that she had nothing to learn from anybody about the natural carriage of a Wingrave, and he even felt convicted by her next words of being, in her eyes, with the troubled story of his check, his weak complaint of his pupil, rather a poor creature. 'If you like him,' she exclaimed, 'for mercy's sake keep him quiet!' Mr Coyle began to explain to her that this was less easy than she appeared to imagine; but it came home to him that she really grasped little of what he said. The more he insisted that the boy had a kind of intellectual independence, the more this struck her as a conclusive proof that her nephew was a Wingrave and a soldier. It was not till he mentioned to her that Owen had spoken of the profession of arms as of something that would be 'beneath' him, it was not till her attention was arrested by this intenser light on the complexity of the problem, that she broke out after a moment's stupefied reflection: 'Send him to see me at once!'

'That's exactly what I wanted to ask your leave to do. But I've wanted also to prepare you for the worst, to make you understand that he strikes me as really obstinate, and to suggest to you that the most powerful arguments at your command – especially if you should be able to put your hand on some intensely practical one – will be none too effective.'

'I think I've got a powerful argument' – and Miss Wingrave looked hard at her visitor. He didn't know in the least what this engine might be, but he begged her to drag it without delay into the field. He promised their young man should come to Baker Street that evening, mentioning however that he had already urged him to spend a couple of the very next days at Eastbourne. This led Jane Wingrave to enquire with surprise what virtue there might be in *that* expensive remedy, and to reply with decision when he had said 'The virtue of a little rest, a little change, a little relief to overwrought nerves,' 'Ah don't coddle him – he's costing us a great deal of money! I'll talk to him and I'll take him down to Paramore; he'll be dealt with there, and I'll send him back to you straightened out.'

Spencer Coyle hailed this pledge superficially with satisfaction, but before he quitted the strenuous lady he knew he had really taken on a new anxiety – a restlessness that made him say to himself, groaning inwardly: 'Oh she *is* a grenadier at bottom, and she'll have no tact. I don't know what her powerful argument is; I'm only afraid she'll be stupid and make him worse. The old man's better – *he's* capable of tact, though he's not quite an extinct volcano. Owen will probably put him in a rage. In short, it's a difficulty that the boy's the best of them.'

He felt afresh that evening at dinner that the boy was the best of them. Young Wingrave – who, he was pleased to observe, had not yet proceeded to the seaside – appeared at the repast as usual, looking inevitably a little self-conscious, but not too original for Bayswater.[10] He talked very naturally to Mrs Coyle, who had thought him from the first the most beautiful young man they had ever received; so that the person most ill at ease was poor Lechmere, who took great trouble, as if from the deepest delicacy, not to meet the eye of his misguided mate. Spencer Coyle however paid the price of his own profundity in feeling more and more worried; he could so easily see that there were all sorts of things in his young friend that the people of Paramore wouldn't understand. He began even already to react against the notion of his being harassed – to reflect that after all he had a right to his ideas – to remember that he was of a substance too fine to be handled with blunt fingers. It was in this way that the ardent little crammer, with his whimsical perceptions and complicated sympathies, was generally condemned not to settle down comfortably either to his displeasures or to his enthusiasms. His love of the real truth never gave him a chance to enjoy them. He mentioned to Wingrave after dinner the propriety of an immediate visit to Baker Street, and the young man, looking 'queer', as he thought – that is smiling again with the perverse high spirit in a wrong cause that he had shown in their recent interview – went off to face the ordeal. Spencer Coyle was sure he was scared – he was afraid of his aunt; but somehow this didn't strike him as a sign of pusillanimity. *He* should have been scared, he was well aware, in the poor boy's place, and the sight of his pupil marching up to the battery in spite of his terrors was a positive suggestion of the temperament of the soldier. Many a plucky youth would have funked this special exposure.

'He *has* got ideas!' young Lechmere broke out to his instructor after his comrade had quitted the house. He was bewildered and rather rueful – he had an emotion to work off. He had before dinner gone straight at his friend, as Mr Coyle had requested, and had elicited from him that his scruples were founded on an overwhelming conviction of the stupidity – the 'crass barbarism' he called it – of war. His great complaint was that people hadn't invented anything cleverer, and he was determined to show, the only way he could, that *he* wasn't so dull a brute.

'And he thinks all the great generals ought to have been shot, and that Napoleon Bonaparte in particular, the greatest, was a scoundrel, a criminal, a monster for whom language has no adequate name!' Mr

Coyle rejoined, completing young Lechmere's picture. 'He favoured you, I see, with exactly the same pearls of wisdom that he produced for me. But I want to know what *you* said.'

'I said they were awful rot!' Young Lechmere spoke with emphasis and was slightly surprised to hear Mr Coyle laugh, out of tune, at this just declaration, and then after a moment continue: 'It's all very curious – I dare say there's something in it. But it's a pity!'

'He told me when it was that the question began to strike him in that light. Four or five years ago, when he did a lot of reading about all the great swells and their campaigns – Hannibal and Julius Caesar, Marlborough and Frederick and Bonaparte.[11] He *has* done a lot of reading, and he says it opened his eyes. He says that a wave of disgust rolled over him. He talked about the "immeasurable misery" of wars, and asked me why nations don't tear to pieces the governments, the rulers that go in for them. He hates poor old Bonaparte worst of all.'

'Well, poor old Bonaparte *was* a scoundrel. He was a frightful ruffian,' Mr Coyle unexpectedly declared. 'But I suppose you didn't admit that.'

'Oh I dare say he was objectionable, and I'm very glad we laid him on his back. But the point I made to Wingrave was that his own behaviour would excite no end of remark.' And young Lechmere hung back but an instant before adding: 'I told him he must be prepared for the worst.'

'Of course he asked you what you meant by the "worst",' said Spencer Coyle.

'Yes, he asked me that, and do you know what I said? I said people would call his conscientious scruples and his wave of disgust a mere pretext. Then he asked, "A pretext for what?"'

'Ah he rather had you there!' Mr Coyle returned with a small laugh that was mystifying to his pupil.

'Not a bit – for I told him.'

'What did you tell him?'

Once more, for a few seconds, with his conscious eyes in his instructor's, the young man delayed. 'Why what we spoke of a few hours ago. The appearance he'd present of not having – ' The honest youth faltered afresh, but brought it out: 'The military temperament, don't you know? But do you know how he cheeked us on that?' young Lechmere went on.

'Damn the military temperament!' the crammer promptly replied.

Young Lechmere stared. Mr Coyle's tone left him uncertain if he were attributing the phrase to Wingrave or uttering his own opinion, but he exclaimed: 'Those were exactly his words!'

'He doesn't care,' said Mr Coyle.

'Perhaps not. But it isn't fair for him to abuse *us* fellows. I told him it's the finest temperament in the world, and that there's nothing so splendid as pluck and heroism.'

'Ah there you had *him!*'

'I told him it was unworthy of him to abuse a gallant, a magnificent profession. I told him there's no type so fine as that of the soldier doing his duty.'

'That's essentially *your* type, my dear boy.' Young Lechmere blushed; he couldn't make out – and the danger was naturally unexpected to him – whether at that moment he didn't exist mainly for the recreation of his friend. But he was partly reassured by the genial way this friend continued, laying a hand on his shoulder: 'Keep *at* him that way! We may do something. I'm in any case extremely obliged to you.'

Another doubt however remained unassuaged – a doubt which led him to overflow yet again before they dropped the painful subject: 'He *doesn't* care! But it's awfully odd he shouldn't!'

'So it is, but remember what you said this afternoon – I mean about your not advising people to make insinuations to *you*.'

'I believe I should knock the beggar down!' said young Lechmere. Mr Coyle had got up; the conversation had taken place while they sat together after Mrs Coyle's withdrawal from the dinner table, and the head of the establishment administered to his candid charge, on principles that were a part of his thoroughness, a glass of excellent claret. The disciple in question, also on his feet, lingered an instant, not for another 'go', as he would have called it, at the decanter, but to wipe his microscopic moustache with prolonged and unusual care. His companion saw he had something to bring out which required a final effort, and waited for him an instant with a hand on the knob of the door. Then as young Lechmere drew nearer Spencer Coyle grew conscious of an unwonted intensity in the round and ingenuous face. The boy was nervous, but tried to behave like a man of the world. 'Of course it's between ourselves,' he stammered, 'and I wouldn't breathe such a word to anyone who wasn't interested in poor Wingrave as you are. But do you think he funks it?'

Mr Coyle looked at him so hard an instant that he was visibly frightened at what he had said. 'Funks it! Funks what?'

'Why what we're talking about – the service.' Young Lechmere gave a little gulp and added with a want of active wit almost pathetic to Spencer Coyle: 'The dangers, you know!'

'Do you mean he's thinking of his skin?'

Young Lechmere's eyes expanded appealingly, and what his instructor saw in his pink face – even thinking he saw a tear – was the dread of a disappointment shocking in the degree in which the loyalty of admiration had been great.

'Is he – is he beastly *afraid?*' repeated the honest lad with a quaver of suspense.

'Dear no!' said Spencer Coyle, turning his back.

On which young Lechmere felt a little snubbed and even a little ashamed. But still more he felt relieved.

III

Less than a week after this, the elder man received a note from Miss Wingrave, who had immediately quitted London with her nephew. She proposed he should come down to Paramore for the following Sunday – Owen was really so tiresome. On the spot, in that house of examples and memories and in combination with her poor dear father, who was 'dreadfully annoyed', it might be worth their while to make a last stand. Mr Coyle read between the lines of this letter that the party at Paramore had got over a good deal of ground since Miss Wingrave, in Baker Street, had treated his despair as superficial. She wasn't an insinuating woman, but she went so far as to put the question on the ground of his conferring a particular favour on an afflicted family; and she expressed the pleasure it would give them should he be accompanied by Mrs Coyle, for whom she enclosed a separate invitation. She mentioned that she was also writing, subject to Mr Coyle's approval, to young Lechmere. She thought such a nice manly boy might do her wretched nephew some good. The celebrated crammer decided to embrace this occasion; and now it was the case not so much that he was angry as that he was anxious. As he directed his answer to Miss Wingrave's letter, he caught himself smiling at the thought that at bottom he was going to defend his ex-pupil rather than to give him away. He said to his wife, who was a fair fresh slow woman – a person of much more presence than himself – that she had better take Miss Wingrave at her word: it was such an extraordinary, such a fascinating specimen of an old English home. This last allusion was softly sarcastic – he had accused the good lady more than once of being in love with Owen Wingrave. She admitted that she was, she even gloried in her passion; which shows that the subject, between them, was treated in a liberal spirit. She carried out the joke by accepting the invitation with eagerness. Young Lechmere was delighted to do the same; his instructor had good-naturedly taken the view that the little break would freshen him up for his last spurt.

It was the fact that the occupants of Paramore did indeed take their trouble hard that struck our friend after he had been an hour or two in that fine old house. This very short second visit, beginning on the Saturday evening, was to constitute the strangest episode of his life. As soon as he found himself in private with his wife – they had retired to dress for dinner – they called each other's attention with effusion and almost with alarm to the sinister gloom diffused through the place. The house was admirable from its old grey front, which came forward in wings so as to form three sides of a square, but Mrs Coyle made no scruple to declare that if she had known in advance the sort of impression she was going to receive she would never have put her foot in it. She characterised it as 'uncanny' and as looking wicked and weird, and she accused her husband of not having warned her properly. He had named to her in advance some of the appearances she was to expect, but while she almost feverishly dressed she had innumerable questions to ask. He hadn't told her about the girl, the extraordinary girl, Miss Julian – that is, he hadn't told her that this young lady, who in plain terms was a mere dependent, would be in effect, and as a consequence of the way she carried herself, the most important person in the house. Mrs Coyle was already prepared to announce that she hated Miss Julian's affectations. Her husband above all hadn't told her that they should find their young charge looking five years older.

'I couldn't imagine that,' Spencer said, 'nor that the character of the crisis here would be quite so perceptible. But I suggested to Miss Wingrave the other day that they should press her nephew in real earnest, and she has taken me at my word. They've cut off his supplies – they're trying to starve him out. That's not what I meant – but indeed I don't quite *know* today what I meant. Owen feels the pressure, but he won't yield.' The strange thing was that, now he was there, the brooding little coach knew still better, even while half-closing his eyes to it, that his own spirit had been caught up by a wave of reaction. If he was there it was because he was on poor Owen's side. His whole impression, his whole apprehension, had on the spot become much deeper. There was something in the young fanatic's very resistance that began to charm him. When his wife, in the intimacy of the conference I have mentioned, threw off the mask and commended even with extravagance the stand his pupil had taken (he was too good to be a horrid soldier and it was noble of him to suffer for his convictions – wasn't he as upright as a young hero,

even though as pale as a Christian martyr?), the good lady only
expressed the sympathy which, under cover of regarding his late
inmate as a rare exception, he had already recognised in his own
soul.

For, half an hour ago, after they had had superficial tea in the
brown old hall of the house, that searcher into the reasons of things
had proposed to him, before going to dress, a short turn outside, and
had even, on the terrace, as they walked together to one of the far
ends, passed his hand entreatingly into his companion's arm,
permitting himself thus a familiarity unusual between pupil and
master and calculated to show he had guessed whom he could most
depend on to be kind to him. Spencer Coyle had on his own side
guessed something, so that he wasn't surprised at the boy's having a
particular confidence to make. He had felt on arriving that each
member of the party would want to get hold of him first, and he knew
that at that moment Jane Wingrave was peering through the ancient
blur of one of the windows – the house had been modernised so little
that the thick dim panes were three centuries old – to see whether her
nephew looked as if he were poisoning the visitor's mind. Mr Coyle
lost no time therefore in reminding the youth – though careful to
turn it to a laugh as he did so – that he hadn't come down to
Paramore to be corrupted. He had come down to make, face to face,
a last appeal, which he hoped wouldn't be utterly vain. Owen smiled
sadly as they went, asking him if he thought he had the general air of
a fellow who was going to knock under.

'I think you look odd – I think you look ill,' Spencer Coyle said very
honestly. They had paused at the end of the terrace.

'I've had to exercise a great power of resistance, and it rather takes
it out of one.'

'Ah my dear boy, I wish your great power – for you evidently
possess it – were exerted in a better cause!'

Owen Wingrave smiled down at his small but erect instructor. 'I
don't believe that!' Then he added, to explain why: 'Isn't what you
want (if you're so good as to think well of my character) to see me
exert *most* power, in whatever direction? Well, this is the way I exert
most.' He allowed he had had some terrible hours with his grandfather, who had denounced him in a way to make his hair stand up on
his head. He had expected them not to like it, not a bit, but had had
no idea they would make such a row. His aunt was different, but she
was equally insulting. Oh they had made him feel they were ashamed
of him; they accused him of putting a public dishonour on their
name. He was the only one who had ever backed out – he was the first

for three hundred years. Everyone had known he was to go up, and now everyone would know him for a young hypocrite who suddenly pretended to have scruples. They talked of his scruples as you wouldn't talk of a cannibal's god. His grandfather had called him outrageous names. 'He called me – he called me – ' Here Owen faltered and his voice failed him. He looked as haggard as was possible to a young man in such splendid health.

'I probably know!' said Spencer Coyle with a nervous laugh.

His companion's clouded eyes, as if following the last strange consequences of things, rested for an instant on a distant object. Then they met his own and for another moment sounded them deeply. 'It isn't true. No, it isn't. It's not *that!*'

'I don't suppose it is! But what *do* you propose instead of it?'

'Instead of what?'

'Instead of the stupid solution of war. If you take that away, you should suggest at least a substitute.'

'That's for the people in charge, for governments and cabinets,' said Owen. '*They'll* arrive soon enough at a substitute, in the particular case, if they're made to understand that they'll be hanged – and also drawn and quartered – if they don't find one. Make it a capital crime; *that* will quicken the wits of ministers!' His eyes brightened as he spoke, and he looked assured and exalted. Mr Coyle gave a sigh of sad surrender – it was really a stiff obsession. He saw the moment after this when Owen was on the point of asking if he too thought him a coward; but he was relieved to be able to judge that he either didn't suspect him of it or shrank uncomfortably from putting the question to the test. Spencer Coyle wished to show confidence, but somehow a direct assurance that he didn't doubt of his courage was too gross a compliment – it would be like saying he didn't doubt of his honesty. The difficulty was presently averted by Owen's continuing: 'My grandfather can't break the entail,[12] but I shall have nothing but this place, which, as you know, is small and, with the way rents are going, has quite ceased to yield an income. He has some money – not much, but such as it is he cuts me off. My aunt does the same – she has let me know her intentions. She was to have left me her six hundred a year. It was all settled, but now what's definite is that I don't get a penny of it if I give up the army. I must add in fairness that I have from my mother three hundred a year of my own. And I tell you the simple truth when I say I don't care a rap for the loss of the money.' The young man drew the long slow breath of a creature in pain; then he added: '*That's* not what worries me!'

'What are you going to do instead then?' his friend asked without other comment.

'I don't know – perhaps nothing. Nothing great at all events. Only something peaceful!'

Owen gave a weary smile, as if, worried as he was, he could yet appreciate the humorous effect of such a declaration from a Wingrave; but what it suggested to his guest, who looked up at him with a sense that he was after all not a Wingrave for nothing and had a military steadiness under fire, was the exasperation that such a profession, made in such a way and striking them as the last word of the inglorious, might well have produced on the part of his grandfather and his aunt. 'Perhaps nothing' – when he might carry on the great tradition! Yes, he wasn't weak, and he was interesting; but there was clearly a point of view from which he was provoking. 'What *is* it then that worries you?' Mr Coyle demanded.

'Oh the house – the very air and feeling of it. There are strange voices in it that seem to mutter at me – to say dreadful things as I pass. I mean the general consciousness and responsibility of what I'm doing. Of course it hasn't been easy for me – anything rather! I assure you I don't enjoy it.' With a light in them that was like a longing for justice, Owen again bent his eyes on those of the little coach; then he pursued: 'I've started up all the old ghosts. The very portraits glower at me on the walls. There's one of my great-great-grandfather (the one the extraordinary story you know is about – the old fellow who hangs on the second landing of the big staircase) that fairly stirs on the canvas, just heaves a little, when I come near it. I have to go up and down stairs – it's rather awkward! It's what my aunt calls the family circle, and they sit, ever so grimly, in judgement. The circle's all constituted here, it's a kind of awful encompassing presence, it stretches away into the past, and when I came back with her the other day Miss Wingrave told me I wouldn't have the impudence to stand in the midst of it and say such things. I *had* to say them to my grandfather; but now that I've said them it seems to me the question's ended. I want to go away – I don't care if I never come back again.'

'Oh you *are* a soldier; you must fight it out!' Mr Coyle laughed.

The young man seemed discouraged at his levity, but as they turned round, strolling back in the direction from which they had come, he himself smiled faintly after an instant and replied: 'Ah we're tainted all!'

They walked in silence part of the way to the old portico; then the elder of the pair, stopping short after having assured himself he was at a sufficient distance from the house not to be heard, suddenly put the question: 'What does Miss Julian say?'

'Miss Julian?' Owen had perceptibly coloured.

'I'm sure *she* hasn't concealed her opinion.'

'Oh it's the opinion of the family circle, for she's a member of it of course. And then she has her own as well.'

'Her own opinion?'

'Her own family circle.'

'Do you mean her mother – that patient lady?'

'I mean more particularly her father, who fell in battle. And her grandfather, and *his* father, and her uncles and great-uncles – they all fell in battle.'

Mr Coyle, his face now rather oddly set, took it in. 'Hasn't the sacrifice of so many lives been sufficient? Why should she sacrifice *you?*'

'Oh she *hates* me!' Owen declared as they resumed their walk.

'Ah the hatred of pretty girls for fine young men!' cried Spencer Coyle.

He didn't believe in it, but his wife did, it appeared perfectly, when he mentioned this conversation while, in the fashion that has been described, the visitors dressed for dinner. Mrs Coyle had already discovered that nothing could have been nastier than Miss Julian's manner to the disgraced youth during the half-hour the party had spent in the hall; and it was this lady's judgement that one must have had no eyes in one's head not to see that she was already trying outrageously to flirt with young Lechmere. It was a pity they had brought that silly boy: he was down in the hall with the creature at that moment. Spencer Coyle's version was different – he believed finer elements involved. The girl's footing in the house was inexplicable on any ground save that of her being predestined to Miss Wingrave's nephew. As the niece of Miss Wingrave's own unhappy intended, she had been devoted early by this lady to the office of healing by a union with the hope of the race the tragic breach that had separated their elders; and if in reply to this it was to be said that a girl of spirit couldn't enjoy in such a matter having her duty cut out for her, Owen's enlightened friend was ready with the argument that a young person in Miss Julian's position would never be such a fool as really to quarrel with a capital chance. She was familiar at Paramore and she felt safe; therefore she might treat herself to the amusement of pretending she had her option. It was all innocent tricks and airs. She had a curious charm, and it was vain to pretend that the heir of that house wouldn't seem good enough to a girl, clever as she might be, of eighteen. Mrs Coyle reminded her husband that their late charge was precisely now *not* of that house: this question was among the articles that exercised their wits after the two men had taken the turn on the terrace. Spencer then mentioned to his wife that Owen was afraid of the portrait of his great-great-grandfather. He would show it to her, since she hadn't noticed it, on their way downstairs.

'Why of his great-great-grandfather more than of any of the others?'

'Oh because he's the most formidable. He's the one who's sometimes seen.'

'Seen where?' Mrs Coyle had turned round with a jerk.

'In the room he was found dead in – the White Room they've always called it.'

'Do you mean to say the house has a proved *ghost?*' Mrs Coyle almost shrieked. 'You brought me here without telling me?'

'Didn't I mention it after my other visit?'

'Not a word. You only talked about Miss Wingrave.'

'Oh I was full of the story – you've simply forgotten.'

'Then you should have reminded me!'

'If I had thought of it, I'd have held my peace – for you wouldn't have come.'

'I wish indeed I hadn't!' cried Mrs Coyle. 'But what,' she immediately asked, '*is* the story?'

'Oh a deed of violence that took place here ages ago. I think it was in George the Second's time that Colonel Wingrave, one of their ancestors, struck in a fit of passion one of his children, a lad just growing up, a blow on the head of which the unhappy child died. The matter was hushed up for the hour and some other explanation put about. The poor boy was laid out in one of those rooms on the other side of the house, and amid strange smothered rumours the funeral was hurried on. The next morning, when the household assembled, Colonel Wingrave was missing; he was looked for vainly, and at last it occurred to someone that he might perhaps be in the room from which his child had been carried to burial. The seeker knocked without an answer – then opened the door. The poor man lay dead on the floor, in his clothes, as if he had reeled and fallen back, without a wound, without a mark, without anything in his appearance to indicate that he had either struggled or suffered. He was a strong sound man – there was nothing to account for such a stroke. He's supposed to have gone to the room during the night, just before going to bed, in some fit of compunction or some fascination of dread. It was only after this that the truth about the boy came out. But no one ever sleeps in the room.'

Mrs Coyle had fairly turned pale. 'I hope not indeed! Thank heaven they haven't put *us* there!'

'We're at a comfortable distance – I know the scene of the event.'

'Do you mean you've been *in* – ?'

'For a few moments. They're rather proud of the place and my young friend showed it me when I was here before.'

Mrs Coyle stared. 'And what is it like?'

'Simply an empty dull old-fashioned bedroom, rather big and furnished with the things of the "period". It's panelled from floor to ceiling, and the panels evidently, years and years ago, were painted white. But the paint has darkened with time and there are three or four quaint little ancient "samplers",[13] framed and glazed, hung on the walls.'

Mrs Coyle looked round with a shudder. 'I'm glad there are no samplers here! I never heard anything so jumpy! Come down to dinner.'

On the staircase as they went her husband showed her the portrait of Colonel Wingrave – a representation, with some force and style, for the place and period, of a gentleman with a hard handsome face, in a red coat and a peruke. Mrs Coyle pronounced his descendant old Sir Philip wonderfully like him; and her husband could fancy, though he kept it to himself, that if one should have the courage to walk the old corridors of Paramore at night, one might meet a figure that resembled him roaming, with the restlessness of a ghost, hand in hand with the figure of a tall boy. As he proceeded to the drawing-room with his wife he found himself suddenly wishing he had made more of a point of his pupil's going to Eastbourne. The evening however seemed to have taken upon itself to dissipate any such whimsical forebodings, for the grimness of the family circle, as he had preconceived its composition, was mitigated by an infusion of the 'neighbourhood'. The company at dinner was recruited by two cheerful couples, one of them the vicar and his wife, and by a silent young man who had come down to fish. This was a relief to Mr Coyle, who had begun to wonder what was after all expected of him and why he had been such a fool as to come, and who now felt that for the first hours at least the situation wouldn't have directly to be dealt with. Indeed he found, as he had found before, sufficient occupation for his ingenuity in reading the various symptoms of which the social scene that spread about him was an expression. He should probably have a trying day on the morrow: he foresaw the difficulty of the long decorous Sunday and how dry Jane Wingrave's ideas, elicited in strenuous conference, would taste. She and her father would make him feel they depended upon him for the impossible, and if they should try to associate him with too tactless a policy he might end by telling them what he thought of it – an accident not required to make his visit a depressed mistake. The old man's actual design was evidently to let their friends see in it a positive mark of their being all right. The presence of the great London coach was tantamount to a profession of faith in the results of the impending examination. It had clearly been obtained from Owen, rather to the principal visitor's surprise, that he would do nothing to interfere with the apparent concord. He let the allusions to his hard work pass and, holding his tongue about his affairs, talked to the ladies as amicably as if he hadn't been 'cut off'. When Mr Coyle looked at him once or twice across the table, catching his eye, which showed an indefinable passion, he found a puzzling pathos in his laughing face: one couldn't resist a pang for a young lamb so visibly marked for sacrifice. 'Hang him, what a pity he's such a fighter!' he privately sighed – and with a want of logic that was only superficial.

This idea however would have absorbed him more if so much of his attention hadn't been for Kate Julian, who now that he had her well before him struck him as a remarkable and even as a possibly interesting young woman. The interest resided not in any extraordinary prettiness, for if she was handsome, with her long Eastern eyes, her magnificent hair and her general unabashed originality, he had seen complexions rosier and features that pleased him more: it dwelt in a strange impression that she gave of being exactly the sort of person whom, in her position, common considerations, those of prudence and perhaps even a little decorum, would have enjoined on her not to be. She was what was vulgarly termed a dependent – penniless patronised tolerated; but something in all her air conveyed that if her situation was inferior her spirit, to make up for it, was above precautions or submissions. It wasn't in the least that she was aggressive – she was too indifferent for that; it was only as if, having nothing either to gain or to lose, she could afford to do as she liked. It occurred to Spencer Coyle that she might really have had more at stake than her imagination appeared to take account of; whatever this quantity might be, at any rate, he had never seen a young woman at less pains to keep the safe side. He wondered inevitably what terms prevailed between Jane Wingrave and such an inmate as this; but those questions of course were unfathomable deeps. Perhaps keen

Kate lorded it even over her protectress. The other time he was at Paramore he had received an impression that, with Sir Philip beside her, the girl could fight with her back to the wall. She amused Sir Philip, she charmed him, and he liked people who weren't afraid; between him and his daughter moreover there was no doubt which was the higher in command. Miss Wingrave took many things for granted, and most of all the rigour of discipline and the fate of the vanquished and the captive.

But between their clever boy and so original a companion of his childhood what odd relation would have grown up? It couldn't be indifference, and yet on the part of happy handsome youthful creatures it was still less likely to be aversion. They weren't Paul and Virginia,[14] but they must have had their common summer and their idyll: no nice girl could have disliked such a nice fellow for anything but not liking *her*, and no nice fellow could have resisted such propinquity. Mr Coyle remembered indeed that Mrs Julian had spoken to him as if the propinquity had been by no means constant, owing to her daughter's absences at school, to say nothing of Owen's; her visits to a few friends who were so kind as to 'take' her from time to time; her sojourns in London – so difficult to manage, but still managed by God's help – for 'advantages', for drawing and singing, especially drawing, or rather painting in oils, for which she had gained high credit. But the good lady had also mentioned that the young people were quite brother and sister, which *was* a little, after all, like Paul and Virginia. Mrs Coyle had been right, and it was apparent that Virginia was doing her best to make the time pass agreeably for young Lechmere. There was no such whirl of conversation as to render it an effort for our critic to reflect on these things: the tone of the occasion, thanks principally to the other guests, was not disposed to stray – it tended to the repetition of anecdote and the discussion of rents, topics that huddled together like uneasy animals. He could judge how intensely his hosts wished the evening to pass off as if nothing had happened; and this gave him the measure of their private resentment. Before dinner was over he found himself fidgety about his second pupil. Young Lechmere, since he began to cram, had done all that might have been expected of him; but this couldn't blind his instructor to a present perception of his being in moments of relaxation as innocent as a babe. Mr Coyle had considered that the amusements of Paramore would probably give him a fillip, and the poor youth's manner testified to the soundness of the forecast. The fillip had been unmistakeably administered; it had come in the form of a revelation. The light on young Lechmere's brow announced with a candour that was almost an appeal for compassion, or at least a deprecation of ridicule, that he had never seen anything like Miss Julian.

IV

In the drawing-room after dinner, the girl found a chance to approach Owen's late preceptor. She stood before him a moment, smiling while she opened and shut her fan, and then said abruptly, raising her strange eyes: 'I know what you've come for, but it isn't any use.'

'I've come to look after *you* a little. Isn't *that* any use?'

'It's very kind. But I'm not the question of the hour. You won't do anything with Owen.'

Spencer Coyle hesitated a moment. 'What will *you* do with his young friend?'

She stared, looked round her. 'Mr Lechmere? Oh poor little lad! We've been talking about Owen. He admires him so.'

'So do I. I should tell you that.'

'So do we all. That's why we're in such despair.'

'Personally then you'd *like* him to be a soldier?' the visitor asked.

'I've quite set my heart on it. I adore the army and I'm awfully fond of my old playmate,' said Miss Julian.

Spencer recalled the young man's own different version of her attitude; but he judged it loyal not to challenge her. 'It's not conceivable that your old playmate shouldn't be fond of you. He must therefore wish to please you; and I don't see why – between you, such clever young people as you are! – you don't set the matter right.'

'Wish to please me!' Miss Julian echoed. 'I'm sorry to say he shows no such desire. He thinks me an impudent wretch. I've told him what I think of *him*, and he simply hates me.'

'But you think so highly! You just told me you admire him.'

'His talents, his possibilities, yes; even his personal appearance, if I may allude to such a matter. But I don't admire his present behaviour.'

'Have you had the question out with him?' Spencer asked.

'Oh yes, I've ventured to be frank – the occasion seemed to excuse it. He couldn't like what I said.'

'What did you say?'

The girl, thinking a moment, opened and shut her fan again. 'Why – as we're such good old friends – that such conduct doesn't begin to be that of a gentleman!'

After she had spoken her eyes met Mr Coyle's, who looked into their ambiguous depths. 'What then would you have said without that tie?'

'How odd for *you* to ask that – in such a way!' she returned with a laugh. 'I don't understand your position: I thought your line was to *make* soldiers!'

'You should take my little joke. But, as regards Owen Wingrave, there's no "making" needed,' he declared. 'To my sense' – and the little crammer paused as with a consciousness of responsibility for his paradox – 'to my sense he *is*, in a high sense of the term, a fighting man.'

'Ah let him prove it!' she cried with impatience and turning short off.

Spencer Coyle let her go; something in her tone annoyed and even not a little shocked him. There had evidently been a violent passage between these young persons, and the reflection that such a matter was after all none of his business but troubled him the more. It was indeed a military house, and she was at any rate a damsel who placed her ideal of manhood – damsels doubtless always had their ideals of manhood – in the type of the belted warrior. It was a taste like another; but even a quarter of an hour later, finding himself near young Lechmere, in whom this type was embodied, Spencer Coyle was still so ruffled that he addressed the innocent lad with a certain magisterial dryness. 'You're under no pressure to sit up late, you know. That's not what I brought you down for.' The dinner guests were taking leave and the bedroom candles twinkled in a monitory row. Young Lechmere however was too agreeably agitated to be accessible to a snub: he had a happy preoccupation which almost engendered a grin.

'I'm only too eager for bedtime. Do you know there's an awfully jolly room?'

Coyle debated a moment as to whether he should take the allusion – then spoke from his general tension. 'Surely they haven't put you there?'

'No indeed: no one has passed a night in it for ages. But that's exactly what I want to do – it would be tremendous fun.'

'And have you been trying to get Miss Julian's leave?'

'Oh *she* can't give it she says. But she believes in it, and she maintains that no man has ever dared.'

'No man *shall* ever!' said Spencer with decision. 'A fellow in your critical position in particular must have a quiet night.'

Young Lechmere gave a disappointed but reasonable sigh. 'Oh all right. But mayn't I sit up for a little go at Wingrave? I haven't had any yet.'

Mr Coyle looked at his watch. 'You may smoke *one* cigarette.'

He felt a hand on his shoulder and turned round to see his wife tilting candle grease upon his coat. The ladies were going to bed and it was Sir Philip's inveterate hour; but Mrs Coyle confided to her husband that after the dreadful things he had told her she positively declined to be left alone, for no matter how short an interval, in any part of the house. He promised to follow her within three minutes, and after the orthodox handshakes the ladies rustled away. The forms were kept up at Paramore as bravely as if the old house had no present intensity of heartache. The only one of which Coyle noticed the drop was some salutation to himself from Kate Julian. She gave him neither a word nor a glance, but he saw her look hard at Owen. Her mother, timid and pitying, was apparently the only person from whom this young man caught an inclination of the head. Miss Wingrave marshalled the three ladies – her little procession of twinkling tapers – up the wide oaken stairs and past the watching portrait of her ill-fated ancestor. Sir Philip's servant appeared and offered his arm to the old man, who turned a perpendicular back on poor Owen when the boy made a vague movement to anticipate this office. Mr Coyle learned later that before Owen had forfeited favour it had always, when he was at home, been his privilege at bedtime to conduct his grandfather ceremoniously to rest. Sir Philip's habits were contemptuously different now. His apartments were on the lower floor and he shuffled stiffly off to them with his valet's help, after fixing for a moment significantly on the most responsible of his visitors the thick red ray, like the glow of stirred embers, that always made his eyes conflict oddly with his mild manners. They seemed to say to poor Spencer 'We'll let the young scoundrel have it tomorrow!' One might have gathered from them that the young scoundrel, who had now strolled to the other end of the hall, had at least forged a cheque. His friend watched him an instant, saw him drop nervously into a chair and then with a restless movement get up. The same movement brought him back to where Mr Coyle stood addressing a last injunction to young Lechmere.

'I'm going to bed and I should like you particularly to conform to what I said to you a short time ago. Smoke a single cigarette with our host here and then go to your room. You'll have me down on you if I hear of your having, during the night, tried any preposterous games.' Young Lechmere, looking down with his hands in his pockets, said nothing – he only poked at the corner of a rug with his toe; so that his fellow visitor, dissatisfied with so tacit a pledge, presently went on to Owen: 'I must request you, Wingrave, not to keep so sensitive a subject sitting up – and indeed to put him to bed and turn his key in the door.' As Owen stared an instant, apparently not understanding the motive of so much solicitude, he added: 'Lechmere has a morbid curiosity about one of your legends – of your historic rooms. Nip it in the bud.'

'Oh the legend's rather good, but I'm afraid the room's an awful sell!' Owen laughed.

'You know you don't *believe* that, my boy!' young Lechmere returned.

'I don't think he does' – Mr Coyle noticed Owen's mottled flush.

'He wouldn't try a night there himself!' their companion pursued.

'I know who told you that,' said Owen, lighting a cigarette in an embarrassed way at the candle, without offering one to either of his friends.

'Well, what if she did?' asked the younger of these gentlemen, rather red. 'Do you want them *all* yourself?' he continued facetiously, fumbling in the cigarette-box.

Owen Wingrave only smoked quietly; then he brought out: 'Yes – what if she did? But she doesn't know,' he added.

'She doesn't know what?'

'She doesn't know anything! – I'll tuck him in!'

Owen went on gaily to Mr Coyle, who saw that his presence, now a certain note had been struck, made the young men uncomfortable. He was curious, but there were discretions and delicacies, with his pupils, that he had always pretended to practise; scruples which however didn't prevent, as he took his way upstairs, his recommending them not to be donkeys.

At the top of the staircase, to his surprise, he met Miss Julian, who was apparently going down again. She hadn't begun to undress, nor was she perceptibly disconcerted at seeing him. She nevertheless, in a manner slightly at variance with the rigour with which she had overlooked him ten minutes before, dropped the words: 'I'm going down to look for something. I've lost a jewel.'

'A jewel?'

'A rather good turquoise, out of my locket. As it's the only *real* ornament I've the honour to possess – !' And she began to descend.

'Shall I go with you and help you?' asked Spencer Coyle.

She paused a few steps below him, looking back with her Oriental eyes. 'Don't I hear our friends' voices in the hall?'

'Those remarkable young men are there.'

'*They'll* help me.' And Kate Julian passed down.

Spencer Coyle was tempted to follow her, but remembering his standard of tact, he rejoined his wife in their apartment. He delayed nevertheless to go to bed and, though he looked into his dressing-room, couldn't bring himself even to take off his coat. He pretended for half an hour to read a novel; after which, quietly, or perhaps I should say agitatedly, he stepped from the dressing-room into the corridor. He followed this passage to the door of the room he knew to have been assigned to young Lechmere and was comforted to see it closed. Half an hour earlier he had noticed it stand open; therefore he could take for granted the bewildered boy had come to bed. It was of this he had wished to assure himself, and having done so he was on the point of retreating. But at the same instant he heard a sound in the room – the occupant was doing, at the window, something that showed him he might knock without the reproach of waking his pupil up. Young Lechmere came in fact to the door in his shirt and trousers. He admitted his visitor in some surprise, and when the door was closed again the latter said: 'I don't want to make your life a burden, but I had it on my conscience to see for myself that you're not exposed to undue excitement.'

'Oh there's plenty of that!' said the ingenuous youth. 'Miss Julian came down again.'

'To look for a turquoise?'

'So she said.'

'Did she find it?'

'I don't know. I came up. I left her with poor Owen.'

'Quite the right thing,' said Spencer Coyle.

'I don't know,' young Lechmere repeated uneasily. 'I left them quarrelling.'

'What about?'

'I don't understand. They're a quaint pair!'

Spencer turned it over. He had, fundamentally, principles and high decencies, but what he had in particular just now was a curiosity, or rather, to recognise it for what it was, a sympathy, which brushed them away. 'Does it strike you that *she's* down on him?' he permitted himself to enquire.

'Rather! – when she tells him he lies!'

'What do you mean?'

'Why before *me*. It made me leave them; it was getting too hot. I stupidly brought up the question of that bad room again, and said how sorry I was I had had to promise you not to try my luck with it.'

'You can't pry about in that gross way in other people's houses – you can't take such liberties, you know!' Mr Coyle interjected.

'I'm all right – see how good I am. I don't want to go *near* the place!' said young Lechmere confidingly. 'Miss Julian said to me "Oh

I dare say *you'd* risk it, but" – and she turned and laughed at poor Owen – "that's more than we can expect of a gentleman who has taken *his* extraordinary line." I could see that something had already passed between them on the subject – some teasing or challenging of hers. It may have been only chaff, but his chucking the profession had evidently brought up the question of the white feather – I mean of his pluck.'

'And what did Owen say?'

'Nothing at first; but presently he brought out very quietly: "I spent all last night in the confounded place." We both stared and cried out at this and I asked him what he had seen there. He said he had seen nothing, and Miss Julian replied that he ought to tell his story better than that – he ought to make something good of it. "It's not a story – it's a simple fact," said he; on which she jeered at him and wanted to know why, if he had done it, he hadn't told her in the morning, since he knew what she thought of him. "I know, my dear, but I don't care," the poor devil said. This made her angry, and she asked him quite seriously whether he'd care if he should know she believed him to be trying to deceive us.'

'Ah what a brute!' cried Spencer Coyle.

'She's a most extraordinary girl – I don't know what she's up to,' young Lechmere quite panted.

'Extraordinary indeed – to be romping and bandying words at that hour of the night with fast young men!'

But young Lechmere made his distinction. 'I mean because I think she likes him.'

Mr Coyle was so struck with this unwonted symptom of subtlety that he flashed out: 'And do you think he likes *her?*'

It produced on his pupil's part a drop and a plaintive sigh. 'I don't know – I give it up! – But I'm sure he *did* see something or hear something,' the youth added.

'In that ridiculous place? What makes you sure?'

'Well, because he looks as if he had. I've an idea you can tell – in such a case. He behaves as if he had.'

'Why then shouldn't he name it?'

Young Lechmere wondered and found. 'Perhaps it's too bad to mention.'

Spencer Coyle gave a laugh. 'Aren't you glad then *you're* not in it?'

'Uncommonly!'

'Go to bed, you goose,' Spencer said with renewed nervous derision. 'But before you go, tell me how he met her charge that he was trying to deceive you.'

"'Take me there yourself then and lock me in!'"

'And *did* she take him?'

'I don't know – I came up.'

He exchanged a long look with his pupil. 'I don't think they're in the hall now. Where's Owen's own room?'

'I haven't the least idea.'

Mr Coyle was at a loss; he was in equal ignorance and he couldn't go about trying doors. He bade young Lechmere sink to slumber; after which he came out into the passage. He asked himself if he should be able to find his way to the room Owen had formerly shown him, remembering that in common with many of the others it had its ancient name painted on it. But the corridors of Paramore were intricate; moreover some of the servants would still be up, and he didn't wish to appear unduly to prowl. He went back to his own quarters, where Mrs Coyle soon noted the continuance of his inability to rest. As she confessed for her own part, in the dreadful place, to an increased sense of 'creepiness', they spent the early part of the night in conversation, so that a portion of their vigil was inevitably beguiled by her husband's account of his colloquy with little Lechmere and by their exchange of opinions upon it. Towards two o'clock, Mrs Coyle became so nervous about their persecuted young friend, and so possessed by the fear that that wicked girl had availed herself of his invitation to put him to an abominable test, that she begged her husband to go and look into the matter at whatever cost to his own tranquillity. But Spencer, perversely, had ended, as the perfect stillness of the night settled upon them, by charming himself into a pale acceptance of Owen's readiness to face God knew what unholy strain – an exposure the more trying to excited sensibilities as the poor boy had now learned by the ordeal of the previous night how resolute an effort he should have to make. 'I hope he *is* there,' he said to his wife: 'it puts them all so hideously in the wrong!' At any rate, he couldn't take on himself to explore a house he knew so little. He was inconsequent – he didn't prepare for bed. He sat in the dressing-room with his light and his novel – he waited to find himself nod. At last however Mrs Coyle turned over and ceased to talk, and at last too he fell asleep in his chair. How long he slept he knew afterwards only by computation; what he knew to begin with was that he had started up in confusion and under the shock of an appalling sound. His consciousness cleared itself fast, helped doubtless by a confirmatory cry of horror from his wife's room. But he gave no heed to his wife; he had already bounded into the passage. There the sound was repeated – it was the 'Help! help!' of a woman in agonised terror. It came from a distant quarter of the house, but the quarter was sufficiently indicated. He rushed straight before him, the sound of opening doors and alarmed voices in his ears and the faintness of the early dawn in his eyes. At a turn of one of the passages, he came upon the white figure of a girl in a swoon on a bench, and in the vividness of the revelation he read as he went that Kate Julian, stricken in her pride too late with a chill of compunction for what she had mockingly done, had, after coming to release the victim of her derision, reeled away, overwhelmed, from the catastrophe that was her work – the catastrophe that the next moment he found himself aghast at on the threshold of an open door. Owen Wingrave, dressed as he had last seen him, lay dead on the spot on which his ancestor had been found. He was all the young soldier on the gained field.

The Friends of the Friends

I FIND, as you prophesied, much that's interesting, but little that helps the delicate question – the possibility of publication. Her diaries are less systematic than I hoped; she only had a blessed habit of noting and narrating. She summarised, she saved; she appears seldom indeed to have let a good story pass without catching it on the wing. I allude of course not so much to things she heard as to things she saw and felt. She writes sometimes of herself, sometimes of others, sometimes of the combination. It's under this last rubric that she's usually most vivid. But it's not, you'll understand, when she's most vivid that she's always most publishable. To tell the truth, she's fearfully indiscreet, or has at least all the material for making *me* so. Take as an instance the fragment I send you after dividing it for your convenience into several small chapters. It's the contents of a thin blank-book[1] which I've had copied out and which has the merit of being nearly enough a rounded thing, an intelligible whole. These pages evidently date from years ago. I've read with the liveliest wonder the statement they so circumstantially make and done my best to swallow the prodigy they leave to be inferred. These things would be striking, wouldn't they? to any reader; but can you imagine for a moment my placing such a document before the world, even though, as if she herself had desired the world should have the benefit of it, she has given her friends neither name nor initials? Have you any sort of clue to their identity? I leave her the floor.

I

I know perfectly of course that I brought it upon myself; but that doesn't make it any better. I was the first to speak of her to him – he had never even heard her mentioned. Even if I had happened not to speak, someone else would have made up for it: I tried afterwards to find comfort in that reflection. But the comfort of reflections is thin: the only comfort that counts in life is not to have been a fool. That's a beatitude I shall doubtless never enjoy. 'Why you ought to meet her and talk it over' is what I immediately said. 'Birds of a feather flock together.' I told him who she was and that they were birds of a feather because if he had had in youth a strange adventure she had had about the same time just such another. It was well known to her friends – an incident she was constantly called on to describe. She was charming clever pretty unhappy; but it was none the less the thing to which she had originally owed her reputation.

Being at the age of eighteen somewhere abroad with an aunt, she had had a vision of one of her parents at the moment of death. The parent was in England hundreds of miles away and so far as she knew neither dying nor dead. It was by day, in the museum of some great foreign town. She had passed alone, in advance of her companions, into a small room containing some famous work of art and occupied at that moment by two other persons. One of these was an old custodian; the second, before observing him, she took for a stranger, a tourist. She was merely conscious that he was bareheaded and seated on a bench. The instant her eyes rested on him however, she beheld to her amazement her father, who, as if he had long waited for her, looked at her in singular distress and an impatience that was akin to reproach. She rushed to him with a bewildered cry, 'Papa, what *is* it?' but this was followed by an exhibition of still livelier feeling when on her movement he simply vanished, leaving the custodian and her relations, who were by that time at her heels, to gather round her in dismay. These persons, the official, the aunt, the cousins, were therefore in a manner witnesses of the fact – the fact at least of the impression made on her; and there was the further testimony of a doctor who was attending one of the party and to whom it was immediately afterwards communicated. He gave her a remedy for hysterics, but said to the aunt privately: 'Wait and see if something doesn't happen at home.' Something *had* happened – the poor father, suddenly and violently seized, had died that morning. The aunt, the mother's sister, received before the day was out a telegram announcing the event and requesting her to prepare her niece for it. Her niece was already prepared, and the girl's sense of this visitation remained of course indelible. We had all, as her friends, had it conveyed to us and had conveyed it creepily to each other. Twelve years had elapsed, and as a woman who had made an unhappy marriage and lived apart from her husband, she had become interesting from other sources; but since the name she now bore was a name frequently borne, and since moreover her judicial separation, as things were going, could hardly count as a distinction, it was usual to qualify her as 'the one, you know, who saw her father's ghost'.

As for him, dear man, he had seen his mother's – so there you are! I had never heard of that till this occasion on which our closer, our pleasanter acquaintance led him, through some turn of the subject of our talk, to mention it and to inspire me in so doing with the impulse to let him know that he had a rival in the field – a person with whom he could compare notes. Later on his story became for him, perhaps because of my unduly repeating it, likewise a convenient worldly label; but it hadn't a year before been the ground on which he was introduced to me. He had other merits, just as she, poor thing, had others. I can honestly say that I was quite aware of them from the first – I discovered them sooner than he discovered mine. I remember how it struck me even at the time that his sense of mine was quickened by my having been able to match, though not indeed straight from my own experience, his curious anecdote. It dated, this anecdote, as hers did, from some dozen years before – a year in which, at Oxford, he had for some reason of his own been staying on into the 'Long'.[2] He had been in the August afternoon on the river. Coming back into his room while it was still distinct daylight, he found his mother standing there as if her eyes had been fixed on the door. He had had a letter from her that morning out of Wales, where she was staying with her father. At the sight of him, she smiled with extraordinary radiance and extended her arms to him, and then as he sprang forward and joyfully opened his own, she vanished from the place. He wrote to her that night, telling her what had happened; the letter had been carefully preserved. The next morning, he heard of her death. He was through this chance of our talk extremely struck with the little prodigy I was able to produce for him. He had never encountered another case. Certainly they ought to meet, my friend and he; certainly they would have something in common. I would arrange this, wouldn't I? – if *she* didn't mind; for himself he didn't mind in the least. I had promised to speak to her of the matter as soon as possible, and within the week I was able to do so. She 'minded' as little as he; she was perfectly willing to see him. And yet no meeting was to occur – as meetings are commonly understood.

II

That's just half my tale – the extraordinary way it was hindered. This was the fault of a series of accidents; but the accidents, persisting for years, became, to me and to others, a subject of mirth with either party. They were droll enough at first, then they grew rather a bore. The odd thing was that both parties were amenable: it wasn't a case of their being indifferent, much less of their being indisposed. It was one of the caprices of chance, aided I suppose by some rather settled opposition of their interests and habits. His were centred in his office, his eternal inspectorship, which left him small leisure, constantly calling him away and making him break engagements. He liked society, but he found it everywhere and took it at a run. I never knew at a given moment where he was, and there were times when for months together I never saw him. She was on her side practically suburban: she lived at Richmond[3] and never went 'out'. She was a woman of distinction, but not of fashion, and felt, as people said, her situation. Decidedly proud and rather whimsical, she lived her life as she had planned it. There were things one could do with her, but one couldn't make her come to one's parties. One went indeed a little more than seemed quite convenient to hers, which consisted of her cousin, a cup of tea and the view. The tea was good; but the view was familiar, though perhaps not, like the cousin – a disagreeable old maid who had been of the group at the museum and with whom she now lived – offensively so. This connection with an inferior relative, which had partly an economic motive – she proclaimed her companion a marvellous manager – was one of the little perversities we had to forgive her. Another was her estimate of the proprieties created by her rupture with her husband. That was extreme – many persons called it even morbid. She made no advances; she cultivated scruples; she suspected, or I should perhaps rather say she remembered, slights: she was one of the few women I've known whom that particular predicament had rendered modest rather than bold. Dear thing, she had some delicacy! Especially marked were the limits she had set to possible attentions from men: it was always her thought that her husband only waited to pounce on her. She discouraged if she didn't forbid the visits of male persons not senile: she said she could never be too careful.

When I first mentioned to her that I had a friend whom fate had distinguished in the same weird way as herself, I put her quite at liberty to say 'Oh bring him out to see me!' I should probably have been able to bring him, and a situation perfectly innocent or at any rate comparatively simple would have been created. But she uttered no such word; she only said: 'I must meet him certainly; yes, I shall look out for him!' That caused the first delay, and meanwhile various things happened. One of them was that as time went on she made, charming as she was, more and more friends, and that it regularly befell that these friends were sufficiently also friends of his to bring him up in conversation. It was odd that without belonging, as it were, to the same world or, according to the horrid term, the same set, my baffled pair should have happened in so many cases to fall in with the same people and make them join in the droll chorus. She had friends who didn't know each other but who inevitably and punctually recommended *him*. She had also the sort of originality, the intrinsic interest, that led her to be kept by each of us as a private resource, cultivated jealously, more or less in secret, as a person whom one didn't meet in society, whom it was not for everyone – whom it was not for the vulgar – to approach, and with whom therefore acquaintance was particularly difficult and particularly precious. We saw her separately, with appointments and conditions, and found it made on the whole for harmony not to tell each other. Somebody had always had a note from her still later than somebody else. There was some silly woman who for a long time, among the unprivileged, owed to three simple visits to Richmond a reputation for being intimate with 'lots of awfully clever out-of-the-way people'.

Everyone has had friends it has seemed a happy thought to bring together, and everyone remembers that his happiest thoughts have not been his greatest successes; but I doubt if there was ever a case in which the failure was in such direct proportion to the quantity of influence set in motion. It's really perhaps here the quantity of influence that was most remarkable. My lady and my gentleman each pronounced it to me and others quite a subject for a roaring farce. The reason first given had with time dropped out of sight and fifty better ones flourished on top of it. They were so awfully alike: they had the same ideas and tricks and tastes, the same prejudices and superstitions and heresies; they said the same things and sometimes did them; they liked and disliked the same persons and places, the same books, authors and styles; there were touches of resemblance even in their looks and features. It established much of a propriety that they were in common parlance equally 'nice' and almost equally handsome. But the great sameness, for wonder and chatter, was their rare perversity in regard to being photographed. They were the only persons ever heard of who had never been 'taken' and who had a passionate objection to it. They just *wouldn't* be – no, not for anything anyone could say. I had loudly complained of this; him in particular I had so vainly desired to be able to show on my drawing-room chimney piece in a Bond Street[4] frame. It was at any rate the very liveliest of all the reasons why they ought to know each other – all the lively reasons reduced to naught by the strange law that had made them bang so many doors in each other's face, made them the buckets in the well, the two ends of the seesaw, the two parties in the State, so that when one was up the other was down, when one was out the other was in; neither by any possibility entering a house till the other had left it or leaving it all unawares till the other was at hand. They only arrived when they had been given up, which was precisely also when they departed. They were in a word alternate and incompatible; they missed each other with an inveteracy that could be explained only by its being preconcerted. It was however so far from preconcerted that it had ended – literally after several years – by disappointing and annoying them. I don't think their curiosity was lively till it had been proved utterly vain. A great deal was of course done to help them, but it merely laid wires for them to trip. To give examples, I should have to have taken notes; but I happen to remember that neither had ever been able to dine on the right occasion. The right occasion for each was the occasion that would be wrong for the other. On the wrong one they were most punctual, and there were never any but wrong ones. The very elements conspired and the constitution of man re-enforced them. A cold, a headache, a bereavement, a storm, a fog, an earthquake, a cataclysm, infallibly intervened. The whole business was beyond a joke.

Yet as a joke it had still to be taken, though one couldn't help feeling that the joke had made the situation serious, had produced on the part of each a consciousness, an awkwardness, a positive dread of the last accident of all, the only one with any freshness left, the accident that *would* bring them together. The final effect of its predecessors had been to kindle this instinct. They were quite ashamed – perhaps even a little of each other. So much preparation, so much frustration: what indeed could be good enough for it all to lead up to? A mere meeting would be mere flatness. Did I see them at the end of years, they often asked, just stupidly confronted? If they were bored by the joke, they might be worse bored by something else. They made exactly the same reflections, and each in some manner was sure to hear of the other's. I really think it was this peculiar diffidence that finally controlled the situation. I mean that if they had failed for the first year or two because they couldn't help it, they kept up the habit because they had – what shall I call it? – grown nervous. It really took some lurking volition to account for anything both so regular and so ridiculous.

III

When to crown our long acquaintance I accepted his renewed offer of marriage, it was humorously said, I know, that I had made the gift of his photograph a condition. This was so far true that I had refused to give him mine without it. At any rate, I had him at last, in his high distinction, on the chimney piece, where the day she called to congratulate me she came nearer than she had ever done to seeing him. He had in being taken set her an example that I invited her to follow; he had sacrificed his perversity – wouldn't she sacrifice hers? She too must give me something on my engagement – wouldn't she give me the companion-piece? She laughed and shook her head; she had headshakes whose impulse seemed to come from as far away as the breeze that stirs a flower. The companion-piece to the portrait of my future husband was the portrait of his future wife. She had taken her stand – she could depart from it as little as she could explain it. It was a prejudice, an *entêtement*,[5] a vow – she would live and die unphotographed. Now too she was alone in that state: this was what she liked; it made her so much more original. She rejoiced in the fall of her late associate and looked a long time at his picture, about which she made no memorable remark, though she even turned it over to see the back. About our engagement she was charming – full of cordiality and sympathy. 'You've known him even longer than I've *not*,' she said, 'and that seems a very long time.' She understood how we had jogged together over hill and dale[6] and how inevitable it was that we should now rest together. I'm definite about all this because what followed is so strange that it's a kind of relief to me to mark the point up to which our relations were as natural as ever. It was I myself who in a sudden madness altered and destroyed them. I see now that she gave me no pretext and that I only found one in the way she looked at the fine face in the Bond Street frame. How then would I have had her look at it? What I had wanted from the first was to make her care for him. Well, that was what I still wanted – up to the moment of her having promised me she would on this occasion really aid me to break the silly spell that had kept them asunder. I had arranged with him to do his part if she would as triumphantly do hers. I was on a different footing now – I was on a footing to answer for him. I would positively engage that at five on the following Saturday he should be on that spot. He was out of town on pressing business, but, pledged to keep his promise to the letter, would return on purpose and in abundant time. 'Are you perfectly sure?' I remember she asked, looking grave and considering: I thought she had turned a little pale. She was tired, she was indisposed: it was a pity he was to see her after all at so poor a moment. If he only *could* have seen her five years before! However, I replied that this time I was sure and that success therefore depended simply on herself. At five o'clock on the Saturday she would find him in a particular chair I pointed out, the one in which he usually sat and in which – though this I didn't mention – he had been sitting when, the week before, he put the question of our future to me in the way that had brought me round. She looked at it in silence, just as she had looked at the photograph, while I repeated for the twentieth time that it was too preposterous one shouldn't somehow succeed in introducing to one's dearest friend one's second self. '*Am* I your dearest friend?' she asked with a smile that for a moment brought back her beauty. I replied by pressing her to my bosom; after which she said: 'Well, I'll come. I'm extraordinarily afraid, but you may count on me.'

When she had left me I began to wonder what she was afraid of, for she had spoken as if she fully meant it. The next day, late in the afternoon, I had three lines from her: she had found on getting home the announcement of her husband's death. She hadn't seen him for seven years, but she wished me to know it in this way before I should hear of it in another. It made however in her life, strange and sad to say, so little difference that she would scrupulously keep her appointment. I rejoiced for her – I supposed it would make at least the difference of her having more money; but even in this diversion, far from forgetting she had said she was afraid, I seemed to catch sight of a reason for her being so. Her fear, as the evening went on, became contagious, and the contagion took in my breast the form of a sudden panic. It wasn't jealousy – it just was the dread of jealousy. I called myself a fool for not having been quiet till we were man and wife. After that I should somehow feel secure. It was only a question of waiting another month – a trifle surely for people who had waited so long. It had been plain enough she was nervous, and now she was free her nervousness wouldn't be less. What was it therefore but a sharp foreboding? She had been hitherto the victim of interference, but it was quite possible she would henceforth be the source of it. The victim in that case would be my simple self. What had the interference been but the finger of Providence pointing out a danger? The danger was of course for poor *me*. It had been kept at bay by a series of accidents unexampled in their frequency; but the reign of accident was now visibly at an end. I had an intimate conviction that both parties would keep the tryst. It was more and more impressed on me that they were approaching, converging. They were like the seekers for the hidden object in the game of blindfold; they had one and the other begun to 'burn'. We had talked about breaking the spell; well, it would be effectually broken – unless indeed it should merely take another form and overdo their encounters as it had overdone their escapes. This was something I couldn't sit still for thinking of; it kept me awake – at midnight, I was full of unrest. At last I felt there was only one way of laying the ghost. If the reign of accident was over, I must just take up the succession. I sat down and wrote a hurried note which would meet him on his return and which as the servants had gone to bed I sallied forth bareheaded into the empty gusty street to drop into the nearest pillar box. It was to tell him that I shouldn't be able to be at home in the afternoon as I had hoped and that he must postpone his visit till dinner-time. This was an implication that he would find me alone.

IV

When accordingly at five she presented herself, I naturally felt false and base. My act had been a momentary madness, but I had at least, as they say, to live up to it. She remained an hour; he of course never came; and I could only persist in my perfidy. I had thought it best to let her come; singular as this now seems to me, I held it diminished my guilt. Yet as she sat there so visibly white and weary, stricken with a sense of everything her husband's death had opened up, I felt a really piercing pang of pity and remorse. If I didn't tell her on the spot what I had done, it was because I was too ashamed. I feigned astonishment – I feigned it to the end; I protested that if ever I had had confidence I had had it that day. I blush as I tell my story – I take it as my penance. There was nothing indignant I didn't say about him; I invented suppositions, attenuations; I admitted in stupefaction, as the hands of the clock travelled, that their luck hadn't turned. She smiled at this vision of their 'luck', but she looked anxious – she looked unusual: the only thing that kept me up was the fact that, oddly enough, she wore mourning – no great depths of crape, but simple and scrupulous black. She had in her bonnet three small black feathers. She carried a little muff of astrachan.[7] This put me, by the aid of some acute reflection, a little in the right. She had written to me that the sudden event made no difference for her, but apparently it made as much difference as that. If she was inclined to the usual forms, why didn't she observe that of not going the first day or two out to tea? There was someone she wanted so much to see that she couldn't wait till her husband was buried. Such a betrayal of eagerness made me hard and cruel enough to practise my odious deceit, though at the same time, as the hour waxed and waned, I suspected in her something deeper still than disappointment and somewhat less successfully concealed. I mean a strange underlying relief, the soft low emission of the breath that comes when a danger is past. What happened as she spent her barren hour with me was that at last she gave him up. She let him go for ever. She made the most graceful joke of it that I've ever seen made of anything; but it was for all that a great date in her life. She spoke with her mild gaiety of all the other vain times, the long game of hide-and-seek, the unprecedented queerness of such a relation. For it *was*, or had been, a relation, wasn't it, hadn't it? That was just the absurd part of it. When she got up to go, I said to her that it was more a relation than ever, but that I hadn't the face after what had occurred to propose to her for the present another opportunity. It was plain that the only valid opportunity would be my accomplished marriage. Of course she would be at my wedding? It was even to be hoped that *he* would.

'If *I* am, he won't be!' – I remember the high quaver and the little break of her laugh. I admitted there might be something in that. The thing was therefore to get us safely married first. 'That won't help us. Nothing will help us!' she said as she kissed me farewell. 'I shall never, never see him!' It was with those words she left me.

I could bear her disappointment as I've called it; but when a couple of hours later I received him at dinner, I discovered I couldn't bear his. The way my manoeuvre might have affected him hadn't been particularly present to me; but the result of it was the first word of reproach that had ever yet dropped from him. I say 'reproach' because that expression is scarcely too strong for the terms in which he conveyed to me his surprise that under the extraordinary circumstances I shouldn't have found some means not to deprive him of such an occasion. I might really have managed either not to be obliged to go out or to let their meeting take place all the same. They would probably have got on, in my drawing-room, well enough without me. At this I quite broke down – I confessed my iniquity and the miserable reason of it. I hadn't put her off and I hadn't gone out; she had been there and, after waiting for him an hour, had departed in the belief that he had been absent by his own fault.

'She must think me a precious brute!' he exclaimed. 'Did she say of me' – and I remember the just perceptible catch of breath in his pause – 'what she had a right to say?'

'I assure you she said nothing that showed the least feeling. She looked at your photograph, she even turned round the back of it, on which your address happens to be inscribed. Yet it provoked her to no demonstration. She doesn't care so much as all that.'

'Then why are you afraid of her?'

'It wasn't of her I was afraid. It was of you.'

'Did you think I'd be so sure to fall in love with her? You never alluded to such a possibility before,' he went on as I remained silent. 'Admirable person as you pronounced her, that wasn't the light in which you showed her to me.'

'Do you mean that if it *had* been you'd have managed by this time to catch a glimpse of her? I didn't fear things then,' I added. 'I hadn't the same reason.'

He kissed me at this, and when I remembered that she had done so an hour or two before I felt for an instant as if he were taking from my lips the very pressure of hers. In spite of kisses, the incident had shed a certain chill, and I suffered horribly from the sense that he had seen me guilty of a fraud. He had seen it only through my frank avowal, but I was as unhappy as if I had a stain to efface. I couldn't get over the manner of his looking at me when I spoke of her apparent indifference to his not having come. For the first time since I had known him, he seemed to have expressed a doubt of my word. Before we parted I told him that I'd undeceive her – start the first thing in the morning for Richmond and there let her know he had been blameless. At this he kissed me again. I'd expiate my sin, I said; I'd humble myself in the dust; I'd confess and ask to be forgiven. At this he kissed me once more.

V

In the train the next day, this struck me as a good deal for him to have consented to; but my purpose was firm enough to carry me on. I mounted the long hill to where the view begins, and then I knocked at her door. I was a trifle mystified by the fact that her blinds were still drawn, reflecting that if in the stress of my compunction I had come early I had certainly yet allowed people time to get up.

'At home, mum? She has left home for ever.'

I was extraordinarily startled by this announcement of the elderly parlour-maid. 'She has gone away?'

'She's dead, mum, please.' Then as I gasped at the horrible word: 'She died last night.'

The loud cry that escaped me sounded even in my own ears like some harsh violation of the hour. I felt for the moment as if I had killed her; I turned faint and saw through a vagueness the woman hold out her arms to me. Of what next happened I've no recollection, nor of anything but my friend's poor stupid cousin, in a darkened room, after an interval that I suppose very brief, sobbing at me in a smothered accusatory way. I can't say how long it took me to

understand, to believe and then to press back with an immense effort
that pang of responsibility which, superstitiously, insanely, had been
at first almost all I was conscious of. The doctor, after the fact, had
been superlatively wise and clear: he was satisfied of a long-latent
weakness of the heart, determined probably years before by the
agitations and terrors to which her marriage had introduced her.
She had had in those days cruel scenes with her husband, she had
been in fear of her life. All emotion, everything in the nature of
anxiety and suspense had been after that to be strongly deprecated,
as in her marked cultivation of a quiet life she was evidently well
aware; but who could say that anyone, especially a 'real lady', might
be successfully protected from *every* little rub? She had had one a day
or two before in the news of her husband's death – since there were
shocks of all kinds, not only those of grief and surprise. For that
matter, she had never dreamed of so near a release: it had looked
uncommonly as if he would live as long as herself. Then in the
evening, in town, she had manifestly had some misadventure:
something must have happened there that it would be imperative to
clear up. She had come back very late – it was past eleven o'clock,
and on being met in the hall by her cousin, who was extremely
anxious, had allowed she was tired and must rest a moment before
mounting the stairs. They had passed together into the dining-
room, her companion proposing a glass of wine and bustling to the
sideboard to pour it out. This took but a moment, and when my
informant turned round our poor friend had not had time to seat
herself. Suddenly, with a small moan that was barely audible, she
dropped upon the sofa. She was dead. What unknown 'little rub' had
dealt her the blow? What concussion, in the name of wonder, *had*
awaited her in town? I mentioned immediately the one thinkable
ground of disturbance – her having failed to meet at my house, to
which by invitation for the purpose she had come at five o'clock, the
gentleman I was to be married to, who had been accidentally kept
away and with whom she had no acquaintance whatever. This
obviously counted for little; but something else might easily have
occurred: nothing in the London streets was more possible than an
accident, especially an accident in those desperate cabs. What had
she done, where had she gone on leaving my house? I had taken for
granted she had gone straight home. We both presently remembered that in her excursions to town she sometimes, for
convenience, for refreshment, spent an hour or two at the 'Gentle-
women', the quiet little ladies' club, and I promised that it should be
my first care to make at that establishment an earnest appeal. Then

we entered the dim and dreadful chamber where she lay locked up in death and where, asking after a little to be left alone with her, I remained for half an hour. Death had made her, had kept her beautiful; but I felt above all, as I knelt at her bed, that it had made her, had kept her silent. It had turned the key on something I was concerned to know.

On my return from Richmond and after another duty had been performed, I drove to his chambers. It was the first time, but I had often wanted to see them. On the staircase, which, as the house contained twenty sets of rooms, was unrestrictedly public, I met his servant, who went back with me and ushered me in. At the sound of my entrance he appeared in the doorway of a further room, and the instant we were alone I produced my news: 'She's dead!'

'Dead?' He was tremendously struck, and I noticed he had no need to ask whom, in this abruptness, I meant.

'She died last evening – just after leaving me.'

He stared with the strangest expression, his eyes searching mine as for a trap. 'Last evening – after leaving you?' He repeated my words in stupefaction. Then he brought out, so that it was in stupefaction I heard, 'Impossible! I saw her.'

'You "saw" her?'

'On that spot – where you stand.'

This called back to me after an instant, as if to help me to take it in, the great wonder of the warning of his youth. 'In the hour of death – I understand: as you so beautifully saw your mother.'

'Ah *not as* I saw my mother – not that way, not that way!' He was deeply moved by my news – far more moved, it was plain, than he would have been the day before: it gave me a vivid sense that, as I had then said to myself, there was indeed a relation between them and that he had actually been face to face with her. Such an idea, by its reassertion of his extraordinary privilege, would have suddenly presented him as painfully abnormal hadn't he vehemently insisted on the difference. 'I saw her living. I saw her to speak to her. I saw her as I see you now.'

It's remarkable that for a moment, though only for a moment, I found relief in the more personal, as it were, but also the more natural, of the two odd facts. The next, as I embraced this image of her having come to him on leaving me and of just what it accounted for in the disposal of her time, I demanded with a shade of harshness of which I was aware: 'What on earth did she come for?'

He had now had a minute to think – to recover himself and judge of effects, so that if it was still with excited eyes he spoke, he showed a conscious redness and made an inconsequent attempt to smile away the gravity of his words. 'She came just to see me. She came – after what had passed at your house – so that we *should*, nevertheless at last meet. The impulse seemed to me exquisite, and that was the way I took it.'

I looked round the room where she had been – where *she* had been and I never had till now. 'And was the way you took it the way she expressed it?'

'She only expressed it by being here and by letting me look at her. That was enough!' he cried with an extraordinary laugh.

I wondered more and more. 'You mean she didn't speak to you?'

'She said nothing. She only looked at me as I looked at her.'

'And you didn't speak either?'

He gave me again his painful smile. 'I thought of *you*. The situation was every way delicate. I used the finest tact. But she saw she had pleased me.' He even repeated his dissonant laugh.

'She evidently "pleased" you!' Then I thought a moment. 'How long did she stay?'

'How can I say? It seemed twenty minutes, but it was probably a good deal less.'

'Twenty minutes of silence!' I began to have my definite view and now in fact quite to clutch at it. 'Do you know you're telling me a thing positively monstrous?'

He had been standing with his back to the fire; at this, with a pleading look, he came to me. 'I beseech you, dearest, to take it kindly.'

I could take it kindly, and I signified as much; but I couldn't somehow, as he rather awkwardly opened his arms, let him draw me to him. So there fell between us for an appreciable time the discomfort of a great silence.

VI

He broke it by presently saying: 'There's absolutely no doubt of her death?'

'Unfortunately none. I've just risen from my knees by the bed where they've laid her out.'

He fixed his eyes hard on the floor; then he raised them to mine. 'How does she look?'

'She looks – at peace.'

He turned away again while I watched him; but after a moment he began: 'At what hour then – ?'

'It must have been near midnight. She dropped as she reached her house – from an affection of the heart which she knew herself and her physician knew her to have, but of which, patiently, bravely, she had never spoken to me.'

He listened intently and for a minute was unable to speak. At last he broke out with an accent of which the almost boyish confidence, the really sublime simplicity, rings in my ears as I write: 'Wasn't she *wonderful!*' Even at the time I was able to do it justice enough to answer that I had always told him so; but the next minute, as if after speaking he had caught a glimpse of what he might have made me feel, he went on quickly: 'You can easily understand that if she didn't get home till midnight – '

I instantly took him up. 'There was plenty of time for you to have seen her? How so,' I asked, 'when you didn't leave my house till late? I don't remember the very moment – I was preoccupied. But you know that though you said you had lots to do, you sat for some time after dinner. She, on her side, was all the evening at the "Gentle-women", I've just come from there – I've ascertained. She had tea there; she remained a long long time.'

'What was she doing all the long long time?'

I saw him eager to challenge at every step my account of the matter; and the more he showed this the more I was moved to emphasise that version, to prefer with apparent perversity an explanation which only deepened the marvel and the mystery, but which, of the two prodigies it had to choose from, my reviving jealousy found easiest to accept. He stood there pleading with a candour that now seems to me beautiful for the privilege of having in spite of supreme defeat known the living woman; while I, with a passion I wonder at today, though it still smoulders in a manner in its ashes, could only reply that, through a strange gift shared by her with his mother and on her own side likewise hereditary, the miracle of his youth had been renewed for him, the miracle of hers for her. She had been to him – yes, and by an impulse as charming as he liked; but oh she hadn't been in the body! It was a simple question of evidence. I had had, I maintained, a definite statement of what she had done – most of the time – at the little club. The place was almost empty, but the servants had noticed her. She had sat motionless in a deep chair by the drawing-room fire; she had leaned back her head, she had closed her eyes, she had seemed softly to sleep.

'I see. But till what o'clock?'

'There,' I was obliged to answer, 'the servants fail me a little. The portress in particular is unfortunately a fool, even though she too is supposed to be a gentlewoman. She was evidently at that period of the evening, without a substitute and against regulations, absent for some little time from the cage in which it's her business to watch the comings and goings. She's muddled, she palpably prevaricates; so I can't positively, from her observation, give you an hour. But it was remarked towards half-past ten that our poor friend was no longer in the club.'

It suited him down to the ground. 'She came straight here, and from here she went straight to the train.'

'She couldn't have run it so close,' I declared. 'That was a thing she particularly never did.'

'There was no need of running it close, my dear – she had plenty of time. Your memory's at fault about my having left you late: I left you, as it happens, unusually early. I'm sorry my stay with you seemed long, for I was back here by ten.'

'To put yourself into your slippers,' I retorted, 'and fall asleep in your chair. You slept till morning – you saw her in a dream!' He looked at me in silence and with sombre eyes – eyes that showed me he had some irritation to repress. Presently I went on: 'You had a visit, at an extraordinary hour, from a lady – *soit*:[8] nothing in the world's more probable. But there are ladies and ladies. How in the name of goodness, if she was unannounced and dumb and you had into the bargain never seen the least portrait of her – how could you identify the person we're talking of?'

'Haven't I to absolute satiety heard her described? I'll describe her for you in every particular.'

'Don't!' I cried with a promptness that made him laugh once more. I coloured at this, but I continued: 'Did your servant introduce her?'

'He wasn't here – he's always away when he's wanted. One of the features of this big house is that from the street door the different floors are accessible practically without challenge. My servant makes love to a young person employed in the rooms above these, and he had a long bout of it last evening. When he's out on that job he leaves my outer door, on the staircase, so much ajar as to enable him to slip back without a sound. The door then only requires a push. She pushed it – that simply took a little courage.'

'A little? It took tons! And it took all sorts of impossible calculations.'

'Well, she had them – she made them. Mind you, I don't deny for a moment,' he added, 'that it was very very wonderful!'

Something in his tone kept me a time from trusting myself to speak. At last I said: 'How did she come to know where you live?'

'By remembering the address on the little label the shop-people happily left sticking to the frame I had had made for my photograph.'

'And how was she dressed?'

'In mourning, my own dear. No great depths of crape, but simple and scrupulous black. She had in her bonnet three small black feathers. She carried a little muff of astrachan. She has near the left eye,' he continued, 'a tiny vertical scar – '

I stopped him short. 'The mark of a caress from her husband.' Then I added: 'How close you must have been to her!' He made no answer to this, and I thought he blushed, observing which I broke straight off. 'Well, goodbye.'

'You won't stay a little?' He came to me again tenderly, and this time I suffered him. 'Her visit had its beauty,' he murmured as he held me, 'but yours has a greater one.'

I let him kiss me, but I remembered, as I had remembered the day before, that the last kiss she had given, as I supposed, in this world had been for the lips he touched. 'I'm life, you see,' I answered. 'What you saw last night was death.'

'It was life – it was life!'

He spoke with a soft stubbornness – I disengaged myself. We stood looking at each other hard. 'You describe the scene – so far as you describe it at all – in terms that are incomprehensible. She was in the room before you knew it?'

'I looked up from my letter-writing – at that table under the lamp I had been wholly absorbed in it – and she stood before me.'

'Then what did you do?'

'I sprang up with an ejaculation, and she, with a smile, laid her finger, ever so warningly, yet with a sort of delicate dignity, to her lips. I knew it meant silence, but the strange thing was that it seemed immediately to explain and to justify her. We at any rate stood for a time that, as I've told you, I can't calculate, face to face. It was just as you and I stand now.'

'Simply staring?'

He shook an impatient head. 'Ah! *we're* not staring!'

'Yes, but we're talking.'

'Well, *we* were – after a fashion.' He lost himself in the memory of it. 'It was as friendly as this.' I had on my tongue's end to ask if that was saying much for it, but I made the point instead that what they had evidently done was to gaze in mutual admiration. Then I asked if his recognition of her had been immediate. 'Not quite,' he replied, 'for of course I didn't expect her; but it came to me long before she went who she was – who only she could be.'

I thought a little. 'And how did she at last go?'

'Just as she arrived. The door was open behind her and she passed out.'

'Was she rapid – slow?'

'Rather quick. But looking behind her,' he smiled to add. 'I let her go, for I perfectly knew I was to take it as she wished.'

I was conscious of exhaling a long vague sigh. 'Well, you must take it now as *I* wish – you must let *me* go.'

At this he drew near me again, detaining and persuading me, declaring with all due gallantry that I was a very different matter. I'd have given anything to have been able to ask him if he had touched her, but the words refused to form themselves: I knew to the last tenth of a tone how horrid and vulgar they'd sound. I said something else – I forget exactly what; it was feebly tortuous and intended, meanly enough, to make him tell me without my putting the question. But he didn't tell me; he only repeated, as from a glimpse of the propriety of soothing and consoling me, the sense of his declaration of some minutes before – the assurance that she was indeed exquisite, as I had always insisted, but that I was his 'real' friend and his very own for ever. This led me to reassert, in the spirit of my previous rejoinder, that I had at least the merit of being alive; which in turn drew from him again the flash of contradiction I dreaded. 'Oh *she* was alive! She was, she was!'

'She was dead, she was dead!' I asseverated with an energy, a determination it should *be* so, which comes back to me now almost as grotesque. But the sound of the word as it rang out filled me suddenly with horror, and all the natural emotion the meaning of it might have evoked in other conditions gathered and broke in a flood. It rolled over me that here was a great affection quenched and how much I had loved and trusted her. I had a vision at the same time of the lonely beauty of her end. 'She's gone – she's lost to us for ever!' I burst into sobs.

'That's exactly what I feel,' he exclaimed, speaking with extreme kindness and pressing me to him for comfort. 'She's gone; she's lost to us for ever: so what does it matter now?' He bent over me, and when his face had touched mine I scarcely knew if it were wet with my tears or with his own.

VII

It was my theory, my conviction, it became, as I may say, my attitude, that they had still never 'met'; and it was just on this ground I felt it generous to ask him to stand with me at her grave. He did so very modestly and tenderly, and I assumed, though he himself clearly cared nothing for the danger, that the solemnity of the occasion, largely made up of persons who had known them both and had a sense of the long joke, would sufficiently deprive his presence of all light association. On the question of what had happened the evening of her death little more passed between us; I had been taken by a horror of the element of evidence. On either hypothesis it was gross and prying. He on his side lacked producible corroboration – everything, that is, but a statement of his house-porter, on his own admission a most casual and intermittent personage – that between the hours of ten o'clock and midnight no less than three ladies in deep black had flitted in and out of the place. This proved far too much; we had neither of us any use for three. He knew I considered I had accounted for every fragment of her time, and we dropped the matter as settled; we abstained from further discussion. What *I* knew however was that he abstained to please me rather than because he yielded to my reasons. He didn't yield – he was only indulgent; he clung to his interpretation because he liked it better. He liked it better, I held, because it had more to say to his vanity.

That, in a similar position, wouldn't have been its effect on me, though I had doubtless quite as much; but these are things of individual humour and as to which no person can judge for another. I should have supposed it more gratifying to be the subject of one of those inexplicable occurrences that are chronicled in thrilling books and disputed about at learned meetings; I could conceive, on the part of a being just engulfed in the infinite and still vibrating with human emotion, of nothing more fine and pure, more high and august, than such an impulse of reparation, of admonition, or even of curiosity. *That* was beautiful, if one would, and I should in his place have thought more of myself for being so distinguished and so selected. It was public that he had already, that he had long figured in that light, and what was such a fact in itself but almost a proof? Each of the strange visitations contributed to establish the other. He had a different feeling; but he had also, I hasten to add, an unmistakeable desire not to make a stand or, as they say, a fuss about it. I might believe what I liked – the more so that the whole thing was in a manner a mystery of my producing. It was an event of my history, a puzzle of my consciousness, not of his; therefore he would take about it any tone that struck me as convenient. We had both at all events other business on hand; we were pressed with preparations for our marriage.

Mine were assuredly urgent, but I found as the days went on that to believe what I 'liked' was to believe what I was more and more intimately convinced of. I found also that I didn't like it so much as that came to, or that the pleasure at all events was far from being the cause of my conviction. My obsession, as I may really call it and as I began to perceive, refused to be elbowed away, as I had hoped, by my sense of paramount duties. If I had a great deal to do I had still more to think of, and the moment came when my occupations were gravely menaced by my thoughts. I see it all now, I feel it, I live it over. It's terribly void of joy, it's full indeed to overflowing of bitterness; and yet I must do myself justice – I couldn't have been other than I was. The same strange impressions, had I to meet them again, would produce the same deep anguish, the same sharp doubts, the same still sharper certainties. Oh it's all easier to remember than to write, but even could I retrace the business hour by hour, could I find terms for the inexpressible, the ugliness and the pain would quickly stay my hand. Let me then note very simply and briefly that a week before our wedding day, three weeks after her death, I knew in all my fibres that I had something very serious to look in the face and that if I was to make this effort I must make it on the spot and before another hour should elapse. My unextinguished jealousy – that was the Medusa-mask.[9] It hadn't died with her death, it had lividly survived, and it was fed by suspicions unspeakable. They *would* be unspeakable today, that is, if I hadn't felt the sharp need of uttering them at the time. This need took possession of me – to save me, as it seemed, from my fate. When once it had done so I saw – in the urgency of the case, the diminishing hours and shrinking interval – only one issue, that of absolute promptness and frankness. I could at least not do him the wrong of delaying another day; I could at least treat my difficulty as too fine for a subterfuge. Therefore very quietly, but none the less abruptly and hideously, I put it before him on a certain evening that we must reconsider our situation and recognise that it had completely altered.

He stared bravely. 'How in the world altered?'

'Another person has come between us.'

He took but an instant to think. 'I won't pretend not to know whom you mean.' He smiled in pity for my aberration, but he meant to be kind. 'A woman dead and buried!'

'She's buried, but she's not dead. She's dead for the world – she's dead for me. But she's not dead for you.'

'You hark back to the different construction we put on her appearance that evening?'

'No,' I answered, 'I hark back to nothing. I've no need of it. I've more than enough with what's before me.'

'And pray, darling, what may that be?'

'You're completely changed.'

'By that absurdity?' he laughed.

'Not so much by that one as by other absurdities that have followed it.'

'And what may *they* have been?'

We had faced each other fairly, with eyes that didn't flinch; but his had a dim strange light, and my certitude triumphed in his perceptible paleness. 'Do you really pretend,' I asked, 'not to know what they are?'

'My dear child,' he replied, 'you describe them too sketchily!'

I considered a moment. 'One may well be embarrassed to finish the picture! But from that point of view – and from the beginning – what was ever more embarrassing than your idiosyncrasy?'

He invoked his vagueness – a thing he always did beautifully. 'My idiosyncrasy?'

'Your notorious, your peculiar power.'

He gave a great shrug of impatience, a groan of overdone disdain. 'Oh my peculiar power!'

'Your accessibility to forms of life,' I coldly went on, 'your command of impressions, appearances, contacts, closed – for our gain or our loss – to the rest of us. That was originally a part of the deep interest with which you inspired me – one of the reasons I was amused, I was indeed positively proud, to know you. It was a magnificent distinction; it's a magnificent distinction still. But of course I had no prevision then of the way it would operate now; and even had that been the case, I should have had none of the extraordinary way in which its action would affect me.'

'To what in the name of goodness,' he pleadingly enquired, 'are you fantastically alluding?' Then as I remained silent, gathering a tone for my charge, 'How in the world *does* it operate?' he went on; 'and how in the world are you affected?'

'She missed you for five years,' I said, 'but she never misses you now. You're making it up!'

'Making it up?' He had begun to turn from white to red.

'You see her – you see her: you see her every night!' He gave a loud sound of derision, but I felt it ring false. 'She comes to you as she came that evening,' I declared; 'having tried it she found she liked it!' I was able, with God's help, to speak without blind passion or vulgar violence; but those were the exact words – and far from 'sketchy' they then appeared to me – that I uttered. He had turned away in his laughter, clapping his hands at my folly, but in an instant he faced me again with a change of expression that struck me. 'Do you dare to deny,' I then asked, 'that you habitually see her?'

He had taken the line of indulgence, of meeting me halfway and kindly humouring me. At all events he to my astonishment suddenly said: 'Well, my dear, what if I do?'

'It's your natural right: it belongs to your constitution and to your wonderful if not perhaps quite enviable fortune. But you'll easily understand that it separates us. I unconditionally release you.'

'Release me?'

'You must choose between me and her.'

He looked at me hard. 'I see.' Then he walked away a little, as if grasping what I had said and thinking how he had best treat it. At last he turned on me afresh. 'How on earth do you know such an awfully private thing?'

'You mean because you've tried so hard to hide it? It *is* awfully private, and you may believe I shall never betray you. You've done your best, you've acted your part, you've behaved, poor dear! loyally and admirably. Therefore I've watched you in silence, playing my part too; I've noted every drop in your voice, every absence in your eyes, every effort in your indifferent hand: I've waited till I was utterly sure and miserably unhappy. How *can* you hide it when you're abjectly in love with her, when you're sick almost to death with the joy of what she gives you?' I checked his quick protest with a quicker gesture. 'You love her as you've *never* loved, and, passion for passion, she gives it straight back! She rules you, she holds you, she has you all! A woman, in such a case as mine, divines and feels and sees; she's not a dull dunce who has to be "credibly informed". You come to me mechanically, compunctiously, with the dregs of your tenderness and the remnant of your life. I can renounce you, but I can't share you: the best of you is hers, I know what it is and freely give you up to her for ever!'

He made a gallant fight, but it couldn't be patched up; he repeated his denial, he retracted his admission, he ridiculed my charge, of which I freely granted him moreover the indefensible extravagance. I didn't pretend for a moment that we were talking of common things; I didn't pretend for a moment that he and she were common people.

Pray, if they *had* been, how should I ever have cared for them? They had enjoyed a rare extension of being and they had caught me up in their flight; only I couldn't breathe in such air and I promptly asked to be set down. Everything in the facts was monstrous, and most of all my lucid perception of them; the only thing allied to nature and truth was my having to act on that perception. I felt after I had spoken in this sense that my assurance was complete; nothing had been wanting to it but the sight of my effect on him. He disguised indeed the effect in a cloud of chaff, a diversion that gained him time and covered his retreat. He challenged my sincerity, my sanity, almost my humanity, and that of course widened our breach and confirmed our rupture. He did everything in short but convince me either that I was wrong or that he was unhappy: we separated and I left him to his inconceivable communion.

He never married, any more than I've done. When six years later, in solitude and silence, I heard of his death, I hailed it as a direct contribution to my theory. It was sudden, it was never properly accounted for, it was surrounded by circumstances in which – for oh I took them to pieces! – I distinctly read an intention, the mark of his own hidden hand. It was the result of a long necessity, of an unquenchable desire. To say exactly what I mean, it was a response to an irresistible call.

The Turn of the Screw

PROLOGUE

THE STORY had held us, round the fire, sufficiently breathless, but except the obvious remark that it was gruesome, as on Christmas Eve in an old house a strange tale should essentially be, I remember no comment uttered till somebody happened to note it as the only case he had met in which such a visitation had fallen on a child. The case, I may mention, was that of an apparition in just such an old house as had gathered us for the occasion – an appearance, of a dreadful kind, to a little boy sleeping in the room with his mother and waking her up in the terror of it; waking her not to dissipate his dread and soothe him to sleep again, but to encounter also herself, before she had succeeded in doing so, the same sight that had shocked him. It was this observation that drew from Douglas – not immediately, but later in the evening – a reply that had the interesting consequence to which I call attention. Someone else told a story not particularly effective, which I saw he was not following. This I took for a sign that he had himself something to produce and that we should only have to wait. We waited in fact till two nights later; but that same evening, before we scattered, he brought out what was in his mind.

'I quite agree – in regard to Griffin's ghost, or whatever it was – that its appearing first to the little boy, at so tender an age, adds a particular touch. But it's not the first occurrence of its charming kind that I know to have been concerned with a child. If the child gives the effect another turn of the screw, what do you say to *two* children – ?'

'We say, of course,' somebody exclaimed, 'that two children give two turns! Also that we want to hear about them.'

I can see Douglas there before the fire, to which he had got up to present his back, looking down at this converser with his hands in his pockets. 'Nobody but me, till now, has ever heard. It's quite too horrible.' This was naturally declared by several voices to give the thing the utmost price, and our friend, with quiet art, prepared his triumph by turning his eyes over the rest of us and going on: 'It's beyond everything. Nothing at all that I know touches it.'

'For sheer terror?' I remember asking.

He seemed to say it wasn't so simple as that; to be really at a loss how to qualify it. He passed his hand over his eyes, made a little wincing grimace. 'For dreadful – dreadfulness!'

'Oh, how delicious!' cried one of the women.

He took no notice of her; he looked at me, but as if, instead of me, he saw what he spoke of. 'For general uncanny ugliness and horror and pain.'

'Well, then,' I said, 'just sit right down and begin.'

He turned round to the fire, gave a kick to a log, watched it an instant. Then as he faced us again: 'I can't begin. I shall have to send to town.' There was a unanimous groan at this, and much reproach; after which, in his preoccupied way, he explained. 'The story's written. It's in a locked drawer – it has not been out for years. I could write to my man and enclose the key; he could send down the packet as he finds it.' It was to me in particular that he appeared to propound this – appeared almost to appeal for aid not to hesitate. He had broken a thickness of ice, the formation of many a winter; had had his reasons for a long silence. The others resented postponement, but it was just his scruples that charmed me. I adjured him to write by the first post and to agree with us for an early hearing; then I asked him if the experience in question had been his own. To this his answer was prompt. 'Oh, thank God, no!'

'And is the record yours? You took the thing down?'

'Nothing but the impression. I took that *here*' – he tapped his heart. 'I've never lost it.'

'Then your manuscript – ?'

'Is in old faded ink and in the most beautiful hand.' He hung fire again. 'A woman's. She has been dead these twenty years. She sent me the pages in question before she died.' They were all listening now, and of course there was somebody to be arch, or at any rate to draw the inference. But if he put the inference by without a smile it was also without irritation. 'She was a most charming person, but she was ten years older than I. She was my sister's governess,' he quietly said. 'She was the most agreeable woman I've ever known in her position; she would have been worthy of any whatever. It was long ago, and this episode was long before. I was at Trinity,[1] and I found her at home on my coming down the second summer. I was much there that year – it was a beautiful one; and we had, in her off-hours, some strolls and talks in the garden – talks in which she struck me as awfully clever and nice. Oh, yes; don't grin: I liked her extremely and am glad to this day to think she liked me too. If she hadn't she wouldn't have told me. She had never told anyone. It wasn't simply that she said so, but that I knew she hadn't. I was sure; I could see. You'll easily judge why when you hear.'

'Because the thing had been such a scare?'

He continued to fix me. 'You'll easily judge,' he repeated; '*you* will.'

I fixed him too. 'I see. She was in love.'

He laughed for the first time. 'You *are* acute. Yes, she was in love. That is, she *had* been. That came out – she couldn't tell her story without its coming out. I saw it, and she saw I saw it; but neither of us spoke of it. I remember the time and the place – the corner of the lawn, the shade of the great beeches and the long hot summer afternoon. It wasn't a scene for a shudder; but oh – !' He quitted the fire and dropped back into his chair.

'You'll receive the packet Thursday morning?' I said.

'Probably not till the second post.'

'Well then; after dinner – '

'You'll all meet me here?' He looked us round again. 'Isn't anybody going?' It was almost the tone of hope.

'Everybody will stay!'

'*I* will – and *I* will!' cried the ladies whose departure had been fixed. Mrs Griffin, however, expressed the need for a little more light. 'Who was it she was in love with?'

'The story will tell,' I took upon myself to reply.

'Oh, I can't wait for the story!'

'The story *won't* tell,' said Douglas; 'not in any literal, vulgar way.'

'More's the pity then. That's the only way I ever understand.'

'Won't *you* tell, Douglas?' somebody else inquired.

He sprang to his feet again. 'Yes – tomorrow. Now I must go to bed. Good-night.' And, quickly catching up a candlestick, he left us slightly bewildered. From our end of the great brown hall we heard his step on the stair; whereupon Mrs Griffin spoke. 'Well, if I don't know who she was in love with I know who *he* was.'

'She was ten years older,' said her husband.

'*Raison de plus*[2] – at that age! But it's rather nice, his long reticence.'

'Forty years!' Griffin put in.

'With this outbreak at last.'

'The outbreak,' I returned, 'will make a tremendous occasion of Thursday night'; and everyone so agreed with me that in the light of it we lost all attention for everything else. The last story, however incomplete and like the mere opening of a serial, had been told; we handshook and 'candlestuck', as somebody said, and went to bed.

I knew the next day that a letter containing the key had, by the first post, gone off to his London apartments; but in spite of – or perhaps just on account of – the eventual diffusion of this knowledge we quite let him alone till after dinner, till such an hour of the evening in fact as might best accord with the kind of emotion on which our hopes were fixed. Then he became as communicative as we could desire, and indeed gave us his best reason for being so. We had it from him again before the fire in the hall, as we had had our mild wonders of the previous night. It appeared that the narrative he had promised to read us really required for a proper intelligence a few words of prologue. Let me say here distinctly, to have done with it, that this narrative, from an exact transcript of my own made much later, is what I shall presently give. Poor Douglas, before his death – when it was in sight – committed to me the manuscript that reached him on the third of these days and that, on the same spot, with immense effect, he began to read to our hushed little circle on the night of the fourth. The departing ladies who had said they would stay didn't, of course, thank heaven, stay: they departed, in consequence of arrangements made, in a rage of curiosity, as they professed, produced by the touches with which he had already worked us up. But that only made his little final auditory more compact and select, kept it round the hearth subject to a common thrill.

The first of these touches conveyed that the written statement took up the date at a point after it had, in a manner, begun. The fact to be in possession of was therefore that his old friend, the youngest of several daughters of a poor country parson, had at the age of twenty, on taking service for the first time in the schoolroom, come up to London, in trepidation, to answer in person an advertisement that had already placed her in brief correspondence with the advertiser. This person proved, on her presenting herself for judgement at a house in Harley Street[3] that impressed her as vast and imposing – this prospective patron proved a gentleman, a bachelor in the prime of life, such a figure as had never risen, save in a dream or an old novel, before a fluttered, anxious girl out of a Hampshire vicarage. One could easily fix his type; it never, happily, dies out. He was handsome and bold and pleasant, offhand and gay and kind. He struck her, inevitably, as gallant and splendid, but what took her most of all and gave her the courage she afterwards showed was that he put the whole thing to her as a favour, an obligation he should gratefully incur. She figured him as rich, but as fearfully extravagant – saw him all in a glow of high fashion, of good looks, of expensive habits, of charming ways with women. He had for his town residence a big house filled with the spoils of travel and the trophies of the chase; but it was to his country home, an old family place in Essex, that he wished her immediately to proceed.

He had been left, by the death of their parents in India, guardian to a small nephew and a small niece, children of a younger, a military brother whom he had lost two years before. These children were, by the strangest of chances for a man in his position – a lone man without the right sort of experience or a grain of patience – very heavy on his hands. It had all been a great worry and, on his own part doubtless, a series of blunders, but he immensely pitied the poor chicks and had done all he could; had in particular sent them down to his other house, the proper place for them being of course the country, and kept them there from the first with the best people he could find to look after them, parting even with his own servants to wait on them and going down himself, whenever he might, to see how they were doing. The awkward thing was that they had practically no other relations and that his own affairs took up all his time. He had put them in possession of Bly, which was healthy and secure, and had placed at the head of their little establishment – but below stairs only – an excellent woman, Mrs Grose, whom he was sure his visitor would like and who had formerly been maid to his mother. She was now housekeeper and was also acting for the time as superintendent to the little girl, of whom, without children of her own, she was by good luck extremely fond. There were plenty of people to help, but of course the young lady who should go down as governess would be in supreme authority. She would also have, in holidays, to look after the small boy, who had been for a term at school – young as he was to be sent, but what else could be done? – and who, as the holidays were about to begin, would be back from one day to the other. There had been for the two children at first a young lady, whom they had had the misfortune to lose. She had done for them quite beautifully – she was a most respectable person – till her death, the great awkwardness of which had, precisely, left no alternative but the school for little Miles. Mrs Grose, since then, in the way of manners and things, had done as she could for Flora; and there were further, a cook, a housemaid, a dairywoman, an old pony, an old groom and an old gardener, all likewise thoroughly respectable.

So far had Douglas presented his picture when someone put a question. 'And what did the former governess die of? Of so much respectability?'

Our friend's answer was prompt. 'That will come out. I don't anticipate.'

'Pardon me – I thought that was just what you *are* doing.'

'In her successor's place,' I suggested, 'I should have wished to learn if the office brought with it – '

'Necessary danger to life?' Douglas completed my thought. 'She did wish to learn, and she did learn. You shall hear tomorrow what she learnt Meanwhile of course the prospect struck her as slightly grim. She was young, untried, nervous: it was a vision of serious duties and little company, of really great loneliness. She hesitated – took a couple of days to consult and consider. But the salary offered much exceeded her modest measure, and on a second interview she faced the music, she engaged.' And Douglas, with this, made a pause that, for the benefit of the company, moved me to throw in: 'The moral of which was of course the seduction exercised by the splendid young man. She succumbed to it.'

He got up and, as he had done the night before, went to the fire, gave a stir to a log with his foot, then stood a moment with his back to us. 'She saw him only twice.'

'Yes, but that's just the beauty of her passion.'

A little to my surprise, on this, Douglas turned round to me. 'It *was* the beauty of it. There were others,' he went on, 'who hadn't succumbed. He told her frankly all his difficulty – that for several applicants the conditions had been prohibitive. They were somehow simply afraid. It sounded dull – it sounded strange; and all the more so because of his main condition.'

'Which was – ?'

'That she should never trouble him – but never, never: neither appeal nor complain nor write about anything; only meet all questions herself, receive all moneys from his solicitor, take the whole thing over and let him alone. She promised to do this, and she mentioned to me that when, for a moment, disburdened, delighted, he held her hand, thanking her for the sacrifice, she already felt rewarded.'

'But was that all her reward?' one of the ladies asked.

'She never saw him again.'

'Oh!' said the lady; which, as our friend immediately again left us, was the only other word of importance contributed to the subject till, the next night, by the corner of the hearth, in the best chair, he opened the faded red cover of a thin, old-fashioned, gilt-edged album. The whole thing took indeed more nights than one, but on on the first occasion the same lady put another question. 'What's your title?'

'I haven't one.'

'Oh, *I* have!' I said. But Douglas, without heeding me, had begun to read with a fine clearness that was like a rendering to the ear of the beauty of his author's hand.

CHAPTER ONE

I REMEMBER the whole beginning as a succession of flights and drops, a little seesaw of the right throbs and the wrong. After rising, in town, to meet his appeal I had at all events a couple of very bad days – found all my doubts bristle again, felt indeed sure I had made a mistake. In this state of mind I spent the long hours of bumping swinging coach that carried me to the stopping-place at which I was to be met by a vehicle from the house. This convenience, I was told, had been ordered, and I found, towards the close of the June afternoon, a commodious fly in waiting for me. Driving at that hour, on a lovely day, through a country the summer sweetness of which served as a friendly welcome, my fortitude revived and, as we turned into the avenue, took a flight that was probably but a proof of the point to which it had sunk. I suppose I had expected, or had dreaded, something so dreary that what greeted me was a good surprise. I remember as a thoroughly pleasant impression the broad, clear front, its open windows and fresh curtains and the pair of maids looking out; I remember the lawn and the bright flowers and the crunch of my wheels on the gravel and the clustered treetops over which the rooks circled and cawed in the golden sky. The scene had a greatness that made it a different affair from my own scant home, and there immediately appeared at the door, with a little girl in her hand, a civil person who dropped me as decent a curtsy as if I had been the mistress or a distinguished visitor. I had received in Harley Street a narrower notion of the place, and that, as I recalled it, made me think the proprietor still more of a gentleman, suggested that what I was to enjoy might be a matter beyond his promise.

I had no drop again till the next day, for I was carried triumphantly through the following hours by my introduction to the younger of my pupils. The little girl who accompanied Mrs Grose affected me on the spot as a creature too charming not to make it a great fortune to have to do with her. She was the most beautiful child I had ever seen, and I afterwards wondered why my employer hadn't made more of a point to me of this. I slept little that night – I was too much excited; and this astonished me too, I recollect, remained with me, adding to my sense of the liberality with which I was treated. The large, impressive room, one of the best in the house, the great state bed as I almost felt it, the figured full curtains, the long glasses in which, for the first time, I could see myself from head to foot, all struck me – like the wonderful appeal of my small charge – as so many things thrown in. It was thrown in as well, from the first moment, that I should get on with Mrs Grose in a relation over which, on my way, in the coach, I fear I had rather brooded. The one appearance indeed that in this early outlook might have made me shrink again was that of her being so inordinately glad to see me. I felt within half an hour that she was so glad – stout, simple, plain, clean, wholesome woman – as to be positively on her guard against showing it too much. I wondered even then a little why she should wish *not* to show it, and that, with reflection, with suspicion, might of course have made me uneasy.

But it was a comfort that there could be no uneasiness in a connection with anything so beatific as the radiant image of my little girl, the vision of whose angelic beauty had probably more than anything else to do with the restlessness that, before morning, made me several times rise and wander about my room to take in the whole picture and prospect; to watch from my open window the faint summer dawn, to look at such stretches of the rest of the house as I could catch, and to listen, while in the fading dusk the first birds began to twitter, for the possible recurrence of a sound or two, less natural and not without but within, that I had fancied I heard. There had been a moment when I believed I recognised, faint and far, the cry of a child; there had been another when I found myself just consciously starting as at the passage, before my door, of a light footstep. But these fancies were not marked enough not to be thrown off, and it is only in the light, or the gloom, I should rather say, of other and subsequent matters that they now come back to me. To watch, teach, 'form' little Flora would too evidently be the making of a happy and useful life. It had been agreed between us downstairs that after this first occasion I should have her as a matter of course at night, her small white bed being already arranged, to that end, in my room. What I had undertaken was the whole care of her, and she had remained just this last time with Mrs Grose only as an effect of our consideration for my inevitable strangeness and her natural timidity. In spite of this timidity – which the child herself, in the oddest way in the world, had been perfectly frank and brave about, allowing it, without a sign of uncomfortable consciousness, with the deep, sweet serenity indeed of one of Raphael's[4] holy infants, to be discussed, to be imputed to her and to determine us – I felt quite sure she would presently like me. It was part of what I already liked Mrs Grose herself for, the pleasure I could see her feel in my admiration and wonder as I sat at supper with four tall candles and with my pupil, in a high chair and a bib, brightly facing me between them over bread and milk. There were naturally things that in Flora's presence could pass between us only as prodigious and gratified looks, obscure and roundabout allusions.

'And the little boy – does he look like her? Is he, too, so very remarkable?'

One wouldn't, it was already conveyed between us, too grossly flatter a child. 'Oh, miss, *most* remarkable. If you think well of this one!' – and she stood there with a plate in her hand, beaming at our companion, who looked from one of us to the other with placid, heavenly eyes that contained nothing to check us.

'Yes; if I do – ?'

'You *will* be carried away by the little gentleman!'

'Well, that, I think, is what I came for – to be carried away. I'm afraid, however,' I remember feeling the impulse to add, 'I'm rather easily carried away. I was carried away in London!'

I can still see Mrs Grose's broad face as she took this in.

'In Harley Street?'

'In Harley Street.'

'Well, miss, you're not the first – and you won't be the last.'

'Oh, I've no pretensions,' I could laugh, 'to being the only one. My other pupil, at any rate, as I understand, comes back tomorrow?'

'Not tomorrow – Friday, miss. He arrives, as you did, by the coach, under care of the guard, and is to be met by the same carriage.'

I forthwith wanted to know if the proper as well as the pleasant and friendly thing wouldn't therefore be that on the arrival of the public conveyance I should await him with his little sister; a proposition to which Mrs Grose assented so heartily that I somehow took her manner as a kind of comforting pledge – never falsified, thank heaven! – that we should on every question be quite at one. Oh, she was glad I was there!

What I felt the next day was, I suppose, nothing that could be fairly called a reaction from the cheer of my arrival; it was probably at the most only a slight oppression produced by a fuller measure of the scale, as I walked round them, gazed up at them, took them in, of my new circumstances. They had, as it were, an extent and mass for which I had not been prepared and in the presence of which I found myself, freshly, a little scared not less than a little proud. Regular lessons, in this agitation, certainly suffered some wrong; I reflected that my first duty was, by the gentlest arts I could contrive, to win the child into the sense of knowing me. I spent the day with her out of doors; I arranged with her, to her great satisfaction, that it should be she, she only, who might show me the place. She showed it step by step and room by room and secret by secret, with droll, delightful, childish talk about it, and with the result, in half an hour, of our becoming tremendous friends. Young as she was I was struck, throughout our little tour, with her confidence and courage, with the way, in empty chambers and dull corridors, on crooked staircases that made me pause, and even on the summit of an old machicolated square tower[5] that made me dizzy, her morning music, her disposition to tell me so many more things than she asked, rang out and led me on. I have not seen Bly since the day I left it, and I dare say that to my present older and more informed eyes it would show a very reduced importance. But as my little conductress, with her hair of gold and her frock of blue, danced before me round corners and pattered down passages, I had the view of a castle of romance inhabited by a rosy sprite, such a place as would somehow, for diversion of the young idea, take all colour out of storybooks and fairytales. Wasn't it just a storybook over which I had fallen a-doze and a-dream? No: it was a big, ugly, antique but convenient house, embodying a few features of a building still older, half-displaced and half-utilised, in which I had the fancy of our being almost as lost as a handful of passengers in a great drifting ship. Well, I was strangely at the helm!

CHAPTER TWO

THIS CAME HOME to me when, two days later, I drove over with Flora to meet, as Mrs Grose said, the little gentleman; and all the more for an incident that, presenting itself the second evening, had deeply disconcerted me. The first day had been, on the whole, as I have expressed, reassuring; but I was to see it wind up to a change of note. The postbag that evening – it came late – contained a letter for me which, however, in the hand of my employer, I found to be composed but of a few words enclosing another, addressed to himself, with a seal still unbroken. 'This, I recognise, is from the headmaster, and the headmaster's an awful bore. Read him, please; deal with him; but mind you don't report. Not a word. I'm off!' I broke the seal with a great effort – so great a one that I was a long time coming to it; took the unopened missive at last up to my room and only attacked it just before going to bed. I had better have let it wait till morning, for it gave me a second sleepless night. With no counsel to take, the next day, I was full of distress; and it finally got so the better of me that I determined to open myself at least to Mrs Grose.

'What does it mean? The child's dismissed his school.'

She gave me a look that I remarked at the moment; then, visibly, with a quick blankness, seemed to try to take it back. 'But aren't they all – ?'

'Sent home – yes. But only for the holidays. Miles may never go back at all.'

Consciously, under my attention, she reddened. 'They won't take him?'

'They absolutely decline.'

At this she raised her eyes, which she had turned from me; I saw them fill with good tears. 'What has he done?'

I cast about; then I judged best simply to hand her my document – which, however, had the effect of making her, without taking it, simply put her hands behind her. She shook her head sadly. 'Such things are not for me, miss.'

My counsellor couldn't read! I winced at my mistake, which I attenuated as I could, and opened the letter again to repeat it to her; then, faltering in the act and folding it up once more, I put it back in my pocket. 'Is it really *bad*?'

The tears were still in her eyes. 'Do the gentlemen say so?'

'They go into no particulars. They simply express their regret that it should be impossible to keep him. That can have but one meaning.' Mrs Grose listened with dumb emotion; she forbore to ask me what this meaning might be; so that, presently, to put the thing with some coherence and with the mere aid of her presence to my own mind, I went on: 'That he's an injury to the others.'

At this, with one of the quick turns of simple folk, she suddenly flamed up. 'Master Miles! – *him* an injury?'

There was such a flood of good faith in it that, though I had not yet seen the child, my very fears made me jump to the absurdity of the idea. I found myself, to meet my friend the better, offering it, on the spot, sarcastically. 'To his poor little innocent mates!'

'It's too dreadful,' cried Mrs Grose, 'to say such cruel things! Why, he's scarce ten years old.'

'Yes, yes; it would be incredible.'

She was evidently grateful for such a profession. 'See him, miss, first. *Then* believe it!' I felt forthwith a new impatience to see him; it was the beginning of a curiosity that, all the next hours, was to deepen almost to pain. Mrs Grose was aware, I could judge, of what she had produced in me, and she followed it up with assurance. 'You might as well believe it of the little lady. Bless her,' she added the next moment – '*look* at her!'

I turned and saw that Flora, whom, ten minutes before, I had established in the schoolroom with a sheet of white paper, a pencil and a copy of nice 'round O's,' now presented herself to view at the open door. She expressed in her little way an extraordinary detachment from disagreeable duties, looking at me, however, with a great childish light that seemed to offer it as a mere result of the affection she had conceived for my person, which had rendered necessary that she should follow me. I needed nothing more than this to feel the full force of Mrs Grose's comparison, and, catching my pupil in my arms, covered her with kisses in which there was a sob of atonement.

None the less, the rest of the day, I watched for further occasion to approach my colleague, especially as, towards evening, I began to fancy she rather sought to avoid me. I overtook her, I remember, on the staircase; we went down together and at the bottom I detained her, holding her there with a hand on her arm. 'I take what you said to me at noon as a declaration that you've never known him to be bad.'

She threw back her head; she had clearly by this time, and very honestly, adopted an attitude. 'Oh, never known him – I don't pretend *that*!'

I was upset again. 'Then you *have* known him – ?'

'Yes indeed, miss, thank God!'

On reflection I accepted this. 'You mean that a boy who never is – ?'

'Is no boy for *me*!'

I held her tighter. 'You like them with the spirit to be naughty?' Then, keeping pace with her answer, 'So do I!' I eagerly brought out. 'But not to the degree to contaminate – '

'To contaminate?' – my big word left her at a loss.

I explained it. 'To corrupt.'

She stared, taking my meaning in; but it produced in her an odd laugh. 'Are you afraid he'll corrupt *you*?' She put the question with such a fine bold humour that with a laugh, a little silly doubtless, to match her own, I gave way for the time to the apprehension of ridicule.

But the next day, as the hour for my drive approached, I cropped up in another place. 'What was the lady who was here before?'

'The last governess? She was also young and pretty – almost as young and almost as pretty, miss, even as you.'

'Ah, then I hope her youth and her beauty helped her!' I recollect throwing off. 'He seems to like us young and pretty!'

'Oh, he *did*,' Mrs Grose assented; 'It was the way he liked everyone!' She had no sooner spoken, indeed, than she caught herself up. 'I mean that's his way – the master's.'

I was struck. 'But of whom did you speak first?'

She looked blank, but she coloured. 'Why, of *him*.'

'Of the master?'

'Of who else?'

There was so obviously no one else that the next moment I had lost my impression of her having accidentally said more than she meant; and I merely asked what I wanted to know. 'Did *she* see anything in the boy – ?'

'That wasn't right? She never told me.'

I had a scruple, but I overcame it. 'Was she careful – particular?'

Mrs Grose appeared to try to be conscientious. 'About some things – yes.'

'But not about all?'

Again she considered. 'Well, miss – she's gone. I won't tell tales.'

'I quite understand your feeling,' I hastened to reply; but I thought it after an instant not opposed to this concession to pursue: 'Did she die here?'

'No – she went off.'

I don't know what there was in this brevity of Mrs Grose's that struck me as ambiguous. 'Went off to die?' Mrs Grose looked straight out of the window, but I felt that, hypothetically, I had a right to know what young persons engaged for Bly were expected to do. 'She was taken ill, you mean, and went home?'

'She was not taken ill, so far as appeared, in this house. She left it, at the end of the year, to go home, as she said, for a short holiday, to which the time she had put in had certainly given her a right. We had then a young woman – a nursemaid who had stayed on and who was a good girl and clever; and *she* took the children altogether for the interval. But our young lady never came back, and at the very moment I was expecting her I heard from the master that she was dead.'

I turned this over. 'But of what?'

'He never told me! But please, miss,' said Mrs Grose, 'I must get to my work.'

CHAPTER THREE

HER THUS TURNING her back on me was fortunately not, for my just preoccupations, a snub that could check the growth of our mutual esteem. We met, after I had brought home little Miles, more intimately than ever on the ground of my stupefaction, my general emotion: so monstrous was I then ready to pronounce it that such a child as had now been revealed to me should be under an interdict. I was a little late on the scene of his arrival, and I felt, as he stood wistfully looking out for me before the door of the inn at which the coach had put him down, that I had seen him on the instant, without and within, in the great glow of freshness, the same positive fragrance of purity, in which I had from the first moment seen his little sister. He was incredibly beautiful, and Mrs Grose had put her finger on it: everything but a sort of passion of tenderness for him was swept away by his presence. What I then and there took him to my heart for was something divine that I have never found to the same degree in any child – his indescribable little air of knowing nothing in the world but love. It would have been impossible to carry a bad name with a greater sweetness of innocence, and by the time I had got back to Bly with him I remained merely bewildered – so far, that is, as I was not outraged – by the sense of the horrible letter locked up in one of the drawers in my room. As soon as I could compass a private word with Mrs Grose, I declared to her that it was grotesque.

She promptly understood me. 'You mean the cruel charge – ?'

'It doesn't live an instant. My dear woman, look at him!'

She smiled at my pretension to have discovered his charm. 'I assure you, miss, I do nothing else! What will you say then?' she immediately added.

'In answer to the letter?' I had made up my mind. 'Nothing at all.'

'And to his uncle?'

I was incisive. 'Nothing at all.'

'And to the boy himself?'

I was wonderful. 'Nothing at all.'

She gave with her apron a great wipe to her mouth. 'Then I'll stand by you. We'll see it out.'

'We'll see it out!' I ardently echoed, giving her my hand to make it a vow.

She held me there a moment, then whisked up her apron again with her detached hand. 'Would you mind, miss, if I used the freedom – '

'To kiss me? No!' I took the good creature in my arms and, after we had embraced like sisters, felt still more fortified and indignant.

This, at all events, was for the time: a time so full that as I recall the way it went it reminds me of all the art I now need to make it a little distinct. What I look back at with amazement is the situation I accepted. I had undertaken, with my companion, to see it out, and I was under a charm apparently that could smooth away the extent and the far and difficult connections of such an effort. I was lifted aloft on a great wave of infatuation and pity. I found it simple, in my ignorance, my confusion and perhaps my conceit, to assume that I could deal with a boy whose education for the world was all on the point of beginning. I am unable even to remember at this day what proposal I framed for the end of his holidays and the resumption of his studies. Lessons with me indeed, that charming summer, we all had a theory that he was to have; but I now feel that for weeks the lessons must have been rather my own. I learnt something – at first certainly – that had not been one of the teachings of my small, smothered life; learnt to be amused, and even amusing, and not to think for the morrow. It was the first time, in a manner, that I had known space and air and freedom, all the music of summer and all the mystery of nature. And then there was consideration – and consideration was sweet. Oh, it was a trap – not designed but deep – to my imagination, to my delicacy, perhaps to my vanity; to whatever in me was most excitable. The best way to picture it all is to say that I was off my guard. They gave me so little trouble – they were of a gentleness so extraordinary. I used to speculate – but even this with a dim disconnectedness – as to how the rough future (for all futures are rough!) would handle them and might bruise them. They had the bloom of health and happiness; and yet, as if I had been in charge of a pair of little grandees, of princes of the blood, for whom everything, to be right, would have to be fenced about and ordered and arranged, the only form that in my fancy the after-years could take for them was that of a romantic, a really royal extension of the garden and the park. It may be of course above all what suddenly broke into this gives the previous time a charm of stillness – that hush in which something gathers or crouches. The change was actually like the spring of a beast.

In the first weeks, the days were long; they often, at their finest, gave me what I used to call my own hour, the hour when, for my pupils, teatime and bedtime having come and gone, I had before my final retirement a small interval alone. Much as I liked my companions, this hour was the thing in the day I liked most; and I liked it best of all when, as the light faded – or rather, I should say, the day lingered and the last calls of the last birds sounded, in a flushed sky, from the old trees – I could take a turn into the grounds and enjoy, almost with a sense of property that amused and flattered me, the beauty and dignity of the place. It was a pleasure at these moments to feel myself tranquil and justified; doubtless perhaps also to reflect that by my discretion, my quiet good sense and general high propriety, I was giving pleasure – if he ever thought of it! – to the person to whose pressure I had yielded. What I was doing was what he had earnestly hoped and directly asked of me, and that I *could*, after all, do it proved even a greater joy that I had expected. I dare say I fancied myself, in short, a remarkable young woman and took comfort in the faith that this would more publicly appear. Well, I needed to be remarkable to offer a front to the remarkable things that presently gave their first sign.

It was plump, one afternoon, in the middle of my very hour: the children were tucked away and I had come out for my stroll. One of the thoughts that, as I don't in the least shrink now from noting, used to be with me in these wanderings was that it would be as charming as a charming story suddenly to meet someone. Someone would appear there at the turn of a path and would stand before me and smile and approve. I didn't ask more than that – I only asked that he should know; and the only way to be sure he knew would be to see it, and the kind light of it, in his handsome face. That was exactly present to me – by which I mean the face was – when, on the first of these occasions, at the end of a long June day, I stopped short on emerging from one of the plantations and coming into view of the house. What arrested me on the spot – and with a shock much greater than any vision had allowed for – was the sense that my imagination had, in a flash, turned real. He did stand there! – but high up, beyond the lawn and at the very top of the tower to which, on that first morning, little Flora had conducted me. This tower was one of a pair – square, incongruous, crenellated structures – that were distinguished, for some reason, though I could see little difference, as the new and the old. They flanked opposite ends of the house and were probably architectural absurdities, redeemed in a measure, indeed, by not being wholly disengaged nor of a height too pretentious, dating, in their ginger-bread antiquity, from a romantic revival that was already a respectable past. I admired them, had fancies about them, for we could all profit in a degree, especially when they loomed through the dusk, by the grandeur of their actual battlements; yet it was not at such an elevation that the figure I had so often invoked seemed most in place.

It produced in me, this figure, in the clear twilight, I remember, two distinct gasps of emotion, which were, sharply, the shock of my first and that of my second surprise. My second was a violent perception of the mistake of my first: the man who met my eyes was not the person I had precipitately supposed. There came to me thus a bewilderment of vision of which, after these years, there is no living view that I can hope to give. An unknown man in a lonely place is a permitted object of fear to a young woman privately bred; and the figure that faced me was – a few more seconds assured me – as little anyone else I knew as it was the image that had been in my mind. I had not seen it in Harley Street – I had not seen it anywhere. The place, moreover, in the strangest way in the world, had on the instant and by the very fact of its appearance become a solitude. To me at least, making my statement here with a deliberation with which I have never made it, the whole feeling of the moment returns. It was as if, while I took in what I did take in, all the rest of the scene had been stricken with death. I can hear again, as I write, the intense hush in which the sounds of evening dropped. The rooks stopped cawing in the golden sky and the friendly hour lost for the unspeakable minute all its voice. But there was no other change in nature, unless indeed it were a change that I saw with a stranger sharpness. The gold was still in the sky, the clearness in the air, and the man who looked at me over the battlements was as definite as a picture in a frame. That's how I thought, with extraordinary quickness, of each person he might have been and that he wasn't. We were confronted across our distance quite long enough for me to ask myself with intensity who then he was and to feel, as an effect of my inability to say, a wonder that in a few seconds more became intense.

The great question, or one of these, is afterwards, I know, with regard to certain matters, the question of how long they have lasted. Well, this matter of mine, think what you will of it, lasted while I caught at a dozen possibilities, none of which made a difference for the better, that I could see, in there having been in the house – and for how long, above all? – a person of whom I was in ignorance. It lasted while I just bridled a little with the sense of how my office seemed to require that there should be no such ignorance and no such person. It lasted while this visitant, at all events – and there was a touch of the strange freedom, as I remember, in the sign of familiarity of his wearing no hat – seemed to fix me, from his position, with just the question, just the scrutiny through the fading light, that his own presence provoked. We were too far apart to call to each other, but there was a moment at which, at shorter range, some challenge between us, breaking the hush, would have been the right result of our straight mutual stare. He was in one of the angles, the one away from the house, very erect, as it struck me, and with both hands on the ledge. So I saw him as I see the letters I form on this page; then, exactly, after a minute, as if to add to the spectacle, he slowly changed his place – passed, looking at me hard all the while, to the opposite corner of the platform. Yes, it was intense to me that during this transit he never took his eyes from me, and I can see at this moment the way his hand as he went, moved from one of the crenellations to the next. He stopped at the other corner, but less long, and even as he turned away still markedly fixed me. He turned away; that was all I knew.

CHAPTER FOUR

It was not that I didn't wait, on this occasion, for more, since I was as deeply rooted as shaken. Was there a 'secret' at Bly – a mystery of Udolpho or an insane, an unmentionable relative kept in unsuspected confinement?[6] I can't say how long I turned it over, or how long, in a confusion of curiosity and dread, I remained where I had had my collision; I only recall that when I re-entered the house, darkness had quite closed in. Agitation, in the interval, certainly had held me and driven me, for I must, in circling about the place, have walked three miles; but I was to be later on so much more overwhelmed that this mere dawn of alarm was a comparatively human chill. The most singular part of it, in fact – singular as the rest had been – was the part I became, in the hall, aware of in meeting Mrs Grose. This picture comes back to me in the general train – the impression, as I received it on my return, of the wide white panelled space, bright in the lamplight and with its portraits and red carpets, and of the good surprised look of my friend, which immediately told me she had missed me. It came to me straightaway, under her contact, that, with plain heartiness, mere relieved anxiety at my appearance, she knew nothing whatever that could bear upon the incident I had there ready for her. I had not suspected in advance that her comfortable face would pull me up, and I somehow measured the importance of what I had seen by my thus finding myself hesitate to mention it. Scarce anything in the whole history seems to me so odd as this fact that my real beginning of fear was one, as I may say, with the instinct of sparing my companion. On the spot, accordingly, in the pleasant hall and with her eyes on me, I, for a reason that I couldn't then have phrased, achieved an inward revolution – offered a vague pretext for my lateness and, with the idea of the beauty of the night and of the heavy dew and wet feet, went as soon as possible to my room.

Here it was another affair; here, for many days after, it was a queer affair enough. There were hours, from day to day – or at least there were moments, snatched even from clear duties – when I had to shut myself up to think. It wasn't so much yet that I was more nervous than I could bear to be as that I was remarkably afraid of becoming so; for the truth I had now to turn over was simply and clearly the truth that I could arrive at no account whatever of the visitor with whom I had been so inexplicably and yet, as it seemed to me, so intimately concerned. It took me little time to see that I might easily sound, without forms of inquiry and without exciting remark, any domestic complication. The shock I had suffered must have sharpened all my senses; I felt sure, at the end of three days and as the result of mere closer attention, that I had not been practised upon by the servants nor made the object of any 'game'. Of whatever it was that I knew, nothing was known around me. There was but one sane inference: someone had taken a liberty rather monstrous. That was what, repeatedly, I dipped into my room and locked the door to say to myself. We had been, collectively, subject to an intrusion; some unscrupulous traveller, curious in old houses, had made his way in unobserved, enjoyed the prospect from the best point of view and then stolen out as he came. If he had given me such a bold, hard stare, that was but a part of his indiscretion. The good thing, after all, was that we should surely see no more of him.

This was not so good a thing, I admit, as not to leave me to judge that what, essentially, made nothing else much signify was simply my charming work. My charming work was just my life with Miles and Flora, and through nothing could I so like it as through feeling that to throw myself into it was to throw myself out of my trouble. The attraction of my small charges was a constant joy, leading me to wonder afresh at the vanity of my original fears, the distaste I had begun by entertaining for the probable grey prose of my office. There was to be no grey prose, it appeared, and no long grind; so how could work not be charming that presented itself as daily beauty? It was all the romance of the nursery and the poetry of the schoolroom. I don't mean by this, of course, that we studied only fiction and verse; I mean that I can express no otherwise the sort of interest my companions inspired. How can I describe that except by saying that instead of growing deadly used to them – and it's a marvel for a governess: I call the sisterhood to witness! – I made constant fresh discoveries. There was one direction, assuredly, in which these discoveries stopped: deep obscurity continued to cover the region of the boy's conduct at school. It had been promptly given me, I have noted, to face that mystery without a pang. Perhaps even it would be nearer the truth to say that – without a word – he himself had cleared it up. He had made the whole charge absurd. My conclusion bloomed there with the real rose-flush of his innocence: he was only too fine and fair for the little horrid, unclean school-world, and he had paid a price for it. I reflected acutely that the sense of such individual differences, such superiorities of quality, always, on the part of the majority – which could include even stupid sordid headmasters – turns infallibly to the vindictive.

Both the children had a gentleness – it was their only fault, and it never made Miles a muff – that kept them (how shall I express it?) almost impersonal and certainly quite unpunishable. They were like those cherubs of the anecdote[7] who had – morally, at any rate – nothing to whack! I remember feeling with Miles especially as if he had had, as it were, nothing to call even an infinitesimal history. We expect of a small child scant enough 'antecedents', but there was in this beautiful little boy something extraordinarily sensitive, yet extraordinarily happy, that, more than in any creature of his age I have seen, struck me as beginning anew each day. He had never for a second suffered. I took this as a direct disproof of his having really been chastised. If he had been wicked he would have 'caught' it, and I should have caught it by the rebound – I should have found the trace, should have felt the wound and the dishonour. I could reconstitute nothing at all, and he was therefore an angel. He never spoke of his school, never mentioned a comrade or a master; and I, for my part, was quite too much disgusted to allude to them. Of course I was under the spell, and the wonderful part is that, even at the time, I perfectly knew I was. But I gave myself up to it; it was an antidote to any pain, and I had more pains than one. I was in receipt in these days of disturbing letters from home, where things were not going well. But with this joy of my children, what things in the world mattered? That was the question I used to put to my scrappy retirements. I was dazzled by their loveliness.

There was a Sunday – to get on – when it rained with such force and for so many hours that there could be no procession to church; in consequence of which, as the day declined, I had arranged with Mrs Grose that, should the evening show improvement, we would attend together the late service. The rain happily stopped, and I prepared for our walk, which, through the park and by the good road to the village, would be a matter of twenty minutes. Coming downstairs to meet my colleague in the hall, I remembered a pair of gloves that had required three stitches and that had received them – with a publicity perhaps not edifying – while I sat with the children at their tea, served on Sundays, by exception, in that cold clean temple of mahogany and brass, the 'grown-up' dining-room. The gloves had been dropped there, and I turned in to recover them. The day was grey enough, but the afternoon light still lingered, and it enabled me, on crossing the threshold, not only to recognise, on a chair near the wide window, then closed, the articles I wanted, but to become aware of a person on the other side of the window and looking straight in. One step into the room had sufficed; my vision was instantaneous; it was all there. The person looking straight in was the person who had already appeared to me. He appeared thus again with I won't say greater distinctness, for that was impossible, but with a nearness that represented a forward stride in our intercourse and made me, as I met him, catch my breath and turn cold. He was the same – he was the same, and seen, this time, as he had been seen before, from the waist up, the window, though the dining-room was on the ground floor, not going down to the terrace on which he stood. His face was close to the glass, yet the effect of this better view was, strangely, just to show me how intense the former had been. He remained but a few seconds – long enough to convince me he also saw and recognised; but it was as if I had been looking at him for years and had known him always. Something, however, happened this time that had not happened before; his stare into my face, through the glass and across the room, was as deep and hard as then, but it quitted me for a moment during which I could still watch it, see it fix successively several other things. On the spot there came to me the added shock of a certitude that it was not for me he had come. He had come for someone else.

The flash of this knowledge – for it was knowledge in the midst of dread – produced in me the most extraordinary effect, starting, as I stood there, a sudden vibration of duty and courage. I say courage because I was beyond all doubt already far gone. I bounded straight out of the door again, reached that of the house, got in an instant upon the drive and, passing along the terrace as fast as I could rush, turned a corner and came full in sight. But it was in sight of nothing now – my visitor had vanished. I stopped, almost dropped, with the real relief of this; but I took in the whole scene – I gave him time to reappear. I call it time, but how long was it? I can't speak to the purpose today of the duration of these things. That kind of measure must have left me: they couldn't have lasted as they actually appeared to me to last. The terrace and the whole place, the lawn and the garden behind it, all I could see of the park, were empty with a great emptiness. There were shrubberies and big trees, but I remember the clear assurance I felt that none of them concealed him. He was there or was not there: not there if I didn't see him. I got hold of this; then, instinctively, instead of returning as I had come, went to the window. It was confusedly present to me that I ought to place myself where he had stood. I did so; I applied my face to the pane and looked, as he had looked, into the room. As if, at this moment, to show me exactly what his range had been, Mrs Grose, as I had done for himself just before, came in from the hall. With this I had the full image of a repetition of what had already occurred. She saw me as I had seen my own visitant; she pulled up short as I had done; I gave her something of the shock that I had received. She turned white, and this made me ask myself if I had blanched as much. She stared, in short, and retreated just on *my* lines, and I knew she had then passed out and come round to me and that I should presently meet her. I remained where I was, and while I waited I thought of more things than one. But there's only one I take space to mention. I wondered why *she* should be scared.

CHAPTER FIVE

OH, SHE LET ME KNOW as soon as, round the corner of the house, she loomed again into view. 'What in the name of goodness is the matter – ?' She was now flushed and out of breath.

I said nothing till she came quite near. 'With me?' I must have made a wonderful face. 'Do I show it?'

'You're as white as a sheet. You look awful.'

I considered; I could meet on this, without scruple – any degree of innocence. My need to respect the bloom of Mrs Grose's had dropped, without a rustle from my shoulders, and if I wavered for the instant it was not with what I kept back. I put out my hand to her and she took it; I held her hard a little, liking to feel her close to me. There was a kind of support in the shy heave of her surprise. 'You came for me for church, of course, but I can't go.'

'Has anything happened?'

'Yes. You must know now. Did I look very queer?'

'Through this window? Dreadful!'

'Well,' I said, 'I've been frightened.' Mrs Grose's eyes expressed plainly that *she* had no wish to be, yet also that she knew too well her place not to be ready to share with me any marked inconvenience. Oh, it was quite settled that she *must* share! 'Just what you saw from the dining-room a minute ago was the effect of that. What *I* saw – just before – was much worse.'

Her hand tightened. 'What was it?'

'An extraordinary man. Looking in.'

'What extraordinary man?'

'I haven't the least idea.'

Mrs Grose gazed round us in vain. 'Then where is he gone?'

'I know still less.'

'Have you seen him before?'

'Yes – once. On the old tower.'

She could only look at me harder. 'Do you mean he's a stranger?'

'Oh, very much!'

'Yet you didn't tell me?'

'No – for reasons. But now that you've guessed – '

Mrs Grose's round eyes encountered this charge. 'Ah, I haven't guessed!' she said very simply. 'How can I if *you* don't imagine?'

'I don't in the very least.'

'You've seen him nowhere but on the tower?'

'And on this spot just now.'

Mrs Grose looked round again. 'What was he doing on the tower?'

'Only standing there and looking down at me.'

She thought a minute. 'Was he a gentleman?'

I found I had no need to think. 'No.' She gazed in deeper wonder. 'No.'

'Then nobody about the place? Nobody from the village?'

'Nobody – nobody. I didn't tell you, but I made sure.'

She breathed a vague relief: this was, oddly, so much to the good. It only went indeed a little way. 'But if he isn't a gentleman – '

'What *is* he? He's a horror.'

'A horror?'

'He's – God help me if I know *what* he is!'

Mrs Grose looked round once more; she fixed her eyes on the duskier distance and then, pulling herself together, turned to me with full inconsequence. 'It's time we should be at church.'

'Oh, I'm not fit for church!'

'Won't it do you good?'

'It won't do them – !' I nodded at the house.

'The children?'

'I can't leave *them* now.'

'You're afraid – ?'

I spoke boldly. 'I'm afraid of *him*.'

Mrs Grose's large face showed me, at this, for the first time, the far-away faint glimmer of a consciousness more acute: I somehow made out in it the delayed dawn of an idea I myself had not given her and that was as yet quite obscure to me. It comes back to me that I thought instantly of this as something I could get from her; and I felt it to be connected with the desire she presently showed to know more. 'When was it – on the tower?'

'About the middle of the month. At this same hour.'

'Almost at dark,' said Mrs Grose.

'Oh, no, not nearly. I saw him as I see you.'

'Then how did he get in?'

'And how did he get out?' I laughed. 'I had no opportunity to ask him! This evening, you see,' I pursued, 'he has not been able to get in.'

'He only peeps?'

'I hope it will be confined to that!' She had now let go my hand; she turned away a little. I waited an instant; then I brought out: 'Go to church. Goodbye. I must watch.'

Slowly she faced me again. 'Do you fear for them?'

We met in another long look. 'Don't *you*?' Instead of answering she came nearer to the window and, for a minute, applied her face to the glass. 'You see how he could see,' I meanwhile went on.

She didn't move. 'How long was he here?'

'Till I came out. I came to meet him.'

Mrs Grose at last turned round, and there was still more in her face: '*I* couldn't have come out.'

'Neither could I!' I laughed again. 'But I did come. I've my duty.'

'So have I mine,' she replied; after which she added: 'What's he like?'

'I've been dying to tell you. But he's like nobody.'

'Nobody?' she echoed.

'He has no hat.' Then seeing in her face that she already, in this, with a deeper dismay, found a touch of picture, I quickly added stroke to stroke. 'He has red hair, very red, close-curling, and a pale face, long in shape, with straight, good features and little, rather queer whiskers that are as red as his hair. His eyebrows are somehow darker; they look particularly arched and as if they might move a good deal. His eyes are sharp, strange – awfully; but I only know clearly that they're rather small and very fixed. His mouth's wide and his lips are thin, and except for his little whiskers he's quite clean-shaven. He gives me a sort of sense of looking like an actor.'

'An actor!' It was impossible to resemble one less, at least, than Mrs Grose at that moment.

'I've never seen one, but so I suppose them. He's tall, active, erect,' I continued, 'but never – no, never! – a gentleman.'

My companion's face had blanched as I went on; her round eyes started and her mild mouth gaped. 'A gentleman?' she gasped, confounded, stupefied: 'a gentleman *he*?'

'You know him then?'

She visibly tried to hold herself. 'But he *is* handsome?'

I saw the way to help her. 'Remarkably!'

'And dressed – ?'

'In somebody's clothes. They're smart, but they're not his own.'

She broke into a breathless affirmative groan. 'They're the master's!'

I caught it up. 'You *do* know him?'

She faltered but a second. 'Quint!' she cried.

'Quint?'

'Peter Quint – his own man, his valet, when he was here!'

'When the master was?'

Gaping still, but meeting me, she pieced it all together. 'He never wore his hat, but he did wear – well, there were waistcoats missed! They were both here – last year. Then the master went, and Quint was alone.'

I followed, but halting a little. 'Alone?'

'Alone with *us*.' Then as from a deeper depth, 'In charge,' she added.

'And what became of him?'

She hung fire so long that I was still more mystified. 'He went too,' she brought out at last.

'Went where?'

Her expression, at this, became extraordinary. 'God knows where! He died.'

'Died?' I almost shrieked.

She seemed fairly to square herself, plant herself more firmly to express the wonder of it. 'Yes. Mr Quint's dead.'

CHAPTER SIX

It took of course more than that particular passage to place us
together in presence of what we had now to live with as we could, my
dreadful liability to impressions of the order so vividly exemplified,
and my companion's knowledge henceforth – a knowledge half
consternation and half compassion – of that liability. There had been
this evening, after the revelation that left me for an hour so
prostrate – there had been for either of us no attendance on any
service but a little service of tears and vows, of prayers and promises,
a climax to the series of mutual challenges and pledges that had
straightaway ensued on our retreating together to the schoolroom
and shutting ourselves up there to have everything out. The result of
our having everything out was simply to reduce our situation to the
last rigour of its elements. She herself had seen nothing, not the
shadow of a shadow, and nobody in the house but the governess was
in the governess's plight; yet she accepted without directly impugn-
ing my sanity the truth as I gave it to her, and ended by showing me
on this ground an awestricken tenderness, a deference to my more
than questionable privilege, of which the very breath has remained
with me as that of the sweetest of human charities.

What was settled between us accordingly that night was that we
thought we might bear things together; and I was not even sure that
in spite of her exemption it was she who had the best of the burden. I
knew at this hour, I think, as well as I knew later, what I was capable
of meeting to shelter my pupils; but it took me some time to be
wholly sure of what my honest comrade was prepared for to keep
terms with so stiff an agreement. I was queer company enough –
quite as queer as the company I received; but as I trace over what we
went through, I see how much common ground we must have found
in the one idea that, by good fortune, *could* steady us. It was the idea,
the second movement, that led me straight out, as I may say, of the
inner chamber of my dread. I could take the air in the court, at least,
and there Mrs Grose could join me. Perfectly can I recall now the
particular way strength came to me before we separated for the night.
We had gone over and over every feature of what I had seen.

'He was looking for someone else, you say – someone who was not
you?'

'He was looking for little Miles.' A portentous clearness now
possessed me. '*That's* whom he was looking for.'

'But how do you know?'

'I know, I know, I know!' My exaltation grew. 'And *you* know, my dear!'

She didn't deny this, but I required, I felt, not even so much telling as that. She took it up again in a moment. 'What if *he* should see him?'

'Little Miles? That's what he wants!'

She looked immensely scared again. 'The child?'

'Heaven forbid! The man. He wants to appear to *them*.' That he might was an awful conception, and yet somehow I could keep it at bay; which moreover, as we lingered there, was what I succeeded in practically proving. I had an absolute certainty that I should see again what I had already seen, but something within me said that by offering myself bravely as the sole subject of such experience, by accepting, by inviting, by surmounting it all, I should serve as an expiatory victim and guard the tranquillity of the rest of the household. The children especially I should thus fence about and absolutely save. I recall one of the last things I said that night to Mrs Grose.

'It does strike me that my pupils have never mentioned – !'

She looked at me hard as I musingly pulled up. 'His having been here and the time they were with him?'

'The time they were with him, and his name, his presence, his history, in any way. They've never alluded to it.'

'Oh, the little lady doesn't remember. She never heard or knew.'

'The circumstances of his death?' I thought with some intensity. 'Perhaps not. But Miles would remember – Miles would know.'

'Ah, don't try him!' broke from Mrs Grose.

I returned her the look she had given me. 'Don't be afraid.' I continued to think. 'It *is* rather odd.'

'That he has never spoken of him?'

'Never by the least reference. And you tell me they were "great friends"?'

'Oh, it wasn't *him*!' Mrs Grose with emphasis declared. 'It was Quint's own fancy. To play with him, I mean – to spoil him.' She paused a moment; then she added: 'Quint was much too free.'

This gave me, straight from my vision of his face – *such* a face! – a sudden sickness of disgust. 'Too free with *my* boy?'

'Too free with everyone!'

I forbore for the moment to analyse this description further than by the reflection that a part of it applied to several of the members of the household, of the half-dozen maids and men who were still of our small colony. But there was everything, for our apprehension, in the lucky fact that no discomfortable legend, no perturbation of scullions, had ever, within anyone's memory, attached to the kind old place. It had neither bad name nor ill fame, and Mrs Grose, most apparently, only desired to cling to me and to quake in silence. I even put her, the very last thing of all, to the test. It was when, at midnight, she had her hand on the schoolroom door to take leave. 'I *have* it from you, then – for it's of great importance – that he was definitely and admittedly bad?'

'Oh, not admittedly. I knew it – but the master didn't.'

'And you never told him?'

'Well, he didn't like tale bearing – he hated complaints. He was terribly short with anything of that kind, and if people were all right to *him* – '

'He wouldn't be bothered with more?' This squared well enough with my impression of him: he was not a trouble-loving gentleman, nor so very particular perhaps about some of the company he himself kept. All the same, I pressed my informant. 'I promise you, *I* would have told!'

She felt my discrimination. 'I dare say I was wrong. But really I was afraid.'

'Afraid of what?'

'Of things that man could do. Quint was so clever – he was so deep.'

I took this in still more than I probably showed. 'You weren't afraid of anything else? Not of his effect – ?'

'His effect?' she repeated with a face of anguish and waiting while I faltered.

'On innocent little precious lives. They were in your charge.'

'No, they weren't in mine!' she roundly and distressfully returned. 'The master believed in him and placed him here because he was supposed not to be quite in health and the country air so good for him. So he had everything to say. Yes' – she let me have it – 'even about *them.*'

'Them – that creature?' I had to smother a kind of howl. 'And you could bear it?'

'No. I couldn't – and I can't now!' And the poor woman burst into tears.

A rigid control, from the next day, was, as I have said, to follow them; yet how often and how passionately, for a week, we came back together to the subject! Much as we had discussed it that Sunday night, I was, in the immediate later hours especially – for it may be imagined whether I slept – still haunted with the shadow of something she had not told me. I myself had kept back nothing, but there was a word Mrs

Grose had kept back. I was sure, moreover, by morning that this was not from a failure of frankness, but because on every side there were fears. It seems to me indeed, in raking it all over, that by the time the morrow's sun was high I had restlessly read into the facts before us almost all the meaning they were to receive from subsequent and more cruel occurrences. What they gave me, above all, was just the sinister figure of the living man – the dead one would keep awhile! – and of the months he had continuously passed at Bly, which, added up made a formidable stretch. The limit of this evil time had arrived only when, on the dawn of a winter's morning, Peter Quint was found, by a labourer going to early work, stone dead on the road from the village: a catastrophe explained – superficially at least – by a visible wound to his head, such a wound as might have been produced (and as, on the final evidence, *had* been) by a fatal slip, in the dark and after leaving the public house, on the steepish icy slope, a wrong path altogether, at the bottom of which he lay. The icy slope, the turn mistaken at night and in liquor, accounted for much – practically, in the end and after the inquest and boundless chatter, for everything; but there had been matters in his life – strange passages and perils, secret disorders, vices more than suspected, that would have accounted for a good deal more.

I scarce know how to put my story into words that shall be a credible picture of my state of mind; but I was in these days literally able to find a joy in the extraordinary flight of heroism the occasion demanded of me. I now saw that I had been asked for a service admirable and difficult; and there would be a greatness in letting it be seen – oh, in the right quarter! – that I could succeed where many another girl might have failed. It was an immense help to me – I confess I rather applaud myself as I look back! – that I saw my response so strongly and so simply. I was there to protect and defend the little creatures in the world the most bereaved and the most lovable, the appeal of whose helplessness had suddenly become only too explicit, a deep, constant ache of one's own engaged affection. We were cut off, really, together; we were united in our danger. They had nothing but me, and I – well, I had them. It was, in short, a magnificent chance. This chance presented itself to me in an image richly material. I was a screen – I was to stand before them. The more I saw the less they would. I began to watch them in a stifled suspense, a disguised tension, that might well, had it continued too long, have turned to something like madness. What saved me, as I now see, was that it turned to another matter altogether. It didn't last as suspense – it was superseded by horrible proofs. Proofs, I say, yes – from the moment I really took hold.

This moment dated from an afternoon hour that I happened to spend in the grounds with the younger of my pupils alone. We had left Miles indoors, on the red cushion of a deep window-seat; he had wished to finish a book, and I had been glad to encourage a purpose so laudable in a young man whose only defect was a certain ingenuity of restlessness. His sister, on the contrary, had been alert to come out, and I strolled with her half an hour, seeking the shade, for the sun was still high and the day exceptionally warm. I was aware afresh with her, as we went, of how, like her brother, she contrived – it was the charming thing in both children – to let me alone without appearing to drop me and to accompany me without appearing to oppress. They were never importunate and yet never listless. My attention to them all really went to seeing them amuse themselves immensely without me: this was a spectacle they seemed actively to prepare and that employed me as an active admirer. I walked in a world of their invention – they had no occasion whatever to draw upon mine; so that my time was taken only with being for them some remarkable person or thing that the game of the moment required and that was merely, thanks to my superior, my exalted stamp, a happy and highly distinguished sinecure. I forget what I was on the present occasion; I only remember that I was something very important and very quiet and that Flora was playing very hard. We were on the edge of the lake, and, as we had lately begun geography, the lake was the Sea of Azov.[8]

Suddenly, amid these elements, I became aware that on the other side of the Sea of Azov we had an interested spectator. The way this knowledge gathered in me was the strangest thing in the world – the strangest, that is, except the very much stranger in which it quickly merged itself. I had sat down with a piece of work – for I was something or other that could sit – on the old stone bench which overlooked the pond; and in this position I began to take in with certitude and yet without direct vision the presence, a good way off, of a third person. The old trees, the thick shrubbery, made a great and pleasant shade, but it was all suffused with the brightness of the hot, still hour. There was no ambiguity in anything; none whatever, at least, in the conviction I from one moment to another found myself forming as to what I should see straight before me and across the lake as a consequence of raising my eyes. They were attached at this juncture to the stitching in which I was engaged, and I can feel once more the spasm of my effort not to move them till I should so have steadied myself as to be able to make up my mind what to do. There was an alien object in view – a figure whose right of presence

I instantly and passionately questioned. I recollect counting over perfectly the possibilities, reminding myself that nothing was more natural, for instance, than the appearance of one of the men about the place, or even of a messenger, a postman or a tradesman's boy, from the village. That reminder had as little effect on my practical certitude as I was conscious – still even without looking – of its having upon the character and attitude of our visitor. Nothing was more natural than that these things should be the other things they absolutely were not.

Of the positive identity of the apparition I would assure myself as soon as the small clock of my courage should have ticked out the right second; meanwhile, with an effort that was already sharp enough, I transferred my eyes straight to little Flora, who, at the moment, was about ten yards away. My heart had stood still for an instant with the wonder and terror of the question whether she too would see; and I held my breath while I waited for what a cry from her, what some sudden innocent sign either of interest or of alarm, would tell me. I waited, but nothing came; then in the first place – and there is something more dire in this, I feel, than in anything I have to relate – I was determined by a sense that within a minute all spontaneous sounds from her had dropped; and in the second by the circumstance that also within the minute she had, in her play, turned her back to the water. This was her attitude when I at last looked at her – looked with the confirmed conviction that we were still, together, under direct personal notice. She had picked up a small, flat piece of wood which happened to have in it a little hole that had evidently suggested to her the idea of sticking in another fragment that might figure as a mast and make the thing a boat. This second morsel, as I watched her, she was very markedly and intently attempting to tighten in its place. My apprehension of what she was doing sustained me so that after some seconds I felt I was ready for more. Then I again shifted my eyes – I faced what I had to face.

CHAPTER SEVEN

I GOT HOLD OF Mrs Grose as soon after this as I could; and I can give no intelligible account of how I fought out the interval. Yet I still hear myself cry as I fairly threw myself into her arms: 'They *know* – it's too monstrous: they know, they know!'

'And what on earth – ?' I felt her incredulity as she held me.

'Why, all that *we* know – and heaven knows what more besides!'

Then as she released me I made it out to her, made it out perhaps only now with full coherency even to myself. 'Two hours ago, in the garden' – I could scarce articulate – 'Flora *saw!*'

Mrs Grose took it as she might have taken a blow in the stomach. 'She has told you?' she panted.

'Not a word – that's the horror. She kept it to herself! The child of eight, *that* child!' Unutterable still for me was the stupefaction of it.

Mrs Grose of course could only gape the wider. 'Then how do you know?'

'I was there – I saw with my eyes: saw she was perfectly aware.'

'Do you mean aware of *him?*'

'No – of *her.*' I was conscious as I spoke that I looked prodigious things, for I got the slow reflection of them in my companion's face. 'Another person – this time; but a figure of quite as unmistakable horror and evil: a woman in black, pale and dreadful – with such an air also, and such a face! – on the other side of the lake. I was there with the child – quiet for the hour; and in the midst of it she came.'

'Came how – from where?'

'From where they come from! She just appeared and stood there – but not so near.'

'And without coming nearer?'

'Oh, for the effect and the feeling she might have been as close as you!'

My friend, with an odd impulse, fell back a step. 'Was she someone you've never seen?'

'Never. But someone the child has. Someone *you* have.' Then to show how I had thought it all out: 'My predecessor – the one who died.'

'Miss Jessel?'

'Miss Jessel. You don't believe me?' I pressed.

She turned right and left in her distress. 'How can you be sure?'

This drew from me, in the state of my nerves, a flash of impatience. 'Then ask Flora – she's sure!' But I had no sooner spoken than I caught myself up. 'No, for God's sake, *don't.* She'll say she isn't – she'll lie!'

Mrs Grose was not too bewildered instinctively to protest. 'Ah, how *can* you?'

'Because I'm clear. Flora doesn't want me to know.'

'It's only then to spare you.'

'No, no – there are depths, depths! The more I go over it the more I see in it, and the more I see in it the more I fear. I don't know what I *don't* see – what I *don't* fear!'

Mrs Grose tried to keep up with me. 'You mean you're afraid of seeing her again?'

'Oh, no; that's nothing – now!' Then I explained. 'It's of *not* seeing her.'

But my companion only looked wan. 'I don't understand.'

'Why, it's that the child may keep it up – and that the child assuredly *will* – without my knowing it.'

At the image of this possibility Mrs Grose for a moment collapsed, yet presently to pull herself together again as from the positive force of the sense of what, should we yield an inch, there would really be to give way to. 'Dear, dear – we must keep our heads! And after all, if she doesn't mind it – !' She even tried a grim joke. 'Perhaps she likes it!'

'Like *such* things – a scrap of an infant!'

'Isn't it just a proof of her blest innocence?' my friend bravely inquired.

She brought me, for the instant, almost round. 'Oh, we must clutch at that – we must cling to it! If it isn't a proof of what you say, it's a proof of – God knows what! For the woman's a horror of horrors.'

Mrs Grose, at this, fixed her eyes a minute on the ground; then at last raising them, 'Tell me how you know,' she said.

'Then you admit it's what she was?' I cried.

'Tell me how you know,' my friend simply repeated.

'Know? By seeing her! By the way she looked.'

'At you, do you mean – so wickedly?'

'Dear me, no – I could have borne that. She gave me never a glance. She only fixed the child.'

Mrs Grose tried to see it. 'Fixed her?'

'Ah, with such awful eyes!'

She stared at mine as if they might really have resembled them. 'Do you mean of dislike?'

'God help us, no. Of something much worse.'

'Worse than dislike?' – this left her indeed at a loss.

'With a determination – indescribable. With a kind of fury of intention.'

I made her turn pale. 'Intention?'

'To get hold of her.' Mrs Grose – her eyes just lingering on mine – gave a shudder and walked to the window; and while she stood there looking out I completed my statement. 'That's what Flora knows.'

After a little she turned round. 'The person was in black, you say?'

'In mourning – rather poor, almost shabby. But – yes – with extraordinary beauty.' I now recognised to what I had at last, stroke by stroke, brought the victim of my confidence, for she quite visibly weighed this. 'Oh, handsome – very, very,' I insisted; 'wonderfully handsome. But infamous.'

She slowly came back to me. 'Miss Jessel – *was* infamous.' She once more took my hand in both her own, holding it as tight as if to fortify me against the increase of alarm I might draw from this disclosure. 'They were both infamous,' she finally said.

So for a little we faced it once more together; and I found absolutely a degree of help in seeing it now so straight. 'I appreciate,' I said, 'the great decency of your not having hitherto spoken; but the time has certainly come to give me the whole thing.' She appeared to assent to this, but still only in silence; seeing which I went on: 'I must have it now. Of what did she die? Come, there was something between them.'

'There was everything.'

'In spite of the difference – ?'

'Oh, of their rank, their condition' – she brought it woefully out. '*She* was a lady.'

I turned it over; I again saw. 'Yes – she was a lady.'

'And he so dreadfully below,' said Mrs Grose.

I felt that I doubtless needn't press too hard, in such company, on the place of a servant in the scale; but there was nothing to prevent an acceptance of my companion's own measure of my predecessor's abasement. There was a way to deal with that, and I dealt; the more readily for my full vision – on the evidence – of our employer's late good-looking 'own' man; impudent, assured, spoiled, depraved. 'The fellow was a hound.'

Mrs Grose considered as if it were perhaps a little a case for a sense of shades. 'I've never seen one like him. He did what he wished.'

'With *her*?'

'With them all.'

It was as if now in my friend's own eyes Miss Jessel had again appeared. I seemed at any rate for an instant to trace their evocation of her as distinctly as I had seen her by the pond; and I brought out with decision: 'It must have been also what *she* wished!'

Mrs Grose's face signified that it had been indeed, but she said at the same time: 'Poor woman – she paid for it!'

'Then you do know what she died of?' I asked.

'No – I know nothing. I wanted not to know; I was glad enough I didn't – and I thanked heaven she was well out of this!'

'Yet you had then your idea – '

'Of her real reason for leaving? Oh, yes – as to that. She couldn't have stayed. Fancy it here – for a governess! And afterwards I imagined – and I still imagine. And what I imagine is dreadful.'

'Not so dreadful as what *I* do,' I replied; on which I must have shown her – as I was indeed but too conscious – a front of miserable defeat. It brought out again all her compassion for me, and at the renewed touch of her kindness, my power to resist broke down. I burst, as I had the other time made her burst, into tears; she took me to her motherly breast, and my lamentation overflowed. 'I don't do it!' I sobbed in despair. 'I don't save or shield them! It's far worse than I dreamed. They're lost!

CHAPTER EIGHT

WHAT I HAD SAID to Mrs Grose was true enough. There were in the matter I had put before her depths and possibilities that I lacked resolution to sound, so that when we met once more in the wonder of it, we were of a common mind about the duty of resistance to extravagant fancies. We were to keep our heads if we should keep nothing else – difficult indeed as that might be in the face of all that, in our prodigious experience, seemed least to be questioned. Late that night, while the house slept, we had another talk in my room; when she went all the way with me as to its being beyond doubt that I had seen exactly what I had seen. I found that to keep her thoroughly in the grip of this I had only to ask her how, if I had 'made it up', I came to be able to give, of each of the persons appearing to me, a picture disclosing, to the last detail, their special marks a portrait on the exhibition of which she had instantly recognised and named them. She wished, of course – small blame to her! – to sink the whole subject; and I was quick to assure her that my own interest in it had now violently taken the form of a search for the way to escape from it. I closed with her cordially on the article of the likelihood that with recurrence – for recurrence we took for granted – I should get used to my danger; distinctly professing that my personal exposure had suddenly become the least of my discomforts. It was my new suspicion that was intolerable; and yet even to this complication the later hours of the day had brought a little ease.

On leaving her, after my first outbreak, I had of course returned to my pupils, associating the right remedy for my dismay with that sense of their charm which I had already recognised as a resource I could positively cultivate and which had never failed me yet. I had simply, in other words, plunged afresh into Flora's special society and there become aware – it was almost a luxury! – that she could put her little conscious hand straight upon the spot that ached. She had looked at me in sweet speculation and then had accused me to my face of having 'cried'. I had supposed the ugly signs of it brushed away; but I could literally – for the time, at all events – rejoice, under this fathomless charity, that they had not entirely disappeared. To gaze into the depths of blue of the child's eyes and pronounce their loveliness a trick of premature cunning was to be guilty of a cynicism in preference to which I naturally preferred to abjure my judgement and, so far as might be, my agitation. I couldn't abjure for merely wanting to, but I could repeat to Mrs Grose – as I did there, over and over, in the small hours – that with our small friends, voices in the air, their pressure on one's heart and their fragrant faces against one's cheek, everything fell to the ground but their incapacity and their beauty. It was a pity that, somehow, to settle this once for all, I had equally to re-enumerate the signs of subtlety that, in the afternoon, by the lake, had made a miracle of my show of self-possession. It was a pity to be obliged to reinvestigate the certitude of the moment itself and repeat how it had come to me as a revelation that the inconceivable communion I then surprised must have been for both parties a matter of habit. It was a pity I should have had to quaver out again, the reasons for my not having, in my delusion, so much as questioned that the little girl saw our visitant even as I actually saw Mrs Grose herself, and that she wanted, by just so much as she did thus see, to make me suppose she didn't, and at the same time, without showing anything, arrive at a guess as to whether I myself did! It was a pity I needed to recapitulate the portentous little activities by which she sought to divert my attention – the perceptible increase of movement, the greater intensity of play, the singing, the gabbling of nonsense and the invitation to romp.

Yet if I had not indulged, to prove there was nothing in it, in this review, I should have missed the two or three dim elements of comfort that still remained to me. I shouldn't, for instance, have been able to asseverate to my friend that I was certain – which was so much to the good – that *I* at least had not betrayed myself. I shouldn't have been prompted, by stress of need, by desperation of mind – I scarce know what to call it – to invoke such further aid to intelligence as might spring from pushing my colleague fairly to the wall. She had told me, bit by bit, under pressure, a great deal; but a small shifty spot on the wrong side of it all still sometimes brushed my brow like the wing of a bat; and I remember how on this occasion – for the sleeping house and the concentration alike of our danger and our watch seemed to help – I felt the importance of giving the last jerk to the curtain. 'I don't believe anything so horrible,' I recollect saying; 'no, let us put it definitely, my dear, that I don't. But if I did, you know, there's a thing I should require now, just without sparing you the least bit more – oh, not a scrap, come! – to get out of you. What was it you had in mind when, in our distress, before Miles came back, over the letter from his school, you said, under my insistence, that you didn't pretend for him he hadn't literally *ever* been "bad"? He has *not*, truly, "ever", in these weeks that I myself have lived with him and so closely watched him; he has been an imperturbable little prodigy of delightful, lovable goodness. Therefore you might perfectly have made the claim for him if you had not, as it happened, seen an exception to take. What was your exception, and to what passage in your personal observation of him did you refer?'

It was a straight question enough, but levity was not our note, and in any case I had, before the grey dawn admonished us to separate, got my answer. What my friend had had in mind proved immensely to the purpose. It was neither more nor less than the particular fact that for a period of several months Quint and the boy had been perpetually together. It was, indeed, the very appropriate item of evidence of her having ventured to criticise the propriety, to hint at the incongruity, of so close an alliance, and even to go so far on the subject as a frank overture to Miss Jessel would take her. Miss Jessel had, with a very high manner about it, requested her to mind her business, and the good woman had on this directly approached little Miles. What she had said to him, since I pressed, was that *she* liked to see young gentlemen not forget their station.

I pressed again, of course, the closer for that. 'You reminded him that Quint was only a base menial?'

'As you might say! And it was his answer, for one thing, that was bad.'

'And for another thing?' I waited. 'He repeated your words to Quint?'

'No, not that. It's just what he *wouldn't*!' she could still impress on me. 'I was sure, at any rate,' she added, 'that he didn't. But he denied certain occasions.'

'What occasions?'

'When they had been about together quite as if Quint were his tutor – and a very grand one – and Miss Jessel only for the little lady. When he had gone off with the fellow, I mean, and spent hours with him.'

'He then prevaricated about it – he said he hadn't?' Her assent was clear enough to cause me to add in a moment: 'I see. He lied.'

'Oh!' Mrs Grose mumbled. This was a suggestion that it didn't matter; which indeed she backed up by a further remark. 'You see, after all, Miss Jessel didn't mind. She didn't forbid him.'

I considered. 'Did he put that to you as a justification?'

At this she dropped again. 'No, he never spoke of it.'

'Never mentioned her in connection with Quint?'

She saw, visibly flushing, where I was coming out. 'Well, he didn't show anything. He denied,' she repeated; 'he denied.'

Lord, how I pressed her now! 'So that you could see he knew what was between the two wretches?'

'I don't know – I don't know!' the poor woman wailed.

'You do know, you dear thing,' I replied; 'only you haven't my dreadful boldness of mind, and you keep back, out of timidity, and modesty and delicacy, even the impression that in the past, when you had, without my aid, to flounder about in silence, most of all made you miserable. But I shall get it out of you yet! There was something in the boy that suggested to you,' I continued, 'his covering and concealing their relation.'

'Oh, he couldn't prevent – '

'Your learning the truth? I dare say! But, heavens,' I fell, with vehemence, a-thinking, 'what it shows that they must, to that extent, have succeeded in making of him!'

'Ah, nothing that's not nice *now*!' Mrs Grose lugubriously pleaded.

'I don't wonder you looked queer,' I persisted, 'when I mentioned to you the letter from his school!'

'I doubt if I looked as queer as you!' she retorted with homely force. 'And if he was so bad then as that comes to, how is he such an angel now?'

'Yes, indeed – and if he was a fiend at school! How, how, how? Well,' I said in my torment, 'you must put it to me again, though I shall not be able to tell you for some days. Only put it to me again!' I cried in a way that made my friend stare. 'There are directions in which I mustn't for the present let myself go.' Meanwhile I returned to her first example – the one to which she had just previously referred – of the boy's happy capacity for an occasional slip. 'If Quint – on your remonstrance at the time you speak of – was a base menial, one of the things Miles said to you, I find myself guessing, was that you were another.' Again her admission was so adequate that I continued: 'And you forgave him that?'

'Wouldn't *you*?'

'Oh, yes!' And we exchanged there, in the stillness, a sound of the oddest amusement. Then I went on: 'At all events, while he was with the man – '

'Miss Flora was with the woman. It suited them all!'

It suited me too, I felt, only too well; by which I mean that it suited exactly the particular deadly view I was in the very act of forbidding myself to entertain. But I so far succeeded in checking the expression of this view that I will throw, just here, no further light on it than may be offered by the mention of my final observation to Mrs Grose. 'His having lied and been impudent are, I confess, less engaging specimens than I had hoped to have from you of the outbreak in him of the little natural man. Still,' I mused, 'they must do, for they make me feel more than ever that I must watch.'

It made me blush, the next minute, to see in my friend's face how much more unreservedly she had forgiven him than her anecdote struck me as pointing out to my own tenderness any way to do. This was marked when, at the schoolroom door, she quitted me. 'Surely you don't accuse *him* – '

'Of carrying on an intercourse that he conceals from me? Ah, remember that, until further evidence, I now accuse nobody.' Then before shutting her out to go by another passage to her own place. 'I must just wait,' I wound up.

CHAPTER NINE

I WAITED AND WAITED, and the days took as they elapsed something from my consternation. A very few of them, in fact, passing, in constant sight of my pupils, without a fresh incident, sufficed to give to grievous fancies and even to odious memories a kind of brush of the sponge. I have spoken of the surrender to their extraordinary childish grace as a thing I could actively promote in myself, and it may be imagined if I neglected now to apply at this source for whatever balm it would yield. Stranger than I can express, certainly, was the effort to struggle against my new lights. It would doubtless have been a greater tension still, however, had it not been so frequently successful. I used to wonder how my little charges could help guessing that I thought strange things about them; and the circumstance that these things only made them more interesting was not by itself a direct aid to keeping them in the dark. I trembled lest they should see that they *were* so immensely more interesting. Putting things at the worst, at all events, as in meditation I so often did, any clouding of their innocence could only be – blameless and foredoomed as they were – a reason the more for taking risks. There were moments when I knew myself to catch them up by an irresistible impulse and press them to my heart. As soon as I had done so, I used to wonder: 'What will they think of that? Doesn't it betray too much?' It would have been easy to get into a sad wild tangle about how much I might betray; but the real account, I feel, of the hours of peace I could still enjoy was that the immediate charm of my companions was a beguilement still effective even under the shadow of the possibility that it was studied. For if it occurred to me that I might occasionally excite suspicion by the little outbreaks of my sharper passion for them, so too I remember asking if I mightn't see a queerness in the traceable increase of their own demonstrations.

They were at this period extravagantly and preternaturally fond of me; which, after all, I could reflect was no more than a graceful response in children perpetually bowed down over and hugged. The homage of which they were so lavish succeeded in truth for my nerves quite as well as if I never appeared to myself, as I may say, literally to catch them at a purpose in it. They had never, I think, wanted to do so many things for their poor protectress; I mean – though they got their lessons better and better, which was naturally what would please her most – in the way of diverting, entertaining, surprising her; reading her passages, telling her stories, acting her charades, pouncing out at her in disguises, as animals and historical characters and above all, astonishing her by the 'pieces' they had secretly got by heart and could interminably recite. I should never get to the bottom – were I to let myself go even now – of the prodigious private commentary, all under still more private correction, with which I in these days overscored their full hours. They had shown me from the first a facility for everything, a general faculty which, taking a fresh start, achieved remarkable flights. They got their little tasks as if they loved them; they indulged, from the mere exuberance of the gift, in the most unimposed little miracles of memory. They not only popped out at me as tigers and as Romans, but as Shakespearians, astronomers, and navigators. This was so singularly the case that it had presumably much to do with the fact as to which, at the present day, I am at a loss for a different explanation: I allude to my unnatural composure on the subject of another school for Miles. What I remember is that I was content for the time not to open the question, and that contentment must have sprung from the sense of his perpetually striking show of cleverness. He was too clever for a bad governess, for a parson's daughter, to spoil; and the strangest if not the brightest thread in the pensive embroidery I just spoke of was the impression I might have got, if I had dared to work it out, that he was under some influence operating in his small intellectual life as a tremendous incitement.

If it was easy to reflect, however, that such a boy could postpone school, it was at least as marked that for such a boy to have been 'kicked out' by a schoolmaster was a mystification without end. Let me add that in their company now – and I was careful almost never to be out of it – I could follow no scent very far. We lived in a cloud of music and affection and success and private theatricals. The musical sense in each of the children was of the quickest, but the elder especially had a marvellous knack of catching and repeating. The schoolroom piano broke into all gruesome fancies; and when that failed there were confabulations in corners, with a sequel of one of them going out in the highest spirits in order to 'come in' as something new. I had had brothers myself, and it was no revelation to me that little girls could be slavish idolaters of little boys. What surpassed everything was that there was a little boy in the world who could have for the inferior age, sex, and intelligence so fine a consideration. They were extraordinarily at one, and to say that they never either quarrelled or complained is to make the note of praise coarse for their quality of sweetness. Sometimes perhaps indeed (when I dropped into coarseness) I came across traces of little understandings between them by which one of them should keep me occupied while the other slipped away. There is a naïf side, I suppose, in all diplomacy; but if my pupils practised upon me it was surely with the minimum of grossness. It was all in the other quarter that, after a lull, the grossness broke out.

I find that I really hang back; but I must take my horrid plunge. In going on with the record of what was hideous at Bly I not only challenge the most liberal faith – for which I little care; but (and this is another matter) I renew what I myself suffered, I again push my dreadful way through it to the end. There came suddenly an hour after which, as I look back, the business seems to me to have been all pure suffering; but I have at least reached the heart of it, and the straightest road out is doubtless to advance. One evening – with nothing to lead up or prepare it – I felt the cold touch of the impression that had breathed on me the night of my arrival and which, much lighter then as I have mentioned, I should probably have made little of in memory had my subsequent sojourn been less agitated. I had not gone to bed; I sat reading by a couple of candles. There was a roomful of old books at Bly – last-century fiction some of it, which, to the extent of a distinctly deprecated renown, but never to so much as that of a stray specimen, had reached the sequestered home and appealed to the unavowed curiosity of my youth. I remember that the book I had in my hand was Fielding's *Amelia*;[9]

also that I was wholly awake. I recall further both a general conviction that it was horribly late and a particular objection to looking at my watch. I figure finally that the white curtain draping, in the fashion of those days, the head of Flora's little bed, shrouded, as I had assured myself long before, the perfection of childish rest. I recollect in short that though I was deeply interested in my author, I found myself, at the turn of a page and with his spell all scattered, looking straight up from him and hard at the door of my room. There was a moment during which I listened, reminded of the faint sense I had had, the first night, of there being something undefinably astir in the house, and noted the soft breath of the open casement just move the half-drawn blind. Then, with all the marks of a deliberation that must have seemed magnificent had there been anyone to admire it, I laid down my book, rose to my feet and, taking a candle, went straight out of the room and, from the passage, on which my light made little impression, noiselessly closed and locked the door.

I can say now neither what determined nor what guided me, but I went straight along the lobby, holding my candle high, till I came within sight of the tall window that presided over the great turn of the staircase. At this point, I precipitately found myself aware of three things. They were practically simultaneous, yet they had flashes of succession. My candle, under a bold flourish, went out, and I perceived, by the uncovered window, that the yielding dusk of earliest morning rendered it unnecessary. Without it, the next instant, I knew that there was a figure on the stair. I speak of sequences, but I required no lapse of seconds to stiffen myself for a third encounter with Quint. The apparition had reached the landing halfway up and was therefore on the spot nearest the window, where, at sight of me, it stopped short and fixed me exactly as it had fixed me from the tower and from the garden. He knew me as well as I knew him; and so, in the cold faint twilight, with a glimmer in the high glass and another on the polish of the oak stair below, we faced each other in our common intensity. He was absolutely, on this occasion, a living, detestable, dangerous presence. But that was not the wonder of wonders; I reserve this distinction for quite another circumstance: the circumstance that dread had unmistakably quitted me and that there was nothing in me unable to meet and measure him.

I had plenty of anguish after that extraordinary moment, but I had, thank God, no terror. And he knew I hadn't – I found myself at the end of an instant magnificently aware of this. I felt, in a fierce rigour of confidence, that if I stood my ground a minute I should cease – for the time at least – to have him to reckon with; and during the minute, accordingly, the thing was as human and hideous as a real interview: hideous just because it *was* human, as human as to have met alone, in the small hours, in a sleeping house, some enemy, some adventurer, some criminal. It was the dead silence of our long gaze at such close quarters that gave the whole horror, huge as it was, its only note of the unnatural. If I had met a murderer in such a place and at such an hour we still at least would have spoken. Something would have passed, in life, between us; if nothing had passed, one of us would have moved. The moment was so prolonged that it would have taken but little more to make me doubt if even *I* were in life. I can't express what followed it save by saying that the silence itself – which was indeed in a manner an attestation of my strength – became the element into which I saw the figure disappear; in which I definitely saw it turn, as I might have seen the low wretch to which it had once belonged turn on receipt of an order, and pass, with my eyes on the villainous back that no hunch could have more disfigured, straight down the staircase and into the darkness in which the next bend was lost.

CHAPTER TEN

I REMAINED awhile at the top of the stair, but with the effect presently of understanding that when my visitor had gone, he had gone; then I returned to my room. The foremost thing I saw there by the light of the candle I had left burning was that Flora's little bed was empty; and on this I caught my breath with all the terror that, five minutes before, I had been able to resist. I dashed at the place in which I had left her lying and over which – for the small silk counterpane and the sheets were disarranged – the white curtains had been deceivingly pulled forward; then my step, to my unutterable relief, produced an answering sound: I noticed an agitation of the window-blind, and the child, ducking down, emerged rosily from the other side of it. She stood there in so much of her candour and so little of her nightgown, with her pink bare feet and the golden glow of her curls. She looked intensely grave and I had never had such a sense of losing an advantage acquired (the thrill of which had just been so prodigious) as on my consciousness that she addressed me with a reproach: 'You naughty: where *have* you been?' Instead of challenging her own irregularity, I found myself arraigned and explaining. She herself explained, for that matter, with the loveliest, eagerest simplicity. She had known suddenly, as she lay there, that I was out of the room and had jumped up to see what had become of me. I had dropped, with the joy of her reappearance, back into my chair – feeling then, and then only, a little faint; and she had pattered straight over to me, thrown herself upon my knee, given herself to be held with the flame of the candle full in the wonderful little face that was still flushed with sleep. I remember closing my eyes an instant, yieldingly, consciously, as before the excess of something beautiful that shone out of the blue of her own. 'You were looking for me out of the window?' I said. 'You thought I might be walking in the grounds?'

'Well, you know, I thought someone was' – she never blanched as she smiled out that at me.

Oh, how I looked at her now! 'And did you see anyone?'

'Ah, *no*!' she returned almost (with the full privilege of childish inconsequence) resentfully, though with a long sweetness in her little drawl of the negative.

At the moment, in the state of my nerves, I absolutely believed she lied, and if I once more closed my eyes it was before the dazzle of the three or four possible ways in which I might take this up. One of these for a moment tempted me with such singular force that, to resist it, I must have gripped my little girl with a spasm that, wonderfully, she submitted to without a cry or a sign of fright. Why not break out at her on the spot and have it all over? – give it to her straight in her lovely little lighted face? 'You see, you see, you *know* that you do and that you already quite suspect I believe it; therefore why not frankly confess it to me, so that we may at least live with it together and learn perhaps, in the strangeness of our fate, where we are and what it means?' This solicitation dropped, alas, as it came: if I could immediately have succumbed to it I might have spared myself – well, you'll see what. Instead of succumbing, I sprang again to my feet, looked at her bed and took a helpless middle way. 'Why did you pull the curtain over the place to make me think you were still there?'

Flora luminously considered; after which, with her little divine smile: 'Because I don't like to frighten you!'

'But if I had, by your idea, gone out – ?'

She absolutely declined to be puzzled; she turned her eyes to the flame of the candle as if the question were as irrelevant, or at any rate as impersonal, as Mrs Marcet or nine-times-nine.[10] 'Oh, but you know,' she quite adequately answered, 'that you might come back, you dear, and that you *have*!' And after a little, when she had got into bed, I had, a long time, by almost sitting on her for the retention of her hand, to show how I recognised the pertinence of my return.

You may imagine the general complexion, from that moment, of my nights. I repeatedly sat up till I didn't know when; I selected moments when my room-mate unmistakably slept, and, stealing out, took noiseless turns in the passage. I even pushed as far as to where I had last met Quint. But I never met him there again, and I may as well say at once that I on no other occasion saw him in the house. I just missed, on the staircase, nevertheless, a different adventure. Looking down it from the top I once recognised the presence of a woman seated on one of the lower steps with her back presented to me, her body half-bowed and her head, in an attitude of woe, in her hands. I had been there but an instant, however, when she vanished without looking round at me. I knew, for all that, exactly what dreadful face she had to show; and I wondered whether, if instead of being above I had been below, I should have had the same nerve for going up that I had lately shown Quint. Well, there continued to be plenty of call for nerve. On the eleventh night after my latest encounter with that gentleman – they were all numbered now – I had an alarm that perilously skirted it and that indeed, from the particular quality of its unexpectedness, proved quite my sharpest shock. It was precisely the first night during this series, that, weary with vigils, I had conceived I might again without laxity lay myself down at my old hour. I slept immediately and, as I afterwards knew, till about one o'clock; but when I woke it was to sit straight up as completely roused as if a hand had shaken me. I had left a light burning, but it was now out, and I felt an instant certainty that Flora had extinguished it. This brought me to my feet and straight, in the darkness, to her bed, which I found she had left. A glance at the window enlightened me further, and the striking of a match completed the picture.

The child had again got up – this time blowing out the taper, and had again, for some purpose of observation or response, squeezed in behind the blind and was peering out into the night. That she now saw as she had not, I had satisfied myself, the previous time – was proved to me by the fact that she was disturbed neither by my re-illumination nor by the haste I made to get into slippers and into a wrap. Hidden, protected, absorbed, she evidently rested on the sill – the casement opened forward – and gave herself up. There was a great still moon to help her, and this fact had counted in my quick decision. She was face to face with the apparition we had met at the lake, and could now communicate with it as she had not then been able to do. What I, on my side, had to care for was, without disturbing her, to reach, from the corridor, some other window turned to the same quarter. I got to the door without her hearing me; I got out of it, closed it, and listened from the other side for some sound from her. While I stood in the passage I had my eyes on her brother's door, which was but ten steps off and which, indescribably, produced in me a renewal of the strange impulse that I lately spoke of as my temptation. What if I should go straight in and march to *his* window? – what if, by risking to his boyish bewilderment a revelation of my motive, I should throw across the rest of the mystery the long halter of my boldness?

This thought held me sufficiently to make me cross to his threshold and pause again. I preternaturally listened; I figured to myself what might portentously be; I wondered if his bed were also empty and he also secretly at watch. It was a deep soundless minute, at the end of which my impulse failed. He was quiet; he might be innocent; the risk was hideous; I turned away. There was a figure in the grounds – a figure prowling for a sight, the visitor with whom Flora was engaged; but it wasn't the visitor most concerned with my boy. I hesitated afresh, but on other grounds and only a few seconds; then I had made my choice. There were empty rooms enough at Bly, and it was only a question of choosing the right one. The right one suddenly presented itself to me as the lower one – though high above the gardens – in the solid corner of the house that I have spoken of as the old tower. This was a large, square chamber, arranged with some state as a bedroom, the extravagant size of which made it so inconvenient that it had not for years, though kept by Mrs Grose in exemplary order, been occupied. I had often admired it and I knew my way about in it; I had only, after just faltering at the first chill gloom of its disuse, to pass across it and unbolt in all quietness one of the shutters. Achieving this transit I uncovered the glass without a sound and, applying my face to the pane, was able, the darkness without being much less than within, to see that I commanded the right direction. Then I saw something more. The moon made the night extraordinarily penetrable and showed me on the lawn a person, diminished by distance, who stood there motionless and as if fascinated, looking up to where I had appeared looking, that is, not so much straight at me as at something that was apparently above me. There was clearly another person above me – there was a person on the tower; but the presence on the lawn was not in the least what I had conceived and had confidently hurried to meet. The presence on the lawn – I felt sick as I made it out – was poor little Miles himself.

CHAPTER ELEVEN

IT WAS NOT TILL LATE next day that I spoke to Mrs Grose; the rigour with which I kept my pupils in sight making it often difficult to meet her privately; the more as we each felt the importance of not provoking – on the part of the servants quite as much as on that of the children – any suspicion of a secret flurry or of a discussion of mysteries. I drew a great security in this particular from her mere smooth aspect. There was nothing in her fresh face to pass on to others the least of my horrible confidences. She believed me, I was sure, absolutely: if she hadn't I don't know what would have become of me, for I couldn't have borne the strain alone. But she was a magnificent monument to the blessing of a want of imagination, and if she could see in our little charges nothing but their beauty and amiability, their happiness and cleverness, she had no direct communication with the sources of my trouble. If they had been at all visibly blighted or battered, she would doubtless have grown, on tracing it back, haggard enough to match them; as matters stood, however, I could feel her, when she surveyed them with her large white arms folded and the habit of serenity in all her look, thank the Lord's mercy that if they were ruined the pieces would still serve. Flights of fancy gave place, in her mind, to a steady fireside glow, and I had already begun to perceive how, with the development of the conviction that – as time went on without a public accident – our young things could, after all, look out for themselves, she addressed her greatest solicitude to the sad case presented by their deputy-guardian. That, for myself, was a sound simplification: I could engage that, to the world, my face should tell no tales, but it would have been, in the conditions, an immense added worry to find myself anxious about hers.

At the hour I now speak of she had joined me, under pressure, on the terrace, where, with the lapse of the season, the afternoon sun was now agreeable; and we sat there together while before us and at a distance, yet within call if we wished, the children strolled to and fro in one of their most manageable moods. They moved slowly, in unison, below us, over the lawn, the boy, as they went, reading aloud from a story-book and passing his arm round his sister to keep her quite in touch. Mrs Grose watched them with positive placidity; then I caught the suppressed intellectual creak with which she conscientiously turned to take from me a view of the back of the tapestry. I had made her a receptacle of lurid things, but there was an odd recognition of my superiority – my accomplishments and my function – in her patience under my pain. She offered her mind to my disclosures as, had I wished to mix a witch's broth and proposed it with assurance, she would have held out a large, clean saucepan. This had become thoroughly her attitude by the time that, in my recital of the events of the night, I reached the point of what Miles had said to me when, after seeing him, at such a monstrous hour, almost on the very spot where he happened now to be, I had gone down to bring him in; choosing then, at the window with a concentrated need of not alarming the house, rather that method than any noisier process. I had left her meanwhile in little doubt of my small hope of representing with success even to her actual sympathy my sense of the real splendour of the little inspiration with which, after I had got him into the house, the boy met my final articulate challenge. As soon as I appeared in the moonlight on the terrace, he had come to me as straight as possible; on which I had taken his hand without a word and led him, through the dark spaces, up the staircase where Quint had so hungrily hovered for him, along the lobby where I had listened and trembled, and so to his forsaken room.

Not a sound, on the way, had passed between us and I had wondered – oh, *how* I had wondered! – if he were groping about in his dreadful little mind for something plausible and not too grotesque. It would tax his invention certainly, and I felt, this time, over his real embarrassment, a curious thrill of triumph. It was a sharp trap for any game hitherto successful. He could play no longer at perfect propriety, nor could he pretend to it; so how the deuce would he get out of the scrape? There beat in me indeed, with the passionate throb of this question, an equal dumb appeal as to how the deuce *I* should. I was confronted at last, as never yet, with all the risk attached even now to sounding my own horrid note. I remember, in fact, that as we pushed into his little chamber, where the bed had not been slept in at all and the window, uncovered to the moonlight, made the place so clear that there was no need of striking a match – I remember how I suddenly dropped, sank upon the edge of the bed from the force of the idea that he must know how he really, as they say, 'had' me. He could do what he liked, with all his cleverness to help him, so long as I should continue to defer to the old tradition of the criminality of those caretakers of the young who minister to superstitions and fears. He 'had' me indeed, and in a cleft stick; for who would ever absolve me, who would consent that I should be unhung, if, by the faintest tremor of an overture, I were the first to introduce into our perfect intercourse an element so dire? No, no: it was useless to attempt to convey to Mrs Grose, just as it is scarcely less so to attempt to suggest here, how, during our short, stiff brush there in the dark, he fairly shook me with admiration. I was of course thoroughly kind and merciful; never, never yet had I placed on his small shoulders hands of such tenderness as those with which, while I rested against the bed, I held him there well under fire. I had no alternative but, in form at least, to put it to him.

'You must tell me now – and all the truth. What did you go out for? What were you doing there?'

I can still see his wonderful smile, the whites of his beautiful eyes and the uncovering of his clear teeth, shine to me in the dusk. 'If I tell you why, will you understand?' My heart, at this, leaped into my mouth. *Would* he tell me why? I found no sound on my lips to press it, and I was aware of answering only with a vague, repeated, grimacing nod. He was gentleness itself, and while I wagged my head at him he stood there more than ever a little fairy prince. It was his brightness indeed that gave me a respite. Would it be so great if he were really going to tell me? 'Well,' he said at last, 'just exactly in order that you should do this.'

'Do what?'

'Think me – for a change – *bad*!' I shall never forget the sweetness and gaiety with which he brought out the word, nor how, on top of it, he bent forward and kissed me. It was practically the end of everything. I met his kiss and I had to make, while I folded him for a minute in my arms, the most stupendous effort not to cry. He had given exactly the account of himself that permitted least my going behind it, and it was only with the effect of confirming my acceptance of it that, as I presently glanced about the room, I could say: 'Then you didn't undress at all?'

He fairly glittered in the gloom. 'Not at all. I sat up and read.'

'And when did you go down?'

'At midnight. When I'm bad I *am* bad!'

'I see, I see – it's charming. But how could you be sure I should know it?'

'Oh, I arranged that with Flora.' His answers rang out with a readiness! 'She was to get up and look out.'

'Which is what she did do.' It was I who fell into the trap!

'So she disturbed you, and, to see what she was looking at, you also looked – you saw.'

'While you,' I concurred, 'caught your death in the night air!'

He literally bloomed so from this exploit that he could afford radiantly to assent. 'How otherwise should I have been bad enough?' he asked. Then, after another embrace, the incident and our interview closed on my recognition of all the reserves of goodness that, for his joke, he had been able to draw upon.

CHAPTER TWELVE

THE PARTICULAR IMPRESSION I had received proved in the morning light, I repeat, not quite successfully presentable to Mrs Grose, though I re-enforced it with the mention of still another remark that he had made before we separated. 'It all lies in half a dozen words,' I said to her, 'words that really settle the matter. "Think, you know, what I *might* do!" He threw that off to show me how good he is. He knows down to the ground what he "might do". That's what he gave them a taste of at school.'

'Lord, you do change!' cried my friend.

'I don't change – I simply make it out. The four, depend upon it, perpetually meet. If on either of these last nights you had been with either child you'd clearly have understood. The more I've watched and waited the more I've felt that if there were nothing else to make it sure it would be made so by the systematic silence of each. Never, by a slip of the tongue, have they so much as alluded to either of their old friends, any more than Miles has alluded to his expulsion. Oh, yes, we may sit here and look at them, and they may show off to us there to their fill; but even while they pretend to be lost in their fairytale they're steeped in their vision of the dead restored to them. He's not reading to her,' I declared; 'they're talking of *them* – they're talking horrors! I go on, I know, as if I were crazy; and it's a wonder I'm not. What I've seen would have made *you* so; but it has only made me more lucid, made me get hold of still other things.'

My lucidity must have seemed awful, but the charming creatures who were victims of it, passing and repassing in their interlocked sweetness, gave my colleague something to hold on by; and I felt how tight she held as, without stirring in the breath of my passion, she covered them still with her eyes. 'Of what other things have you got hold?'

'Why, of the very things that have delighted, fascinated and yet, at bottom, as I now so strangely see, mystified and troubled me. Their more than earthly beauty, their absolutely unnatural goodness. It's a game,' I went on; 'it's a policy and a fraud!'

'On the part of little darlings – ?'

'As yet mere lovely babies? Yes, mad as that seems!' The very act of bringing it out really helped me to trace it – follow it all up and piece it all together. 'They haven't been good – they've only been absent. It has been easy to live with them because they're simply leading a life of their own. They're not mine – they're not ours. They're his and they're hers!'

'Quint's and that woman's?'

'Quint's and that woman's. They want to get to them.'

Oh, how, at this, poor Mrs Grose appeared to study them! 'But for what?'

'For the love of all the evil that, in those dreadful days, the pair put into them. And to ply them with that evil still, to keep up the work of demons, is what brings the others back.'

'Laws!' said my friend under her breath. The exclamation was homely, but it revealed a real acceptance of my further proof of what, in the bad time – for there had been a worse even than this – must have occurred. There could have been no such justification for me as the plain assent of her experience to whatever depth of depravity I found credible in our brace of scoundrels. It was in obvious submission of memory that she brought out after a moment: 'They *were* rascals! But what can they now do?' she pursued.

'Do?' I echoed so loud that Miles and Flora, as they passed at their distance, paused an instant in their walk and looked at us. 'Don't they do enough?' I demanded in a lower tone, while the children, having smiled and nodded and kissed hands to us, resumed their exhibition. We were held by it a minute; then I answered: 'They can destroy them!' At this my companion did turn, but the appeal she launched was a silent one, the effect of which was to make me more explicit. 'They don't know as yet quite how – but they're trying hard. They're seen only across, as it were, and beyond – in strange places and on high places, the top of towers, the roof of houses, the outside of windows, the farther edge of pools; but there's a deep design on either side, to shorten the distance and overcome the obstacle: so the success of the tempters is only a question of time. They've only to keep to their suggestions of danger.'

'For the children to come?'

'And perish in the attempt!' Mrs Grose slowly got up, and I scrupulously added: 'Unless, of course, we can prevent!'

Standing there before me while I kept my seat, she visibly turned things over. 'Their uncle must do the preventing. He must take them away.'

'And who's to make him?'

She had been scanning the distance, but she now dropped on me a foolish face. 'You, miss.'

'By writing to him that his house is poisoned and his nephew and niece mad?'

'But if they *are*, miss?'

'And if I am myself, you mean? That's charming news to be sent him by a person enjoying his confidence and whose prime undertaking was to give him no worry.'

Mrs Grose considered, following the children again. 'Yes, he do hate worry. That was the great reason – '

'Why those fiends took him in so long? No doubt, though his indifference must have been awful. As I'm not a fiend, at any rate, I shouldn't take him in.'

My companion, after an instant and for all answer, sat down again and grasped my arm. 'Make him at any rate come to you.'

I stared. 'To *me*?' I had a sudden fear of what she might do. ' "Him?" '

'He ought to *be* here – he ought to help.'

I quickly rose and I think I must have shown her a queerer face than ever yet. 'You see me asking him for a visit?' No, with her eyes on my face she evidently couldn't. Instead of it even – as a woman reads another – she could see what I myself saw: his derision, his amusement, his contempt for the breakdown of my resignation at being left alone and for the fine machinery I had set in motion to attract his attention to my slighted charms. She didn't know – no one knew – how proud I had been to serve him and to stick to our terms; yet she none the less took the measure, I think, of the warning I now gave her. 'If you should so lose your head as to appeal to him for me – '

She was really frightened. 'Yes, miss?'

'I would leave, on the spot, both him and you.'

CHAPTER THIRTEEN

IT WAS ALL VERY WELL to join them, but speaking to them proved quite as much as ever an effort beyond my strength – offered, in close quarters, difficulties as insurmountable as before. This situation continued a month, and with new aggravations and particular notes, the note above all, sharper and sharper, of the small ironic consciousness on the part of my pupils. It was not, I am as sure today as I was sure then, my mere infernal imagination: it was absolutely traceable that they were aware of my predicament and that this strange relation made, in a manner, for a long time, the air in which we moved. I don't mean that they had their tongues in their cheeks or did anything vulgar, for that was not one of their dangers: I do mean, on the other hand, that the element of the unnamed and untouched became, between us, greater than any other, and that so much avoidance couldn't have been made successful without a great deal of tacit arrangement. It was as if, at moments, we were perpetually coming into sight of subjects before which we must stop short, turning suddenly out of alleys that we perceived to be blind, closing with a little bang that made us look at each other – for, like all bangs, it was something louder than we had intended – the doors we had indiscreetly opened. All roads lead to Rome, and there were times when it might have struck us that almost every branch of study or subject of conversation skirted forbidden ground. Forbidden ground was the question of the return of the dead in general and of whatever, especially, might survive, for memory, of the friends little children had lost. There were days when I could have sworn that one of them had, with a small invisible nudge, said to the other: 'She thinks she'll do it this time – but she *won't*!' To 'do it' would have been to indulge, for instance – and for once in a way – in some direct reference to the lady who had prepared them for my discipline. They had a delightful endless appetite for passages in my own history to which I had again and again treated them; they were in possession of everything that had ever happened to me, had had, with every circumstance, the story of my smallest adventures and of those of my brothers and sisters and of the cat and the dog at home, as well as many particulars of the whimsical bent of my father, of the furniture and arrangement of our house and of the conversation of the old women of our village. There were things enough, taking one with another, to chatter about, if one went very fast and knew by instinct when to go round. They pulled with an art of their own the strings of my invention and my memory; and nothing else perhaps, when I thought of such occasions afterwards, gave me so the suspicion of being watched from under cover. It was in any case over *my* life, *my* past and *my* friends alone that we could take anything like our ease; a state of affairs that led them sometimes without the least pertinence to break out into sociable reminders. I was invited – with no visible connection – to repeat afresh Goody Gosling's[11] celebrated *mot* or to confirm the details already supplied as to the cleverness of the vicarage pony.

It was partly at such junctures as these and partly at quite different ones that, with the turn my matters had now taken, my predicament, as I have called it, grew most sensible. The fact that the days passed for me without another encounter ought, it would have appeared, to have done something towards soothing my nerves. Since the light brush, that second night on the upper landing, of the presence of a woman at the foot of the stair, I had seen nothing, whether in or out of the house, that one had better not have seen. There was many a corner round which I expected to come upon Quint, and many a situation that, in a merely sinister way, would have favoured the appearance of Miss Jessel. The summer had turned, the summer had gone; the autumn had dropped upon Bly and had blown out half our lights. The place, with its grey sky and withered garlands, its bared spaces and scattered dead leaves, was like a theatre after the performance – all strewn with crumpled playbills. There were exactly states of the air, conditions of sound and of stillness, unspeakable impressions of the *kind* of ministering moment, that brought back to me, long enough to catch it, the feeling of the medium in which, that June evening out of doors, I had had my first sight of Quint, and in which too, at those other instants, I had, after seeing him through the window, looked for him in vain in the circle of shrubbery. I recognised the signs, the portents – I recognised the moment, the spot. But they remained unaccompanied and empty, and I continued unmolested; if unmolested one could call a young woman whose sensibility had, in the most extraordinary fashion, not declined but deepened. I had said in my talk with Mrs Grose on that horrid scene of Flora's by the lake – and had perplexed her by so saying – that it would from that moment distress me much more to lose my power than to keep it. I had then expressed what was vividly in my mind: the truth that, whether the children really saw or not – since, that is, it was not yet definitely proved – I greatly preferred, as a safeguard, the fullness of my own exposure. I was ready to know the very worst that was to be known. What I had then had an ugly glimpse of was that my eyes might be sealed just while theirs were most opened. Well, my eyes *were* sealed, it appeared, at present – a consummation for which it seemed blasphemous not to thank God. There was, alas, a difficulty about that: I would have thanked Him with all my soul had I not had in a proportionate measure this conviction of the secret of my pupils.

How can I retrace today the strange steps of my obsession? There were times of our being together when I would have been ready to swear that, literally, in my presence, but with my direct sense of it closed, they had visitors who were known and were welcome. Then it was that, had I not been deterred by the very chance that such an injury might prove greater than the injury to be averted, my exaltation would have broken out. 'They're here, they're here, you little wretches,' I would have cried, 'and you can't deny it now!' The little wretches denied it with all the added volume of their sociability and their tenderness, just in the crystal depths of which – like the flash of a fish in a stream – the mockery of their advantage peeped up. The shock had in truth sunk into me still deeper than I knew on the night when, looking out either for Quint or for Miss Jessel under the stars, I had seen there the boy over whose rest I watched and who had immediately brought in with him – had straightaway there turned on me – the lovely upward look with which, from the battlements above us, the hideous apparition of Quint had played. If it was a question of a scare, my discovery on this occasion had scared me more than any other, and it was essentially in the scared state that I drew my actual conclusions. They harassed me so that sometimes, at odd moments, I shut myself up audibly to rehearse – it was at once a fantastic relief and a renewed despair – the manner in which I might come to the point. I approached it from one side and the other while, in my room, I flung myself about, but I always broke down in the monstrous utterances of names. As they died away on my lips I said to myself that I should indeed help them to represent something infamous if by pronouncing them I should violate as rare a little case of instinctive delicacy as any schoolroom probably had ever known. When I said to myself: '*They* have the manners to be silent, and you, trusted as you are, the baseness to speak!' I felt myself crimson and covered my face with my hands. After these secret scenes I chattered more than ever, going on volubly enough till one of our prodigious, palpable hushes occurred – I can call them nothing else – the strange, dizzy lift or swim (I try for terms!) into a stillness, a pause of all life, that had nothing to do with the more or less noise we at the moment might be engaged in making and that I could hear through any intensified mirth or quickened recitation or louder strum of the piano. Then it was that the others, the outsiders, were there. Though they were not angels they 'passed', as the French say, causing me, while they stayed, to tremble with the fear of their addressing to their younger victims some yet more infernal message or more vivid image than they had thought good enough for myself.

What it was least possible to get rid of was the cruel idea that, whatever I had seen, Miles and Flora saw *more* – things terrible and unguessable and that sprang from dreadful passages of intercourse in the past. Such things naturally left on the surface, for the time, a chill that we vociferously denied we felt; and we had all three, with repetition, got into such splendid training that we went, each time, to mark the close of the incident, almost automatically through the very same movements. It was striking of the children at all events to kiss me inveterately with a wild irrelevance and never to fail – one or the other – of the precious question that had helped us through many a peril. 'When do you think he *will* come? Don't you think we *ought* to write?' – there was nothing like that inquiry, we found by experience, for carrying off an awkwardness. 'He', of course, was their uncle in Harley Street; and we lived in much profusion of theory that he might at any moment arrive to mingle in our circle. It was impossible to have given less encouragement than he had administered to such a doctrine, but if we had not had the doctrine to fall back upon, we should have deprived each other of some of our finest exhibitions. He never wrote to them – that may have been selfish, but it was a part of the flattery of his trust of myself; for the way in which a man pays his highest tribute to a woman is apt to be put by the more festal celebration of one of the sacred laws of his comfort. So I held that I carried out the spirit of the pledge given not to appeal to him when I let our young friends understand that their own letters were but charming literary exercises. They were too beautiful to be posted; I kept them myself; I have them all to this hour. This was a rule, indeed, which only added to the satiric effect of my being plied with the supposition that he might at any moment be among us. It was exactly as if our young friends knew how almost more awkward than anything else that might be for me. There appears to me, moreover, as I look back, no note in all this more extraordinary than the mere fact that, in spite of my tension and of their triumph, I never lost patience with them. Adorable they must in truth have been, I now feel, since I didn't in these days hate them! Would exasperation, however, if relief had longer been postponed, finally have betrayed me? It little matters, for relief arrived. I call it relief though it was only the relief that a snap brings to a strain or the burst of a thunderstorm to a day of suffocation. It was at least change, and it came with a rush.

CHAPTER FOURTEEN

WALKING TO CHURCH a certain Sunday morning, I had little Miles at my side and his sister, in advance of us and at Mrs Grose's, well in sight. It was a crisp, clear day, the first of its order for some time; the night had brought a touch of frost and the autumn air, bright and sharp, made the church bells almost gay. It was an odd accident of thought that I should have happened at such a moment to be particularly and very gratefully struck with the obedience of my little charges. Why did they never resent my inexorable, my perpetual society? Something or other had brought nearer home to me that I had all but pinned the boy to my shawl, and that in the way our companions were marshalled before me I might have appeared to provide against some danger of rebellion. I was like a jailer with an eye to possible surprises and escapes. But all this belonged – I mean their magnificent little surrender – just to the special array of the facts that were most abysmal. Turned out for Sunday by his uncle's tailor, who had had a free hand and a notion of pretty waistcoats and of his grand little air, Miles's whole title to independence, the rights of his sex and situation, were so stamped upon him that if he had suddenly struck for freedom I should have had nothing to say. I was by the strangest of chances wondering how I should meet him when the revolution unmistakably occurred. I call it a revolution because I now see how, with the word he spoke, the curtain rose on the last act of my dreadful drama and the catastrophe was precipitated. 'Look here, my dear, you know,' he charmingly said, 'when in the world, please, am I going back to school?'

Transcribed here the speech sounds harmless enough, particularly as uttered in the sweet, high, casual pipe with which, at all interlocutors, but above all at his eternal governess, he threw off intonations as if he were tossing roses. There was something in them that always made one 'catch', and I caught at any rate now so effectually that I stopped as short as if one of the trees of the park had fallen across the road. There was something new, on the spot, between us, and he was perfectly aware I recognised it, though to enable me to do so he had no need to look a whit less candid and charming than usual. I could feel in him how he already, from my at first finding nothing to reply, perceived the advantage he had gained. I was so slow to find anything that he had plenty of time, after a minute, to continue with his suggestive but inconclusive smile: 'You know, my dear, that for a fellow to be with a lady *always* – !' His 'my dear' was constantly on his lips for me, and nothing could have expressed more the exact shade of the sentiment with which I desired to inspire my pupils than its fond familiarity. It was so respectfully easy.

But oh, how I felt that at present I must pick my own phrases! I remember that, to gain time, I tried to laugh, and I seemed to see in the beautiful face with which he watched me how ugly and queer I looked. 'And always with the same lady?' I returned.

He neither blenched nor winked. The whole thing was virtually out between us. 'Ah, of course she's a jolly "perfect" lady; but after all I'm a fellow, don't you see? who's – well, getting on.'

I lingered there with him an instant ever so kindly. 'Yes, you're getting on.' Oh, but I felt helpless!

I have kept to this day the heartbreaking little idea of how he seemed to know that and to play with it. 'And you can't say I've not been awfully good, can you?'

I laid my hand on his shoulder, for though I felt how much better it would have been to walk on, I was not yet quite able. 'No, I can't say that, Miles.'

'Except just that one night, you know – !'

'That one night?' I couldn't look as straight as he.

'Why, when I went down – went out of the house.'

'Oh, yes. But I forget what you did it for.'

'You forget?' – he spoke with the sweet extravagance of childish reproach. 'Why, it was just to show you I could!'

'Oh, yes – you could.'

'And I can again.'

I felt I might perhaps after all succeed in keeping my wits about me. 'Certainly. But you won't.'

'No, not *that* again. It was nothing.'

'It was nothing,' I said. 'But we must go on.'

He resumed our walk with me, passing his hand into my arm. 'Then when *am* I going back?'

I wore, in turning it over, my most responsible air. 'Were you very happy at school?'

He just considered. 'Oh, I'm happy enough anywhere!'

'Well, then,' I quavered, 'if you're just as happy here – !'

'Ah, but that isn't everything! Of course *you* know a lot – '

'But you hint that you know almost as much?' I asked as he paused.

'Not half I want to!' Miles honestly professed. 'But it isn't so much that.'

'What is it, then?'

'Well – I want to see more life.'

'I see; I see.' We had arrived within sight of the church and of various persons, including several of the household of Bly, on their way to it and clustered about the door to see us go in. I quickened our step; I wanted to get there before the question between us opened up much further; I reflected hungrily that he would have for more than an hour to be silent, and I thought with envy of the comparative dusk of the pew and of the almost spiritual help of the hassock on which I might bend my knees. I seemed literally to be running a race with some confusion to which he was about to reduce me, but I felt he had got in first when, before we had entered the churchyard, he threw out: 'I want my own sort!'

It literally made me bound forward. 'There aren't many of your own sort, Miles!' I laughed. 'Unless perhaps dear little Flora!'

'You really compare me to a baby girl?'

This found me singularly weak. 'Don't you then *love* our sweet Flora?'

'If I didn't – and you too; if I didn't – !' he repeated as if retreating for a jump, yet leaving his thought so unfinished that, after we had come into the gate, another stop, which he imposed on me by the pressure of his arm, had become inevitable. Mrs Grose and Flora had passed into the church, the other worshippers had followed and we were, for the minute, alone among the old, thick graves. We had paused, on the path from the gate, by a low, oblong, table-like tomb.

'Yes, if you didn't – ?'

He looked, while I waited, about at the graves. 'Well, you know what!' But he didn't move, and he presently produced something that made me drop straight down on the stone slab as if suddenly to rest. 'Does my uncle think what *you* think?'

I markedly rested. 'How do you know what I think?'

'Ah, well, of course I don't; for it strikes me you never tell me. But I mean does *he* know?'

'Know what, Miles?'

'Why, the way I'm going on.'

I recognised quickly enough that I could make, to this inquiry, no answer that wouldn't involve something of a sacrifice of my employer. Yet it struck me that we were all, at Bly, sufficiently sacrificed to make that venial. 'I don't think your uncle much cares.'

Miles, on this, stood looking at me. 'Then don't you think he can be made to?'

'In what way?'

'Why, by his coming down.'

'But who'll get him to come down?'

'*I* will!' the boy said with extraordinary brightness and emphasis. He gave me another look charged with that expression and then marched off alone into church.

CHAPTER FIFTEEN

THE BUSINESS was practically settled from the moment I never followed him. It was a pitiful surrender to agitation, but my being aware of this had somehow no power to restore me. I only sat there on my tomb and read into what our young friend had said to me the fullness of its meaning; by the time I had grasped the whole of which, I had also embraced, for absence, the pretext that I was ashamed to offer my pupils and the rest of the congregation such an example of delay. What I said to myself, above all, was that Miles had got something out of me and that the gauge of it for him would be just this awkward collapse. He had got out of me that there was something I was much afraid of, and that he should probably be able to make use of my fear to gain, for his own purpose, more freedom. My fear was of having to deal with the intolerable question of the grounds of his dismissal from school, since that was really but the question of the horrors gathered behind. That his uncle should arrive to treat with me of these things was a solution that, strictly speaking, I ought now to have desired to bring on; but I could so little face the ugliness and the pain of it that I simply procrastinated and lived from hand to mouth. The boy, to my deep discomposure, was immensely in the right, was in a position to say to me: 'Either you clear up with my guardian the mystery of this interruption of my studies, or you cease to expect me to lead with you a life that's so unnatural for a boy.' What was so unnatural for the particular boy I was concerned with was this sudden revelation of a consciousness and a plan.

That was what really overcame me, what prevented my going in. I walked round the church hesitating, hovering; I reflected that I had already with him, hurt myself beyond repair. Therefore I could patch up nothing and it was too extreme an effort to squeeze beside him into the pew: he would be so much more sure than ever to pass his arm into mine and make me sit there for an hour in close silent contact with his commentary on our talk. For the first minute since his arrival, I wanted to get away from him. As I paused beneath the high east window and listened to the sounds of worship, I was taken with an impulse that might master me, I felt, and completely, should I give it the least encouragement. I might easily put an end to my ordeal by getting away altogether. Here was my chance; there was no one to stop me; I could give the whole thing up – turn my back and bolt. It was only a question of hurrying again, for a few preparations, to the house which the attendance at church of so many of the servants would practically have left unoccupied. No one, in short, could blame me if I should just drive desperately off. What was it to get away if I should get away only till dinner? That would be in a couple of hours, at the end of which – I had the acute prevision – my little pupils would play at innocent wonder about my nonappearance in their train.

'What *did* you do, you naughty bad thing? Why in the world, to worry us so – and take our thoughts off too, don't you know? – did you desert us at the very door?' I couldn't meet such questions nor, as they asked them, their false little lovely eyes; yet it was all so exactly what I should have to meet that, as the prospect grew sharp to me, I at last let myself go.

I got, so far as the immediate moment was concerned, away; I came straight out of the churchyard and, thinking hard, retraced my steps through the park. It seemed to me that by the time I reached the house I had made up my mind to cynical flight. The Sunday stillness both of the approaches and of the interior, in which I met no one, fairly stirred me with a sense of opportunity. Were I to get off quickly this way I should get off without a scene, without a word. My quickness would have to be remarkable, however, and the question of a conveyance was the great one to settle. Tormented, in the hall, with difficulties and obstacles, I remember sinking down at the foot of the staircase – suddenly collapsing there on the lowest step and then, with a revulsion, recalling that it was exactly where, more than a month before, in the darkness of night and just so bowed with evil things, I had seen the spectre of the most horrible of women. At this I was able to straighten myself; I went the rest of the way up; I made, in my turmoil, for the schoolroom, where there were objects belonging to me that I should have to take. But I opened the door to find again, in a flash, my eyes unsealed. In the presence of what I saw, I reeled straight back upon resistance.

Seated at my own table in the clear noonday light I saw a person whom, without my previous experience, I should have taken at the first blush for some housemaid who might have stayed at home to look after the place and who, availing herself of rare relief from observation and of the schoolroom table and my pens, ink, and paper, had applied herself to the considerable effort of a letter to her sweetheart. There was an effort in the way that, while her arms rested on the table, her hands, with evident weariness, supported her head; but at the moment I took this in I had already become aware that, in spite of my entrance, her attitude strangely persisted. Then it was – with the very act of its announcing itself – that her identity flared up in a change of posture. She rose, not as if she had heard me, but with an indescribable grand melancholy of indifference and detachment, and, within a dozen feet of me, stood there as my vile predecessor. Dishonoured and tragic, she was all before me; but even as I fixed and, for memory, secured it, the awful image passed away. Dark as midnight in her dark dress, her haggard beauty and her unutterable woe, she had looked at me long enough to appear to say that her right to sit at my table was as good as mine to sit at hers. While these instants lasted indeed I had the extraordinary chill of a feeling that it was I who was the intruder. It was as a wild protest against it that, actually addressing her – 'You terrible, miserable woman!' – I heard myself break into a sound that, by the open door, rang through the long passage and the empty house. She looked at me as if she heard me, but I had recovered myself and cleared the air. There was nothing in the room the next minute but the sunshine and the sense that I must stay.

CHAPTER SIXTEEN

I HAD SO PERFECTLY expected the return of the others to be marked by a demonstration that I was freshly upset at having to find them merely dumb and discreet about my desertion. Instead of gaily denouncing and caressing me they made no allusion to my having failed them, and I was left, for the time, on perceiving that she too said nothing, to study Mrs Grose's odd face. I did this to such purpose that I made sure they had in some way bribed her to silence; a silence that, however, I would engage to break down on the first private opportunity. This opportunity came before tea: I secured five minutes with her in the housekeeper's room, where, in the twilight, amid a smell of lately-baked bread, but with the place all swept and garnished,[12] I found her sitting in pained placidity before the fire. So I see her still, so I see her best: facing the flame from her straight chair in the dusky, shining room, a large, clean picture of the 'put away' – of drawers closed and locked and rest without a remedy.

'Oh, yes, they asked me to say nothing; and to please them – so long as they were there – of course I promised. But what had happened to you?'

'I only went with you for the walk,' I said. 'I had then to come back to meet a friend.'

She showed her surprise. 'A friend – *you?*'

'Oh, yes, I've a couple!' I laughed. 'But did the children give you a reason?'

'For not alluding to your leaving us? Yes; they said you'd like it better. *Do* you like it better?'

My face had made her rueful. 'No, I like it worse!' But after an instant I added: 'Did they say why I should like it better?'

'No; Master Miles only said, "We must do nothing but what she likes"!'

'I wish indeed he would! And what did Flora say?'

'Miss Flora was too sweet. She said, "Oh, of course, of course!" – and I said the same.'

I thought a moment. 'You were too sweet, too – I can hear you all. But none the less, between Miles and me, it's now all out.'

'All out?' My companion stared. 'But what, miss?'

'Everything. It doesn't matter. I've made up my mind. I came home, my dear,' I went on, 'for a talk with Miss Jessel.'

I had by this time formed the habit of having Mrs Grose literally well in hand in advance of my sounding that note; so that even now, as she bravely blinked under the signal of my word, I could keep her comparatively firm. 'A talk! Do you mean she spoke?'

'It came to that. I found her, on my return, in the schoolroom.'

'And what did she say?' I can hear the good woman still, and the candour of her stupefaction.

'That she suffers the torments – !'

It was this, of a truth, that made her, as she filled out my picture, gape. 'Do you mean,' she faltered ' – of the lost?'

'Of the lost. Of the damned. And that's why, to share them – ' I faltered myself with the horror of it.

But my companion, with less imagination, kept me up. 'To share them – ?'

'She wants Flora.' Mrs Grose might, as I gave it to her, fairly have fallen away from me had I not been prepared. I still held her there, to show I was. 'As I've told you, however, it doesn't matter.'

'Because you've made up your mind? But to what?'

'To everything.'

'And what do you call "everything"?'

'Why, to sending for their uncle.'

'Oh, miss, in pity do,' my friend broke out.

'Ah, but I will, I *will*! I see it's the only way. What's "out", as I told you, with Miles is that if he thinks I'm afraid to – and has ideas of what he gains by that – he shall see he's mistaken. Yes, yes, his uncle shall have it here from me on the spot (and before the boy himself if necessary) that if I'm to be reproached with having done nothing again about more school – '

'Yes, miss – ' my companion pressed me.

'Well, there's that awful reason.'

There were now clearly so many of these for my poor colleague that she was excusable for being vague. 'But – a – which?'

'Why, the letter from his old place.'

'You'll show it to the master?'

'I ought to have done so on the instant.'

'Oh, no!' said Mrs Grose with decision.

'I'll put it before him,' I went on inexorably, 'that I can't undertake to work the question on behalf of a child who has been expelled – '

'For we've never in the least known what!' Mrs Grose declared.

'For wickedness. For what else – when he's so clever and beautiful and perfect? Is he stupid? Is he untidy? Is he infirm? Is he ill-natured? He's exquisite – so it can be only *that*; and that would open up the whole thing. After all,' I said, 'it's their uncle's fault. If he left here such people – !'

'He didn't really in the least know them. The fault's mine.' She had turned quite pale.

'Well, you shan't suffer,' I answered.

'The children shan't!' she emphatically returned.

I was silent awhile; we looked at each other. 'Then what am I to tell him?'

'You needn't tell him anything. I'*ll* tell him.'

I measured this. 'Do you mean you'll write – ?' Remembering she couldn't, I caught myself up. 'How do you communicate?'

'I tell the bailiff. *He* writes.'

'And should you like him to write our story?'

My question had a sarcastic force that I had not fully intended, and it made her after a moment inconsequently break down. The tears were again in her eyes. 'Ah, miss, you write!'

'Well – tonight,' I at last returned; and on this we separated.

CHAPTER SEVENTEEN

I went so far, in the evening, as to make a beginning. The weather had changed back, a great wind was abroad, and beneath the lamp, in my room, with Flora at peace beside me, I sat for a long time before a blank sheet of paper and listened to the lash of the rain and the batter of the gusts. Finally I went out, taking a candle; I crossed the passage and listened a minute at Miles's door. What, under my endless obsession, I had been impelled to listen for was some betrayal of his not being at rest, and I presently caught one, but not in the form I had expected. His voice tinkled out. 'I say, you there – come in.' It was gaiety in the gloom!

I went in with my light and found him in bed, very wideawake but very much at his ease. 'Well, what are *you* up to?' he asked with a grace of sociability in which it occurred to me that Mrs Grose, had she been present, might have looked in vain for proof that anything was 'out'.

I stood over him with my candle. 'How did you know I was there?'

'Why, of course, I heard you. Did you fancy you made no noise? You're like a troop of cavalry!' he beautifully laughed.

'Then you weren't asleep?'

'Not much! I lie awake and think.'

I had put my candle, designedly, a short way off, and then, as he held out his friendly old hand to me, had sat down on the edge of his bed. 'What is it,' I asked, 'that you think of?'

'What in the world, my dear, but *you*?'

'Ah, the pride I take in your appreciation doesn't insist on that! I had so far rather you slept.'

'Well, I think also, you know, of this queer business of ours.'

I marked the coolness of his firm little hand. 'Of what queer business, Miles?'

'Why, the way you bring me up. And all the rest!'

I fairly held my breath a minute, and even from my glimmering taper there was light enough to show how he smiled up at me from his pillow. 'What do you mean by all the rest?'

'Oh, you know, you know!'

I could say nothing for a minute, though I felt as I held his hand and our eyes continued to meet that my silence had all the air of admitting his charge and that nothing in the whole world of reality was perhaps at that moment so fabulous as our actual relation. 'Certainly you shall go back to school,' I said, 'if it be that that troubles you. But not to the old place – we must find another, a better. How could I know it did trouble you, this question, when you never told me so, never spoke of it at all?' His clear listening face, framed in its smooth whiteness, made him for the minute as appealing as some wistful patient in a children's hospital; and I would have given, as the resemblance came to me, all I possessed on earth really to be the nurse or the sister of charity who might have helped to cure him. Well, even as it was I perhaps might help! 'Do you know you've never said a word to me about your school – I mean the old one; never mentioned it in any way?'

He seemed to wonder; he smiled with the same loveliness. But he clearly gained time; he waited, he called for guidance. 'Haven't I?' It wasn't for *me* to help him – it was for the thing I had met!

Something in his tone and the expression of his face, as I got this from him, set my heart aching with such a pang as it had never yet known; so unutterably touching was it to see his little brain puzzled and his little resources taxed to play, under the spell laid on him, a part of innocence and consistency. 'No, never – from the hour you came back. You've never mentioned to me one of your masters, one of your comrades, nor the least little thing that ever happened to you at school. Never, little Miles – no, never – have you given me an inkling of anything that *may* have happened there. Therefore you can fancy how much I'm in the dark. Until you came out, that way, this morning, you had since the first hour I saw you scarce even made a reference to anything in your previous life. You seemed so perfectly to accept the present.' It was extraordinary how my absolute conviction of his secret precocity – or whatever I might call the poison of an influence that I dared but half-phrase – made him, in spite of the faint breath of his inward trouble, appear as accessible as an older person, forced me to treat him as an intelligent equal. 'I thought you wanted to go on as you are.'

It struck me that at this he just faintly coloured. He gave, at any rate, like a convalescent slightly fatigued, a languid shake of his head. 'I don't – I don't. I want to get away.'

'You're tired of Bly?'

'Oh, no, I like Bly.'

'Well, then – ?'

'Oh, *you* know what a boy wants!'

I felt I didn't know so well as Miles, and I took temporary refuge. 'You want to go to your uncle?'

Again, at this, with his sweet ironic face, he made a movement on the pillow. 'Ah, you can't get off with that!'

I was silent a little, and it was I now, I think, who changed colour. 'My dear, I don't want to get off!'

'You can't even if you do. You can't, you can't!' – he lay beautifully staring. 'My uncle must come down and you must completely settle things.'

'If we do,' I returned with some spirit, 'you may be sure it will be to take you quite away.'

'Well, don't you understand that that's exactly what I'm working for? You'll have to *tell* him – about the way you've let it all drop: you'll have to tell him a tremendous lot!'

The exultation with which he uttered this helped me somehow for the instant to meet him rather more. 'And how much will *you*, Miles, have to tell him? There are things he'll ask you!'

He turned it over. 'Very likely. But what things?'

'The things you've never told me. To make up his mind what to do with you. He can't send you back –'

'I don't want to go back!' he broke in. 'I want a new field.'

He said it with admirable serenity, with positive, unimpeachable gaiety; and doubtless it was that very note that most evoked for me the poignancy, the unnatural childish tragedy, of his probable reappearance at the end of three months with all this bravado and still more dishonour. It overwhelmed me now that I should never be able to bear that, and it made me let myself go. I threw myself upon him and in the tenderness of my pity embraced him. 'Dear little Miles, dear little Miles – !'

My face was close to his, and he let me kiss him, simply taking it with indulgent good-humour. 'Well, old lady?'

'Is there nothing – nothing at all that you want to tell me?'

He turned off a little, facing round towards the wall and holding up his hand to look at as one had seen sick children look. 'I've told you – I told you this morning.'

Oh, I was sorry for him! 'That you just want me not to worry you?'

He looked round at me now as if in recognition of my understanding him; then ever so gently, 'To let me alone,' he replied.

There was even a strange little dignity in it, something that made me release him, yet, when I had slowly risen, linger beside him. God knows I never wished to harass him, but I felt that merely, at this, to turn my back on him was to abandon or, to put it more truly, to lose him. 'I've just begun a letter to your uncle,' I said.

'Well, then, finish it!'

I waited a minute. 'What happened before?'

He gazed up at me again. 'Before what?'

'Before you came back. And before you went away.'

For some time he was silent, but he continued to meet my eyes. 'What happened?'

It made me, the sound of the words, in which it seemed to me I caught for the very first time a small faint quaver of consenting consciousness – it made me drop to my knees beside the bed and seize once more the chance of possessing him. 'Dear little Miles, dear little Miles, if you knew how I want to help you! It's only that, it's nothing but that, and I'd rather die than give you a pain or do you a wrong – I'd rather die than hurt a hair of you. Dear little Miles' – oh I brought it out now even if I *should* go too far – 'I just want you to help me to save you!' But I knew in a moment after this that I had gone too far. The answer to my appeal was instantaneous, but it came in the form of an extraordinary blast and chill, a gust of frozen air and a shake of the room as great as if, in the wild wind, the casement had crashed in. The boy gave a loud, high shriek which, lost in the rest of the shock of sound, might have seemed, indistinctly, though I was so close to him, a note either of jubilation or of terror. I jumped to my feet again and was conscious of darkness. So for a moment we remained, while I stared about me and saw the drawn curtains unstilted and the window tight. 'Why, the candle's out!' I then cried.

'It was I who blew it, dear!' said Miles.

CHAPTER EIGHTEEN

THE NEXT DAY, after lessons, Mrs Grose found a moment to say to me quietly: 'Have you written, miss?'

'Yes – I've written.' But I didn't add – for the hour – that my letter, sealed and directed, was still in my pocket. There would be time enough to send it before the messenger should go to the village. Meanwhile there had been on the part of my pupils no more brilliant, more exemplary morning. It was exactly as if they had both had at heart to gloss over any recent little friction. They performed the dizziest feats of arithmetic, soaring quite out of *my* feeble range, and perpetrated, in higher spirits than ever, geographical and historical jokes. It was conspicuous of course in Miles in particular that he appeared to wish to show how easily he could let me down. This child, to my memory, really lives in a setting of beauty and misery that no words can translate; there was a distinction all his own in every impulse he revealed; never was a small natural creature, to the uninformed eye all frankness and freedom, a more ingenious, a more extraordinary little gentleman. I had perpetually to guard against the wonder of contemplation into which my initiated view betrayed me; to check the irrelevant gaze and discouraged sigh in which I constantly both attacked and renounced the enigma of what such a little gentleman could have done that deserved a penalty. Say that, by the dark prodigy I knew, the imagination of all evil had been opened up to him: all the justice within me ached for the proof that it could ever have flowered into an act.

He had never at any rate been such a little gentleman as when, after our early dinner on this dreadful day, he came round to me and asked if I shouldn't like him for half an hour to play to me. David playing to Saul[13] could never have shown a finer sense of the occasion. It was literally a charming exhibition of tact, of magnanimity, and quite tantamount to his saying outright: 'The true knights we love to read about never push an advantage too far. I know what you mean now: you mean that – to be let alone yourself and not followed up – you'll cease to worry and spy upon me, won't keep me so close to you, will let me go and come. Well, I "come", you see – but I don't go! There'll be plenty of time for that. I do really delight in your society and I only want to show you that I contended for a principle.' It may be imagined whether I resisted this appeal or failed to accompany him again, hand in hand, to the schoolroom. He sat down at the old piano and played as he had never played; and if there are those who think he had better have been kicking a football, I can only say that I wholly agree with them. For at the end of a time that under his influence I had quite ceased to measure, I started up with a strange sense of having literally slept at my post. It was after luncheon, and by the schoolroom fire, and yet I hadn't really in the least slept; I had only done something much worse – I had forgotten. Where all this time was Flora? When I put the question to Miles, he played on a minute before answering, and then could only say: 'Why, my dear, how do I know?' – breaking moreover into a happy laugh which immediately after, as if it were a vocal accompaniment, he prolonged into incoherent, extravagant song.

I went straight to my room, but his sister was not there; then, before going downstairs, I looked into several others. As she was nowhere about she would surely be with Mrs Grose, whom in the comfort of that theory I accordingly proceeded in quest of. I found her where I had found her the evening before, but she met my quick challenge with blank scared ignorance. She had only supposed that, after the repast, I had carried off both the children; as to which she was quite in her right, for it was the very first time I had allowed the little girl out of my sight without some special provision. Of course now indeed she might be with the maids, so that the immediate thing was to look for her without an air of alarm. This we promptly arranged between us; but when, ten minutes later and in pursuance of our arrangement, we met in the hall, it was only to report on either side that after guarded inquiries we had altogether failed to trace her. For a minute there, apart from observation, we exchanged mute alarms, and I could feel with what high interest my friend returned me all those I had from the first given her.

'She'll be above,' she presently said – 'in one of the rooms you haven't searched.'

'No; she's at a distance.' I had made up my mind. 'She has gone out.'

Mrs Grose stared. 'Without a hat!'

I naturally also looked volumes. 'Isn't that woman always without one?'

'She's with *her*?'

'She's with *her*!' I declared. 'We must find them.'

My hand was on my friend's arm, but she failed for the moment, confronted with such an account of the matter, to respond to my pressure. She communed on the contrary, where she stood, with her uneasiness. 'And where's Master Miles?'

'Oh, *he's* with Quint. They'll be in the schoolroom.'

'Lord, miss!' My view, I was myself aware – and therefore I suppose my tone – had never yet reached so calm an assurance.

'The trick's played,' I went on; 'they've successfully worked their plan. He found the most divine little way to keep me quiet while she went off.'

' "Divine"?' Mrs Grose bewilderedly echoed.

'Infernal, then!' I almost cheerfully rejoined. 'He has provided for himself as well. But come!'

She had helplessly gloomed at the upper regions. 'You leave him – ?'

'So long with Quint? Yes – I don't mind that now.'

She always ended at these moments by getting possession of my hand, and in this manner she could at present still stay me. But after gasping an instant at my sudden resignation, 'Because of your letter?' she eagerly brought out.

I quickly, by way of answer, felt for my letter, drew it forth, held it up, and then, freeing myself, went and laid it on the great hall-table. 'Luke will take it,' I said as I came back. I reached the house-door and opened it; I was already on the steps.

My companion still demurred: the storm of the night and the early morning had dropped, but the afternoon was damp and grey. I came down to the drive while she stood in the doorway. 'You go with nothing on?'

'What do I care when the child has nothing? I can't wait to dress,' I cried, 'and if you must do so I leave you. Try meanwhile yourself upstairs.'

'With *them*?' Oh, on this the poor woman promptly joined me!

CHAPTER NINETEEN

We went straight to the lake, as it was called at Bly, and I dare say rightly called, though it may have been a sheet of water less remarkable than my untravelled eyes supposed it. My acquaintance with sheets of water was small, and the pool of Bly, at all events on the few occasions of my consenting, under the protection of my pupils, to affront its surface in the old flat-bottomed boat moored there for our use, had impressed me both with its extent and its agitation. The usual place of embarkation was half a mile from the house, but I had an intimate conviction that, wherever Flora might be, she was not near home. She had not given me the slip for any small adventure, and, since the day of the very great one that I had shared with her by the pond, I had been aware in our walks, of the quarter to which she most inclined. This was why I had now given to Mrs Grose's steps so marked a direction – a direction making her, when she perceived it, oppose a resistance that showed me she was freshly mystified. 'You're going to the water, miss? – you think she's *in* – ?'

'She may be, though the depth is, I believe, nowhere very great. But what I judge most likely is that she's on the spot from which, the other day, we saw together what I told you.'

'When she pretended not to see – ?'

'With that astounding self-possession! I've always been sure she wanted to go back alone. And now her brother has managed it for her.'

Mrs Grose still stood where she had stopped. 'You suppose they really *talk* of them?'

I could meet this with an assurance! 'They say things that, if we heard them, would simply appal us.'

'And if she *is* there – ?'

'Yes?'

'Then Miss Jessel is?'

'Beyond a doubt. You shall see.'

'Oh, thank you!' my friend cried, planted so firm that, taking it in, I went straight on without her. By the time I reached the pool, however, she was close behind me, and I knew that, whatever, to her apprehension, might befall me, the exposure of sticking to me struck her as her least danger. She exhaled a moan of relief as we at last came in sight of the greater part of the water without a sight of the child. There was no trace of Flora on that nearer side of the bank where my observation of her had been most startling, and none on the opposite edge, where, save for a margin of some twenty yards, a thick copse came down to the water. This expanse, oblong in shape, was so narrow compared to its length that, with its ends out of view, it might have been taken for a scant river. We looked at the empty stretch, and then I felt the suggestion in my friend's eyes. I knew what she meant and I replied with a negative headshake.

'No, no; wait! She has taken the boat.'

My companion stared at the vacant mooring-place and then again across the lake. 'Then where is it?'

'Our not seeing it is the strongest of proofs. She has used it to go over, and then has managed to hide it.'

'All alone – that child?'

'She's not alone, and at such times she's not a child: she's an old, old woman.' I scanned all the visible shore while Mrs Grose took again, into the queer element I offered her, one of her plunges of submission; then I pointed out that the boat might perfectly be in a small refuge formed by one of the recesses of the pool, an indentation masked, for the hither side, by a projection of the bank and by a clump of trees growing close to the water.

'But if the boat's there, where on earth's *she*?' my colleague anxiously asked.

'That's exactly what we must learn.' And I started to walk farther.

'By going all the way round?'

'Certainly, far as it is. It will take us but ten minutes, yet it's far enough to have made the child prefer not to walk. She went straight over.'

'Laws!' cried my friend again; the chain of my logic was ever too strong for her. It dragged her at my heels even now, and when we had got halfway round – a devious tiresome process, on ground much broken and by a path choked with overgrowth – I paused to give her breath. I sustained her with a grateful arm, assuring her that she might hugely help me; and this started us afresh, so that in the course of but few minutes more we reached a point from which we found the boat to be where I had supposed it. It had been intentionally left as much as possible out of sight and was tied to one of the stakes of a fence that came, just there, down to the brink and that had been an assistance to disembarking. I recognised, as I looked at the pair of short, thick oars, quite safely drawn up, the prodigious character of the feat for a little girl; but I had by this time lived too long among wonders and had panted to too many livelier measures. There was a gate in the fence, through which we passed, and that brought us after a trifling interval more into the open. Then 'There she is!' we both exclaimed at once.

Flora, a short way off, stood before us on the grass and smiled as if her performance had now become complete. The next thing she did, however, was to stoop straight down and pluck – quite as if it were all she was there for – a big, ugly spray of withered fern. I at once felt sure she had just come out of the copse. She waited for us, not herself taking a step, and I was conscious of the rare solemnity with which we presently approached her. She smiled and smiled, and we met; but it was all done in a silence by this time flagrantly ominous. Mrs Grose was the first to break the spell: she threw herself on her knees and, drawing the child to her breast, clasped in a long embrace the little, tender, yielding body. While this dumb convulsion lasted I could only watch it – which I did the more intently when I saw Flora's face peep at me over our companion's shoulder. It was serious now – the flicker had left it; but it strengthened the pang with which I at that moment envied Mrs Grose the simplicity of *her* relation. Still, all this while, nothing more passed between us save that Flora had let her foolish fern again drop to the ground. What she and I had virtually said to each other was that pretexts were useless now. When Mrs Grose finally got up, she kept the child's hand, so that the two were still before me; and the singular reticence of our communion was even more marked in the frank look she addressed me. 'I'll be hanged,' it said, 'if *I'll* speak!'

It was Flora who, gazing all over me in candid wonder, was the first. She was struck with our bareheaded aspect. 'Why, where are your things?'

'Where yours are, my dear!' I promptly returned.

She had already got back her gaiety and appeared to take this as an answer quite sufficient. 'And where's Miles?' she went on.

There was something in the small valour of it that quite finished me: these three words from her were in a flash like the glitter of a drawn blade, the jostle of the cup that my hand for weeks and weeks had held high and full to the brim and that now, even before speaking, I felt overflow in a deluge. 'I'll tell you if you'll tell *me* – ' I heard myself say, then heard the tremor in which it broke.

'Well, what?'

Mrs Grose's suspense blazed at me, but it was too late now, and I brought the thing out handsomely. 'Where, my pet, is Miss Jessel?'

CHAPTER TWENTY

JUST AS in the churchyard with Miles, the whole thing was upon us. Much as I had made of the fact that this name had never once, between us, been sounded, the quick smitten glare with which the child's face now received it fairly likened my breach of the silence to the smash of a pane of glass. It added to the interposing cry, as if to stay the blow, that Mrs Grose at the same instant uttered over my violence – the shriek of a creature scared, or rather wounded, which, in turn, within a few seconds, was completed by a gasp of my own. I seized my colleague's arm. 'She's there, she's there!'

Miss Jessel stood before us on the opposite bank exactly as she had stood the other time, and I remember, strangely, as the first feeling now produced in me, my thrill of joy at having brought on a proof. She was there, so I was justified; she was there, so I was neither cruel nor mad. She was there for poor scared Mrs Grose, but she was there most for Flora; and no moment of my monstrous time was perhaps so extraordinary as that in which I consciously threw out to her – with the sense that, pale and ravenous demon as she was, she would catch and understand it – an inarticulate message of gratitude. She rose erect on the spot my friend and I had lately quitted, and there wasn't in all the long reach of her desire an inch of her evil that fell short. This first vividness of vision and emotion were things of a few seconds, during which Mrs Grose's dazed blink across to where I pointed struck me as showing that she too at last saw, just as it carried my own eyes precipitately to the child. The revelation then of the manner in which Flora was affected startled me in truth far more than it would have done to find her also merely agitated, for direct dismay was of course not what I had expected. Prepared and on her guard as our pursuit had actually made her, she would repress every betrayal; and I was therefore at once shaken by my first glimpse of the particular one for which I had not allowed. To see her, without a convulsion of her small pink face, not even feign to glance in the direction of the prodigy I announced, but only, instead of that, turn at *me* an expression of hard, still gravity, an expression absolutely new and unprecedented and that appeared to read and accuse and judge me – this was a stroke that somehow converted the little girl herself into a figure portentous. I gaped at her coolness even though my certitude of her thoroughly seeing was never greater than at that instant, and then, in the immediate need to defend myself, I called

her passionately to witness. 'She's there, you little unhappy thing –
there, there, *there*, and you know it as well as you know me!' I had said
shortly before to Mrs Grose that she was not at these times a child,
but an old, old woman, and my description of her couldn't have been
more strikingly confirmed than in the way in which, for all notice of
this, she simply showed me, without an expressional concession or
admission, a countenance of deeper and deeper, of indeed suddenly
quite fixed reprobation. I was by this time – if I can put the whole
thing at all together – more appalled at what I may properly call her
manner than at anything else, though it was quite simultaneously
that I became aware of having Mrs Grose also, and very formidably,
to reckon with. My elder companion, the next moment, at any rate,
blotted out everything but her own flushed face and her loud shocked
protest, a burst of high disapproval. 'What a dreadful turn, to be sure,
miss! Where on earth do you see anything?'

I could only grasp her more quickly yet, for even while she spoke
the hideous plain presence stood undimmed and undaunted. It had
already lasted a minute, and it lasted while I continued, seizing my
colleague, quite thrusting her at it and presenting her to it, to insist
with my pointing hand. 'You don't see her exactly as *we* see? – you
mean to say you don't now – *now*? She's as big as a blazing fire! Only
look, dearest woman, *look* – !' She looked, just as I did, and gave me,
with her deep groan of negation, repulsion, compassion – the
mixture with her pity of her relief at her exemption – a sense,
touching to me even then, that she would have backed me up if she
had been able. I might well have needed that, for with this hard blow
of the proof that her eyes were hopelessly sealed, I felt my own
situation horribly crumble, I felt – I *saw* – my livid predecessor press,
from her position, on my defeat, and I took the measure, more than
all, of what I should have from this instant to deal with in the
astounding little attitude of Flora. Into this attitude Mrs Grose
immediately and violently entered, breaking, even while there
pierced through my sense of ruin a prodigious private triumph, into
breathless reassurance.

'She isn't there, little lady, and nobody's there – and you never see
nothing, my sweet! How can poor Miss Jessel – when poor Miss
Jessel's dead and buried? *We* know, don't we, love?' – and she
appealed, blundering in, to the child. 'It's all a mere mistake and a
worry and a joke – and we'll go home as fast as we can!'

Our companion, on this, had responded with a strange quick
primness of propriety, and they were again, with Mrs Grose on her
feet, united, as it were, in shocked opposition to me. Flora continued

to fix me with her small mask of disaffection, and even at that minute
I prayed God to forgive me for seeming to see that, as she stood there
holding tight to our friend's dress, her incomparable childish beauty
had suddenly failed, had quite vanished. I've said it already – she was
literally, she was hideously hard; she had turned common and almost
ugly. 'I don't know what you mean. I see nobody. I see nothing. I never
have. I think you're cruel. I don't like you!' Then, after this
deliverance, which might have been that of a vulgarly pert little girl in
the street, she hugged Mrs Grose more closely and buried in her skirts
the dreadful little face. In this position she launched an almost furious
wail. 'Take me away, take me away – oh, take me away from *her*!'

'From *me*?' I panted.

'From you – from you!' she cried.

Even Mrs Grose looked across at me dismayed, while I had nothing
to do but communicate again with the figure that, on the opposite
bank, without a movement, as rigidly still as if catching, beyond the
interval, our voices, was as vividly there for my disaster as it was not
there for my service. The wretched child had spoken exactly as if she
had got from some outside source each of her stabbing little words,
and I could therefore, in the full despair of all I had to accept, but
sadly shake my head at her. 'If I had ever doubted, all my doubt would
at present have gone. I've been living with the miserable truth, and
now it has only too much closed round me. Of course I've lost you:
I've interfered, and you've seen, under *her* dictation' – with which I
faced, over the pool again, our infernal witness – 'the easy and perfect
way to meet it. I've done my best, but I've lost you. Goodbye.' For
Mrs Grose I had an imperative, an almost frantic 'Go, go!' before
which, in infinite distress, but mutely possessed of the little girl and
clearly convinced, in spite of her blindness, that something awful had
occurred and some collapse engulfed us, she retreated, by the way we
had come, as fast as she could move.

Of what first happened when I was left alone I had no subsequent
memory. I only knew that at the end of, I suppose, a quarter of an
hour, an odorous dampness and roughness, chilling and piercing my
trouble, had made me understand that I must have thrown myself, on
my face, to the ground and given way to a wildness of grief. I must
have lain there long and cried and wailed, for when I raised my head
the day was almost done. I got up and looked a moment, through the
twilight, at the grey pool and its blank haunted edge, and then I took,
back to the house, my dreary and difficult course. When I reached
the gate in the fence the boat, to my surprise, was gone, so that I had
a fresh reflection to make on Flora's extraordinary command of the

situation. She passed that night, by the most tacit and, I should add, were not the word so grotesque a false note, the happiest of arrangements, with Mrs Grose. I saw neither of them on my return, but on the other hand I saw, as by an ambiguous compensation, a great deal of Miles. I saw – I can use no other phrase – so much of him that it fairly measured more than it had ever measured. No evening I had passed at Bly was to have had the portentous quality of this one; in spite of which – and in spite also of the deeper depths of consternation that had opened beneath my feet – there was literally, in the ebbing actual, an extraordinarily sweet sadness. On reaching the house I had never so much as looked for the boy; I had simply gone straight to my room to change what I was wearing and to take in, at a glance, much material testimony to Flora's rupture. Her little belongings had all been removed. When later, by the schoolroom fire, I was served with tea by the usual maid, I indulged, on the article of my other pupil, in no inquiry whatever. He had his freedom now – he might have it to the end! Well, he did have it; and it consisted – in part at least – of his coming in at about eight o'clock and sitting down with me in silence. On the removal of the tea things, I had blown out the candles and drawn my chair closer: I was conscious of a mortal coldness and felt as if I should never again be warm. So when he appeared I was sitting in the glow with my thoughts. He paused a moment by the door as if to look at me; then – as if to share them – came to the other side of the hearth and sank into a chair. We sat there in absolute stillness; yet he wanted, I felt, to be with me.

CHAPTER TWENTY-ONE

BEFORE A NEW DAY, in my room, had fully broken, my eyes opened to Mrs Grose, who had come to my bedside with worse news. Flora was so markedly feverish that an illness was perhaps at hand; she had passed a night of extreme unrest, a night agitated above all by fears that had for their subject not in the least her former but wholly her present governess. It was not against the possible re-entrance of Miss Jessel on the scene that she protested – it was conspicuously and passionately against mine. I was at once on my feet, and with an immense deal to ask; the more that my friend had discernibly now girded her loins to meet me afresh. This I felt as soon as I had put to her the question of her sense of the child's sincerity as against my own. 'She persists in denying to you that she saw, or has ever seen, anything?'

My visitor's trouble truly was great. 'Ah, miss, it isn't a matter on which I can push her. Yet it isn't either, I must say, as if I much needed to. It has made her, every inch of her, quite old.'

'Oh, I see her perfectly from here. She resents, for all the world like some high little personage, the imputation on her truthfulness and, as it were, her respectability. "Miss Jessel indeed – *she*!" Ah, she's "respectable", the chit! The impression she gave me there yesterday was, I assure you, the very strangest of all; it was quite beyond any of the others. I *did* put my foot in it! She'll never speak to me again.'

Hideous and obscure as it all was, it held Mrs Grose briefly silent; then she granted my point with a frankness which, I made sure, had more behind it. 'I think indeed, miss, she never will. She do have a grand manner about it!'

'And that manner' – I summed it up – 'is practically what's the matter with her now.'

Oh, that manner, I could see in my visitor's face, and not a little else besides! 'She asks me every three minutes if I think you're coming in.'

'I see – I see.' I too, on my side, had so much more than worked it out. 'Has she said to you since yesterday – except to repudiate her familiarity with anything so dreadful – a single other word about Miss Jessel?'

'Not one, miss. And of course, you know,' my friend added, 'I took it from her by the lake that just then and there at least there *was* nobody.'

'Rather! And naturally you take it from her still.'

'I don't contradict her. What else can I do?'

'Nothing in the world! You've the cleverest little person to deal with. They've made them – their two friends, I mean – still cleverer even than nature did; for it was wondrous material to play on! Flora has now her grievance, and she'll work it to the end.'

'Yes, miss; but to *what* end?'

'Why, that of dealing with me to her uncle. She'll make me out to him the lowest creature – !'

I winced at the fair show of the scene in Mrs Grose's face; she looked for a minute as if she sharply saw them together. 'And him who thinks so well of you!'

'He has an odd way – it comes over me now,' I laughed, ' – of proving it! But that doesn't matter. What Flora wants of course is to get rid of me.'

My companion bravely concurred. 'Never again to so much as look at you.'

'So that what you've come to me now for,' I asked, 'is to speed me on my way?' Before she had time to reply, however, I had her in check. 'I've a better idea – the result of my reflections. My going *would* seem the right thing, and on Sunday I was terribly near it. Yet that won't do. It's *you* who must go. You must take Flora.'

My visitor, at this, did speculate. 'But where in the world – ?'

'Away from here. Away from *them*. Away, even most of all, now, from me. Straight to her uncle.'

'Only to tell on you – ?'

'No, not "only"! To leave me, in addition, with my remedy.'

She was still vague. 'And what *is* your remedy?'

'Your loyalty, to begin with. And then Miles's.'

She looked at me hard. 'Do you think he – ?'

'Won't, if he has the chance, turn on me? Yes, I venture still to think it. At all events I want to try. Get off with his sister as soon as possible and leave me with him alone.' I was amazed, myself, at the spirit I had still in reserve, and therefore perhaps a trifle the more disconcerted at the way in which, in spite of this fine example of it, she hesitated. 'There's one thing, of course,' I went on: 'they mustn't, before she goes, see each other for three seconds.' Then it came over me that, in spite of Flora's presumable sequestration from the instant of her return from the pool, it might already be too late. 'Do you mean,' I anxiously asked, 'that they *have* met?'

At this she quite flushed. 'Ah, miss, I'm not such a fool as that! If I've been obliged to leave her three or four times, it has been each time with one of the maids, and at present, though she's alone, she's locked in safe. And yet – and yet!' There were too many things.

'And yet what?'

'Well, are you so sure of the little gentleman?'

'I'm not sure of anything but *you*. But I have, since last evening, a new hope. I think he wants to give me an opening. I do believe that – poor little exquisite wretch! – he wants to speak. Last evening, in the firelight and the silence, he sat with me for two hours as if it were just coming.'

Mrs Grose looked hard through the window at the grey gathering day. 'And did it come?'

'No, though I waited and waited I confess it didn't, and it was without a breach of the silence, or so much as a faint allusion to his sister's condition and absence, that we at last kissed for good-night. All the same,' I continued, 'I can't, if her uncle sees her, consent to his seeing her brother without my having given the boy – and most of all because things have got so bad – a little more time.'

My friend appeared on this ground more reluctant than I could quite understand. 'What do you mean by more time?'

'Well, a day or two – really to bring it out. He'll then be on *my* side – of which you see the importance. If nothing comes, I shall only fail, and you at the worst have helped me by doing on your arrival in town whatever you may have found possible.' So I put it before her, but she continued for a little so lost in other reasons that I came again to her aid. 'Unless indeed,' I wound up, 'you really want *not* to go.'

I could see it, in her face, at last clear itself; she put out her hand to me as a pledge. 'I'll go – I'll go. I'll go this morning.'

I wanted to be very just. 'If you *should* wish still to wait, I'd engage she shouldn't see me.'

'No, no: it's the place itself. She must leave it.' She held me a moment with heavy eyes, then brought out the rest. 'Your idea's the right one. I myself, miss – '

'Well?'

'I can't stay.'

The look she gave me with it made me jump at possibilities. 'You mean that, since yesterday, you *have* seen – ?'

She shook her head with dignity. 'I've *heard* – !'

'Heard?'

'From that child – horrors! There!' she sighed with tragic relief. 'On my honour, miss, she says things – !' But at this evocation she broke down; she dropped with a sudden cry upon my sofa and, as I had seen her do before, gave way to all the anguish of it.

It was in quite another manner that I for my part let myself go. 'Oh, thank God!'

She sprang up again at this, drying her eyes with a groan. ' "Thank God"?'

'It so justifies me!'

'It does that, miss!'

I couldn't have desired more emphasis, but I just waited. 'She's so horrible?'

I saw my colleague scarce knew how to put it. 'Really shocking.'

'And about me?'

'About you, miss – since you must have it. It's beyond everything, for a young lady; and I can't think wherever she must have picked up – '

'The appalling language she applies to me? I can, then!' I broke in with a laugh that was doubtless significant enough.

It only in truth left my friend still more grave. 'Well, perhaps I

ought to also – since I've heard some of it before! Yet I can't bear it,'
the poor woman went on while with the same movement she glanced,
on my dressing-table, at the face of my watch. 'But I must go back.'

I kept her, however. 'Ah, if you can't bear it – !'

'How can I stop with her, you mean? Why, just *for* that: to get her
away. Far from this,' she pursued, 'far from *them* – '

'She may be different? She may be free?' I seized her almost with
joy. 'Then in spite of yesterday you *believe* – '

'In such doings?' Her simple description of them required, in the
light of her expression, to be carried no further, and she gave me the
whole thing as she had never done. 'I believe.'

Yes, it was a joy, and we were still shoulder to shoulder: if I might
continue sure of that I should care but little what else happened. My
support in the presence of disaster would be the same as it had been
in my early need of confidence, and if my friend would answer for my
honesty, I would answer for all the rest. On the point of taking leave
of her, none the less, I was to some extent embarrassed. 'There's one
thing of course – it occurs to me – to remember. My letter, giving the
alarm, will have reached town before you.'

I now felt still more how she had been beating about the bush and
how weary at last it had made her. 'Your letter won't have got there.
Your letter never went.'

'What then became of it?'

'Goodness knows! Master Miles – '

'Do you mean *he* took it?' I gasped.

She hung fire, but she overcame her reluctance. 'I mean that I saw
yesterday, when I came back with Miss Flora, that it wasn't where
you had put it. Later in the evening I had the chance to question
Luke, and he declared that he had neither noticed nor touched it.'
We could only exchange, on this, one of our deeper mutual
soundings, and it was Mrs Grose who first brought up the plumb
with an almost elate 'You see!'

'Yes, I see that if Miles took it instead, he probably will have read it
and destroyed it.'

'And don't you see anything else?'

I faced her a moment with a sad smile. 'It strikes me that by this
time your eyes are open even wider than mine.'

They proved to be so indeed, but she could still almost blush to
show it. 'I make out now what he must have done at school.' And she
gave, in her simple sharpness, an almost droll disillusioned nod. 'He
stole!'

I turned it over – I tried to be more judicial. 'Well – perhaps.'

She looked as if she found me unexpectedly calm. 'He stole *letters*!'

She couldn't know my reasons for a calmness after all pretty shallow; so I showed them off as I might. 'I hope then it was to more purpose than in this case! The note, at all events, that I put on the table yesterday,' I pursued, 'will have given him so scant an advantage – for it contained only the bare demand for an interview – that he's already much ashamed of having gone so far for so little, and that which he had on his mind last evening was precisely the need of confession.' I seemed to myself for the instant to have mastered it, to see it all. 'Leave us, leave us' – I was already, at the door, hurrying her off. 'I'll get it out of him. He'll meet me. He'll confess. If he confesses he's saved. And if he's saved – '

'Then *you* are?' The dear woman kissed me on this, and I took her farewell. 'I'll save you without him!' she cried as she went.

CHAPTER TWENTY-TWO

YET IT WAS when she had got off – and I missed her on the spot – that the great pinch really came. If I had counted on what it would give me to find myself alone with Miles I quickly recognised that it would give me at least a measure. No hour of my stay in fact was so assailed with apprehensions as that of my coming down to learn that the carriage containing Mrs Grose and my younger pupil had already rolled out of the gates. Now I was, I said to myself, face to face with the elements, and for much of the rest of the day, while I fought my weakness, I could consider that I had been supremely rash. It was a tighter place still than I had yet turned round in; all the more that, for the first time, I could see in the aspect of others a confused reflection of the crisis. What had happened naturally caused them all to stare; there was too little of the explained, throw out whatever we might, in the suddenness of my colleague's act. The maids and the men looked blank; the effect of which on my nerves was an aggravation until I saw the necessity of making it a positive aid. It was in short by just clutching the helm that I avoided total wreck; and I dare say that, to bear up at all, I became that morning very grand and very dry. I welcomed the consciousness that I was charged with much to do, and I caused it to be known as well that, left thus to myself, I was quite remarkably firm. I wandered with that manner, for the next hour or two, all over the place and looked, I have no doubt, as if I were ready for any onset. So, for the benefit of whom it might concern, I paraded with a sick heart.

The person it appeared least to concern proved to be, till dinner, little Miles himself. My perambulations had given me meanwhile no glimpse of him, but they had tended to make more public the change taking place in our relation as a consequence of his having at the piano, the day before, kept me, in Flora's interest, so beguiled and befooled. The stamp of publicity had of course been fully given by her confinement and departure, and the change itself was now ushered in by our non-observance of the regular custom of the schoolroom. He had already disappeared when, on my way down, I pushed open his door, and I learned below that he had breakfasted – in the presence of a couple of the maids – with Mrs Grose and his sister. He had then gone out, as he said, for a stroll; than which nothing, I reflected, could better have expressed his frank view of the abrupt transformation of my office. What he would now permit this office to consist of was yet to be settled: there was at least a queer relief – I mean for myself especially – in the renouncement of one pretension. If so much had sprung to the surface I scarce put it too strongly in saying that what had perhaps sprung highest was the absurdity of our prolonging the fiction that I had anything more to teach him. It sufficiently stuck out that, by tacit little tricks in which even more than myself he carried out the care for my dignity, I had had to appeal to him to let me off straining to meet him on the ground of his true capacity. He had at any rate his freedom now; I was never to touch it again; as I had amply shown, moreover, when, on his joining me in the schoolroom the previous night, I uttered, in reference to the interval just concluded, neither challenge nor hint. I had too much, from this moment, my other ideas. Yet when he at last arrived the difficulty of applying them, the accumulations of my problem, were brought straight home to me by the beautiful little presence on which what had occurred had as yet, for the eye, dropped neither stain nor shadow.

To mark, for the house, the high state I cultivated I decreed that my meals with the boy should be served, as we called it, downstairs; so that I had been awaiting him in the ponderous pomp of the room outside the window of which I had had from Mrs Grose, that first scared Sunday, my flash of something it would scarce have done to call light. Here at present I felt afresh – for I had felt it again and again – how my equilibrium depended on the success of my rigid will, the will to shut my eyes as tight as possible to the truth that what I had to deal with was, revoltingly, against nature. I could only get on at all by taking 'nature' into my confidence and my account, by treating my monstrous ordeal as a push in a direction unusual, of course, and unpleasant, but demanding after all, for a fair front, only another turn of the screw of ordinary human virtue. No attempt, none the less, could well require more tact than just this attempt to supply, oneself, *all* the nature. How could I put even a little of that article into a suppression of reference to what had occurred? How on the other hand could I make a reference without a new plunge into the hideous obscure? Well, a sort of answer, after a time, had come to me, and it was so far confirmed as that I was met, incontestably, by the quickened vision of what was rare in my little companion. It was, indeed, as if he had found even now – as he had so often found at lessons – still some other delicate way to ease me off. Wasn't there light in the fact which, as we shared our solitude, broke out with a specious glitter it had never yet quite worn? – the fact that (opportunity aiding, precious opportunity which had now come) it would be preposterous, with a child so endowed, to forgo the help one might wrest from absolute intelligence? What had his intelligence been given him for but to save him? Mightn't one, to reach his mind, risk the stretch of a stiff arm across his character? It was as if, when we were face to face in the dining-room, he had literally shown me the way. The roast mutton was on the table, and I had dispensed with attendance. Miles, before he sat down, stood a moment with his hands in his pockets and looked at the joint, on which he seemed on the point of passing some humorous judgement. But what he presently produced was: 'I say, my dear, is she really very awfully ill?'

'Little Flora? Not so bad but that she'll presently be better. London will set her up. Bly had ceased to agree with her. Come here and take your mutton.'

He alertly obeyed me, carried the plate carefully to his seat and, when he was established, went on. 'Did Bly disagree with her so terribly all at once?'

'Not so suddenly as you might think. One had seen it coming on.'

'Then why didn't you get her off before?'

'Before what?'

'Before she became too ill to travel.'

I found myself prompt. 'She's *not* too ill to travel: she only might have become so if she had stayed. This was just the moment to seize. The journey will dissipate the influence' – oh, I was grand! – 'and carry it off.'

'I see, I see' – Miles, for that matter, was grand too. He settled to his repast with the charming little 'table manner' that, from the day of his arrival, had relieved me of all grossness of admonition. Whatever he had been expelled from school for, it wasn't for ugly feeding. He was irreproachable, as always, today; but was unmistakably more conscious. He was discernibly trying to take for granted more things than he found, without assistance, quite easy; and he dropped into peaceful silence while he felt his situation. Our meal was of the briefest – mine a vain pretence, and I had the things immediately removed. While this was done, Miles stood again with his hands in his little pockets and his back to me – stood and looked out of the wide window through which, that other day, I had seen what pulled me up. We continued silent while the maid was with us – as silent, it whimsically occurred to me, as some young couple who, on their wedding journey, at the inn, feel shy in the presence of the waiter. He turned round only when the waiter had left us. 'Well – so we're alone!'

CHAPTER TWENTY-THREE

'Oh, MORE OR LESS.' I imagine my smile was pale. 'Not absolutely. We shouldn't like that!' I went on.

'No – I suppose we shouldn't. Of course, we've the others.'

'We've the others – we've, indeed, the others,' I concurred.

'Yet even though we have them,' he returned, still with his hands in his pockets and planted there in front of me, 'they don't much count, do they?'

I made the best of it, but I felt wan. 'It depends on what you call "much"!'

'Yes' – with all accommodation – 'everything depends!' On this, however, he faced to the window again and presently reached it with his vague, restless, cogitating step. He remained there awhile with his forehead against the glass, in contemplation of the stupid shrubs I knew and the dull things of November. I had always my hypocrisy of 'work', behind which I now gained the sofa. Steadying myself with it there as I had repeatedly done at those moments of torment that I have described as the moments of my knowing the children to be given to something from which I was barred, I sufficiently obeyed my habit of being prepared for the worst. But an extraordinary impression dropped on me as I extracted a meaning from the boy's embarrassed back – none other than the impression that I was not barred now. This inference grew in a few minutes to sharp intensity and seemed bound up with the direct perception that it was positively *he* who was. The frames and squares of the great window were a kind of image, for him, of a kind of failure. I felt that I saw him, in any case, shut in or shut out. He was admirable but not comfortable: I took it in with a throb of hope. Wasn't he looking through the haunted pane for something he couldn't see? – and wasn't it the first time in the whole business that he had known such a lapse? The first, the very first: I found it a splendid portent. It made him anxious, though he watched himself; he had been anxious all day and, even while in his usual sweet little manner he sat at table, had needed all his small strange genius to give it a gloss. When he at last turned round to meet me it was almost as if this genius had succumbed. 'Well, I think I'm glad Bly agrees with me!'

'You'd certainly seemed to have seen, these twenty-four hours, a good deal more of it than for some time before. I hope,' I went on bravely, 'that you've been enjoying yourself.'

'Oh, yes, I've been ever so far; all round about – miles and miles away. I've never been so free.'

He had really a manner of his own, and I could only try to keep up with him. 'Well, do you like it?'

He stood there smiling; then at last he put into two words – 'Do *you*?' – more discrimination than I had ever heard two words contain. Before I had time to deal with that, however, he continued as if with the sense that this was an impertinence to be softened. 'Nothing could be more charming than the way you take it, for of course if we're alone together now it's you that are alone most. But I hope,' he threw in, 'you don't particularly mind!'

'Having to do with you?' I asked. 'My dear child, how can I help minding? Though I've renounced all claim to your company – you're so beyond me – I at least greatly enjoy it. What else should I stay on for?'

He looked at me more directly, and the expression of his face, graver now, struck me as the most beautiful I had ever found in it. 'You stay on just for *that*?'

'Certainly. I stay on as your friend and from the tremendous interest I take in you till something can be done for you that may be more worth your while. That needn't surprise you.' My voice trembled so that I felt it impossible to suppress the shake. 'Don't you remember how I told you, when I came and sat on your bed the night of the storm, that there was nothing in the world I wouldn't do for you?'

'Yes, yes!' He, on his side, more and more visibly nervous, had a tone to master; but he was so much more successful than I that, laughing out through his gravity, he could pretend we were pleasantly jesting. 'Only that, I think, was to get me to do something for *you*!'

'It was partly to get you to do something,' I conceded. 'But, you know, you didn't do it.'

'Oh, yes,' he said with the brightest superficial eagerness, 'you wanted me to tell you something.'

'That's it. Out, straight out. What you have on your mind, you know.'

'Ah, then is *that* what you've stayed over for?'

He spoke with a gaiety through which I could still catch the finest little quiver of resentful passion; but I can't begin to express the effect upon me of an implication of surrender even so faint. It was as if what I had yearned for had come at last only to astonish me. 'Well, yes – I may as well make a clean breast of it. It was precisely for that.'

He waited so long that I supposed it for the purpose of repudiating the assumption on which my action had been founded; but what he finally said was: 'Do you mean now – here?'

'There couldn't be a better place or time.' He looked round him uneasily, and I had the rare – oh, the queer! – impression of the very first symptom I had seen in him of the approach of immediate fear. It was as if he were suddenly afraid of me – which struck me, indeed, as perhaps the best thing to make him. Yet in the very pang of the effort I felt it vain to try sternness, and I heard myself the next instant so gentle as to be almost grotesque. 'You want so to go out again?'

'Awfully!' He smiled at me heroically, and the touching little bravery of it was enhanced by his actually flushing with pain. He had picked up his hat, which he had brought in, and stood twirling it in a way that gave me, even as I was just nearly reaching port, a perverse horror of what I was doing. To do it in *any* way was an act of violence, for what did it consist of but the obtrusion of the idea of grossness and guilt on a small, helpless creature who had been for me a revelation of the possibilities of beautiful intercourse? Wasn't it base to create for a being so exquisite a mere alien awkwardness? I suppose I now read into our situation a clearness it couldn't have had at the time, for I seem to see our poor eyes already lighted with some spark of a prevision of the anguish that was to come. So we circled about with terrors and scruples, fighters not daring to close. But it was for each other we feared! That kept us a little longer suspended and unbruised. 'I'll tell you everything,' Miles said – 'I mean I'll tell you anything you like. You'll stay on with me, and we shall both be all right, and I *will* tell you – I *will*. But not now.'

'Why not now?'

My resistance turned him from me and kept him once more at his window in a silence during which, between us, you might have heard a pin drop. Then he was before me again with the air of a person for whom, outside, someone who had frankly to be reckoned with was waiting. 'I have to see Luke.'

I had not yet reduced him to quite so vulgar a lie, and I felt proportionately ashamed. But, horrible as it was, his lies made up my truth. I achieved thoughtfully a few loops of my knitting.

'Well, then go to Luke, and I'll wait for what you promise. Only in return for that satisfy, before you leave me, one very much smaller request.'

He looked as if he felt he had succeeded enough to be able still a little to bargain. 'Very much smaller – ?'

'Yes, a mere fraction of the whole. Tell me' – oh, my work preoccupied me, and I was offhand! – 'if, yesterday afternoon, from the table in the hall, you took, you know, my letter.'

CHAPTER TWENTY-FOUR

MY GRASP of how he received this suffered for a minute from something that I can describe only as a fierce split of my attention – a stroke that at first, as I sprang straight up, reduced me to the mere blind movement of getting hold of him, drawing him close and, while I just fell for support against the nearest piece of furniture, instinctively keeping him with his back to the window. The appearance was full upon us that I had already had to deal with here: Peter Quint had come into view like a sentinel before a prison. The next thing I saw was that, from outside, he had reached the window, and then I knew that, close to the glass and glaring in through it, he offered once more to the room his white face of damnation. It represents but grossly what took place within me at the sight to say that on the second my decision was made; yet I believe that no woman so overwhelmed ever in so short a time recovered her command of the act. It came to me in the very horror of the immediate presence that the act would be, seeing and facing what I saw and faced, to keep the boy himself unaware. The inspiration – I can call it by no other name – was that I felt how voluntarily, how transcendently, I *might*. It was like fighting with a demon for a human soul, and when I had fairly so appraised it I saw how the human soul – held out, in the tremor of my hands, at arms' length – had a perfect dew of sweat on a lovely childish forehead. The face that was close to mine was as white as the face against the glass, and out of it presently came a sound, not low nor weak, but as if from much farther away, that I drank like a waft of fragrance.

'Yes – I took it.'

At this, with a moan of joy, I enfolded, I drew him close; and while I held him to my breast, where I could feel in the sudden fever of his little body the tremendous pulse of his little heart, I kept my eyes on the thing at the window and saw it move and shift its posture. I have likened it to a sentinel, but its slow wheel, for a moment, was rather the prowl of a baffled beast. My present quickened courage, however, was such that, not too much to let it through, I had to shade, as it were, my flame. Meanwhile the glare of the face was again at the window, the scoundrel fixed as if to watch and wait. It was the very confidence that I might now defy him, as well as the positive certitude, by this time, of the child's unconsciousness, that made me go on. 'What did you take it for?'

'To see what you said about me.'

'You opened the letter?'

'I opened it.'

My eyes were now, as I held him off a little again, on Miles's own face, in which the collapse of mockery showed me how complete was the ravage of uneasiness. What was prodigious was that at last, by my success, his sense was sealed and his communication stopped: he knew that he was in presence, but knew not of what, and knew still less that I also was and that I did know. And what did this strain of trouble matter when my eyes went back to the window only to see that the air was clear again and – by my personal triumph – the influence quenched? There was nothing there. I felt that the cause was mine and that I should surely get *all*. 'And you found nothing!' – I let my elation out.

He gave me the most mournful, thoughtful little headshake. 'Nothing.'

'Nothing, nothing!' I almost shouted in my joy.

'Nothing, nothing,' he sadly repeated.

I kissed his forehead; it was drenched. 'So what have you done with it?'

'I've burnt it.'

'Burnt it?' It was now or never. 'Is that what you did at school?'

Oh, what this brought up! 'At school?'

'Did you take letters? – or other things?'

'Other things?' He appeared now to be thinking of something far off and that reached him only through the pressure of his anxiety. Yet it did reach him. 'Did I *steal*?'

I felt myself redden to the roots of my hair as well as wonder if it were more strange to put to a gentleman such a question or to see him take it with allowances that gave the very distance of his fall in the world. 'Was it for that you mightn't go back?'

The only thing he felt was rather a dreary little surprise. 'Did you know I mightn't go back?'

'I know everything.'

He gave me at this the longest and strangest look. 'Everything?'

'Everything. Therefore *did* you – ?' But couldn't say it again.

Miles could, very simply. 'No. I didn't steal.'

My face must have shown him I believed him utterly; yet my hands – but it was for pure tenderness – shook him as if to ask him why, if it was all for nothing, he had condemned me to months of torment. 'What then did you do?'

He looked in vague pain all round the top of the room and drew his breath, two or three times over, as if with difficulty. He might have been standing at the bottom of the sea and raising his eyes to some faint green twilight. 'Well – I said things.'

'Only that?'

'They thought it was enough!'

'To turn you out for?'

Never, truly, had a person 'turned out' shown so little to explain it as this little person! He appeared to weigh my question, but in a manner quite detached and almost helpless. 'Well, I suppose I oughtn't.'

'But to whom did you say them?'

He evidently tried to remember, but it dropped – he had lost it. 'I don't know!'

He almost smiled at me in the desolation of his surrender, which was, indeed, practically, by this time, so complete that I ought to have left it there. But I was infatuated – I was blind with victory though even then the very effect that was to have brought him so much nearer was already that of added separation. 'Was it to everyone?' I asked.

'No; it was only to – ' But he gave a sick little headshake. 'I don't remember their names.'

'Were they then so many?'

'No – only a few. Those I liked.'

Those he liked? I seemed to float not into clearness, but into a darker obscure, and within a minute there had come to me out of my very pity the appalling alarm of his being perhaps innocent. It was for the instant confounding and bottomless, for if he *were* innocent what then on earth was I? Paralysed, while it lasted, by the mere brush of the question, I let him go a little, so that, with a deep-drawn sigh, he turned away from me again; which, as he faced towards the clear window, I suffered, feeling that I had nothing now there to keep him from. 'And did they repeat what you said?' I went on after a moment.

He was soon at some distance from me, still breathing hard and again with the air, though now without anger for it, of being confined against his will. Once more, as he had done before, he looked up at the dim day as if, of what had hitherto sustained him, nothing was left but an unspeakable anxiety. 'Oh, yes,' he nevertheless replied – 'they must have repeated them. To those *they* liked,' he added.

There was somehow less of it than I had expected; but I turned it over. 'And these things came round – ?'

'To the masters? Oh, yes!' he answered very simply. 'But I didn't know they'd tell.'

'The masters? They didn't – they've never told. That's why I ask you.'

He turned to me again his little beautiful fevered face. 'Yes, it was too bad.'

'Too bad?'

'What I suppose I sometimes said. To write home.'

I can't name the exquisite pathos of the contradiction given to such a speech by such a speaker; I only know that the next instant I heard myself throw off with homely force: 'Stuff and nonsense!' But the next after that I must have sounded stern enough. 'What *were* these things?'

My sternness was all for his judge, his executioner; yet it made him avert himself again, and that movement made *me*, with a single bound and an irrepressible cry, spring straight upon him. For there again, against the glass, as if to blight his confession and stay his answer, was the hideous author of our woe – the white face of damnation. I felt a sick swim at the drop of my victory and all the return of my battle, so that the wildness of my veritable leap only served as a great betrayal. I saw him, from the midst of my act, meet it with a divination, and on the perception that even now he only guessed, and that the window was still to his own eyes free, I let the impulse flame up to convert the climax of his dismay into the very proof of his liberation. 'No more, no more, no more!' I shrieked to my visitant as I tried to press him against me.

'Is she *here*?' Miles panted as he caught with his sealed eyes the direction of my words. Then as his strange 'she' staggered me and, with a gasp, I echoed it, 'Miss Jessel, Miss Jessel!' he with sudden fury gave me back.

I seized, stupefied, his supposition – some sequel to what we had done to Flora, but this made me only want to show him that it was better still than that. 'It's not Miss Jessel! But it's at the window – straight before us. It's *there* – the coward horror, there for the last time!'

At this, after a second in which his head made the movement of a baffled dog's on a scent and then gave a frantic little shake for air and light, he was at me in a white rage, bewildered, glaring vainly over the place and missing wholly, though it now, to my sense, filled the room like the taste of poison, the wide overwhelming presence. 'It's *he*?'

I was so determined to have all my proof that I dashed into ice to challenge him. 'Whom do you mean by "he"?'

'Peter Quint – you devil!' His face gave again round the room, its convulsed supplication. '*Where*?'

They are in my ears still, his supreme surrender of the name and his tribute to my devotion. 'What does he matter now, my own? – what will he *ever* matter? *I* have you,' I launched at the beast, 'but he has lost you for ever!' Then, for the demonstration of my work, 'There, *there*!' I said to Miles.

But he had already jerked straight round, stared, glared again, and seen but the quiet day. With the stroke of the loss I was so proud of he uttered the cry of a creature hurled over an abyss, and the grasp with which I recovered him might have been that of catching him in his fall. I caught him, yes, I held him – it may be imagined with what a passion; but at the end of a minute I began to feel what it truly was that I held. We were alone with the quiet day, and his little heart, dispossessed, had stopped.

The Real Right Thing

I

WHEN, after the death of Ashton Doyne – but three months after – George Withermore was approached, as the phrase is, on the subject of a 'volume', the communication came straight from his publishers, who had been, and indeed much more, Doyne's own; but he was not surprised to learn, on the occurrence of the interview they next suggested, that a certain pressure as to the early issue of a Life had been applied them by their late client's widow. Doyne's relations with his wife had been to Withermore's knowledge a special chapter – which would present itself, by the way, as a delicate one for the biographer; but a sense of what she had lost, and even of what she had lacked, had betrayed itself, on the poor woman's part, from the first days of her bereavement, sufficiently to prepare an observer at all initiated for some attitude of reparation, some espousal even exaggerated of the interests of a distinguished name. George Withermore was, as he felt, initiated; yet what he had not expected was to hear that she had mentioned him as the person in whose hands she would most promptly place the materials for a book.

These materials – diaries, letters, memoranda, notes, documents of many sorts – were her property and wholly in her control, no conditions at all attaching to any portion of her heritage; so that she was free at present to do as she liked – free in particular to do nothing. What Doyne would have arranged had he had time to arrange could be but supposition and guess. Death had taken him too soon and too suddenly, and there was all the pity that the only wishes he was known to have expressed were wishes leaving it positively out. He had broken short off – that was the way of it; and the end was ragged and needed trimming. Withermore was conscious, abundantly, of how close he had stood to him, but also was not less aware of his comparative obscurity. He was young, a journalist, a critic, a hand-to-mouth character, with little, as yet, of any striking sort, to show. His writings were few and small, his relations scant and vague. Doyne, on the other hand, had lived long enough – above all had had talent enough – to become great, and among his many friends gilded also with greatness were several to whom his wife would have affected those who knew her as much more likely to appeal.

The preference she had at all events uttered – and uttered in a roundabout considerate way that left him a measure of freedom – made our young man feel that he must at least see her and that there would be in any case a good deal to talk about. He immediately wrote to her, she as promptly named an hour, and they had it out. But he came away with his particular idea immensely strengthened. She was a strange woman, and he had never thought her an agreeable, yet there was something that touched him now in her bustling blundering zeal. She wanted the book to make up, and the individual whom, of her husband's set, she probably believed she might most manipulate was in every way to help it to do so. She hadn't taken Doyne seriously enough in life, but the biography should be a full reply to every imputation on herself. She had scantly known how such books were · constructed, but she had been looking and had learned something. It alarmed Withermore a little from the first to see that she'd wish to go in for quantity. She talked of 'volumes', but he had his notion of that.

'My thought went straight to *you*, as his own would have done,' she had said almost as soon as she rose before him there in her large array of mourning – with her big black eyes, her big black wig, her big black fan and gloves, her general gaunt ugly tragic, but striking and, as might have been thought from a certain point of view, 'elegant' presence. 'You're the one he liked most; oh *much!*' – and it had quite sufficed to turn Withermore's head. It little mattered that he could afterwards wonder if she had known Doyne enough, when it came to that, to be sure. He would have said for himself indeed that her testimony on such a point could scarcely count. Still, there was no smoke without fire; she knew at least what she meant, and he wasn't a person she could have an interest in flattering. They went up together without delay to the great man's vacant study at the back of the house and looking over the large green garden – a beautiful and inspiring scene to poor Withermore's view – common to the expensive row.

'You can perfectly work here, you know,' said Mrs Doyne: 'you shall have the place quite to yourself – I'll give it all up to you; so that in the evenings in particular, don't you see? it will be perfection for quiet and privacy.'

Perfection indeed, the young man felt as he looked about – having explained that, as his actual occupation was an evening paper and his earlier hours, for a long time yet, regularly taken up, he should have to come always at night. The place was full of their lost friend; everything in it had belonged to him; everything they touched had been part of his life. It was all at once too much for Withermore – too great an honour and even too great a care; memories still recent came back to him, so that, while his heart beat faster and his eyes filled with tears, the pressure of his loyalty seemed almost more than he could carry. At the sight of his tears Mrs Doyne's own rose to her lids, and the two for a minute only looked at each other. He half-expected her to break out 'Oh help me to feel as I know you know I want to feel!' And after a little, one of them said, with the other's deep assent – it didn't matter which: 'It's here that we're *with* him.' But it was definitely the young man who put it, before they left the room, that it was there he was with themselves.

The young man began to come as soon as he could arrange it, and then it was, on the spot, in the charmed stillness, between the lamp and the fire and with the curtains drawn, that a certain intenser consciousness set in for him. He escaped from the black London November; he passed through the large hushed house and up the red-carpeted staircase where he only found in his path the whisk of a soundless trained maid or the reach, out of an open room, of Mrs Doyne's queenly weeds[1] and approving tragic face; and then, by a mere touch of the well-made door that gave so sharp and pleasant a click, shut himself in for three or four warm hours with the spirit – as he had always distinctly declared it – of his master. He was not a little frightened when, even the first night, it came over him that he had really been most affected, in the whole matter, by the prospect, the privilege and the luxury, of this sensation. He hadn't, he could now reflect, definitely considered the question of the book – as to which there was here even already much to consider: he had simply let his affection and admiration – to say nothing of his gratified pride – meet to the full the temptation Mrs Doyne had offered them.

How did he know without more thought, he might begin to ask himself, that the book was on the whole to be desired? What warrant had he ever received from Ashton Doyne himself for so direct and, as it were, so familiar an approach? Great was the art of biography, but there were lives and lives, there were subjects and subjects. He confusedly recalled, so far as that went, old words dropped by Doyne over contemporary compilations, suggestions of how he himself discriminated as to other heroes and other panoramas. He even remembered how his friend would at moments have shown himself as holding that the 'literary' career might – save in the case of a Johnson and a Scott, with a Boswell and a Lockhart[2] to help – best content itself to be represented. The artist was what he *did* – he was nothing else. Yet how on the other hand wasn't *he*, George Withermore, poor devil, to have jumped at the chance of spending his winter in an intimacy so rich? It had been simply dazzling – that was the fact. It hadn't been the 'terms', from the publishers – though these were, as they said at the office, all right; it had been Doyne himself, his company and contact and presence, it had been just what it was turning out, the possibility of an intercourse closer than that of life. Strange that death, of the two things, should have the fewer mysteries and secrets! The first night our young man was alone in the room it struck him his master and he were really for the first time together.

II

Mrs Doyne had for the most part let him expressively alone, but she had on two or three occasions looked in to see if his needs had been met, and he had had the opportunity of thanking her on the spot for the judgement and zeal with which she had smoothed his way. She had to some extent herself been looking things over and had been able already to muster several groups of letters; all the keys of drawers and cabinets she had moreover from the first placed in his hands, with helpful information as to the apparent whereabouts of different matters. She had put him, to be brief, in the fullest possible possession, and whether or no her husband had trusted her she at least, it was clear, trusted her husband's friend. There grew upon Withermore nevertheless the impression that in spite of all these offices she wasn't yet at peace and that a certain unassuageable anxiety continued even to keep step with her confidence. Though so full of consideration she was at the same time perceptibly *there*: he felt her, through a supersubtle sixth sense that the whole connection had already brought into play, hover, in the still hours, at the top of landings and on the other side of doors; he gathered from the soundless brush of her skirts the hint of her watchings and waitings. One evening when, at his friend's table, he had lost himself in the depths of correspondence, he was made to start and turn by the suggestion that someone was behind him. Mrs Doyne had come in without his hearing the door, and she gave a strained smile as he sprang to his feet. 'I hope,' she said, 'I haven't frightened you.'

'Just a little – I was so absorbed. It was as if, for the instant,' the young man explained, 'it had been himself.'

The oddity of her face increased in her wonder. 'Ashton?'

'He does seem so near,' said Withermore.

'To you too?'

This naturally struck him. 'He does then to you?'

She waited, not moving from the spot where she had first stood, but looking round the room as if to penetrate its duskier angles. She had a way of raising to the level of her nose the big black fan which she apparently never laid aside and with which she thus covered the lower half of her face, her rather hard eyes, above it, becoming the more ambiguous. 'Sometimes.'

'Here,' Withermore went on, 'it's as if he might at any moment come in. That's why I jumped just now. The time's so short since he really used to – it only *was* yesterday. I sit in his chair, I turn his books, I use his pens, I stir his fire – all exactly as if, learning he would presently be back from a walk, I had come up here contentedly to wait. It's delightful – but it's strange.'

Mrs Doyne, her fan still up, listened with interest. 'Does it worry you?'

'No – I like it.'

Again she faltered. 'Do you ever feel as if he were – a – quite – a – personally in the room?'

'Well, as I said just now,' her companion laughed, 'on hearing you behind me I seemed to take it so. What do we want, after all,' he asked, 'but that he shall be with us?'

'Yes, as you said he'd be – that first time.' She gazed in full assent. 'He *is* with us.'

She was rather portentous, but Withermore took it smiling. 'Then we must keep him. We must do only what he'd like.'

'Oh only that of course – only. But if he *is* here – ?' And her sombre eyes seemed to throw it out in vague distress over her fan.

'It proves he's pleased and wants only to help? Yes, surely; it must prove that.'

She gave a light gasp and looked again round the room. 'Well,' she said as she took leave of him, 'remember that I too want only to help.' On which, when she had gone, he felt sufficiently that she had come in simply to see he was all right.

He was all right more and more, it struck him after this, for as he began to get into his work he moved, as it appeared to him, but the closer to the idea of Doyne's personal presence. When once this fancy had begun to hang about him he welcomed it, persuaded it, encouraged it, quite cherished it, looking forward all day to feeling it renew itself in the evening, and waiting for the growth of dusk very much as one of a pair of lovers might wait for the hour of their appointment. The smallest accidents humoured and confirmed it, and by the end of three or four weeks he had come fully to regard it as the consecration of his enterprise. Didn't it just settle the question of what Doyne would have thought of what they were doing? What they were doing was what he wanted done, and they could go on from step to step without scruple or doubt. Withermore rejoiced indeed at moments to feel this certitude: there were times of dipping deep into some of Doyne's secrets when it was particularly pleasant to be able to hold that Doyne desired him, as it were, to know them. He was learning many things he hadn't suspected – drawing many curtains, forcing many doors, reading many riddles, going, in general, as they said, behind almost everything. It was at an occasional sharp turn of some of the duskier of these wanderings 'behind' that he really, of a sudden, most felt himself, in the intimate sensible way, face to face with his friend; so that he could scarce have told, for the instant, if their meeting occurred in the narrow passage and tight squeeze of the past or at the hour and in the place that actually held him. Was it a matter of '67? – or but of the other side of the table?

Happily, at any rate, even in the vulgarest light publicity could ever shed, there would be the great fact of the way Doyne was 'coming out'. He was coming out too beautifully – better yet than such a partisan as Withermore could have supposed. All the while as well, nevertheless, how would this partisan have represented to anyone else the special state of his own consciousness? It wasn't a thing to talk about – it was only a thing to feel. There were moments for instance when, while he bent over his papers, the light breath of his dead host was as distinctly in his hair as his own elbows were on the table before him. There were moments when, had he been able to look up, the other side of the table would have shown him this companion as vividly as the shaded lamplight showed him his page. That he couldn't at such a juncture look up was his own affair, for the situation was ruled – that was but natural – by deep delicacies and fine timidities, the dread of too sudden or too rude an advance. What was intensely in the air was that if Doyne *was* there it wasn't nearly so much for himself as for the young priest of his altar. He hovered and lingered, he came and went, he might almost have been, among the books and the papers, a hushed discreet librarian, doing the particular things, rendering the quiet aid, liked by men of letters.

Withermore himself meanwhile came and went, changed his place, wandered on quests either definite or vague; and more than once when, taking a book down from a shelf and finding in it marks of Doyne's pencil, he got drawn on and lost, he had heard documents on the table behind him gently shifted and stirred, had literally, on his return, found some letter mislaid pushed again into view, some thicket cleared by the opening of an old journal at the very date he wanted. How should he have gone so, on occasion, to the special box or drawer, out of fifty receptacles, that would help him, had not his mystic assistant happened, in fine prevision, to tilt its lid or pull it half-open, just in the way that would catch his eye? – in spite, after all, of the fact of lapses and intervals in which, *could* one have really looked, one would have seen somebody standing before the fire a trifle detached and over-erect – somebody fixing one the least bit harder than in life.

III

That this auspicious relation had in fact existed, had continued, for two or three weeks, was sufficiently shown by the dawn of the distress with which our young man found himself aware of having, for some reason, from the close of a certain day, begun to miss it. The sign of that was an abrupt surprised sense – on the occasion of his mislaying a marvellous unpublished page which, hunt where he would, remained stupidly irrecoverably lost – that his protected state was, with all said, exposed to some confusion and even to some depression. If, for the joy of the business, Doyne and he had, from the start, been together, the situation had within a few days of his first suspicion of it suffered the odd change of their ceasing to be so. That was what was the matter, he mused, from the moment an impression of mere mass and quantity struck him as taking, in his happy outlook at his material, the place of the pleasant assumption of a clear course and a quick pace. For five nights he struggled; then, never at his table, wandering about the room, taking up his references only to lay them down, looking out of the window, poking the fire, thinking strange thoughts and listening for signs and sounds not as he suspected or imagined, but as he vainly desired and invoked them, he yielded to the view that he was for the time at least forsaken.

The extraordinary thing thus became that it made him not only sad but in a high degree uneasy not to feel Doyne's presence. It was somehow stranger he shouldn't be there than it had ever been he *was* – so strange indeed at last that Withermore's nerves found themselves quite illogically touched. They had taken kindly enough to what was of an order impossible to explain, perversely reserving their sharpest state for the return to the normal, the supersession of the false. They were remarkably beyond control when finally, one night after his resisting them an hour or two, he simply edged out of the room. It had now but for the first time become impossible to him to stay. Without design, but panting a little and positively as a man scared, he passed along his usual corridor and reached the top of the staircase. From this point he saw Mrs Doyne look up at him from the bottom quite as if she had known he would come; and the most singular thing of all was that, though he had been conscious of no motion to resort to her, had only been prompted to relieve himself by escape, the sight of her position made him recognise it as just, quickly feel it as a part of some monstrous oppression that was closing over them both. It was wonderful how, in the mere modern London hall, between the Tottenham Court Road rugs and the electric light, it came up to him from the tall black lady, and went again from him down to her, that he knew what she meant by looking as if he would know. He descended straight, she turned into her own little lower room, and there, the next thing, with the door shut, they were, still in silence and with queer faces, confronted over confessions that had taken sudden life from these two or three movements. Withermore gasped as it came to him why he had lost his friend. 'He has been with *you*?'

With this it was all out – out so far that neither had to explain and that, when 'What do you suppose is the matter?' quickly passed between them, one appeared to have said it as much as the other. Withermore looked about at the small bright room in which, night after night, she had been living her life as he had been living his own upstairs. It was pretty, cosy, rosy; but she had by turns felt in it what he had felt and heard in it what he had heard. Her effect there – fantastic black, plumed and extravagant, upon deep pink – was that of some 'decadent'[3] coloured print, some poster of the newest school. 'You understood he had left me?' he asked.

She markedly wished to make it clear. 'This evening – yes. I've made things out.'

'You knew – before – that he was with me?'

She hesitated again. 'I felt he wasn't with *me*. But on the stairs – '

'Yes?'

'Well – he passed; more than once. He was in the house. And at your door – '

'Well?' he went on as she once more faltered.

'If I stopped I could sometimes tell. And from your face,' she added, 'tonight, at any rate, I knew your state.'

'And that was why you came out?'

'I thought you'd come to me.'

He put out to her, on this, his hand, and they thus for a minute of silence held each other clasped. There was no peculiar presence for either now – nothing more peculiar than that of each for the other. But the place had suddenly become as if consecrated, and Withermore played over it again his anxiety. 'What *is* then the matter?'

'I only want to do the real right thing,' she returned after her pause.

'And aren't we doing it?'

'I wonder. Aren't *you?*'

He wondered too. 'To the best of my belief. But we must think.'

'We must think,' she echoed. And they did think – thought with intensity the rest of that evening together, and thought independently (Withermore at least could answer for himself) during many days that followed. He intermitted a little his visits and his work, trying, all critically, to catch himself in the act of some mistake that might have accounted for their disturbance. Had he taken, on some important point – or looked as if he might take – some wrong line or wrong view? had he somewhere benightedly falsified or inadequately insisted? He went back at last with the idea of having guessed two or three questions he might have been on the way to muddle; after which he had abovestairs, another period of agitation, presently followed by another interview below with Mrs Doyne, who was still troubled and flushed.

'He's there?'

'He's there.'

'I knew it!' she returned in an odd gloom of triumph. Then as to make it clear: 'He hasn't been again with *me.*'

'Nor with me again to help,' said Withermore.

She considered. 'Not to help?'

'I can't make it out – I'm at sea. Do what I will I feel I'm wrong.'

She covered him a moment with her pompous pain. 'How do you feel it?'

'Why by things that happen. The strangest things. I can't describe them – and you wouldn't believe them.'

'Oh yes I should!' Mrs Doyne cried.

'Well, he intervenes.' Withermore tried to explain. 'However I turn I find him.'

She earnestly followed. ' "Find" him?'

'I meet him. He seems to rise there before me.'

Staring, she waited a little. 'Do you mean you see him?'

'I feel as if at any moment I may. I'm baffled. I'm checked.' Then he added: 'I'm afraid.'

'Of *him?*' asked Mrs Doyne.

He thought. 'Well – of what I'm doing.'

'Then what, that's so awful, *are* you doing?'

'What you proposed to me. Going into his life.'

She showed, in her present gravity, a new alarm. 'And don't you *like* that?'

'Doesn't *he?* That's the question. We lay him bare. We serve him up. What is it called? We give him to the world.'

Poor Mrs Doyne, as if on a menace to her hard atonement, glared at this for an instant in deeper gloom. 'And why shouldn't we?'

'Because we don't know. There are natures, there are lives, that shrink. He mayn't wish it,' said Withermore. 'We never asked him.'

'How *could* we?'

He was silent a little. 'Well, we ask him now. That's after all what our start has so far represented. We've put it to him.'

'Then – if he has been with us – we've had his answer.'

Withermore spoke now as if he knew what to believe. 'He hasn't been "with" us – he has been against us.'

'Then why did you think – '

'What I *did* think at first – that what he wishes to make us feel is his sympathy? Because I was in my original simplicity mistaken. I was – I don't know what to call it – so excited and charmed that I didn't understand. But I understand at last. He only wanted to communicate. He strains forward out of his darkness, he reaches towards us out of his mystery, he makes us dim signs out of his horror.'

' "Horror"?' Mrs Doyne gasped with her fan up to her mouth.

'At what we're doing.' He could by this time piece it all together. 'I see now that at first – '

'Well, what?'

'One had simply to feel he was there and therefore not indifferent. And the beauty of that misled me. But he's there as a protest.'

'Against *my* Life?' Mrs Doyne wailed.

'Against *any* Life. He's there to *save* his Life. He's there to be let alone.'

'So you give up?' she almost shrieked.

He could only meet her. 'He's there as a warning.'

For a moment, on this, they looked at each other deep. 'You *are* afraid!' she at last brought out.

It affected him, but he insisted. 'He's there as a curse!'

With that they parted, but only for two or three days; her last word to him continuing to sound so in his ears that, between his need really to satisfy her and another need presently to be noted, he felt he mightn't yet take up his stake. He finally went back at his usual hour and found her in her usual place. 'Yes, I *am* afraid,' he announced as if he had turned that well over and knew now all it meant. 'But I gather you're not.'

She faltered, reserving her word. 'What is it you fear?'

'Well, that if I go on I *shall* see him.'

'And then – ?'

'Oh then,' said George Withermore, 'I *should* give up!'

She weighed it with her proud but earnest air. 'I think, you know, we must have a clear sign.'

'You wish me to try again?'

She debated. 'You see what it means – for me – to give up.'

'Ah but *you* needn't,' Withermore said.

She seemed to wonder, but in a moment went on.

'It would mean that he won't take from me – ' But she dropped for despair.

'Well, what?'

'Anything,' said poor Mrs Doyne.

He faced her a moment more. 'I've thought myself of the clear sign. I'll try again.'

As he was leaving her however she remembered. 'I'm only afraid that tonight there's nothing ready – no lamp and no fire.'

'Never mind,' he said from the foot of the stairs; 'I'll find things.'

To which she answered that the door of the room would probably at any rate be open; and retired again as to wait for him. She hadn't long to wait; though, with her own door wide and her attention fixed, she may not have taken the time quite as it appeared to her visitor. She heard him, after an interval, on the stair, and he presently stood at her entrance, where, if he hadn't been precipitate, but rather, for step and sound, backward and vague, he showed at least as livid and blank.

'I give up.'

'Then you've seen him?'

'On the threshold – guarding it.'

'Guarding it?' She glowed over her fan. 'Distinct?'

'Immense. But dim. Dark. Dreadful,' said poor George Withermore.

She continued to wonder. 'You didn't go in?'

The young man turned away. 'He forbids!'

'You say *I* needn't,' she went on after a moment. 'Well then need I?'

'See him?' George Withermore asked.

She waited an instant. 'Give up.'

'You must decide.' For himself he could at last but sink to the sofa with his bent face in his hands.

He wasn't quite to know afterwards how long he had sat so; it was enough that what he did next know was that he was alone among her favourite objects. Just as he gained his feet however, with this sense and that of the door standing open to the hall, he found himself afresh confronted, in the light, the warmth, the rosy space, with her big black perfumed presence. He saw at a glance, as she offered him a huger bleaker stare over the mask of her fan, that she had been above; and so it was that they for the last time faced together their strange question. 'You've seen him?' Withermore asked.

He was to infer later on from the extraordinary way she closed her eyes and, as if to steady herself, held them tight and long, in silence, that beside the unutterable vision of Ashton Doyne's wife his own might rank as an escape. He knew before she spoke that all was over. 'I give up.'

The Third Person

I

WHEN, a few years since, two good ladies, previously not intimate nor indeed more than slightly acquainted, found themselves domiciled together in the small but ancient town of Marr,[1] it was as a result, naturally, of special considerations. They bore the same name and were second cousins; but their paths had not hitherto crossed; there had not been coincidence of age to draw them together; and Miss Frush, the more mature, had spent much of her life abroad. She was a bland, shy, sketching person, whom fate had condemned to a monotony – triumphing over variety – of Swiss and Italian *pensions*;[2] in any one of which, with her well-fastened hat, her gauntlets and her stout boots, her camp-stool, her sketchbook, her Tauchnitz novel,[3] she would have served with peculiar propriety as a frontispiece to the natural history of the English old maid. She would have struck you indeed, poor Miss Frush, as so happy an instance of the type that you would perhaps scarce have been able to equip her with the dignity of the individual. This was what she enjoyed, however, for those brought nearer – a very insistent identity, once even of prettiness, but which now, blanched and bony, timid and inordinately queer, with its utterance all vague interjection and its aspect all eyeglass and teeth, might be acknowledged without inconvenience and deplored without reserve. Miss Amy, her kinswoman, who, ten years her junior, showed a different figure – such as, oddly enough, though formed almost wholly in English air, might have appeared much more to betray a foreign influence – Miss Amy was brown, brisk, and expressive: when really young she had even been pronounced showy. She had an innocent vanity on the subject of her foot, a member which she somehow regarded as a guarantee of her wit, or at least of her good taste. Even had it not been pretty, she flattered herself it would have been shod: she would never – no, never, like Susan – have given it up. Her bright brown eye was comparatively bold, and she had accepted Susan once for all as a frump. She even thought her, and silently deplored her as, a goose. But she was none the less herself a lamb.

They had benefited, this innocuous pair, under the will of an old aunt, a prodigiously ancient gentlewoman, of whom, in her later time, it had been given them, mainly by the office of others, to see almost nothing; so that the little property they came in for had the happy effect of a windfall. Each, at least, pretended to the other that she had never dreamed – as in truth there had been small encouragement for dreams in the sad character of what they now spoke of as the late lady's 'dreadful *entourage*'.[4] Terrorised and deceived, as they considered, by her own people, Mrs Frush was scantily enough to have been counted on for an act of almost inspired justice. The good luck of her husband's nieces was that she had really outlived, for the most part, their ill-wishers and so, at the very last, had died without the blame of diverting fine Frush property from fine Frush use. Property quite of her own she had done as she liked with; but she had pitied poor expatriated Susan and had remembered poor unhusbanded Amy, though lumping them together perhaps a little roughly in her final provision. Her will directed that, should no other arrangement be more convenient to her executors, the old house at Marr might be sold for their joint advantage. What befell, however, in the event, was that the two legatees, advised in due course, took an early occasion – and quite without concert – to judge their prospects on the spot. They arrived at Marr, each on her own side, and they were so pleased with Marr that they remained. So it was that they met: Miss Amy, accompanied by the office-boy of the local solicitor, presented herself at the door of the house to ask admittance of the caretaker. But when the door opened, it offered to sight not the caretaker, but an unexpected, unexpecting lady in a very old waterproof, who held a long-handled eyeglass very much as a child holds a rattle. Miss Susan, already in the field, roaming, prying, meditating in the absence on an errand of the woman in charge, offered herself in this manner as in settled possession; and it was on that idea that, through the eyeglass, the cousins viewed each other with some penetration even before Amy came in. Then at last when Amy did come in it was not, any more than Susan, to go out again.

It would take us too far to imagine what might have happened had Mrs Frush made it a condition of her benevolence that the subjects of it should inhabit, should live at peace together, under the roof she left them; but certain it is that as they stood there they had at the same moment the same unprompted thought. Each became aware on the spot that the dear old house itself was exactly what she, and exactly what the other, wanted; it met in perfection their longing for a quiet harbour and an assured future; each, in short, was willing to take the other in order to get the house. It was therefore not sold; it was made, instead, their own, as it stood, with the dead lady's extremely 'good' old appurtenances not only undisturbed and undivided, but piously reconstructed and infinitely admired, the agents of her testamentary purpose rejoicing meanwhile to see the business so simplified. They might have had their private doubts – or their wives might have; might cynically have predicted the sharpest of quarrels, before three months were out, between the deluded yoke-fellows, and the dissolution of the partnership with every circumstance of recrimination. All that need be said is that such prophets would have prophesied vulgarly. The Misses Frush were not vulgar; they had drunk deep of the cup of singleness and found it prevailingly bitter; they were not unacquainted with solitude and sadness, and they recognised with due humility the supreme opportunity of their lives. By the end of three months, moreover, each knew the worst about the other. Miss Amy took her evening nap before dinner, an hour at which Miss Susan could never sleep – it was so odd; whereby Miss Susan took hers after that meal, just at the hour when Miss Amy was keenest for talk. Miss Susan, erect and unsupported, had feelings as to the way in which, in almost any posture that could pass for a seated one, Miss Amy managed to find a place in the small of her back for two out of the three sofa-cushions – a smaller place, obviously, than they had ever been intended to fit.

But when this was said all was said; they continued to have, on either side, the pleasant consciousness of a personal soil, not devoid of fragmentary ruins, to dig in. They had a theory that their lives had been immensely different, and each appeared now to the other to have conducted her career so perversely only that she should have an unfamiliar range of anecdote for her companion's ear. Miss Susan, at foreign *pensions*, had met the Russian, the Polish, the Danish, and even an occasional flower of the English, nobility, as well as many of the most extraordinary Americans, who, as she said, had made everything of her and with whom she had remained, often, in correspondence; while Miss Amy, after all less conventional, at the end of long years of London, abounded in reminiscences of literary, artistic, and even – Miss Susan heard it with bated breath – theatrical society, under the influence of which she had written – there, it came out! – a novel that had been anonymously published and a play that had been strikingly type-copied.[5] Not the least charm, clearly, of this picturesque outlook at Marr would be the support that might be drawn from it for getting back, as she hinted, with 'general society' bravely sacrificed, to 'real work'. She had in her head hundreds of

plots – with which the future, accordingly, seemed to bristle for Miss
Susan. The latter, on her side, was only waiting for the wind to go
down to take up again her sketching. The wind at Marr was often
high, as was natural in a little old huddled, red-roofed, historic south-
coast town which had once been in a manner mistress, as the cousins
reminded each other, of the 'Channel',[6] and from which, high and
dry on its hilltop though it might be, the sea had not so far receded as
not to give, constantly, a taste of temper. Miss Susan came back to
English scenery with a small sigh of fondness to which the consciousness of Alps and Apennines only gave more of a quaver; she had
picked out her subjects and, with her head on one side and a sense
that they were easier abroad, sat sucking her watercolour brush and
nervously – perhaps even a little inconsistently – waiting and
hesitating. What had happened was that they had, each for herself,
rediscovered the country; only Miss Amy, emergent from
Bloomsbury lodgings, spoke of it as primroses and sunsets, and Miss
Susan, rebounding from the Arno and the Reuss,[7] called it, with a
shy, synthetic pride, simply England.

The country was at any rate in the house with them as well as in
the little green girdle and in the big blue belt. It was in the objects
and relics that they handled together and wondered over, finding in
them a ground for much inferred importance and invoked romance,
stuffing large stories into very small openings and pulling every
faded bell-rope that might jingle rustily into the past. They were still
here in the presence, at all events, of their common ancestors, as to
whom, more than ever before, they took only the best for granted.
Was not the best, for that matter – the best, that is, of little
melancholy, middling, disinherited Marr – seated in every stiff chair
of the decent old house and stitched into the patchwork of every
quaint old counterpane? Two hundred years of it squared themselves in the brown, panelled parlour, creaked patiently on the wide
staircase, and bloomed herbaceously in the red-walled garden.
There was nothing anyone had ever done or been at Marr that a
Frush hadn't done it or been it. Yet they wanted more of a picture
and talked themselves into the fancy of it; there were portraits – half
a dozen, comparatively recent (they called 1800 comparatively
recent), and something of a trial to a descendant who had copied
Titian at the Pitti;[8] but they were curious of detail and would have
liked to people a little more thickly their backward space, to set it up
behind their chairs as a screen embossed with figures. They threw
off theories and small imaginations, and almost conceived themselves engaged in researches; all of which made for pomp and

circumstance. Their desire was to discover something, and, embold-
ened by the broader sweep of wing of her companion, Miss Susan
herself was not afraid of discovering something bad. Miss Amy it was
who had first remarked, as a warning, that this was what it might all
lead to. It was she, moreover, to whom they owed the formula that,
had anything *very* bad ever happened at Marr, they should be sorry if
a Frush hadn't been in it. This was the moment at which Miss
Susan's spirit had reached its highest point: she had declared, with
her odd, breathless laugh, a prolonged, an alarmed or alarming gasp,
that she should really be quite ashamed. And so they rested awhile;
not saying quite how far they were prepared to go in crime – not
giving the matter a name. But there would have been little doubt for
an observer that each supposed the other to mean that she not only
didn't draw the line at murder, but stretched it so as to take in – well,
gay deception. If Miss Susan could conceivably have asked whether
Don Juan[9] had ever touched at that port, Miss Amy would, to a
certainty, have wanted to know by way of answer at what port he had
not touched. It was only unfortunately true that no one of the
portraits of gentlemen looked at all like him and no one of those of
ladies suggested one of his victims.

At last, none the less, the cousins had a find, came upon a box of
old odds and ends, mainly documentary; partly printed matter,
newspapers and pamphlets yellow and grey with time, and, for the
rest, epistolary – several packets of letters, faded, scarce decipher-
able, but clearly sorted for preservation and tied, with sprigged
ribbon of a faraway fashion, into little groups. Marr, below ground,
is solidly founded – underlaid with great straddling cellars, sound
and dry, that are like the groined crypts of churches and that present
themselves to the meagre modern conception as the treasure-
chambers of stout merchants and bankers in the old bustling days. A
recess in the thickness of one of the walls had yielded up, on resolute
investigation – that of the local youth employed for odd jobs and
who had happened to explore in this direction on his own account –
a collection of rusty superfluities among which the small chest in
question had been dragged to light. It produced of course an instant
impression and figured as a discovery; though indeed as rather a
deceptive one on its having, when forced open, nothing better to
show, at the best, than a quantity of rather illegible correspondence.
The good ladies had naturally had for the moment a fluttered hope
of old golden guineas – a miser's hoard; perhaps even of a hatful of
those foreign coins of old-fashioned romance, ducats, doubloons,
pieces of eight, as are sometimes found to have come to hiding, from

over seas, in ancient ports. But they had to accept their disappointment – which they sought to do by making the best of the papers, by
agreeing, in other words, to regard them as wonderful. Well, they
were, doubtless, wonderful; which didn't prevent them, however,
from appearing to be, on superficial inspection, also rather a weary
labyrinth. Baffling, at any rate, to Miss Susan's unpractised eyes, the
little pale-ribboned packets were, for several evenings, round the
fire, while she luxuriously dozed, taken in hand by Miss Amy; with
the result that on a certain occasion when, towards nine o'clock,
Miss Susan woke up, she found her fellow-labourer fast asleep. A
slightly irritated confession of ignorance of the Gothic character[10]
was the further consequence, and the upshot of this, in turn, was the
idea of appeal to Mr Patten. Mr Patten was the vicar and was known
to interest himself, as such, in the ancient annals of Marr; in addition
to which – and to its being even held a little that his sense of the
affairs of the hour was sometimes sacrificed to such inquiries – he
was a gentleman with a humour of his own, a flushed face, a bushy
eyebrow, and a black wideawake[11] worn sociably askew. 'He will tell
us,' said Amy Frush, 'if there's anything in them.'

'Yet if it should be,' Susan suggested, 'anything we mayn't like?'

'Well, that's just what I'm thinking of,' returned Miss Amy in her
offhand way. 'If it's anything we shouldn't know . . . '

'We've only to tell him not to tell us? Oh, certainly,' said mild Miss
Susan. She took upon herself even to give him that warning when, on
the invitation of our friends, Mr Patten came to tea and to talk things
over; Miss Amy sitting by and raising no protest, but distinctly
promising herself that, whatever there might be to be known, and
however objectionable, she would privately get it out of their
initiator. She found herself already hoping that it *would* be something
too bad for her cousin – too bad for anyone else at all – to know, and
that it most properly might remain between them. Mr Patten, at
sight of the papers, exclaimed, perhaps a trifle ambiguously, and by
no means clerically, 'My eye, what a lark!' and retired, after three
cups of tea, in an overcoat bulging with his spoil.

II

At ten o'clock that evening the pair separated, as usual on the upper
landing, outside their respective doors, for the night; but Miss Amy
had hardly set down her candle on her dressing-table before she was
startled by an extraordinary sound, which appeared to proceed not
only from her companion's room, but from her companion's throat.

It was something she would have described, had she ever described it, as between a gurgle and a shriek, and it brought Amy Frush, after an interval of stricken stillness that gave her just time to say to herself 'Someone under her bed!' breathlessly and bravely back to the landing. She had not reached it, however, before her neighbour, bursting in, met her and stayed her.

'There's someone in my room!'

They held each other. 'But who?'

'A man.'

'Under the bed?'

'No – just standing there.'

They continued to hold each other, but they rocked. 'Standing? Where? How?'

'Why, right in the middle – before my dressing-glass.'

Amy's blanched face by this time matched her mate's, but its terror was enhanced by speculation. 'To look at himself?'

'No – with his back to it. To look at *me*,' poor Susan just audibly breathed. 'To keep me off,' she quavered. 'In strange clothes – of another age; with his head on one side.'

Amy wondered. 'On one side?'

'Awfully!' the refugee declared while, clinging together, they sounded each other.

This, somehow, for Miss Amy, was the convincing touch; and on it, after a moment, she was capable of the effort of darting back to close her own door. 'You'll remain then with me.'

'Oh!' Miss Susan wailed with deep assent; quite, as if, had she been a slangy person, she would have ejaculated 'Rather!' So they spent the night together; with the assumption thus marked, from the first, both that it would have been vain to confront their visitor as they didn't even pretend to each other that they would have confronted a housebreaker; and that by leaving the place at his mercy nothing worse could happen than had already happened. It was Miss Amy's approaching the door again as with intent ear and after a hush that had represented between them a deep and extraordinary inter-change – it was this that put them promptly face to face with the real character of the occurrence. 'Ah,' Miss Susan, still under her breath, portentously exclaimed, 'it isn't anyone – '

'No' – her partner was already able magnificently to take her up. 'It isn't anyone – '

'Who can really hurt us' – Miss Susan completed her thought. And Miss Amy, as it proved, had been so indescribably prepared that this thought, before morning, had, in the strangest, finest way, made for itself an admirable place with them. The person the elder of our pair had seen in her room was not – well, just simply was not anyone in from outside. He was a different thing altogether. Miss Amy had felt it as soon as she heard her friend's cry and become aware of her commotion; as soon, at all events, as she saw Miss Susan's face. That was all – and there it was. There had been something hitherto wanting, they felt, to their small state and importance; it was present now, and they were as handsomely conscious of it as if they had previously missed it. The element in question, then, was a third person in their association, a hovering presence for the dark hours, a figure that with its head very much – too much – on one side, could be trusted to look at them out of unnatural places; yet only, it doubtless might be assumed, to look at them. They had it at last – had what was to be had in an old house where many, too many, things had happened, where the very walls they touched and floors they trod could have told secrets and named names, where every surface was a blurred mirror of life and death, of the endured, the remembered, the forgotten. Yes; the place was h – , but they stopped at sounding the word. And by morning, wonderful to say, they were used to it – had quite lived into it.

Not only this indeed, but they had their prompt theory. There was a connection between the finding of the box in the vault and the appearance in Miss Susan's room. The heavy air of the past had been stirred by the bringing to light of what had so long been hidden. The communication of the papers to Mr Patten had had its effect. They faced each other in the morning at breakfast over the certainty that their queer roused inmate was the sign of the violated secret of these relics. No matter; for the sake of the secret they would put up with his attention; and – this, in them, was most beautiful of all – they must, though he was such an addition to their grandeur, keep him quite to themselves. Other people might hear of what was in the letters, but they should never hear of *him*. They were not afraid that either of the maids should see him – he was not a matter for maids. The question indeed was whether – should he keep it up long – they themselves would find that they could really live with him. Yet perhaps his keeping it up would be just what would make them indifferent. They turned these things over, but spent the next nights together; and on the third day, in the course of their afternoon walk, descried at a distance the vicar, who, as soon as he saw them, waved his arms violently – either as a warning or as a joke – and came more than halfway to meet them. It was in the middle – or what passed for such – of the big, bleak, blank, melancholy square of Marr; a public place, as it were, of such an absurd capacity for a crowd; with the great ivy-mantled choir and stopped transept of the nobly planned church, telling of how many centuries ago it had, for its part, given up growing.

'Why, my dear ladies,' cried Mr Patten as he approached, 'do you know what, of all things in the world, I seem to make out for you from your funny old letters?' Then as they waited, extremely on their guard now: 'Neither more nor less, if you please, than that one of your ancestors in the last century – Mr Cuthbert Frush, it would seem, by name – was hanged.'

They never knew afterwards which of the two had first found composure – found even dignity – to respond. 'And pray, Mr Patten, for what?'

'Ah, that's just what I don't yet get hold of. But if you don't mind my digging away' – and the vicar's bushy, jolly brows turned from one of the ladies to the other – 'I think I can run it to earth. They hanged, in those days, you know,' he added as if he had seen something in their faces, 'for almost any trifle!'

'Oh, I hope it wasn't for a trifle!' Miss Susan strangely tittered.

'Yes, of course one would like that, while he was about it – well, it had been, as they say,' Mr Patten laughed, 'rather for a sheep than for a lamb!'

'Did they hang at that time for a sheep?' Miss Amy wonderingly asked.

It made their friend laugh again. 'The question's whether *he* did! But we'll find out. Upon my word, you know, I quite want to myself. I'm awfully busy, but I think I can promise you that you shall hear. You *don't* mind?' he insisted.

'I think we could bear *anything*,' said Miss Amy.

Miss Susan gazed at her, on this, as for reference and appeal. 'And what is he, after all, at this time of day, *to* us?'

Her kinswoman, meeting the eyeglass fixedly, spoke with gravity. 'Oh, an ancestor's always an ancestor.'

'Well said and well felt, dear lady!' the vicar declared. 'Whatever they may have done – '

'It isn't everyone,' Miss Amy replied, 'that has them to be ashamed of.'

'And we're not ashamed *yet!*' Miss Frush jerked out.

'Let me promise you then that you shan't be. Only, for I am busy,' said Mr Patten, 'give me time.'

'Ah, but we want the truth!' they cried with high emphasis as he quitted them. They were much excited now.

He answered by pulling up and turning round as short as if his professional character had been challenged. 'Isn't it just in the truth – and the truth only – that I deal?'

This they recognised as much as his love of a joke, and so they were left there together in the pleasant, if slightly overdone, void of the square, which wore at moments the air of a conscious demonstration, intended as an appeal, of the shrinkage of the population of Marr to a solitary cat. They walked on after a little, but they waited till the vicar was ever so far away before they spoke again; all the more that their doing so must bring them once more to a pause. Then they had a long look. 'Hanged!' said Miss Amy – yet almost exultantly.

This was, however, because it was not she who had seen.

'That's why his head – ' but Miss Susan faltered.

Her companion took it in. 'Oh, has such a dreadful twist?'

'It *is* dreadful!' Miss Susan at last dropped, speaking as if she had been present at twenty executions.

There would have been no saying, at any rate, what it didn't evoke from Miss Amy. 'It breaks their neck,' she contributed after a moment.

Miss Susan looked away. 'That's why, I suppose, the head turns so fearfully awry. It's a most peculiar effect.'

So peculiar, it might have seemed, that it made them silent afresh. 'Well, then, I hope he killed someone!' Miss Amy broke out at last.

Her companion thought. 'Wouldn't it depend on whom – ?'

'No!' she returned with her characteristic briskness – a briskness that set them again into motion.

That Mr Patten was tremendously busy was evident indeed, as even by the end of the week he had nothing more to impart. The whole thing meanwhile came up again – on the Sunday afternoon; as the younger Miss Frush had been quite confident that, from one day to the other, it must. They went inveterately to evening church, to the close of which supper was postponed; and Miss Susan, on this occasion, ready the first, patiently awaited her mate at the foot of the stairs. Miss Amy at last came down, buttoning a glove, rustling the tail of a frock, and looking, as her kinswoman always thought, conspicuously young and smart. There was no one at Marr, she held, who dressed like her; and Miss Amy, it must be owned, had also settled to this view of Miss Susan, though taking it in a different spirit. Dusk had gathered, but our frugal pair were always tardy lighters, and the grey close of day, in which the elder lady, on a high-backed hall chair, sat with hands patiently folded, had for all cheer the subdued glow – always subdued – of the small fire in the drawing-room, visible through a door that stood open. Into the drawing-room Miss Amy passed in search of the prayer book she had laid down there after morning church, and from it, after a minute, without this volume, she returned to her companion. There was something in her movement that spoke – spoke for a moment so largely that nothing more was said till, with a quick unanimity, they had got themselves straight out of the house. There, before the door, in the cold, still twilight of the winter's end, while the church bells rang and the windows of the great choir showed across the empty square faintly red, they had it out again. But it was Miss Susan herself, this time, who had to bring it.

'He's there?'

'Before the fire – with his back to it.'

'Well, now you see!' Miss Susan exclaimed with elation and as if her friend had hitherto doubted her.

'Yes, I see – and what you mean.' Miss Amy was deeply thoughtful. 'About his head?'

'It *is* on one side,' Miss Amy went on. 'It makes him – ' she considered. But she faltered as if still in his presence.

'It makes him awful!' Miss Susan murmured. 'The way,' she softly moaned, 'he looks at you!'

Miss Amy, with a glance, met this recognition. 'Yes – doesn't he?' Then her eyes attached themselves to the red windows of the church. 'But it means something.'

'The Lord knows what it means!' her associate gloomily sighed. Then, after an instant, 'Did he move?' Miss Susan asked.

'No – and *I* didn't.'

'Oh, I did!' Miss Susan declared, recalling her more precipitous retreat.

'I mean I took my time. I waited.'

'To see him fade?'

Miss Amy for a moment said nothing. 'He doesn't fade. That's *it*.'

'Oh, then you did move!' her relative rejoined.

Again for a little she was silent. 'One *has* to. But I don't know what really happened. Of course I came back to you. What I mean is that I took him thoroughly in. He's young,' she added.

'But he's *bad*!' said Miss Susan.

'He's handsome!' Miss Amy brought out after a moment. And she showed herself even prepared to continue: 'Splendidly.'

' "Splendidly"! – with his neck broken and with that terrible look?'

'It's just the look that makes him so. It's the wonderful eyes. They mean something,' Amy Frush brooded.

She spoke with a decision of which Susan presently betrayed the effect. 'And what do they mean?'

Her friend had stared again at the glimmering windows of St Thomas of Canterbury. 'That it's time we should get to church.'

III

The curate that evening did duty alone; but on the morrow the vicar called and, as soon as he got into the room, let them again have it. 'He was hanged for smuggling!'

They stood there before him almost cold in their surprise and diffusing an air in which, somehow, this misdemeanour sounded out as the coarsest of all. '*Smuggling?*' Miss Susan disappointedly echoed – as if it presented itself to the first chill of their apprehension that he had, then, only been vulgar.

'Ah, but they hanged for it freely, you know, and I was an idiot for not having taken it, in his case, for granted. If a man swung, hereabouts, it *was* mostly for that. Don't you know it's on that we stand here today, such as we are – on the fact of what our bold, bad forefathers were not afraid of? It's in the floors we walk on and under the roofs that cover us. They smuggled so hard that they never had time to do anything else; and if they broke a head not their own it was only in the awkwardness of landing their brandy kegs. I mean, dear ladies,' good Mr Patten wound up, 'no disrespect to *your* forefathers when I tell you that – as I've rather been supposing that, like all the rest of us, you were aware – they conveniently lived by it.'

Miss Susan wondered – visibly almost doubted. 'Gentlefolks?'

'It was the gentlefolks who were the worst.'

'They must have been the bravest!' Miss Amy interjected. She had listened to their visitor's free explanation with a rapid return of colour. 'And since if they lived by it they also died for it – '

'There's nothing at all to be said against them? I quite agree with you,' the vicar laughed, 'for all my cloth; and I even go so far as to say, shocking as you may think me, that we owe them, in our shabby little shrunken present, the sense of a bustling background, a sort of undertone of romance. They give us' – he humorously kept it up, verging perilously near, for his cloth, upon positive paradox – 'our little handful of legend and our small possibility of ghosts.' He paused an instant, with his lighter pulpit manner, but the ladies exchanged no look. They were, in fact, already, with an immense revulsion, carried quite as far away. 'Every penny in the place, really, that hasn't been earned by subtler – not nobler – arts in our own virtuous time, and though it's a pity there are not more of 'em: every penny in the place was picked up, somehow, by a clever trick, and at the risk of your neck, when the backs of the king's officers were turned. It's shocking, you know, what I'm saying to you, and I wouldn't say it to everyone, but I think of some of the shabby old things about us, that represent such pickings, with a sort of sneaking kindness – as of relics of our heroic age. What are we now? We were at any rate devils of fellows then!'

Susan Frush considered it all solemnly, struggling with the spell of this evocation. 'But must we forget that they were wicked?'

'Never!' Mr Patten laughed. 'Thank you, dear friend, for reminding me. Only I'm worse than they!'

'But would you do it?'

'Murder a coastguard – ?' The vicar scratched his head.

'I hope,' said Miss Amy rather surprisingly, 'you'd defend yourself.' And she gave Miss Susan a superior glance. 'I would!' she distinctly added.

Her companion anxiously took it up. 'Would you defraud the revenue?'

Miss Amy hesitated but a moment; then with a strange laugh, which she covered, however, by turning instantly away, 'Yes!' she remarkably declared.

Their visitor, at this, amused and amusing, eagerly seized her arm. 'Then may I count on you on the stroke of midnight to help me – ?'

'To help you – ?'

'To land the last new Tauchnitz.'

She met the proposal as one whose fancy had kindled, while her cousin watched them as if they had suddenly improvised a drawing-room charade. 'A service of danger?'

'Under the cliff – when you see the lugger stand in!'

'Armed to the teeth?'

'Yes – but invisibly. Your old waterproof – !'

'Mine is new. I'll take Susan's!'

This good lady, however, had her reserves. 'Mayn't one of them, all the same – here and there – have been sorry?'

Mr Patten wondered. 'For the jobs he muffed?'

'For the wrong – as it *was* wrong – he did.'

' "One" of them?' She had gone too far, for the vicar suddenly looked as if he divined in the question a reference.

They became, however, as promptly unanimous in meeting this danger, as to which Miss Susan in particular showed an inspired presence of mind. 'Two of them!' she sweetly smiled. 'May not Amy and I – ?'

'Vicariously repent?' said Mr Patten. 'That depends – for the true honour of Marr – on how you show it.'

'Oh, we *shan't* show it!' Miss Amy cried.

'Ah, then,' Mr Patten returned, 'though atonements, to be efficient, are supposed to be public, you may do penance in secret as much as you please!'

'Well, *I* shall do it,' said Susan Frush.

Again, by something in her tone, the vicar's attention appeared to be caught. 'Have you then in view a particular form – ?'

'Of atonement?' She coloured now, glaring rather helplessly, in spite of herself, at her companion. 'Oh, if you're sincere you'll always find one.'

Amy came to her assistance. 'The way she often treats me has made her – though there's after all no harm in her – familiar with remorse. Mayn't we, at any rate,' the younger lady continued, 'now have our letters back?' And the vicar left them with the assurance that they should receive the bundle on the morrow.

They were indeed so at one as to shrouding their mystery that no explicit agreement, no exchange of vows, needed to pass between them; they only settled down, from this moment, to an unshared possession of their secret, an economy in the use and, as may even be said, the enjoyment of it, that was part of their general instinct and habit of thrift. It had been the disposition, the practice, the necessity of each to keep, fairly indeed to clutch, everything that, as they often phrased it, came their way; and this was not the first time such an influence had determined for them an affirmation of property in objects to which ridicule, suspicion, or some other inconvenience might attach. It was their simple philosophy that one never knew of what service an odd object might *not* be; and there were days now on which they felt themselves to have made a better bargain with their aunt's executors than was witnessed in those law-papers which they had at first timorously regarded as the record of advantages taken of them in matters of detail. They had got, in short, more than was vulgarly, more than was even shrewdly supposed – such an indescribable unearned increment as might scarce more be divulged as a dread than as a delight. They drew together, old-maidishly, in a suspicious, invidious grasp of the idea that a dread of their very own – and blissfully not, of course, that of a failure of any essential supply – might, on nearer acquaintance, positively turn to a delight.

Upon some such attempted consideration of it, at all events, they found themselves embarking after their last interview with Mr Patten, and understanding conveyed between them in no redundancy of discussion, no flippant repetitions nor profane recurrences, yet resting on a sense of added margin, of appropriated history, of liberties taken with time and space, that would leave them prepared both for the worst and for the best. The best would be that something that would turn out to their advantage might prove to be hidden about the place; the worst would be that they might find themselves growing to depend only too much on excitement. They found themselves amazingly reconciled, on Mr Patten's information, to the particular character thus fixed on their visitor; they knew by tradition and fiction that even the highwaymen of the same picturesque age were often gallant gentlemen; therefore a smuggler, by such a measure, fairly belonged to the aristocracy of crime. When their packet of documents came back from the vicarage, Miss Amy, to whom her associate continued to leave them, took them once more in hand; but with an effect, afresh, of discouragement and languor – a headachy sense of faded ink, of strange spelling and crabbed characters, of allusions she couldn't follow and parts she couldn't match. She placed the tattered papers piously together, wrapping them tenderly in a piece of old figured silken stuff; then, as solemnly as if they had been archives or statues or title deeds, laid them away in one of the several small cupboards lodged in the thickness of the wainscoted walls. What really most sustained our friends in all ways was their consciousness of having, after all – and so contrariwise to what appeared – a man in the house. It removed them from that category of the manless in which no lady really lapses till every issue is closed. Their visitor was an issue – at least to the imagination, and they arrived finally, under provocation, at intensities of flutter in which they felt themselves so compromised by his hoverings that they could only consider with relief the fact of nobody's knowing.

The real complication indeed at first was that for some weeks after their talks with Mr Patten the hoverings quite ceased; a circumstance that brought home to them in some degree a sense of indiscretion and indelicacy. They hadn't mentioned him, no; but they had come perilously near it, and they had doubtless, at any rate, too recklessly let in the light on old buried and sheltered things, old sorrows and shames. They roamed about the house themselves at times, fitfully and singly, when each supposed the other out or engaged; they paused and lingered, like soundless apparitions, in corners, doorways, passages, and sometimes suddenly met, in these experiments, with a suppressed start and a mute confession. They talked of him practically never; but each knew how the other thought – all the more that it was (oh yes, unmistakably!) in a manner different from her own. They were together, none the less, in feeling, while, week after week, he failed again to show, as if they had been guilty of blowing, with an effect of sacrilege, on old-gathered silvery ashes. It frankly came out for them that, possessed as they so strange, yet so ridiculously were, they should be able to settle to nothing till their consciousness was yet again confirmed. Whatever the subject of it might have for them of fear or favour, profit or loss, he had taken the taste from everything else. He had converted *them* into wandering ghosts. At last, one day, with nothing they could afterwards perceive to have determined it, the change came – came, as the previous splash in their stillness had come, by the pale testimony of Miss Susan.

She waited till after breakfast to speak of it – or Miss Amy, rather, waited to hear her; for she showed during the meal the face of controlled commotion that her comrade already knew and that must, with the game loyally played, serve as preface to a disclosure. The younger of the friends really watched the elder, over their tea and toast, as if seeing her for the first time as possibly tortuous, suspecting in her some intention of keeping back what had happened. What had happened was that the image of the hanged man had reappeared in the night; yet only after they had moved together to the drawing-room did Miss Amy learn the facts.

'I was beside the bed – in that low chair; about' – since Miss Amy must know – 'to take off my right shoe. I had noticed nothing before, and had had time partly to undress – had got into my wrapper. So, suddenly – as I happened to look – there he was. And there,' said Susan Frush, 'he stayed.'

'But where do you mean?'

'In the high-backed chair, the old flowered chintz "ear-chair"[12] beside the chimney.'

'All night? – and you in your wrapper?' Then as if this image almost challenged her credulity, 'Why didn't you go to bed?' Miss Amy inquired.

'With a – a person in the room?' her friend wonderfully asked; adding after an instant as with positive pride: 'I never broke the spell!'

'And didn't freeze to death?'

'Yes, almost. To say nothing of not having slept, I can assure you, one wink. I shut my eyes for long stretches, but whenever I opened them he was still there, and I never for a moment lost consciousness.'

Miss Amy gave a groan of conscientious sympathy. 'So that you're feeling now, of course, half dead.'

Her companion turned to the chimney-glass[13] a wan, glazed eye. 'I dare say I *am* looking impossible.'

Miss Amy, after an instant, found herself still conscientious. 'You are.' Her own eyes strayed to the glass, lingering there while she lost herself in thought. 'Really,' she reflected with a certain dryness, 'if that's the kind of thing it's to be . . . !' there would seem, in a word, to be no withstanding it for either. Why, she afterwards asked herself in secret, should the restless spirit of a dead adventurer have addressed itself in its trouble, to such a person as her queer, quaint, inefficient housemate? It was in *her*, she dumbly and somehow sorely argued, that an unappeased soul of the old race should show a confidence. To this conviction she was the more directed by the sense that Susan had, in relation to the preference shown, vain and foolish complacencies. She had her idea of what, in their prodigious predicament, should be, as she called it, 'done', and that was a question that Amy from this time began to nurse the small aggression of not so much as discussing with her. She had certainly, poor Miss Frush, a new, an obscure reticence, and since she wouldn't speak first she should have silence to her fill. Miss Amy, however, peopled the silence with conjectural visions of her kinswoman's secret communion. Miss Susan, it was true, showed nothing, on any particular occasion, more than usual; but this was just a part of the very felicity that had begun to harden and uplift her. Days and nights hereupon elapsed without bringing felicity of any order to Amy Frush. If she had no emotions it was, she suspected, because Susan had them all; and – it would have been preposterous had it not been pathetic – she proceeded rapidly to hug the opinion that Susan was selfish and even something of a sneak. Politeness, between them, still reigned, but confidence had flown, and its place was taken by open ceremonies and confessed precautions. Miss Susan looked blank but resigned; which maintained again, unfortunately, her superior air and the presumption of her duplicity. Her manner was of not knowing where her friend's shoe pinched; but it might have been taken by a jaundiced eye for surprise at the challenge of her monopoly. The unexpected resistance of her nerves was indeed a wonder: was that, then, the result, even for a shaky old woman, of shocks sufficiently repeated? Miss Amy brooded on the rich inference that, if the first of them didn't prostrate and the rest didn't undermine, one might keep them up as easily as – well, say an unavowed acquaintance or a private commerce of letters. She was startled at the comparison into which she fell – but what was this but an intrigue like another? And fancy Susan carrying one on! That history of the long night hours of the pair in the two chairs kept before her – for it was always present – the extraordinary measure.

Was the situation it involved only grotesque – or was it quite grimly grand? It struck her as both; but that was the case with all their situations. Would it be in herself, at any rate, to show such a front? She put herself such questions till she was tired of them. A few good moments of her own would have cleared the air. Luckily they were to come.

IV

It was on a Sunday morning in April, a day brimming over with the turn of the season. She had gone into the garden before church; they cherished alike, with pottering intimacies and opposed theories and a wonderful apparatus of old gloves and trowels and spuds and little botanical cards on sticks, this feature of their establishment, where they could still differ without fear and agree without diplomacy, and which now, with its vernal promise, threw beauty and gloom and light and space, a great good-natured ease, into their wavering scales. She was dressed for church; but when Susan, who had, from a window, seen her wandering, stooping, examining, touching, appeared in the doorway to signify a like readiness, she suddenly felt her intention checked. 'Thank you,' she said, drawing near; 'I think that, though I've dressed, I won't, after all, go. Please, therefore, proceed without me.'

Miss Susan fixed her. 'You're not well?'

'Not particularly. I shall be better – the morning's so perfect – here.'

'Are you really ill?'

'Indisposed; but not enough so, thank you, for you to stay with me.'

'Then it has come on but just now?'

'No – I felt not quite fit when I dressed. But it won't do.'

'Yet you'll stay out here?'

Miss Amy looked about. 'It will depend!'

Her friend paused long enough to have asked what it would depend on, but abruptly, after this contemplation, turned instead and, merely throwing over her shoulder an 'At least take care of yourself!' went rustling, in her stiffest Sunday fashion, about her business. Miss Amy, left alone, as she clearly desired to be, lingered awhile in the garden, where the sense of things was somehow made still more delicious by the sweet, vain sounds from the church tower; but by the end of ten minutes she had returned to the house. The sense of things was not delicious there, for what it had at last come to was that, as they thought of each other what they couldn't say, all their contacts were hard and false. The real wrong was in what Susan thought – as to which she was much too proud and too sore to undeceive her. Miss Amy went vaguely to the drawing-room.

They sat, as usual, after church, at their early Sunday dinner, face to face; but little passed between them save that Miss Amy felt better, that the curate had preached, that nobody else had stayed away, and that everybody had asked why Amy had. Amy, hereupon, satisfied everybody by feeling well enough to go in the afternoon; on which occasion, on the other hand – and for reasons even less luminous than those that had operated with her mate in the morning – Miss Susan remained within. Her comrade came back late, having, after church, paid visits; and found her, as daylight faded, seated in the drawing-room, placid and dressed, but without so much as a Sunday book – the place contained whole shelves of such reading – in her hand. She looked so as if a visitor had just left her that Amy put the question: 'Has anyone called?'

'Dear, no; I've been quite alone.'

This again was indirect, and it instantly determined for Miss Amy a conviction – a conviction that, on her also sitting down just as she was and in a silence that prolonged itself, promoted in its turn another determination. The April dusk gathered, and still, without further speech, the companions sat there. But at last Miss Amy said in a tone not quite her commonest: 'This morning he came – while you were at church. I suppose it must have been really – though of course I couldn't know it – what I was moved to stay at home for.' She spoke now – out of her contentment – as if to oblige with explanations.

But it was strange how Miss Susan met her. 'You stay at home for him? *I* don't!' She fairly laughed at the triviality of the idea.

Miss Amy was naturally struck by it and after an instant even nettled. 'Then why did you do so this afternoon?'

'Oh, it wasn't for *that!*' Miss Susan lightly quavered. She made her distinction. 'I *really* wasn't well.'

At this her cousin brought it out. 'But he has been with you?'

'My dear child,' said Susan, launched unexpectedly even to herself, 'he's with me so often that if I put myself out for him – !' But as if at sight of something that showed, through the twilight, in her friend's face, she pulled herself up.

Amy, however, spoke with studied stillness. 'You've ceased then to put yourself out? You gave me, you remember, an instance of how you once did!' And she tried, on her side, a laugh.

'Oh yes – that was at first. But I've seen such a lot of him since. Do you mean *you* hadn't?' Susan asked. Then as her companion only sat looking at her: 'Has this been really the first time for you – since we last talked?'

Miss Amy for a minute said nothing. 'You've actually believed me –'

'To be enjoying on your own account what *I* enjoy? How couldn't I, at the very least,' Miss Susan cried – 'so grand and strange as you must allow me to say you've struck me?'

Amy hesitated. 'I hope I've sometimes struck you as decent!'

But it was a touch that, in her friend's almost amused preoccupation with the simple fact, happily fell short. 'You've only been waiting for what didn't come?'

Miss Amy coloured in the dusk. 'It came, as I tell you, today.'

'Better late than never!' And Miss Susan got up.

Amy Frush sat looking. 'It's because you thought you had ground for jealousy that *you've* been extraordinary?'

Poor Susan, at this, quite bounced about. 'Jealousy?'

It was a tone – never heard from her before – that brought Amy Frush to her feet; so that for a minute, in the unlighted room where, in honour of the spring, there had been no fire and the evening chill had gathered, they stood as enemies. It lasted, fortunately, even long enough to give one of them time suddenly to find it horrible. 'But why should we quarrel *now*?' Amy broke out in a different voice.

Susan was not too alienated quickly enough to meet it. 'It *is* rather wretched.'

'Now when we're equal,' Amy went on.

'Yes – I suppose we are.' Then, however, as if just to attenuate the admission, Susan had her last lapse from grace. 'They say, you know, that when women do quarrel it's usually about a man.'

Amy recognised it, but also with a reserve. 'Well, then, let there first *be* one!'

'And don't you call *him* – ?'

'No!' Amy declared and turned away, while her companion showed her a vain wonder for what she could in that case have expected. Their identity of privilege was thus established, but it is not certain that the air with which she indicated that the subject had better drop didn't press down for an instant her side of the balance. She knew that she knew most about men.

The subject did drop for the time, it being agreed between them that neither should from that hour expect from the other any confession or report. They would treat all occurrences now as not worth mentioning – a course easy to pursue from the moment the suspicion of jealousy had, on each side, been so completely laid to rest.

They led their life a month or two on the smooth ground of taking everything for granted; by the end of which time, however, try as they would, they had set up no question that – while they met as a pair of gentlewomen living together only must meet – could successfully pretend to take the place of that of Cuthbert Frush. The spring softened and deepened, reached out its tender arms and scattered its shy graces; the earth broke, the air stirred, with emanations that were as touches and voices of the past; our friends bent their backs in their garden and their noses over its symptoms; they opened their windows to the mildness and tracked it in the lanes and by the hedges; yet the plant of conversation between them markedly failed to renew itself with the rest. It was not indeed that the mildness was not within them as well as without; all asperity, at least, had melted away; they were more than ever pleased with their general acquisition, which, at the winter's end, seemed to give out more of its old secrets, to hum, however faintly with more of its old echoes, to creak, here and there, with the expiring throb of old aches. The deepest sweetness of the spring at Marr was just in its being in this way an attestation of age and rest. The place never seemed to have lived and lingered so long as when kind nature, like a maiden blessing a crone, laid rosy hands on its grizzled head. Then the new season was a light held up to show all the dignity of the years, but also all the wrinkles and scars. The good ladies in whom we are interested changed, at any rate, with the happy days, and it finally came out not only that the invidious note had dropped, but that it had positively turned to music. The whole tone of the time made so for tenderness that it really seemed as if at moments they were sad for each other. They had their grounds at last: each found them in her own consciousness; but it was as if each waited, on the other hand, to be sure she could speak without offence. Fortunately, at last, the tense cord snapped.

The old churchyard at Marr is still liberal; it does its immemorial utmost to people, with names and dates and memories and eulogies, with generations foreshortened and confounded, the high empty table at which the grand old cripple of the church looks down over the low wall. It serves as an easy thoroughfare, and the stranger finds himself pausing in it with a sense of respect and compassion for the great maimed, ivied shoulders – as the image strikes him – of stone. Miss Susan and Miss Amy were strangers enough still to have sunk down one May morning on the sun-warmed tablet of an ancient tomb and to have remained looking about them in a sort of anxious peace. Their walks were all pointless now, as if they always stopped and turned, for an unconfessed want of interest, before reaching their object. That object presented itself at every start as the same to each, but they had come back too often without having got near it. This morning, strangely, on the return and almost in sight of their door, they were more in presence of it than they had ever been, and they seemed fairly to touch it when Susan said at last, quite in the air and with no traceable reference: 'I hope you don't mind, dearest, if I'm awfully sorry for you.'

'Oh, I know it,' Amy returned – 'I've felt it. But what does it do for us?' she asked.

Then Susan saw, with wonder and pity, how little resentment for penetration or patronage she had had to fear and out of what a depth of sentiment similar to her own her companion helplessly spoke. 'You're sorry for *me?*'

Amy at first only looked at her with tired eyes, putting out a hand that remained awhile on her arm. 'Dear old girl! You might have told me before,' she went on as she took everything in; 'though, after all, haven't we each really known it?'

'Well,' said Susan, 'we've waited. We could only wait.'

'Then if we've waited together,' her friend returned, 'that *has* helped us.'

'Yes – to keep him in his place. Who would ever believe in him?' Miss Susan wearily wondered. 'If it wasn't for you and for me – '

'Not doubting of each other?' – her companion took her up: 'yes, there wouldn't be a creature. It's lucky for us,' said Miss Amy, 'that we *don't* doubt.'

'Oh, if we did we shouldn't be sorry.'

'No – except, selfishly, for ourselves. I am, I assure you, for *myself* – it has made me older. But, luckily, at any rate, we trust each other.'

'We do,' said Miss Susan.

'We do,' Miss Amy repeated – they lingered a little on that.

'But except making one feel older, what has it done for one?'

'There it is!'

'And though we've kept him in his place,' Miss Amy continued, 'he has also kept us in ours. We've lived with it,' she declared in melancholy justice. 'And we wondered at first if we could!' she ironically added. 'Well, isn't just what we feel now that we can't any longer?'

'No – it must stop. And I've my idea,' said Susan Frush.

'Oh, I assure you I've mine!' her cousin responded.

'Then if you want to act, don't mind me.'

'Because you certainly won't *me?* No, I suppose not. Well!' Amy sighed, as if, merely from this, relief had at last come. Her comrade echoed it; they remained side by side; and nothing could have had more oddity than what was assumed alike in what they had said and in what they still kept back. There would have been this at least in their favour for a questioner of their case, that each, charged dejectedly with her own experience, took, on the part of the other, the extraordinary – the ineffable, in fact – all for granted. They never named it again – as indeed it was not easy to name; the whole matter shrouded itself in personal discriminations and privacies; the comparison of notes had become a thing impossible. What was definite was that they had lived into their queer story, passed through it as through an observed, a studied, eclipse of the usual, a period of reclusion, a financial, social or moral crisis, and only desired now to live out of it again. The questioner we have been supposing might even have fancied that each, on her side, had hoped for something from it that she finally perceived it was never to give, which would have been exactly, moreover, the core of her secret and the explanation of her reserve. They, at least, as the business stood, put each other to no test, and, if they were in fact disillusioned and disappointed, came together, after their long blight, solidly on that. It fully appeared between them that they felt a great deal older. When they got up from their sunwarmed slab, however, reminding each other of luncheon, it was with a visible increase of ease and with Miss Susan's hand drawn, for the walk home into Miss Amy's arm. Thus the 'idea' of each had continued unspoken and ungrudged. It was as if each wished the other to try her own first; from which it might have been gathered that they alike presented difficulty and even entailed expense. The great questions remained. What then did he mean? what then did he want? Absolution, peace, rest, his final reprieve – merely to say *that* saw them no further on the way than they had already come. What were they at last to do for him? What could they give him that he would take? The ideas they respectively nursed still bore no fruit, and at the end of another month Miss Susan was frankly anxious about Miss Amy. Miss Amy as freely admitted that people *must* have begun to notice strange marks in them and to look for reasons. They were changed – they must change back.

V

Yet it was not till one morning at midsummer, on their meeting for breakfast, that the elder lady fairly attacked the younger's last entrenchment. 'Poor, poor Susan!' Miss Amy had said to herself as her cousin came into the room; and a moment later she brought out, for very pity, her appeal. 'What then *is* yours?'

'My idea?' It was clearly, at last, a vague comfort to Miss Susan to be asked. Yet her answer was desolate. 'Oh, it's no use!'

'But how do you know?'

'Why, I tried it – ten days ago, and I thought at first it had answered. But it hasn't.'

'He's back again?'

Wan, tired, Miss Susan gave it up. 'Back again.'

Miss Amy, after one of the long, odd looks that had now become their most frequent form of intercourse, thought it over. 'And just the same?'

'Worse.'

'Dear!' said Miss Amy, clearly knowing what that meant. 'Then what did you do?'

Her friend brought it roundly out. 'I made my sacrifice.'

Miss Amy, though still more deeply interrogative, hesitated. 'But of what?'

'Why, of my little all – or almost.'

The 'almost' seemed to puzzle Miss Amy, who, moreover, had plainly no clue to the property or attribute so described. 'Your "little all"?'

'Twenty pounds.'

'Money?' Miss Amy gasped.

Her tone produced on her companion's part a wonder as great as her own. 'What then is it yours to give?'

'My idea? It's not to *give!*' cried Amy Frush.

At the finer pride that broke out in this poor Susan's blankness flushed. 'What then is it to do?'

But Miss Amy's bewilderment outlasted her reproach. 'Do you mean he takes money?'

'The Chancellor of the Exchequer does – for "conscience".'

Her friend's exploit shone larger. 'Conscience-money? You sent it to government?' Then while, as the effect of her surprise, her mate looked too much a fool, Amy melted to kindness. 'Why, you secretive old thing!'

Miss Susan presently pulled herself more together. 'When your ancestor has robbed the revenue and his spirit walks for remorse – '

'You pay to get rid of him? I see – and it becomes what the vicar called his atonement by deputy. But what if it isn't remorse?' Miss Amy shrewdly asked.

'But it *is* – or it seemed to me so.'

'Never to me,' said Miss Amy.

Again they searched each other. 'Then, evidently, with you he's different.'

Miss Amy looked away. 'I dare say!'

'So what *is* your idea?'

Miss Amy thought. 'I'll tell you only if it works.'

'Then, for God's sake, try it!'

Miss Amy, still with averted eyes and now looking easily wise, continued to think. 'To try it I shall have to leave you. That's why I've waited so long.' Then she fully turned, and with expression: 'Can you face three days alone?'

'Oh – "alone"! I wish I ever were!'

At this her friend, as for very compassion, kissed her; for it seemed really to have come out at last – and welcome! – that poor Susan was the worse beset. 'I'll do it! But I must go up to town. Ask me no questions. All I can tell you now is – '

'Well?' Susan appealed while Amy impressively fixed her.

'It's no more remorse than *I'm* a smuggler.'

'What is it then?'

'It's bravado.'

An 'Oh!' more shocked and scared than any that, in the whole business, had yet dropped from her, wound up poor Susan's share in this agreement, appearing as it did to represent for her a somewhat lurid inference. Amy, clearly, had lights of her own. It was by their aid, accordingly, that she immediately prepared for the first separation they had had yet to suffer; of which the consequence, two days later, was that Miss Susan, bowed and anxious, crept singly, on the return from their parting, up the steep hill that leads from the station of Marr and passed ruefully under the ruined town-gate, one of the old defences, that arches over it.

But the full sequel was not for a month – one hot August night when, under the dim stars, they sat together in their little walled garden. Though they had by this time, in general, found again – as women only can find – the secret of easy speech, nothing, for the half-hour, had passed between them: Susan had only sat waiting for her comrade to wake up. Miss Amy had taken of late to interminable dozing – as if with forfeits and arrears to recover; she might have been a convalescent from fever repairing tissue and getting through time. Susan Frush watched her in the warm dimness, and the question between them was fortunately at last so simple that she had freedom to think her pretty in slumber and to fear that she herself, so unguarded, presented an appearance less graceful. She was impatient, for her need had at last come, but she waited, and while she waited she thought. She had already often done so, but the mystery deepened tonight in the story told, as it seemed to her by her companion's frequent relapses. What had been, three weeks before, the effort intense enough to leave behind such a trail of fatigue? The marks, sure enough, had shown in the poor girl that morning of the termination of the arranged absence for which not three days, but ten, without word or sign, were to prove no more than sufficient. It was at an unnatural hour that Amy had turned up, dusty, dishevelled, inscrutable, confessing for the time to nothing more than a long night-journey. Miss Susan prided herself on having played the game and respected, however tormenting, the conditions. She had her conviction that her friend had been out of the country, and she marvelled, thinking of her own old wanderings and her present settled fears, at the spirit with which a person who, whatever she had previously done, had not travelled, could carry off such a flight. The hour had come at last for this person to name her remedy. What determined it was that as Susan Frush sat there, she took home the fact that the remedy was by this time not to be questioned. It had acted as her own had not, and Amy, to all appearance, had only waited for her to admit it. Well, she was ready when Amy woke – woke immediately to meet her eyes and to show, after a moment, in doing so, a vision of what was in her mind. 'What *was* it now?' Susan finally said.

'My idea? Is it possible you've not guessed?'

'Oh, you're deeper, much deeper,' Susan sighed, 'than I.'

Amy didn't contradict that – seemed indeed, placidly enough, to take it for truth; but she presently spoke as if the difference, after all, didn't matter now. 'Happily for us today – isn't it so? – our case is the same. I can speak, at any rate, for myself. He has left me.'

'Thank God, then!' Miss Susan devoutly murmured. 'For he has left *me*.'

'Are you sure?'

'Oh, I think so.'

'But how?'

'Well,' said Miss Susan after an hesitation, 'how are *you?*'

Amy, for a little, matched her pause. 'Ah, that's what I can't tell you. I can only answer for it that he's gone.'

'Then allow me also to prefer not to explain. The sense of relief has for some reason grown strong in me during the last half-hour. That's such a comfort that it's enough, isn't it?'

'Oh, plenty!' The garden-side of their old house, a window or two dimly lighted, massed itself darkly in the summer night, and, with a common impulse, they gave it, across the little lawn, a long, fond look. Yes, they could be sure. 'Plenty!' Amy repeated. 'He's gone.'

Susan's elder eyes hovered, in the same way, through her elegant glass, at his purified haunt. 'He's gone. And how,' she insisted, '*did* you do it?'

'Why, you dear goose,' – Miss Amy spoke a little strangely – 'I went to Paris.'

'To Paris?'

'To see what I could bring back – that I mightn't, that I shouldn't. To do a stroke with!' Miss Amy brought out.

But it left her friend still vague. 'A stroke – ?'

'To get through the Customs – under their nose.'

It was only with this that, for Miss Susan, a pale light dawned. 'You wanted to smuggle? *That* was your idea?'

'It was *his*,' said Miss Amy. 'He wanted no "conscience-money" spent for him,' she now more bravely laughed; 'it was quite the other way about – he wanted some bold deed done, of the old wild kind; he wanted some big risk taken. And I took it.' She sprang up, rebounding, in her triumph.

Her companion, gasping, gazed at her. 'Might they have hanged you too?'

Miss Amy looked up at the dim stars. 'If I had defended myself. But luckily it didn't come to that. What I brought in I brought' – she rang out, more and more lucid, now, as she talked – 'triumphantly. To appease him – I braved them. I chanced it, at Dover, and they never knew.'

'Then you hid it – ?'

'About my person.'

With the shiver of this Miss Susan got up, and they stood there duskily together. 'It was so small?' the elder lady wonderingly murmured.

'It was big enough to have satisfied him,' her mate replied with just a shade of sharpness. 'I chose it, with much thought, from the forbidden list.'

The forbidden list hung a moment in Miss Susan's eyes, suggesting to her, however, but a pale conjecture. 'A Tauchnitz?'

Miss Amy communed again with the August stars. 'It was the *spirit* of the dead that told.'

'A Tauchnitz?' her friend insisted.

Then at last her eyes again dropped, and the Misses Frush moved together to the house. 'Well, he's satisfied.'

'Yes, and' – Miss Susan mused a little ruefully as they went – 'you got at last your week in Paris!'

The Jolly Corner

I

'EVERYONE ASKS ME what I "think" of everything,' said Spencer Brydon; 'and I make answer as I can – begging or dodging the question, putting them off with any nonsense. It wouldn't matter to any of them really,' he went on, 'for, even were it possible to meet in that stand-and-deliver way so silly a demand on so big a subject, my "thoughts" would still be almost altogether about something that concerns only myself.' He was talking to Miss Staverton, with whom for a couple of months now he had availed himself of every possible occasion to talk; this disposition and this resource, this comfort and support, as the situation in fact presented itself, having promptly enough taken the first place in the considerable array of rather unattenuated surprises attending his so strangely belated return to America. Everything was somehow a surprise; and that might be natural when one had so long and so consistently neglected everything, taken pains to give surprises so much margin for play. He had given them more than thirty years – thirty-three, to be exact; and they now seemed to him to have organised their performance quite on the scale of that licence. He had been twenty-three on leaving New York – he was fifty-six today: unless indeed he were to reckon as he had sometimes, since his repatriation, found himself feeling; in which case he would have lived longer than is often allotted to man. It would have taken a century, he repeatedly said to himself, and said also to Alice Staverton, it would have taken a longer absence and a more averted mind than those even of which he had been guilty, to pile up the differences, the newnesses, the queernesses, above all the bignesses, for the better or the worse, that at present assaulted his vision wherever he looked.

The great fact all the while however had been the incalculability; since he *had* supposed himself, from decade to decade, to be allowing, and in the most liberal and intelligent manner, for brilliancy of change. He actually saw that he had allowed for nothing; he missed what he would have been sure of finding, he found what he would never have imagined. Proportions and values were upside-down; the ugly things he had expected, the ugly things of his faraway youth, when he had too promptly waked up to a sense of the ugly – these uncanny phenomena placed him rather, as it happened, under the charm; whereas the 'swagger' things, the modern, the monstrous, the famous things, those he had more particularly, like thousands of ingenuous enquirers every year, come over to see, were exactly his sources of dismay. They were as so many set traps for displeasure, above all for reaction, of which his restless tread was constantly pressing the spring. It was interesting, doubtless, the whole show, but it would have been too disconcerting hadn't a certain finer truth saved the situation. He had distinctly not, in this steadier light, come over *all* for the monstrosities; he had come, not only in the last analysis but quite on the face of the act, under an impulse with which they had nothing to do. He had come – putting the thing pompously – to look at his 'property', which he had thus for a third of a century not been within four thousand miles of; or, expressing it less sordidly, he had yielded to the humour of seeing again his house on the jolly corner, as he usually, and quite fondly, described it – the one in which he had first seen the light, in which various members of his family had lived and had died, in which the holidays of his overschooled boyhood had been passed and the few social flowers of his chilled adolescence gathered, and which, alienated then for so long a period, had, through the successive deaths of his two brothers and the termination of old arrangements, come wholly into his hands. He was the owner of another, not quite so 'good' – the jolly corner having been, from far back, superlatively extended and consecrated; and the value of the pair represented his main capital, with an income consisting, in these later years, of their respective rents which (thanks precisely to their original excellent type) had never been depressingly low. He could live in 'Europe', as he had been in the habit of living, on the product of these flourishing New York leases, and all the better since that of the second structure, the mere number in its long row, having within a twelvemonth fallen in, renovation at a high advance had proved beautifully possible.

These were items of property indeed, but he had found himself since his arrival distinguishing more than ever between them. The house within the street, two bristling blocks westward, was already in course of reconstruction as a tall mass of flats; he had acceded, some time before, to overtures for this conversion – in which, now that it was going forward, it had been not the least of his astonishments to find himself able, on the spot, and though without a previous ounce of such experience, to participate with a certain intelligence, almost with a certain authority. He had lived his life with his back so turned to such concerns and his face addressed to those of so different an order that he scarce knew what to make of this lively stir, in a compartment of his mind never yet penetrated, of a capacity for business and a sense for construction. These virtues, so common all round him now, had been dormant in his own organism – where it might be said of them perhaps that they had slept the sleep of the just. At present, in the splendid autumn weather – the autumn at least was a pure boon in the terrible place – he loafed about his 'work' undeterred, secretly agitated; not in the least 'minding' that the whole proposition, as they said, was vulgar and sordid, and ready to climb ladders, to walk the plank, to handle materials and look wise about them, to ask questions, in fine, and challenge explanations and really 'go into' figures.

It amused, it verily quite charmed him; and, by the same stroke, it amused, and even more, Alice Staverton, though perhaps charming her perceptibly less. She wasn't however going to be better off for it, as *he* was – and so astonishingly much: nothing was now likely, he knew, ever to make her better off than she found herself, in the afternoon of life, as the delicately frugal possessor and tenant of the small house in Irving Place[1] to which she had subtly managed to cling through her almost unbroken New York career. If he knew the way to it now better than to any other address among the dreadful multiplied numberings which seemed to him to reduce the whole place to some vast ledger-page, overgrown, fantastic, of ruled and criss-crossed lines and figures – if he had formed, for his consolation, that habit, it was really not a little because of the charm of his having encountered and recognised, in the vast wilderness of the wholesale, breaking through the mere gross generalisation of wealth and force and success, a small still scene where items and shades, all delicate things, kept the sharpness of the notes of a high voice perfectly trained, and where economy hung about like the scent of a garden. His old friend lived with one maid and herself dusted her relics and trimmed her lamps and polished her silver; she stood off, in the awful modern crush, when she could, but she sallied forth and did battle when the challenge was really to 'spirit', the spirit she after all confessed to, proudly and a little shyly, as to that of the better time, that of *their* common, their quite faraway and antediluvian social period and order. She made use of the streetcars when need be, the terrible things that people scrambled for as the panic-stricken at sea scramble for the boats; she affronted, inscrutably, under stress, all the public concussions and ordeals; and yet, with that slim mystifying grace of her appearance, which defied you to say if she were a fair young woman who looked older through trouble, or a fine smooth older one who looked young through successful indifference; with her precious reference, above all, to memories and histories into which he could enter, she was as exquisite for him as some pale pressed flower (a rarity to begin with), and, failing other sweetnesses, she was a sufficient reward of his effort. They had communities of knowledge, 'their' knowledge (this discriminating possessive was always on her lips) of presences of the other age, presences all overlaid, in his case, by the experience of a man and the freedom of a wanderer, overlaid by pleasure, by infidelity, by passages of life that were strange and dim to her, just by 'Europe' in short, but still unobscured, still exposed and cherished, under that pious visitation of the spirit from which she had never been diverted.

She had come with him one day to see how his 'apartment-house' was rising; he had helped her over gaps and explained to her plans, and while they were there had happened to have, before her, a brief but lively discussion with the man in charge, the representative of the building firm that had undertaken his work. He had found himself quite 'standing up' to this personage over a failure on the latter's part to observe some detail of one of their noted conditions, and had so lucidly argued his case that, besides ever so prettily flushing, at the time, for sympathy in his triumph, she had afterwards said to him (though to a slightly greater effect of irony) that he had clearly for too many years neglected a real gift. If he had but stayed at home he would have anticipated the inventor of the skyscraper. If he had but stayed at home he would have discovered his genius in time really to start some new variety of awful architectural hare and run it till it burrowed in a goldmine. He was to remember these words, while the weeks elapsed, for the small silver ring they had sounded over the queerest and deepest of his own lately most disguised and most muffled vibrations.

It had begun to be present to him after the first fortnight, it had broken out with the oddest abruptness, this particular wanton wonderment: it met him there – and this was the image under which he himself judged the matter, or at least, not a little, thrilled and flushed with it – very much as he might have been met by some strange figure, some unexpected occupant, at a turn of one of the dim passages of an empty house. The quaint analogy quite hauntingly remained with him, when he didn't indeed rather improve it by a still intenser form: that of his opening a door behind which he would have made sure of finding nothing, a door into a room shuttered and void, and yet so coming, with a great suppressed start, on some quite erect confronting presence, something planted in the middle of the place and facing him through the dusk. After that visit to the house in construction he walked with his companion to see the other and always so much the better one, which in the eastward direction formed one of the corners, the 'jolly' one precisely, of the street now so generally dishonoured and disfigured in its westward reaches, and of the comparatively conservative Avenue. The Avenue still had pretensions, as Miss Staverton said, to decency; the old people had mostly gone, the old names were unknown, and here and there an old association seemed to stray, all vaguely, like some very aged person, out too late, whom you might meet and feel the impulse to watch or follow, in kindness, for safe restoration to shelter.

They went in together, our friends; he admitted himself with his key, as he kept no one there, he explained, preferring, for his reasons, to leave the place empty, under a simple arrangement with a good woman living in the neighbourhood and who came for a daily hour to open windows and dust and sweep. Spencer Brydon had his reasons and was growingly aware of them; they seemed to him better each time he was there, though he didn't name them all to his companion, any more than he told her as yet how often, how quite absurdly often, he himself came. He only let her see for the present, while they walked through the great blank rooms, that absolute vacancy reigned and that, from top to bottom, there was nothing but Mrs Muldoon's broomstick, in a corner, to tempt the burglar. Mrs Muldoon was then on the premises, and she loquaciously attended the visitors, preceding them from room to room and pushing back shutters and throwing up sashes – all to show them, as she remarked, how little there was to see. There was little indeed to see in the great gaunt shell where the main dispositions and the general apportionment of space, the style of an age of ampler allowances, had nevertheless for its master their honest pleading message, affecting him as some good old servant's, some lifelong retainer's appeal for a character,[2] or even for a retiring-pension; yet it was also a remark of Mrs Muldoon's that, glad as she was to oblige him by her noonday round, there was a request she greatly hoped he would never make of her. If he should wish her for any reason to come in after dark she would just tell him, if he 'plased', that he must ask it of somebody else.

The fact that there was nothing to see didn't militate for the worthy woman against what one *might* see, and she put it frankly to Miss Staverton that no lady could be expected to like, could she? 'craping up to thim top storeys in the ayvil hours.' The gas and the electric light were off the house, and she fairly evoked a gruesome vision of her march through the great grey rooms – so many of them as there were too! – with her glimmering taper. Miss Staverton met her honest glare with a smile and the profession that she herself certainly would recoil from such an adventure. Spencer Brydon meanwhile held his peace – for the moment; the question of the 'evil' hours in his old home had already become too grave for him. He had begun some time since to 'crape', and he knew just why a packet of candles addressed to that pursuit had been stowed by his own hand, three weeks before, at the back of a drawer of the fine old sideboard that occupied, as a 'fixture', the deep recess in the dining-room. Just now he laughed at his companion – quickly however changing the subject; for the reason that, in the first place, his laugh struck him even at that moment as starting the odd echo, the conscious human resonance (he scarce knew how to qualify it) that sounds made while he was there alone sent back to his ear or his fancy; and that, in the second, he imagined Alice Staverton for the instant on the point of asking him, with a divination, if he ever so prowled. There were divinations he was unprepared for, and he had at all events averted enquiry by the time Mrs Muldoon had left them, passing on to other parts.

There was happily enough to say, on so consecrated a spot, that could be said freely and fairly; so that a whole train of declarations was precipitated by his friend's having herself broken out, after a yearning look round: 'But I hope you don't mean they want you to pull *this* to pieces!' His answer came, promptly, with his reawakened wrath: it was of course exactly what they wanted, and what they were 'at' him for, daily, with the iteration of people who couldn't for their life understand a man's liability to decent feelings. He had found the place, just as it stood and beyond what he could express, an interest and a joy. There were values other than the beastly rent values, and in short, in short – ! But it was thus Miss Staverton took him up. 'In short you're to make so good a thing of your skyscraper that, living in luxury on *those* ill-gotten gains, you can afford for a while to be sentimental here!' Her smile had for him, with the words, the particular mild irony with which he found half her talk suffused; an irony without bitterness and that came, exactly, from her having so much imagination – not, like the cheap sarcasms with which one heard most people, about the world of 'society', bid for the reputation of cleverness, from nobody's really having any. It was agreeable to him at this very moment to be sure that when he had answered, after a brief demur, 'Well yes: so, precisely, you may put it!' her imagination would still do him justice. He explained that even if never a dollar were to come to him from the other house he would nevertheless cherish this one; and he dwelt, further, while they lingered and wandered, on the fact of the stupefaction he was already exciting, the positive mystification he felt himself create.

He spoke of the value of all he read into it, into the mere sight of the walls, mere shapes of the rooms, mere sound of the floors, mere feel, in his hand, of the old silver-plated knobs of the several mahogany doors, which suggested the pressure of the palms of the dead; the seventy years of the past in fine that these things represented, the annals of nearly three generations, counting his grandfather's, the one that had ended there, and the impalpable ashes of his long-extinct youth, afloat in the very air like microscopic motes. She listened to everything; she was a woman who answered intimately but who utterly didn't chatter. She scattered abroad therefore no cloud of words; she could assent, she could agree, above all she could encourage, without doing that. Only at the last she went a little further than he had done himself. 'And then how do you know? You may still, after all, want to live here.' It rather indeed pulled him up, for it wasn't what he had been thinking, at least in her sense of the words. 'You mean I may decide to stay on for the sake of it?'

'Well, *with* such a home – !' But, quite beautifully, she had too much tact to dot so monstrous an *i*, and it was precisely an illustration of the way she didn't rattle. How could anyone – of any wit – insist on anyone else's 'wanting' to live in New York?

'Oh,' he said, 'I *might* have lived here (since I had my opportunity early in life); I might have put in here all these years. Then everything would have been different enough – and, I dare say, "funny" enough. But that's another matter. And then the beauty of it – I mean of my perversity, of my refusal to agree to a "deal" – is just in the total absence of a reason. Don't you see that if I had a reason about the matter at all it would *have* to be the other way, and would then be inevitably a reason of dollars? There are no reasons here *but* of dollars. Let us therefore have none whatever – not the ghost of one.'

They were back in the hall then for departure, but from where they stood the vista was large, through an open door, into the great square main saloon, with its almost antique felicity of brave spaces between windows. Her eyes came back from that reach and met his own a moment. 'Are you very sure the "ghost" of one doesn't, much rather, serve – ?'

He had a positive sense of turning pale. But it was as near as they were then to come. For he made answer, he believed, between a glare and a grin: 'Oh ghosts – of course the place must swarm with them! I should be ashamed of it if it didn't. Poor Mrs Muldoon's right, and it's why I haven't asked her to do more than look in.'

Miss Staverton's gaze again lost itself, and things she didn't utter, it was clear, came and went in her mind. She might even for the minute, off there in the fine room, have imagined some element dimly gathering. Simplified like the death-mask of a handsome face, it perhaps produced for her just then an effect akin to the stir of an expression in the 'set' commemorative plaster. Yet whatever her impression may have been she produced instead a vague platitude. 'Well, if it were only furnished and lived in – !'

She appeared to imply that in case of its being still furnished he might have been a little less opposed to the idea of a return. But she passed straight into the vestibule, as if to leave her words behind her, and the next moment he had opened the house-door and was standing with her on the steps. He closed the door and, while he re-pocketed his key, looking up and down, they took in the comparatively harsh actuality of the Avenue, which reminded him of the assault of the outer light of the desert on the traveller emerging from an Egyptian tomb. But he risked before they stepped into the street his gathered answer to her speech. 'For me it *is* lived in. For me it *is* furnished.' At which it was easy for her to sigh 'Ah yes – !' all vaguely and discreetly; since his parents and his favourite sister, to say nothing of other kin, in numbers, had run their course and met their end there. That represented, within the walls, ineffaceable life.

It was a few days after this that, during an hour passed with her again, he had expressed his impatience of the too flattering curiosity – among the people he met – about his appreciation of New York. He had arrived at none at all that was socially producible, and as for that matter of his 'thinking' (thinking the better or the worse of anything there) he was wholly taken up with one subject of thought. It was mere vain egoism, and it was moreover, if she liked, a morbid obsession. He found all things come back to the question of what he personally might have been, how he might have led his life and 'turned out', if he had not so, at the outset, given it up. And confessing for the first time to the intensity within him of this absurd speculation – which but proved also, no doubt, the habit of too selfishly thinking – he affirmed the impotence there of any other source of interest, any other native appeal. 'What would it have made of me, what would it have made of me? I keep for ever wondering, all idiotically; as if I could possibly know! I see what it has made of dozens of others, those I meet, and it positively aches within me, to the point of exasperation, that it would have made something of me as well. Only I can't make out *what*, and the worry of it, the small rage of curiosity never to be satisfied, brings back what I remember to have felt, once or twice, after judging best, for reasons, to burn some important letter unopened. I've been sorry,

I've hated it – I've never known what was in the letter. You may of course say it's a trifle – !'

'I don't say it's a trifle,' Miss Staverton gravely interrupted.

She was seated by her fire, and before her, on his feet and restless, he turned to and fro between this intensity of his idea and a fitful and unseeing inspection, through his single eyeglass, of the dear little old objects on her chimney piece. Her interruption made him for an instant look at her harder. 'I shouldn't care if you did!' he laughed, however; 'and it's only a figure, at any rate, for the way I now feel. *Not* to have followed my perverse young course – and almost in the teeth of my father's curse, as I may say; not to have kept it up, so, "over there", from that day to this, without a doubt or a pang; not, above all, to have liked it, to have loved it, so much, loved it, no doubt, with such an abysmal conceit of my own preference: some variation from *that*, I say, must have produced some different effect for my life and for my "form". I should have stuck here – if it had been possible; and I was too young, at twenty-three, to judge, *pour deux sous*,[3] whether it *were* possible. If I had waited I might have seen it was, and then I might have been, by staying here, something nearer to one of these types who have been hammered so hard and made so keen by their conditions. It isn't that I admire them so much – the question of any charm in them, or of any charm, beyond that of the rank money-passion, exerted by their conditions *for* them, has nothing to do with the matter: it's only a question of what fantastic, yet perfectly possible, development of my own nature I mayn't have missed. It comes over me that I had then a strange *alter ego*[4] deep down somewhere within me, as the full-blown flower is in the small tight bud, and that I just took the course, I just transferred him to the climate, that blighted him for once and for ever.'

'And you wonder about the flower,' Miss Staverton said. 'So do I, if you want to know; and so I've been wondering these several weeks. I believe in the flower,' she continued, 'I feel it would have been quite splendid, quite huge and monstrous.'

'Monstrous above all!' her visitor echoed; 'and I imagine, by the same stroke, quite hideous and offensive.'

'You don't believe that,' she returned; 'if you did you wouldn't wonder. You'd know, and that would be enough for you. What you feel – and what I feel *for* you – is that you'd have had power.'

'You'd have liked me that way?' he asked.

She barely hung fire. 'How should I not have liked you?'

'I see. You'd have liked me, have preferred me, a billionaire!'

'How should I not have liked you?' she simply again asked.

He stood before her still – her question kept him motionless. He took it in, so much there was of it; and indeed his not otherwise meeting it testified to that. 'I know at least what I am,' he simply went on; 'the other side of the medal's clear enough. I've not been edifying – I believe I'm thought in a hundred quarters to have been barely decent. I've followed strange paths and worshipped strange gods; it must have come to you again and again – in fact you've admitted to me as much – that I was leading, at any time these thirty years, a selfish frivolous scandalous life. And you see what it has made of me.'

She just waited, smiling at him. 'You see what it has made of *me*.'

'Oh you're a person whom nothing can have altered. You were born to be what you are, anywhere, anyway: you've the perfection nothing else could have blighted. And don't you see how, without my exile, I shouldn't have been waiting till now – ?' But he pulled up for the strange pang.

'The great thing to see,' she presently said, 'seems to me to be that it has spoiled nothing. It hasn't spoiled your being here at last. It hasn't spoiled this. It hasn't spoiled your speaking – ' She also however faltered.

He wondered at everything her controlled emotion might mean. 'Do you believe then – too dreadfully! – that I *am* as good as I might ever have been?'

'Oh no! Far from it!' With which she got up from her chair and was nearer to him. 'But I don't care,' she smiled.

'You mean I'm good enough?'

She considered a little. 'Will you believe it if I say so? I mean will you let that settle your question for you?' And then as if making out in his face that he drew back from this, that he had some idea which, however absurd, he couldn't yet bargain away: 'Oh you don't care either – but very differently: you don't care for anything but yourself.'

Spencer Brydon recognised it – it was in fact what he had absolutely professed. Yet he importantly qualified. '*He* isn't myself. He's the just so totally other person. But I do want to see him,' he added. 'And I can. And I shall.'

Their eyes met for a minute while he guessed from something in hers that she divined his strange sense. But neither of them otherwise expressed it, and her apparent understanding, with no protesting shock, no easy derision, touched him more deeply than anything yet, constituting for his stifled perversity, on the spot, an element that was like breathable air. What she said however was unexpected. 'Well, *I've* seen him.'

'You – ?'

'I've seen him in a dream.'

'Oh a "dream" – !' It let him down.

'But twice over,' she continued. 'I saw him as I see you now.'

'You've dreamed the same dream – ?'

'Twice over,' she repeated. 'The very same.'

This did somehow a little speak to him, as it also gratified him. 'You dream about me at that rate?'

'Ah about *him!*' she smiled.

His eyes again sounded her. 'Then you know all about him.' And as she said nothing more: 'What's the wretch like?'

She hesitated, and it was as if he were pressing her so hard that, resisting for reasons of her own, she had to turn away. 'I'll tell you some other time!'

II

It was after this that there was most of a virtue for him, most of a cultivated charm, most of a preposterous secret thrill, in the particular form of surrender to his obsession and of address to what he more and more believed to be his privilege. It was what in these weeks he was living for – since he really felt life to begin but after Mrs Muldoon had retired from the scene and, visiting the ample house from attic to cellar, making sure he was alone, he knew himself in safe possession and, as he tacitly expressed it, let himself go. He sometimes came twice in the twenty-four hours; the moments he liked best were those of gathering dusk, of the short autumn twilight; this was the time of which, again and again, be found himself hoping most. Then he could, as seemed to him, most intimately wander and wait, linger and listen, feel his fine attention, never in his life before so fine, on the pulse of the great vague place: he preferred the lampless hour and only wished he might have prolonged each day the deep crepuscular spell. Later – rarely much before midnight, but then for a considerable vigil – he watched with his glimmering light; moving slowly, holding it high, playing it far, rejoicing above all, as much as he might, in open vistas, reaches of communication between rooms and by passages; the long straight chance or show, as he would have called it, for the revelation he pretended to invite. It was a practice he found he could perfectly 'work' without exciting remark; no one was in the least the wiser for it; even Alice Staverton, who was moreover a well of discretion, didn't quite fully imagine.

He let himself in and let himself out with the assurance of calm proprietorship; and accident so far favoured him that, if a fat Avenue 'officer' had happened on occasion to see him entering at eleven-thirty, he had never yet, to the best of his belief, been noticed as emerging at two. He walked there on the crisp November nights, arrived regularly at the evening's end; it was as easy to do this after dining out as to take his way to a club or to his hotel. When he left his club, if he hadn't been dining out, it was ostensibly to go to his hotel; and when he left his hotel, if he had spent a part of the evening there, it was ostensibly to go to his club. Everything was easy in fine; everything conspired and promoted: there was truly even in the strain of his experience something that glossed over, something that salved and simplified, all the rest of consciousness. He circulated, talked, renewed, loosely and pleasantly, old relations – met indeed, so far as he could, new expectations and seemed to make out on the whole that in spite of the career, of such different contacts, which he had spoken of to Miss Staverton as ministering so little, for those who might have watched it, to edification, he was positively rather liked than not. He was a dim secondary social success – and all with people who had truly not an idea of him. It was all mere surface sound, this murmur of their welcome, this popping of their corks – just as his gestures of response were the extravagant shadows, emphatic in proportion as they meant little, of some game of *ombres chinoises*.[5] He projected himself all day, in thought, straight over the bristling line of hard unconscious heads and into the other, the real, the waiting life; the life that, as soon as he had heard behind him the click of his great house-door, began for him, on the jolly corner, as beguilingly as the slow opening bars of some rich music follows the tap of the conductor's wand.

He always caught the first effect of the steel point of his stick on the old marble of the hall pavement, large black-and-white squares that he remembered as the admiration of his childhood and that had then made in him, as he now saw, for the growth of an early conception of style. This effect was the dim reverberating tinkle as of some far-off bell hung who should say where? – in the depths of the house, of the past, of that mystical other world that might have flourished for him had he not, for weal or woe, abandoned it. On this impression he did ever same thing; he put his stick noiselessly away in a corner – feeling the place once more in the likeness of some great glass bowl, all precious concave crystal, set delicately humming by the play of a moist finger round its edge. The concave crystal held, as it were, this mystical other world, and the indescribably fine murmur of its rim was the sigh there, the scarce audible pathetic wail to his strained ear, of all the old baffled forsworn possibilities. What he did therefore by

this appeal of his hushed presence was to wake them into such
measure of ghostly life as they might still enjoy. They were shy, all
but unappeasably shy, but they weren't really sinister; at least they
weren't as he had hitherto felt them – before they had taken the form
he so yearned to make them take, the form he at moments saw
himself in the light of fairly hunting on tiptoe, the points of his
evening-shoes, from room to room and from storey to storey.

That was the essence of his vision – which was all rank folly, if one
would, while he was out of the house and otherwise occupied, but
which took on the last verisimilitude as soon as he was placed and
posted. He knew what he meant and what he wanted; it was as clear as
the figure on a cheque presented in demand for cash. His *alter ego*
'walked' – that was the note of his image of him, while his image of his
motive for his own odd pastime was the desire to waylay him and meet
him. He roamed, slowly, warily, but all restlessly, he himself did –
Mrs Muldoon had been right, absolutely, with her figure of their
'craping'; and the presence he watched for would roam restlessly too.
But it would be as cautious and as shifty; the conviction of its
probable, in fact its already quite sensible, quite audible evasion of
pursuit grew for him from night to night, laying on him finally a
rigour to which nothing in his life had been comparable. It had been
the theory of many superficially judging persons, he knew, that he was
wasting that life in a surrender to sensations, but he had tasted of no
pleasure so fine as his actual tension, had been introduced to no sport
that demanded at once the patience and the nerve of this stalking of a
creature more subtle, yet at bay perhaps more formidable, than any
beast of the forest. The terms, the comparisons, the very practices of
the chase positively came again into play; there were even moments
when passages of his occasional experience as a sportsman, stirred
memories, from his younger time, of moor and mountain and desert,
revived for him – and to the increase of his keenness – by the
tremendous force of analogy. He found himself at moments – once he
had placed his single light on some mantelshelf or in some recess –
stepping back into shelter or shade, effacing himself behind a door or
in an embrasure, as he had sought of old the vantage of rock and tree;
he found himself holding his breath and living in the joy of the
instant, the supreme suspense created by big game alone.

He wasn't afraid (though putting himself the question as he
believed gentlemen on Bengal tiger-shoots or in close quarters with
the great bear of the Rockies had been known to confess to having
put it); and this indeed – since here at least he might be frank! –
because of the impression, so intimate and so strange, that he himself

produced as yet a dread, produced certainly a strain, beyond the liveliest he was likely to feel. They fell for him into categories, they fairly became familiar, the signs, for his own perception, of the alarm his presence and his vigilance created; though leaving him always to remark, portentously, on his probably having formed a relation, his probably enjoying a consciousness, unique in the experience of man. People enough, first and last, had been in terror of apparitions, but who had ever before so turned the tables and become himself, in the apparitional world, an incalculable terror? He might have found this sublime had he quite dared to think of it; but he didn't too much insist, truly, on that side of his privilege. With habit and repetition he gained to an extraordinary degree the power to penetrate the dusk of distances and the darkness of corners, to resolve back into their innocence the treacheries of uncertain light, the evil-looking forms taken in the gloom by mere shadows, by accidents of the air, by shifting effects of perspective; putting down his dim luminary he could still wander on without it, pass into other rooms and, only knowing it was there behind him in case of need, see his way about, visually project for his purpose a comparative clearness. It made him feel, this acquired faculty, like some monstrous stealthy cat; he wondered if he would have glared at these moments with large shining yellow eyes, and what it mightn't verily be, for the poor hard-pressed *alter ego*, to be confronted with such a type.

He liked however the open shutters; he opened everywhere those Mrs Muldoon had closed, closing them as carefully afterwards, so that she shouldn't notice: he liked – oh this he did like, and above all in the upper rooms! – the sense of the hard silver of the autumn stars through the windowpanes, and scarcely less the flare of the street-lamps below, the white electric lustre which it would have taken curtains to keep out. This was human actual social; this was of the world he had lived in, and he was more at his ease certainly for the countenance, coldly general and impersonal, that all the while and in spite of his detachment it seemed to give him. He had support of course mostly in the rooms at the wide front and the prolonged side; it failed him considerably in the central shades and the parts at the back. But if he sometimes, on his rounds, was glad of his optical reach, so none the less often the rear of the house affected him as the very jungle of his prey. The place was there more subdivided; a large 'extension' in particular, where small rooms for servants had been multiplied, abounded in nooks and corners, in closets and passages, in the ramifications especially of an ample back staircase over which he leaned, many a time, to look far down – not deterred from his

gravity even while aware that he might, for a spectator, have figured
some solemn simpleton playing at hide-and-seek. Outside in fact he
might himself make that ironic *rapprochement*;[6] but within the walls,
and in spite of the clear windows, his consistency was proof against
the cynical light of New York.

It had belonged to that idea of the exasperated consciousness of his
victim to become a real test for him; since he had quite put it to
himself from the first that, oh distinctly! he could 'cultivate' his
whole perception. He had felt it as above all open to cultivation –
which indeed was but another name for his manner of spending his
time. He was bringing it on, bringing it to perfection, by practice; in
consequence of which it had grown so fine that he was now aware of
impressions, attestations of his general postulate, that couldn't have
broken upon him at once. This was the case more specifically with a
phenomenon at last quite frequent for him in the upper rooms, the
recognition – absolutely unmistakeable, and by a turn dating from a
particular hour, his resumption of his campaign after a diplomatic
drop, a calculated absence of three nights – of his being definitely
followed, tracked at a distance carefully taken and to the express end
that he should the less confidently, less arrogantly, appear to himself
merely to pursue. It worried, it finally quite broke him up, for it
proved, of all the conceivable impressions, the one least suited to his
book. He was kept in sight while remaining himself – as regards the
essence of his position – sightless, and his only recourse then was in
abrupt turns, rapid recoveries of ground. He wheeled about, retracing his steps, as if he might so catch in his face at least the stirred air
of some other quick revolution. It was indeed true that his fully
dislocalised thought of these manoeuvres recalled to him Pantaloon,
at the Christmas farce, buffeted and tricked from behind by ubiqui-
tous Harlequin;[7] but it left intact the influence of the conditions
themselves each time he was re-exposed to them, so that in fact this
association, had he suffered it to become constant, would on a certain
side have but ministered to his intenser gravity. He had made, as I
have said, to create on the premises the baseless sense of a reprieve,
his three absences; and the result of the third was to confirm the
after-effect of the second.

On his return, that night – the night succeeding his last intermission – he stood in the hall and looked up the staircase with a
certainty more intimate than any he had yet known. 'He's *there*, at the
top, and waiting – not, as in general, falling back for disappearance.
He's holding his ground, and it's the first time – which is a proof,
isn't it? that something has happened for him.' So Brydon argued

with his hand on the banister and his foot on the lowest stair; in which position he felt as never before the air chilled by his logic. He himself turned cold in it, for he seemed of a sudden to know what now was involved. 'Harder pressed? – yes, he takes it in, with its thus making clear to him that I've come, as they say, "to stay". He finally doesn't like and can't bear it, in the sense, I mean, that his wrath, his menaced interest, now balances with his dread. I've hunted him till he has "turned" that, up there, is what has happened – he's the fanged or the antlered animal brought at last to bay.' There came to him, as I say – but determined by an influence beyond my notation! – the acuteness of this certainty; under which however the next moment he had broken into a sweat that he would as little have consented to attribute to fear as he would have dared immediately to act upon it for enterprise. It marked none the less a prodigious thrill, a thrill that represented sudden dismay, no doubt, but also represented, and with the selfsame throb, the strangest, the most joyous, possibly the next minute almost the proudest, duplication of consciousness.

'He has been dodging, retreating, hiding, but now, worked up to anger, he'll fight!' – this intense impression made a single mouthful, as it were, of terror and applause. But what was wondrous was that the applause, for the felt fact, was so eager, since, if it was his other self he was running to earth, this ineffable identity was thus in the last resort not unworthy of him. It bristled there – somewhere near at hand, however unseen still – as the hunted thing, even as the trodden worm of the adage *must* at last bristle; and Brydon at this instant tasted probably of a sensation more complex than had ever before found itself consistent with sanity. It was as if it would have shamed him that a character so associated with his own should triumphantly succeed in just skulking, should to the end not risk the open; so that the drop of this danger was, on the spot, a great lift of the whole situation. Yet with another rare shift of the same subtlety he was already trying to measure by how much more he himself might now be in peril of fear; so rejoicing that he could, in another form, actively inspire that fear, and simultaneously quaking for the form in which he might passively know it.

The apprehension of knowing it must after a little have grown in him, and the strangest moment of his adventure perhaps, the most memorable or really most interesting, afterwards, of his crisis, was the lapse of certain instants of concentrated conscious *combat*, the sense of a need to hold on to something, even after the manner of a man slipping and slipping on some awful incline; the vivid impulse, above all, to move, to act, to charge, somehow and upon something –

to show himself, in a word, that he wasn't afraid. The state of 'holding on' was thus the state to which he was momentarily reduced; if there had been anything, in the great vacancy, to seize, he would presently have been aware of having clutched it as he might under a shock at home have clutched the nearest chair-back. He had been surprised at any rate – of this he *was* aware – into something unprecedented since his original appropriation of the place; he had closed his eyes, held them tight, for a long minute, as with that instinct of dismay and that terror of vision. When he opened them the room, the other contiguous rooms, extraordinarily, seemed lighter – so light, almost, that at first he took the change for day. He stood firm, however that might be, just where he had paused; his resistance had helped him – it was as if there were something he had tided over. He knew after a little what this was – it had been in the imminent danger of flight. He had stiffened his will against going; without this he would have made for the stairs, and it seemed to him that, still with his eyes closed, he would have descended them, would have known how, straight and swiftly, to the bottom.

Well, as he had held out, here he was – still at the top, among the more intricate upper rooms and with the gauntlet of the others, of all the rest of the house, still to run when it should be his time to go. He would go at his time – only at his time: didn't he go every night very much at the same hour? He took out his watch – there was light for that: it was scarcely a quarter past one, and he had never withdrawn so soon. He reached his lodgings for the most part at two – with his walk of a quarter of an hour. He would wait for the last quarter – he wouldn't stir till then; and he kept his watch there with his eyes on it, reflecting while he held it that this deliberate wait, a wait with an effort, which he recognised, would serve perfectly for the attestation he desired to make. It would prove his courage – unless indeed the latter might most be proved by his budging at last from his place. What he mainly felt now was that, since he hadn't originally scuttled, he had his dignities – which had never in his life seemed so many – all to preserve and to carry aloft. This was before him in truth as a physical image, an image almost worthy of an age of greater romance. That remark indeed glimmered for him only to glow the next instant with a finer light; since what age of romance, after all, could have matched either the state of his mind or, 'objectively', as they said, the wonder of his situation? The only difference would have been that, brandishing his dignities over his head as in a parchment scroll, he might then – that is in the heroic time – have proceeded downstairs with a drawn sword in his other grasp.

At present, really, the light he had set down on the mantel of the next room would have to figure his sword; which utensil, in the course of a minute, he had taken the requisite number of steps to possess himself of. The door between the rooms was open, and from the second another door opened to a third. These rooms, as he remembered, gave all three upon a common corridor as well, but there was a fourth, beyond them, without issue save through the preceding. To have moved, to have heard his step again, was appreciably a help; though even in recognising this he lingered once more a little by the chimney piece on which his light had rested. When he next moved, just hesitating where to turn, he found himself considering a circumstance that, after his first and comparatively vague apprehension of it, produced in him the start that often attends some pang of recollection, the violent shock of having ceased happily to forget. He had come into sight of the door in which the brief chain of communication ended and which he now surveyed from the nearer threshold, the one not directly facing it. Placed at some distance to the left of this point, it would have admitted him to the last room of the four, the room without other approach or egress, had it not, to his intimate conviction, been closed *since* his former visitation, the matter probably of a quarter of an hour before. He stared with all his eyes at the wonder of the fact, arrested again where he stood and again holding his breath while he sounded its sense. Surely it had been *subsequently* closed – that is it had been on his previous passage indubitably open!

He took it full in the face that something had happened between – that he couldn't not have noticed before (by which he meant on his original tour of all the rooms that evening) that such a barrier had exceptionally presented itself. He had indeed since that moment undergone an agitation so extraordinary that it might have muddled for him any earlier view; and he tried to convince himself that he might perhaps then have gone into the room and, inadvertently, automatically, on coming out, have drawn the door after him. The difficulty was that this exactly was what he never did; it was against his whole policy, as he might have said, the essence of which was to keep vistas clear. He had them from the first, as he was well aware, quite on the brain: the strange apparition, at the far end of one of them, of his baffled 'prey' (which had become by so sharp an irony so little the term now to apply!) was the form of success his imagination had most cherished, projecting into it always a refinement of beauty. He had known fifty times the start of perception that had afterwards dropped; had fifty times gasped to himself, 'There!' under some fond brief hallucination. The house, as the case stood, admirably lent itself; he might wonder at the taste, the native architecture of the particular time, which could rejoice so in the multiplication of doors – the opposite extreme to the modern, the actual almost complete proscription of them; but it had fairly contributed to provoke this obsession of the presence encountered telescopically, as he might say, focused and studied in diminishing perspective and as by a rest for the elbow.

It was with these considerations that his present attention was charged – they perfectly availed to make what he saw portentous. He *couldn't*, by any lapse, have blocked that aperture; and if he hadn't, if it was unthinkable, why what else was clear but that there had been another agent? Another agent? – he had been catching, as he felt, a moment back, the very breath of him; but when had he been so close as in this simple, this logical, this completely personal act? It was so logical, that is, that one might have taken it for personal; yet for what did Brydon take it, he asked himself, while, softly panting, he felt his eyes almost leave their sockets. Ah this time at last they *were*, the two, the opposed projections of him, in presence; and this time, as much as one would, the question of danger loomed. With it rose, as not before, the question of courage – for what he knew the blank face of the door to say to him was, 'Show us how much you have!' It stared, it glared back at him with that challenge; it put to him the two alternatives: should he just push it open or not? Oh to have this consciousness was to *think* – and to think, Brydon knew, as he stood there, was, with the lapsing moments, not to have acted! Not to have acted – that was the misery and the pang – was even still not to act; was in fact *all* to feel the thing in another, in a new and terrible way. How long did he pause and how long did he debate? There was presently nothing to measure it; for his vibration had already changed – as just by the effect of its intensity. Shut up there, at bay, defiant, and with the prodigy of the thing palpably provably *done*, thus giving notice like some stark signboard – under that accession of accent the situation itself had turned; and Brydon at last remarkably made up his mind on what it had turned to.

It had turned altogether to a different admonition; to a supreme hint, for him, of the value of discretion! This slowly dawned, no doubt – for it could take its time; so perfectly, on his threshold, had he been stayed, so little as yet had he either advanced or retreated. It was the strangest of all things that now when, by his taking ten steps and applying his hand to a latch, or even his shoulder and his knee, if necessary, to a panel, all the hunger of his prime need might have been met, his high curiosity crowned, his unrest assuaged – it was amazing, but it was also exquisite and rare, that insistence should have, at a touch, quite dropped from him. Discretion – he jumped at that; and yet not, verily, at such a pitch, because it saved his nerves or his skin, but because, much more valuably, it saved the situation. When I say he 'jumped' at it I feel the consonance of this term with the fact that – at the end indeed of I know not how long – he did move again, he crossed straight to the door. He wouldn't touch it – it seemed now that he might *if* he would: he would only just wait there a little, to show, to prove, that he wouldn't. He had thus another station, close to the thin partition by which revelation was denied him; but with his eyes bent and his hands held off in a mere intensity of stillness. He listened as if there had been something to hear, but this attitude, while it lasted, was his own communication. 'If you won't then – good: I spare you and I give up. You affect me as by the appeal positively for pity: you convince me that for reasons rigid and sublime – what do I know? – we both of us should have suffered. I respect them then, and, though moved and privileged as, I believe, it has never been given to man, I retire, I renounce – never, on my honour, to try again. So rest for ever – and let *me!*'

That, for Brydon was the deep sense of this last demonstration – solemn, measured, directed, as he felt it to be. He brought it to a close, he turned away; and now verily he knew how deeply he had been stirred. He retraced his steps, taking up his candle, burnt, he observed, well-nigh to the socket, and marking again, lighten it as he would, the distinctness of his footfall; after which, in a moment, he knew himself at the other side of the house. He did here what he had not yet done at these hours – he opened half a casement, one of those in the front, and let in the air of the night; a thing he would have taken at any time previous for a sharp rupture of his spell. His spell was broken now, and it didn't matter – broken by his concession and his surrender, which made it idle henceforth that he should ever come back. The empty street – its other life so marked even by the great lamplit vacancy – was within call, within touch; he stayed there as to be in it again, high above it though he was still perched; he watched as for some comforting common fact, some vulgar human note, the passage of a scavenger or a thief, some nightbird however base. He would have blessed that sign of life; he would have welcomed positively the slow approach of his friend the policeman, whom he had hitherto only sought to avoid, and was not sure that if the patrol had come into sight he mightn't have felt the impulse to get into relation with it, to hail it, on some pretext, from his fourth floor.

The pretext that wouldn't have been too silly or too compromising, the explanation that would have saved his dignity and kept his name, in such a case, out of the papers, was not definite to him: he was so occupied with the thought of recording his discretion – as an effect of the vow he had just uttered to his intimate adversary – that the importance of this loomed large and something had overtaken all ironically his sense of proportion. If there had been a ladder applied to the front of the house, even one of the vertiginous perpendiculars employed by painters and roofers and sometimes left standing overnight, he would have managed somehow, astride of the window-sill, to compass by outstretched leg and arm that mode of descent. If there had been some such uncanny thing as he had found in his room at hotels, a workable fire escape in the form of notched cable or a canvas shoot, he would have availed himself of it as a proof – well, of his present delicacy. He nursed that sentiment, as the question stood, a little in vain, and even – at the end of he scarce knew, once more, how long – found it, as by the action on his mind of the failure of response of the outer world, sinking back to vague anguish. It seemed to him he had waited an age for some stir of the great grim hush; the life of the town was itself under a spell – so unnaturally, up and down the whole prospect of known and rather ugly objects, the blankness and the silence lasted. Had they ever, he asked himself, the hard-faced houses, which had begun to look livid in the dim dawn, had they ever spoken so little to any need of his spirit? Great builded voids, great crowded stillnesses put on, often, in the heart of cities, for the small hours, a sort of sinister mask, and it was of this large collective negation that Brydon presently became conscious – all the more that the break of day was, almost incredibly, now at hand, proving to him what a night he had made of it.

He looked again at his watch, saw what had become of his time-values (he had taken hours for minutes – not, as in other tense situations, minutes for hours) and the strange air of the streets was but the weak, the sullen flush of a dawn in which everything was still locked up. His choked appeal from his own open window had been the sole note of life, and he could but break off at last as for a worse despair. Yet while so deeply demoralised he was capable again of an impulse denoting – at least by his present measure – extraordinary resolution; of retracing his steps to the spot where he had turned cold with the extinction of his last pulse of doubt as to there being in the place another presence than his own. This required an effort strong enough to sicken him; but he had his reason, which overmastered for the moment everything else. There was the whole of the rest of the house to traverse, and how should he screw himself to that if the door he had seen closed were at present open? He could hold to the idea that the closing had practically been for him an act of mercy, a chance offered him to descend, depart, get off the ground and never again profane it. This conception held together, it worked; but what it meant for him depended now clearly on the amount of forbearance his recent action, or rather his recent inaction, had engendered. The image of the 'presence', whatever it was, waiting there for him to go – this image had not yet been so concrete for his nerves as when he stopped short of the point at which certainty would have come to him. For, with all his resolution, or more exactly with all his dread, he did stop short – he hung back from really seeing. The risk was too great and his fear too definite: it took at this moment an awful specific form.

He knew – yes, as he had never known anything – that, *should* he see the door open, it would all too abjectly be the end of him. It would mean that the agent of his shame – for his shame was the deep abjection – was once more at large and in general possession; and what glared him thus in the face was the act that this would determine for him. It would send him straight about to the window he had left open, and by that window, be long ladder and dangling rope as absent as they would, he saw himself uncontrollably insanely fatally take his way to the street. The hideous chance of this he at least could avert; but he could only avert it by recoiling in time from assurance. He had the whole house to deal with, this fact was still there; only he now knew that uncertainty alone could start him. He stole back from where he had checked himself – merely to do so was suddenly like safety – and, making blindly for the greater staircase, left gaping rooms and sounding passages behind. Here was the top of the stairs, with a fine large dim descent and three spacious landings to mark off. His instinct was all for mildness, but his feet were harsh on the floors, and, strangely, when he had in a couple of minutes become aware of this, it counted somehow for help. He couldn't have spoken, the tone of his voice would have scared him, and the common conceit or resource of 'whistling in the dark' (whether literally or figuratively) have appeared basely vulgar; yet he liked none the less to hear himself go, and when he had reached his first landing – taking it all with no rush, but quite steadily – that stage of success drew from him a gasp of relief.

The house, withal, seemed immense, the scale of space again inordinate; the open rooms, to no one of which his eyes deflected, gloomed in their shuttered state like mouths of caverns; only the high skylight that formed the crown of the deep well created for him a medium in which he could advance, but which might have been, for queerness of colour, some watery underworld. He tried to think of something noble, as that his property was really grand, a splendid

possession; but this nobleness took the form too of the clear delight
with which he was finally to sacrifice it. They might come in now, the
builders, the destroyers – they might come as soon as they would. At
the end of two flights he had dropped to another zone, and from the
middle of the third, with only one more left, he recognised the
influence of the lower windows, of half-drawn blinds, of the
occasional gleam of streetlamps, of the glazed spaces of the vestibule.
This was the bottom of the sea, which showed an illumination of its
own and which he even saw paved – when at a given moment he drew
up to sink a long look over the banisters – with the marble squares of
his childhood. By that time indubitably he felt, as he might have said
in a commoner cause, better; it had allowed him to stop and draw
breath, and the ease increased with the sight of the old black-and-
white slabs. But what he most felt was that now surely, with the
element of impunity pulling him as by hard firm hands, the case was
settled for what he might have seen above had he dared that last look.
The closed door, blessedly remote now, was still closed – and he had
only in short to reach that of the house.

He came down farther, he crossed the passage forming the access
to the last flight; and if here again he stopped an instant it was almost
for the sharpness of the thrill of assured escape. It made him shut his
eyes – which opened again to the straight slope of the remainder of
the stairs. Here was impunity still, but impunity almost excessive;
inasmuch as the sidelights and the high fan-tracery of the entrance
were glimmering straight into the hall; an appearance produced, he
the next instant saw, by the fact that the vestibule gaped wide, that
the hinged halves of the inner door had been thrown far back. Out
of that again the *question* sprang at him, making his eyes, as he felt,
half-start from his head, as they had done, at the top of the house,
before the sign of the other door. If he had left that one open, hadn't
he left this one closed, and wasn't he now in *most* immediate
presence of some inconceivable occult activity? It was as sharp, the
question, as a knife in his side, but the answer hung fire still and
seemed to lose itself in the vague darkness to which the thin
admitted dawn, glimmering archwise over the whole outer door,
made a semicircular margin, a cold silvery nimbus that seemed to
play a little as he looked – to shift and expand and contract.

It was as if there had been something within it, protected by
indistinctness and corresponding in extent with the opaque surface
behind, the painted panels of the last barrier to his escape, of which
the key was in his pocket. The indistinctness mocked him even while
he stared, affected him as somehow shrouding or challenging

certitude, so that after faltering an instant on his step he let himself go with the sense that here *was* at last something to meet, to touch, to take, to know – something all unnatural and dreadful, but to advance upon which was the condition for him either of liberation or of supreme defeat. The penumbra, dense and dark, was the virtual screen of a figure which stood in it as still as some image erect in a niche or as some black-vizored sentinel guarding a treasure. Brydon was to know afterwards, was to recall and make out, the particular thing he had believed during the rest of his descent. He saw, in its great grey glimmering margin, the central vagueness diminish, and he felt it to be taking the very form towards which, for so many days, the passion of his curiosity had yearned. It gloomed, it loomed, it was something, it was somebody, the prodigy of a personal presence.

Rigid and conscious, spectral yet human, a man of his own substance and stature waited there to measure himself with his power to dismay. This only could it be – this only till he recognised, with his advance, that what made the face dim was the pair of raised hands that covered it and in which, so far from being offered in defiance, it was buried as for dark deprecation. So Brydon, before him, took him in; with every fact of him now, in the higher light, hard and acute – his planted stillness, his vivid truth, his grizzled bent head and white masking hands, his queer actuality of evening-dress, of dangling double eyeglass, of gleaming silk lappet and white linen, of pearl button and gold watchguard and polished shoe. No portrait by a great modern master could have presented him with more intensity, thrust him out of his frame with more art, as if there had been 'treatment', of the consummate sort, in his every shade and salience. The revulsion, for our friend, had become, before he knew it, immense – this drop, in the act of apprehension, to the sense of his adversary's inscrutable manoeuvre. That meaning at least, while he gaped, it offered him; for he could but gape at his other self in this other anguish, gape as a proof that *he*, standing there for the achieved, the enjoyed, the triumphant life, couldn't be faced in his triumph. Wasn't the proof in the splendid covering hands, strong and completely spread? – so spread and so intentional that, in spite of a special verity that surpassed every other, the fact that one of these hands had lost two fingers, which were reduced to stumps, as if accidentally shot away, the face was effectually guarded and saved.

'Saved', though, *would* it be? – Brydon breathed his wonder till the very impunity of his attitude and the very insistence of his eyes produced, as he felt, a sudden stir which showed the next instant as a deeper portent, while the head raised itself, the betrayal of a braver purpose. The hands, as he looked, began to move, to open; then, as if deciding in a flash, dropped from the face and left it uncovered and presented. Horror, with the sight, had leaped into Brydon's throat, gasping there in a sound he couldn't utter; for the bared identity was too hideous as *his*, and his glare was the passion of his protest. The face, *that* face, Spencer Brydon's? – he searched it still, but looking away from it in dismay and denial, falling straight from his height of sublimity. It was unknown, inconceivable, awful, disconnected from any possibility – ! He had been 'sold', he inwardly moaned, stalking such game as this: the presence before him was a presence, the horror within him a horror, but the waste of his nights had been only grotesque and the success of his adventure an irony. Such an identity fitted his at *no* point, made its alternative monstrous. A thousand times yes, as it came upon him nearer now – the face was the face of a stranger. It came upon him nearer now, quite as one of those expanding fantastic images projected by the magic lantern of childhood; for the stranger, whoever he might be, evil, odious, blatant, vulgar, had advanced as for aggression, and he knew himself give ground. Then harder pressed still, sick with the force of his shock, and falling back as under the hot breath and the roused passion of a life larger than his own, a rage of personality before which his own collapsed, he felt the whole vision turn to darkness and his very feet give way. His head went round; he was going; he had gone.

III

What had next brought him back, clearly – though after how long? – was Mrs Muldoon's voice, coming to him from quite near, from so near that he seemed presently to see her as kneeling on the ground before him while he lay looking up at her; himself not wholly on the ground, but half-raised and upheld – conscious, yes, of tenderness of support and, more particularly, of a head pillowed in extraordinary softness and fainly refreshing fragrance. He considered, he wondered, his wit but half at his service; then another face intervened, bending more directly over him, and he finally knew that Alice Staverton had made her lap an ample and perfect cushion to him, and that she had to this end seated herself on the lowest degree of the staircase, the rest of his long person remaining stretched on his old black-and-white slabs. They were cold, these marble squares of his youth; but *he* somehow was not, in this rich return of consciousness – the most wonderful hour, little by little, that he had ever known, leaving him, as it did, so gratefully, so abysmally passive, and yet as with a treasure of intelligence waiting all round him for quiet appropriation; dissolved, he might call it, in the air of the place and producing the golden glow of a late autumn afternoon. He had come back, yes – come back from farther away than any man but himself had ever travelled; but it was strange how with this sense what he had come back *to* seemed really the great thing, and as if his prodigious journey had been all for the sake of it. Slowly but surely his consciousness grew, his vision of his state thus completing itself: he had been miraculously *carried* back – lifted and carefully borne as from where he had been picked up, the uttermost end of an interminable grey passage. Even with this he was suffered to rest, and what had now brought him to knowledge was the break in the long mild motion.

It had brought him to knowledge, to knowledge – yes, this was the beauty of his state; which came to resemble more and more that of a man who has gone to sleep on some news of a great inheritance, and then, after dreaming it away, after profaning it with matters strange to it, has waked up again to serenity of certitude and has only to lie and watch it grow. This was the drift of his patience – that he had only to let it shine on him. He must moreover, with intermissions, still have been lifted and borne; since why and how else should he have known himself, later on, with the afternoon glow intenser, no longer at the foot of his stairs – situated as these now seemed at that dark other end of his tunnel – but on a deep window-bench of his high saloon, over which had been spread, couch-fashion, a mantle of soft stuff lined with grey fur that was familiar to his eyes and that one of his hands kept fondly feeling as for its pledge of truth. Mrs Muldoon's face had gone, but the other, the second he had recognised, hung over him in a way that showed how he was still propped and pillowed. He took it all in, and the more he took it the more it seemed to suffice: he was as much at peace as if he had had food and drink. It was the two women who had found him, on Mrs Muldoon's having plied, at her usual hour, her latchkey – and on her having above all arrived while Miss Staverton still lingered near the house. She had been turning away, all anxiety, from worrying the vain bell-handle – her calculation having been of the hour of the good woman's visit; but the latter, blessedly, had come up while she was still there, and they had entered together. He had then lain, beyond the vestibule, very much as he was lying now – quite, that is, as he appeared to have fallen, but all so wondrously without bruise or gash; only in a depth of stupor. What he most took in, however, at present, with the steadier clearance, was that Alice Staverton had for a long unspeakable moment not doubted he was dead.

'It must have been that I *was*.' He made it out as she held him. 'Yes – I can only have died. You brought me literally to life. Only,' he wondered, his eyes rising to her, 'only, in the name of all the benedictions, how?'

It took her but an instant to bend her face and kiss him, and something in the manner of it, and in the way her hands clasped and locked his head while he felt the cool charity and virtue of her lips, something in all this beatitude somehow answered everything. 'And now I keep you,' she said.

'Oh keep me, keep me!' he pleaded while her face still hung over him: in response to which it dropped again and stayed close, clingingly close. It was the seal of their situation – of which he tasted the impress for a long blissful moment in silence. But he came back. 'Yet how did you know – ?'

'I was uneasy. You were to have come, you remember – and you had sent no word.'

'Yes, I remember – I was to have gone to you at one today.' It caught on to their 'old' life and relation – which were so near and so far. 'I was still out there in my strange darkness – where was it, what was it? I must have stayed there so long.' He could but wonder at the depth and the duration of his swoon.

'Since last night?' she asked with a shade of fear for her possible indiscretion.

'Since this morning – it must have been: the cold dim dawn of today. Where have I been,' he vaguely wailed, 'where have I been?' He felt her hold him close, and it was as if this helped him now to make in all security his mild moan. 'What a long dark day!'

All in her tenderness she had waited a moment. 'In the cold dim dawn?' she quavered.

But he had already gone on piecing together the parts of the whole prodigy. 'As I didn't turn up you came straight – ?'

She barely cast about. 'I went first to your hotel – where they told me of your absence. You had dined out last evening and hadn't been back since. But they appeared to know you had been at your club.'

'So you had the idea of *this* – ?'

'Of what?' she asked in a moment.

'Well – of what has happened.'

'I believed at least you'd have been here. I've known, all along,' she said, 'that you've been coming.'

' "Known" it – ?'

'Well, I've believed it. I said nothing to you after that talk we had a month ago – but I felt sure. I knew you *would*,' she declared.

'That I'd persist, you mean?'

'That you'd see him.'

'Ah but I didn't!' cried Brydon with his long wail. 'There's somebody – an awful beast; whom I brought, too horribly, to bay. But it's not me.'

At this she bent over him again, and her eyes were in his eyes. 'No – it's not you.' And it was as if, while her face hovered, he might have made out in it, hadn't it been so near, some particular meaning blurred by a smile. 'No, thank heaven,' she repeated – 'it's not you! Of course it wasn't to have been.'

'Ah but it *was*,' he gently insisted. And he stared before him now as he had been staring for so many weeks. 'I was to have known myself.'

'You couldn't!' she returned consolingly. And then reverting, and as if to account further for what she had herself done, 'But it wasn't only *that*, that you hadn't been at home,' she went on. 'I waited till the hour at which we had found Mrs Muldoon that day of my going with you; and she arrived, as I've told you, while, failing to bring anyone to the door, I lingered in my despair on the steps. After a little, if she hadn't come, by such a mercy, I should have found means to hunt her up. But it wasn't,' said Alice Staverton, as if once more with her fine intention – 'it wasn't only that.'

His eyes, as he lay, turned back to her. 'What more then?'

She met it, the wonder she had stirred. 'In the cold dim dawn, you say? Well, in the cold dim dawn of this morning I too saw you.'

'Saw *me* – ?'

'Saw *him*,' said Alice Staverton. 'It must have been at the same moment.'

He lay an instant taking it in – as if he wished to be quite reasonable. 'At the same moment?'

'Yes – in my dream again, the same one I've named to you. He came back to me. Then I knew it for a sign. He had come to you.'

At this Brydon raised himself; he had to see her better. She helped him when she understood his movement, and he sat up, steadying himself beside her there on the window-bench and with his right hand grasping her left. '*He* didn't come to me.'

'You came to yourself,' she beautifully smiled.

'Ah I've come to myself now – thanks to you, dearest. But this brute, with his awful face – this brute's a black stranger. He's none of *me*, even as I *might* have been,' Brydon sturdily declared.

But she kept the clearness that was like the breath of infallibility. 'Isn't the whole point that you'd have been different?'

He almost scowled for it. 'As different as *that* – ?'

Her look again was more beautiful to him than the things of this world. 'Haven't you exactly wanted to know *how* different? So this morning,' she said, 'you appeared to me.'

'Like *him*?'

'A black stranger!'

'Then how did you know it was I?'

'Because, as I told you weeks ago, my mind, my imagination, had worked so over what you might, what you mightn't have been – to show you, you see, how I've thought of you. In the midst of that you came to me – that my wonder might be answered. So I knew,' she went on; 'and believed that, since the question held you too so fast, as you told me that day, you too would see for yourself. And when this morning I again saw I knew it would be because you had – and also then, from the first moment, because you somehow wanted me. *He* seemed to tell me of that. So why,' she strangely smiled, 'shouldn't I like him?'

It brought Spencer Brydon to his feet. 'You "like" that horror – ?'

'I *could* have liked him. And to me,' she said, 'he was no horror. I had accepted him.'

' "Accepted" – ?' Brydon oddly sounded.

'Before, for the interest of his difference – yes. And as I didn't disown him, as I knew him – which you at last, confronted with him in his difference, so cruelly didn't, my dear – well, he must have been, you see, less dreadful to me. And it may have pleased him that I pitied him.'

She was beside him on her feet, but still holding his hand – still with her arm supporting him. But though it all brought for him thus a dim light, 'You "pitied" him?' he grudgingly, resentfully asked.

'He has been unhappy, he has been ravaged,' she said.

'And haven't I been unhappy? Am not I – you've only to look at me! – ravaged?'

'Ah I don't say I like him *better*,' she granted after a thought. 'But he's grim, he's worn – and things have happened to him. He doesn't make shift, for sight, with your charming monocle.'

'No' – it struck Brydon: 'I couldn't have sported mine "down-town". They'd have guyed me there.'

'His great convex pince-nez – I saw it, I recognised the kind – is for his poor ruined sight. And his poor right hand – !'

'Ah!' Brydon winced – whether for his proved identity or for his lost fingers. Then, 'He has a million a year,' he lucidly added. 'But he hasn't you.'

'And he isn't – no, he isn't – *you!*' she murmured as he drew her to his breast.

NOTES TO THE PREFACES

A note on the texts of the Prefaces

The texts of the excerpts here are from Vols XII and XVII of *The Novels and Tales of Henry James* (1908–9). Volume XII, which contained 'The Turn of the Screw', also included 'The Aspern Papers', and Vol. XVII also included 'The Altar of the Dead', 'The Beast in the Jungle', 'The Birthplace' and 'Julia Bride'.

On 'The Turn of the Screw'

1 (p. 4) *Cinderella . . . Brothers Grimm*   Cinderella was the heroine of the ancient Eastern fairytale, popularised by Charles Perrault (1628–1703) in his *Tales of Mother Goose* (1697) and included in the collection of the Brothers Grimm (see below); *Bluebeard*: see Note 10 to 'The Ghostly Rental' (p. 50); *Hop o' my Thumb*: hero of the fairytale *Little Thumb* from the French of Charles Perrault, translated by Robert Samber (?1729); *Little Red Riding Hood*: traditional European fairy-story, popularised by Charles Perrault in his *Contes du Temps* (Tales of the Times); *the Brothers Grimm*: Jacob Ludwig Carl Grimm (1785–1863) and Wilhelm Carl Grimm (1786–1859), scholars of German philology, law, mythology and folklore, chiefly known in England for their collection of fairytales translated into English in 1823 by Edgar Taylor.

2 (p. 4) *Arabian Nights*   See Note 15 to 'The Ghostly Rental' (p. 337)

3 (p. 5) *amusette*   (French) toy, plaything

4 (p. 6) *déjà très-joli*   (French, literally 'already very pretty') already very appealing

5 (p. 8) *the Pit*   i.e. Hell

On 'The Private Life', 'Owen Wingrave', 'The Friends of the Friends', 'Sir Edmund Orme', 'The Real Right Thing', 'The Jolly Corner'

1 (p. 12) *that most accomplished artist and most dazzling of men of the world* James based the figure of Lord Mellifont on Lord Leighton (see Introduction, pp. xiv–xv).

2 (p. 13) *solus*   (Latin) alone

3 (p. 15) *bêtises*   (French) absurdities

4 (p. 20) *Thackerayan Brighton*   William Makepeace Thackeray (1811–63) set part of his most famous novel *Vanity Fair* (1847) in the Brighton of the Regency period. There is a lively description of the town in Chapter XXII.

NOTES TO THE STORIES

A note on the texts used in this edition

The text of the 'The Romance of Certain Old Clothes' is that of its first book publication in *A Passionate Pilgrim* (1875), and that of 'The Ghostly Rental' is from its only publication in James's lifetime, in *Scribner's Monthly* (1876). The text of 'The Third Person' is that of its first publication in *The Soft Side* (1900). The texts of all the other stories are those of the New York Edition, *The Novels and Tales of Henry James* (1907–9).

The Romance of Certain Old Clothes

First published in the *Atlantic Monthly*, February 1868

1 (p. 21) *Viola . . . Perdita*   major female characters in, respectively, Shakespeare's *Twelfth Night* and *The Winter's Tale*

2 (p. 22) *brusquerie*   (French) abruptness, bluntness

3 (p. 23) *belle jeunesse*   (French, literally 'beautiful youth') fashionable young people

4 (p. 25) *the Vicar of Wakefield*   hero of the novel of that name (published 1764) by Oliver Goldsmith (1728–74)

5 (p. 28) *trousseau*   a bride's outfit of clothes (from French for 'bundle')

6 (p. 33) *Petrarch*   Francesco Petrarca (1304–74), Italian poet whose sonnets and other poems to Laura became a model of ideal love for subsequent European poets

The Ghostly Rental

First published in *Scribner's Monthly*, 1876

1 (p. 38) *Dr Channing*   William Ellery Channing (1780–1842) was a notable Boston theologian who opposed the strict Puritan doctrines of Calvinism and became a proponent of the milder and more rationalistic doctrines of Unitarianism.

2 (p. 38) *the old Divinity School*   part of Harvard University

3 (p. 38) *Cambridge*   town in Massachusetts, just outside Boston; home of Harvard University

4 (p. 38) *Overbeck and Ary Scheffer*   Friedrich Overbeck (1789–1869), a German painter of religious subjects who was inspired by the German and Italian Primitives and whose ideals were similar to those of the Pre-Raphaelite Brotherhood in England; Ary Scheffer (1795–1858), a Dutch painter and engraver of sentimental scenes of classical subjects

5 (p. 38) *Plotinus and St Augustine*   Plotinus (*c.*205–270) was a Greek theologian whose *Enneads* had a great influence on Christian theology; St Augustine (354–430) was bishop of Hippo in N. Africa and author of the great theological works *The City of God* (412–27) and *On Christian Doctrine*, and the autobiographical *Confessions* (*c.*400).

6 (p. 41) *Yankee*   inhabitant of New England (from Dutch 'Janke', a diminutive of the name Jan, used derisively)

7 (p. 43) *Andrew Jackson*   (1767–1845) 7th president of the United States (1828–37)

8 (p. 43) *Hoffmann's tales*   E. T. A. Hoffmann (1776–1822) was a German Romantic author of several fantastic and ghostly tales, like 'The Golden Flowerpot' (1814) and 'The Sandman' (1817), which were widely read in translation in England and America.

9 (p. 43) *flambeaux*   (from French) large, decorated candlesticks

10 (p. 50) *Bluebeard's wife*   Bluebeard was the villain who murdered several wives in the traditional tale, best known in the version in *Contes du Temps* (1697) by the French author Charles Perrault (1628–1703).

11 (p. 51) *He toils not, neither does he spin*   Matthew 6:28: 'Consider the lilies of the field, how they grow; they toil not, neither do they spin.'

12 (p. 52) *salaam*   oriental bow (from Arabic *salam*)

13 (p. 53) *Jonathan Edwards and Dr Hopkins*   Jonathan Edwards (1703–58), influential New England pastor and theologian from

Connecticut; Dr Samuel Hopkins (1721–1803), a theologian, also from Connecticut, and a noted opponent of slavery

14 (p. 54) *Pascal's 'Thoughts'* Blaise Pascal (1623–62), French mathematician, physicist and moralist, published his highly influential *Pensées sur la Religion* (Thoughts on Religion), a series of notes and fragments towards an uncompleted defence of the Christian religion, in 1670.

15 (p. 60) *The Arabian Nights* a collection of stories, *The Arabian Nights' Entertainments* or *The Thousand and One Nights*, written in Arabic and translated into French in the early eighteenth century. James would probably have known E. W. Lane's bowdlerised version of 1839–41.

16 (p. 60) *Gothic* in the Gothic or medieval style of the twelfth–fifteenth centuries, and also suggesting the uncouth and the strange, associated with the 'Gothic' literary style of the late eighteenth and early nineteenth centuries.

Sir Edmund Orme

First published in the Christmas number (the first) of *Black and White* in 1891

1 (p. 67) *Brighton* fashionable seaside town on the south coast of England, in the county of Sussex. The Marine Parade and the King's Road run along the sea-front.

2 (p. 72) *a little wrong in the upper storey* slightly mad

3 (p. 72) *beaters* hired employees of an estate, who go through woods and copses with sticks, shouting and striking trees and bushes to scare the pheasants and other game into flight, during a shoot.

4 (p. 73) *decent rustics* respectable country people

5 (p. 75) *flags* flagstones (of the terrace)

6 (p. 80) *pilot* pilot of a ship (responsible for taking it in and out of harbour)

7 (p. 81) *third volume of a novel* Novels in the later part of the nineteenth century were often published in three volumes, known as 'triple-deckers'.

8 (p. 85) *régimes* (French) diets, courses of exercise

9 (p. 87) *the visiting on the children of the sins of the mothers* an allusion to Exodus 20:5: 'I the Lord thy God am a jealous God, visiting the iniquity of the fathers upon the children unto the third and fourth generation of them that hate me.'

10 (p. 88) *Saint Martin's summer*   a particularly fine late autumn. St Martin's Day is 11 November.

The Private Life

First published in the *Atlantic Monthly*, 1892

1 (p. 92) *fleur des pois*   (French, literally 'flower of the peas') 'the pick of the bunch', the best

2 (p. 92) *Lord Mellifont . . . Clare Vawdrey*   See Introduction, pp. XIV–XV.

3 (p. 92) *shibboleths*   (from Hebrew) A shibboleth is a 'test word or principle or behaviour or opinion, the use of or the inability to use which reveals one's party, nationality, orthodoxy, etc' (*Concise Oxford Dictionary*); in this case, tests of class or social group.

4 (p. 95) *bugles*   tube shaped beads

5 (p. 95) *Queen of Night*   the queen in Mozart's opera *The Magic Flute* (1791).

6 (p. 97) *gilded obelisk*   funerary monument

7 (p. 98) *salle-à-manger*   (French) dining-room

8 (p. 98) *the old English and the new French*   the classics of English drama and new French plays

9 (p. 99) *Sheridan . . . Bowdler*   Richard Brinsley Sheridan, English comic dramatist (1751–1816); Bowdler is probably an invented playwright, but the name echoes that of Thomas Bowdler (1754–1825), who published his *Family Shakespeare* in 1818, an edition of the plays which tried to remove all 'obscenity' and 'profaneness' from the texts. His edition was very popular, but it is unlikely that it was used much for professional productions, and Bowdler wrote no plays himself.

10 (p. 99) *cher grand maître*   (French, literally 'dear great master') 'Cher maître' was a respectful form of address to a senior artist or writer.

11 (p. 99) *haricots verts*   (French) green beans

12 (p. 100) *régal*   (French) treat

13 (p. 100) *débit*   (French) vocal delivery

14 (p. 100) *Comédie Française*   the famous Parisian theatre and acting company

15 (p. 101) *contretemps*   (French) embarrassing occurrence, mishap

16 (p. 106) *Où voulez-vous en venir?*   (French) What are you getting at?

17 (p. 110) *a fortiori*   (Latin) even more strongly, more conclusively

18 (p. 110) *entr'acte* (French) interval

19 (p. 110) *raison d'être* (French) reason for existing

20 (p. 115) *y pensez-vous?* (French) how could you think that?

21 (p. 116) *Oberkellner* (German) head-waiter

22 (p. 119) *Manfred* eponymous hero of the 'dramatic poem' (1817) by Byron (1788–1824), which like James's story is set in the Alps

Owen Wingrave

First published in the Christmas number of *The Graphic*, 1892

1 (p. 123) *Napoleon* Napoleon Bonaparte (1769–1821), great military general and first emperor of France

2 (p. 123) *Eastbourne* Seaside resort on the Sussex coast, somewhat quieter and more staid than Brighton (see 'Sir Edmund Orme', Note 1, p. 338)

3 (p. 123) *well up* well prepared for his examinations

4 (p. 124) *Baker Street* residential (in the nineteenth century) street in London

5 (p. 124) *Kensington Gardens* a large park in West London, close to the flat in De Vere Gardens where James lived for a time. See Introduction, p. XII.

6 (p. 125) *corrupting the youth of Athens* an allusion to the Greek philosopher and teacher Socrates (469–399 BC), who was accused by the authorities in Athens of 'corrupting the minds of the young' (Plato, *Apology*, 24b)

7 (p. 127) *Afghan sabre* The British fought wars in Afghanistan in 1838–42 and 1878. Since the story appears to be set in the present or the recent past, Owen Wingrave the elder, the father of the hero of the story, must have died in the second of these.

8 (p. 127) *Jacobean* from the time of King James I (1603–25)

9 (p. 128) *the Indian Mutiny* the revolt in 1857 against British colonial rule

10 (p. 131) *Bayswater* a respectable and (James implies) conventional residential district of London

11 (p. 132) *Hannibal and Julius Caesar, Marlborough and Frederick and Bonaparte* great military leaders: the Carthaginian general Hannibal (247–182 BC) won victories against the Roman Empire; the Roman emperor Julius Caesar (102–44 BC) conquered Gaul and won victories in Syria, Asia Minor and Africa; John Churchill,

first Duke of Marlborough (1650–1722), won several victories during the War of the Spanish Succession (1702–1714); Frederick the Great (1712–86), second King of Prussia, won famous victories against Silesia and Austria; for Bonaparte, see Note 1.

12 (p. 137) *entail*   'settlement of succession of landed estate so that it cannot be bequeathed at pleasure or sold' (*Concise Oxford Dictionary*)

13 (p. 141) '*samplers*'   pieces of embroidery, often of a picture, proverb or homely saying

14 (p. 143) *Paul and Virginia*   The novel *Paul et Virginie* (1788) by the French philosopher and novelist Jacques-Henri Bernardin de Saint-Pierre (1737–1814) was a pastoral romance telling the idyllic story of a boy and girl brought up as brother and sister on a tropical island.

The Friend of the Friends

First published under the title 'The Way It Came' in *Chap Book* and *Chapman's Magazine of Fiction* in 1896

1 (p. 152) *blank-book*   notebook with blank pages

2 (p. 154) *the 'Long'*   the long (summer) vacation

3 (p. 155) *Richmond*   a town on the Thames, near London

4 (p. 156) *Bond Street frame*   picture frame bought from the fashionable London shopping street

5 (p. 158) *entêtement*   (French) obstinacy

6 (p. 158) *jogged together over hill and dale*   (metaphorical) been everywhere together

7 (p. 160) *astrachan*   dark curly lamb's fleece, or cloth imitating this

8 (p. 167) *soit*   (French) so be it, all right

9 (p. 171) *Medusa-mask*   mask like the face of Medusa, the female monster in Greek mythology whose face was so terrible that all who looked on her turned to stone

The Turn of the Screw

First published in weekly instalments in *Collier's* magazine, from 27 January 1898 to 16 April 1899.

1 (p. 176) *Trinity*   Trinity College, Cambridge. E. W. Benson, the Archbishop of Canterbury from whom James said that he heard the anecdote on which the story of *The Turn of the Screw* was based, had also been a member of Trinity College. He,

together with F. W. H. Myers and Henry Sidgwick, were founder members of the Society for Psychical Research. See also Introduction pp. VIII and XIV.

2 (p. 177) *Raison de plus* (French) all the more reason

3 (p. 178) *Harley Street* a fashionable residential street in London (not yet noted, as it later became, for its number of doctors' consulting rooms)

4 (p. 182) *Raphael* Italian painter (1483–1520), who painted several pictures of the Virgin Mary and the infant Jesus

5 (p. 184) *machicolated square tower* a tower with openings between the corbels (supporting projections) on its parapets.

6 (p. 192) *a mystery of Udolpho . . . unmentionable relative kept in unsuspected confinement* references, respectively, to *The Mysteries of Udolpho* (1794) by Ann Radcliffe, in which the heroine is beset by seemingly supernatural terrors; and Charlotte Brontë's *Jane Eyre* (1847), in which the first wife of the governess heroine's employer is insane and kept in an attic room

7 (p. 194) *cherubs of the anecdote* The anecdote apparently derives from a story in Charles Lamb's *Elia* essay, 'Christ's Hospital Thirty Years Ago', in which the poet Coleridge recalled his former headmaster, the Revd James Boyer, who reputedly used to enjoy beating his pupils: 'Poor J.B.! – may all his faults be forgiven; and may he be wafted to bliss by little cherub boys, all head and wings, with no *bottoms* to reproach his sublunary infirmities.'

8 (p. 204) *the Sea of Azof* a gulf on the Russian coast of the Black Sea

9 (p. 215) *Fielding's Amelia* a novel (1751) by Henry Fielding (1707–54)

10 (p. 218) *Mrs Marcet or nine-times-nine* Jane Marcet (1769–1858) wrote textbooks for children, including *Conversations on Chemistry intended more especially for the female sex* (1806) and *Conversations on Political Economy* (1816). Nine-times-nine: nine multiplied by nine, part of the 'multiplication tables' that children learned to recite aloud

11 (p. 228) *Goody Gosling . . . mot* Goody is an abbreviation of 'Goodwife', a 'term of civility formerly applied to a woman, usually a married woman, in humble life' (*OED*). Goody Gosling was presumably part of the governess's household when she was a child; *mot* (French) is a saying or witticism.

12 (p. 236) *swept and garnished*   a phrase from Matthew 12:44. Jesus tells the Pharisees that they are inhabited by an unclean spirit who returns to the house despite the fact that it is 'swept, and garnished'.

13 (p. 243) *David playing to Saul*   The story is in the Old Testament, 1 Samuel 16:14–23. David played before Saul so that 'the evil spirit' should pass from the latter.

The Real Right Thing

First published in *Collier's Weekly*, 1899

1 (p. 269) *weeds*   clothes

2 (p. 269) *Johnson . . . Scott . . . Boswell . . . Lockhart*   James Boswell (1740–95) and John Gibson Lockhart (1794–1854) wrote classic biographies of, respectively, Dr Samuel Johnson (1709–84), the poet and critic, and Sir Walter Scott (1771–1832) the novelist.

3 (p. 274) *'decadent'*   belonging to the literary and artistic fashion of the 1880s and 1890s so described, deriving from France and exemplified by artists like Aubrey Beardsley (1872–98), which favoured supposedly decadent or sensational subjects and styles

The Third Person

Published in James's collection of stories *The Soft Side* (1900); not included in the New York Edition of novels and stories

1 (p. 279) *Marr*   based on Rye in Sussex, where James lived from 1897 to 1913

2 (p. 279) *pensions*   (French) inns, small hotels

3 (p. 279) *Tauchnitz novel*   a novel from the publishing firm Tauchnitz in Leipzig which in 1841 began to issue piratically, then from 1843–1941 by copyright and sanction, a series of volumes eventually entitled 'Collection of British and American Authors'. These were for sale only on the Continent, so they would have been regarded as contraband by English customs officials, a fact which becomes significant later in the story.

4 (p. 280) *entourage*   (French) attendants, circle of friends

5 (p. 281) *type-copied*   copied on a typewriter

6 (p. 282) *the 'Channel'*   the English Channel, between the south coast of England and the north coast of France

7 (p. 282) *Arno . . . Reuss*   the former a river in central Italy which flows though the great artistic city of Florence; the latter a river

in Switzerland which flows south from Lake Lucerne and
through the Alps

8 (p. 282) *Titian . . . the Pitti*   Italian painter (*c.*1487–1576), the
foremost painter in Venice in its greatest artistic period; the Pitti
Palace, the major art gallery in Florence

9 (p. 283) *Don Juan*   legendary Spanish adventurer and lover, best
known to English readers from Byron's epic poem of that name
(1819–24)

10 (p. 284) *Gothic character*   old-fashioned German type of lettering

11 (p. 284) *wideawake*   a 'soft wide-brimmed low-crowned felt hat'
(*Concise Oxford Dictionary*)

12 (p. 294) *'ear-chair'*   upholstered chair with forward-jutting
side-pieces to its high back. The equivalent term today would be
'wing armchair'.

13 (p. 294) *chimney-glass*   mirror on a chimney-piece, usually above
a fireplace

The Jolly Corner

First published in the *English Review*, 1908

1 (p. 308) *Irving Place*   A short street between Fourteenth and
Twentieth Streets in New York. The whole action takes place in
the general area of New York in which James lived as a child
(1847–55).

2 (p. 310) *character*   character reference

3 (p. 314) *pour deux sous*   (French, literally 'for two sous') to the
slightest degree

4 (p. 314) *alter ego*   (Latin) other self

5 (p. 317) *ombres chinoises*   (French, literally 'Chinese shadows')
shadow theatre

6 (p. 320) *rapprochement*   (French) connection

7 (p. 320) *Pantaloon . . . Harlequin*   characters derived from the
Commedia dell'arte, a popular form of Italian comedy (sixteenth
to eighteenth century), who survived into the English pantomime
tradition